D0444063

BLACKOUT

By Simon Scarrow

The *Eagles of the Empire* Series

The Britannia Campaign

Under the Eagle (AD 42–43, Britannia)

The Eagle's Conquest (AD 43, Britannia)

When the Eagle Hunts (AD 44, Britannia)

The Eagle and the Wolves (AD 44, Britannia)

The Eagle's Prey (AD 44, Britannia)

Rome and the Eastern Provinces

The Eagle's Prophecy (AD 45, Rome)

The Eagle in the Sand (AD 46, Judaea)

Centurion (AD 46, Syria)

The Mediterranean

The Gladiator (AD 48–49, Crete)

The Legion (AD 49, Egypt)

Praetorian (AD 51, Rome)

The Return to Britannia

Blood Crows (AD 51, Britannia)

Brothers in Blood (AD 51, Britannia)

Britannia (AD 52, Britannia)

Hispania

Invictus (AD 54, Hispania)

The Return to Rome

Day of the Caesars (AD 54, Rome)

The Eastern Campaign

The Blood of Rome (AD 55, Armenia)

Traitors of Rome (AD 56, Syria)

The Emperor's Exile (AD 57, Sardinia)

The *Wellington and Napoleon* Quartet
Young Bloods
The Generals
Fire and Sword
The Fields of Death

Sword and Scimitar (Great Siege of Malta)

Hearts of Stone (Second World War)

Blackout

Writing with T.J. Andrews
Arena (AD 41, Rome)
Invader (AD 44, Britannia)
Pirata (AD 25, Rome)

The *Gladiator* Series
Gladiator: Fight for Freedom
Gladiator: Street Fighter
Gladiator: Son of Spartacus
Gladiator: Vengeance

Writing with Lee Francis
Playing With Death

SIMON SCARROW

BLACKOUT

PINNACLE BOOKS
KENSINGTON PUBLISHING CORP.
www.kensingtonbooks.com

PINNACLE BOOKS are published by

Kensington Publishing Corp.
119 West 40th Street
New York, NY 10018

Copyright © 2021 by Simon Scarrow

Previously published in Great Britain by Headline Publishing Group.

This book is a work of fiction. Names, characters, businesses, organizations, places, events, and incidents either are the product of the author's imagination or are used fictitiously. Any resemblance to actual persons, living or dead, events, or locales is entirely coincidental.

All rights reserved. No part of this book may be reproduced in any form or by any means without the prior written consent of the Publisher, excepting brief quotes used in reviews.

To the extent that the image or images on the cover of this book depict a person or persons, such person or persons are merely models, and are not intended to portray any character or characters featured in the book.

If you purchased this book without a cover you should be aware that this book is stolen property. It was reported as "unsold and destroyed" to the Publisher and neither the Author nor the Publisher has received any payment for this "stripped book."

All Kensington titles, imprints, and distributed lines are available at special quantity discounts for bulk purchases for sales promotion, premiums, fund-raising, and educational or institutional use.

Special book excerpts or customized printings can also be created to fit specific needs. For details, write or phone the office of the Kensington Sales Manager: Kensington Publishing Corp., 119 West 40th Street, New York, NY 10018. Attn. Sales Department. Phone: 1-800-221-2647.

PINNACLE BOOKS and the Pinnacle logo Reg. U.S. Pat. & TM Off.

First Kensington hardcover printing: April 2022
First Pinnacle mass market paperback printing: January 2023
ISBN-13: 978-0-7860-4931-8
ISBN-13: 978-0-7860-4932-5 (eBook)

10 9 8 7 6 5 4 3 2 1

Printed in the United States of America

Für meinen guten Freund Peter Krämer

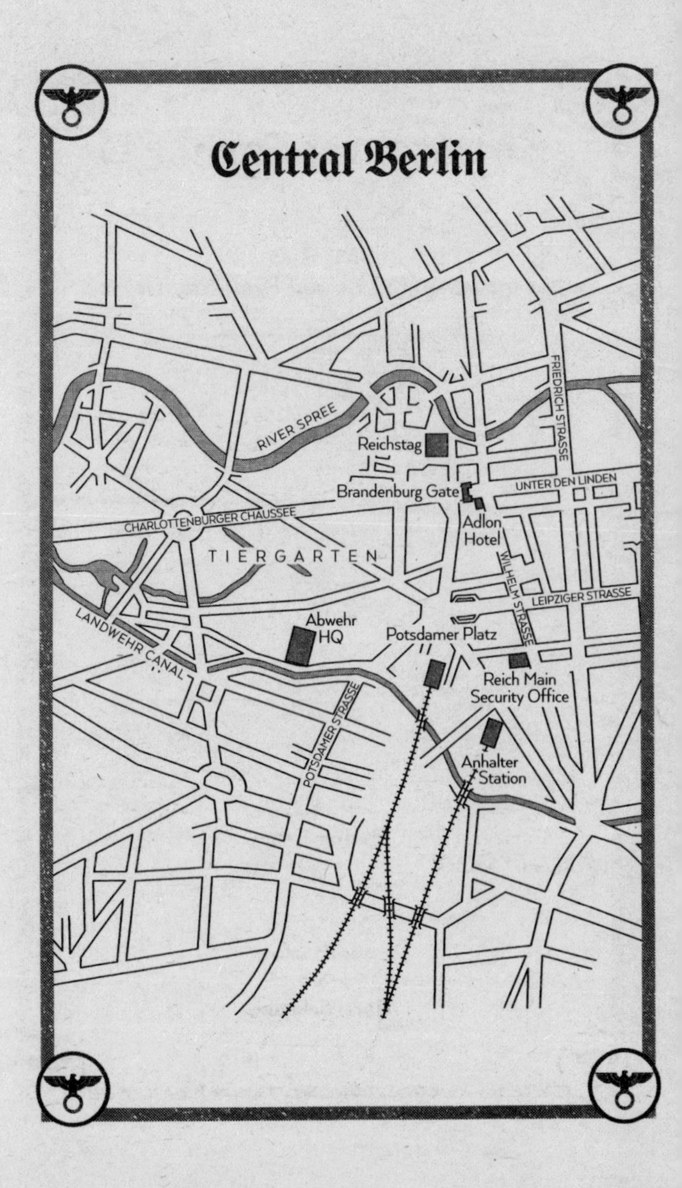
Central Berlin
RIVER SPREE
Reichstag
FRIEDRICH STRASSE
Brandenburg Gate
UNTER DEN LINDEN
CHARLOTTENBURGER CHAUSSEE
Adlon
Hotel
TIERGARTEN
WILHELM STRASSE
LEIPZIGER STRASSE
LANDWEHR CANAL
Abwehr
HQ
Potsdamer Platz
Reich Main
Security Office
POTSDAMER STRASSE
Anhalter
Station

The Chain of Command

The Führer
Adolf Hitler

Reichsführer-SS
Heinrich Himmler

Reichsminister of Public Enlightenment and Propaganda
Josef Goebbels

Chief of the Reich Main Security Office
Reinhard Heydrich

Head of Abwehr (Military Intelligence)
Admiral Wilhelm Canaris

Head of Kriminalpolizei
Arthur Nebe

Head of Gestapo
Heinrich Müller

Head of Pankow Kripo Section
Horst Schenke

Prologue

Berlin, 19 December 1939

The Christmas party had not long begun when Gerda Korzeny and her escort arrived at half past eight that evening. The snow was deep and they kicked the ice off their boots before stepping into the lobby and handing their coats and fur hats to a maid. Gerda removed her boots and placed them by the door before taking some Louis-heeled evening shoes from the bag she had brought with her and slipping them on. She examined herself in a mirror on the lobby wall. Smoothing down her cocktail dress, she reached up and brushed her brown hair lightly into place with her fingertips. She noticed her companion smiling behind her and pouted.

"That's better," she said. "I feel more human now."

He grinned and took her elbow as he stepped up beside her. His black boots gleamed and in his neatly pressed uniform he cut an impressive figure.

"We make a handsome couple," she said, lifting a gloved hand to stroke his chin. "Too bad we're not married. Not to each other, at least."

His smile faded and he steered her through to the large hall beyond. At least half the guests had already arrived;

more than a hundred of the capital's high society stood in clusters beneath the glittering chandelier that illuminated the voluminous space. White-jacketed waiters and aproned waitresses bearing trays of champagne glasses moved from group to group.

Conversation and laughter echoed off the high walls as Gerda scanned the crowd looking for familiar faces. There were people from the film industry whom she knew from her years as a star of the UFA studio. Some were actors, like Emil Jannings, the portly man with the high forehead who was bellowing with laughter. There were also some directors she recognized, as well as producers, screenwriters and composers. Sadly, many of the more familiar faces had long since emigrated. Most to Hollywood, and some to other European nations, where their politics or religion were less likely to land them in trouble with the authorities.

Besides the film people, there were artists and writers, leading figures from the world of sport and those wealthy Germans who acted as their patrons, such as Count Harstein, once a backer of the Silver Arrows motor-racing team. There were also many guests in the uniforms of the army, navy and air force, as well as those who represented branches of the ruling party. One of the latter, an SS officer, returned her gaze with a cold expression.

Gerda turned towards her companion and muttered, "Dear God, that oily creature Fegelein is here. Do me a favor and keep him away from me."

"Why?"

"Because, my dear Oberst Karl Dorner, he is a loathsome hypocrite who will take me to task for cheating on my husband in one breath and attempt to seduce me with the next. I'd rather not have to endure him tonight."

"What would you like me to do about it?"

"If he causes me embarrassment, I would expect you to do the gallant thing and strike him down."

"I am not sure if it would be wise for an army officer to punch one of Himmler's favorites."

"Then think of it as a gentleman teaching a lesson to an unscrupulous arriviste."

"There was a time when I would do that happily," Dorner responded. "But the arrivistes rule Germany now and they are not inclined to allow their betters to forget it. But I will do what I can to keep him occupied."

Gerda smiled. "It's only for an hour or so. Then we can leave. I have the key to a friend's flat. He won't be returning to Berlin until the new year, so the rest of the night will be ours alone."

The officer smiled as he took her hand and kissed it. "I will look forward to that." He felt her tremble beneath his touch.

"Wouldn't you like to be with me every night, my love?" She spoke softly so only he could hear. "Don't we deserve that happiness?"

He sighed. "We have talked about this. I told you, I am not going to divorce my wife until I can afford it. If you leave that dolt you are married to, he will give you nothing. What do you think we will live on then? Eh?"

She glared back. "We will have each other. Isn't that enough for you?"

"No. It isn't. And it certainly isn't enough for you. Not with your tastes. So why not let things stay as they are and we can enjoy what we do have?"

"But I want more than the occasional evening and afternoon with you. I want *you*. All I am to you is a good fuck. Isn't that the truth?"

He froze, and then smiled coldly. "Maybe you are not even that. But at least you are an easy fuck."

"Bastard." She pulled away from him. "You think you're the only man who wants me? You'll see."

She strode towards a group of guests from the film industry and her face lit up in a brilliant smile as she called out a greeting. "Leni!"

A woman dressed in a trouser suit, with shoulder-length dark hair and manly features, smiled back and opened her arms to welcome the new arrival. They exchanged kisses before Gerda greeted others she knew and was introduced to the few she did not.

Dorner watched her for a moment from the edge of the hall before he made for two officers standing by the bottom of the wide staircase that climbed up to a gallery overlooking the hall.

He nodded to them as he approached. One was the aide he worked alongside at his office in the Abwehr, Germany's military intelligence. The other man, General von Tresckow, wore the red collar tabs of a general staff officer. Even though he was not yet forty, his hair had receded, marring his otherwise handsome features.

"Good evening, sir." Dorner bowed his head slightly.

"Dorner, good to see you again," von Tresckow replied. "Tell me, I recognize that woman's face. The one you arrived with."

"I imagine you did, sir. She's an actress. Or at least she was. Gerda retired from the film industry some years ago."

"Ah! *That* Gerda! But I thought she was a blonde."

"She was back then. But brown is her natural color."

The general stared towards the group, which had now arranged itself around Gerda as she began to exert her magnetic charm over her audience. "Blonde or brunette, she is a fine-looking woman. Lucky you."

"Yes, lucky me." Dorner raised his glass, took a sip and stepped in between his superior and Gerda before he continued. "So, General, after Poland, what has the general staff got planned for the Western Front?"

Von Tresckow laughed and wagged his finger. "I am not at liberty to give any details, my friend. But let's just say our

French and British friends are in for a shock when the time comes . . ."

The general began to extol the superiority of German arms and tactics over those of the enemy, but Dorner's attention wavered as his thoughts returned to Gerda. It was not enough that she was there to warm a bed for him when his lust demanded satisfaction. He was a jealous man, and could not tolerate the idea of sharing her with anyone else. It was true that they were both married, but she had assured him that she no longer slept with her husband, a Nazi lawyer. For his part, Dorner had married young to a pleasant girl from a family who owned a large estate below the Harz mountains. But she had proved to be dull. Certainly compared to a former film star like Gerda. And there was the problem. He could choose the comforts of his wife's wealth, or the sophistication of Gerda. But he wanted both.

As more guests arrived, the hall became crowded and it was difficult to hold a conversation over the swelling din. Music started playing from a gramophone in the gallery, an upbeat number by a former cabaret singer still tolerated by the party. At length the general exhausted his shop talk, and his voice, and moved off to get another drink.

Dorner's aide rolled his eyes. "I thought he'd never finish. The man has no idea what social gatherings are for. Who invited him?"

"I have no idea, Schumacher. But I do not intend to let him bore me any further. If he comes back, keep him occupied. There's someone I need to speak to."

"Your friend Gerda? If I were you, I'd not leave it too late." Schumacher nodded behind his superior.

Dorner turned, and his eyes quickly fixed on the far side of the hall, where several couples were dancing to the music. Gerda was amongst them, her arms around a slender young man in a velvet jacket, their bodies pressed close together. She looked over the man's shoulder at Dorner and kissed her dancing partner on the neck. He held her closer still and his right hand slipped from her shoulder to her waist.

"Damn her . . ." Dorner growled. He thrust his empty glass at his aide and strode through the crowd towards her. Pulling her away from the man, he grabbed her by the arms and leaned to speak into her ear. Her dancing partner stood two paces away, uncertain how to react. As the pair continued their tense exchange, he backed away and returned to the large crowd of guests from the film industry. A moment later, Gerda tore herself free and hurried towards the lobby. Dorner glared after her before following.

At the same time, von Tresckow returned to the bottom of the stairs, champagne bottle in one hand and glass in the other. "Oh, where's Dorner gone? I had more I wanted to tell him."

"I think he has decided to leave early, sir." Schumacher lifted his glass in the direction of the lobby, and both men watched as Gerda put on her coat and changed back into her boots. Dorner addressed her earnestly, but she shrugged off his attempt to take her hand and turned to open the door. Dorner clenched his fists and snatched up his coat and hat before setting off after her, leaving a footman to close the door behind them.

"What was that about?" asked von Tresckow.

"I'm not sure, sir." Schumacher raised his glass and took a sip. "But I'd say there's trouble brewing tonight . . ."

Gerda broke into a run to put some distance between her and Dorner as he emerged from the house. Her boots crunched over a thin layer of fresh snow that had fallen while they had been at the party. The sky was clear and stars glinted sharply against a velvet blackness.

"Wait!" he called. "What do you think you are doing? Gerda!"

She heard his footsteps as he followed at a quick stride. She had reached the end of the street when he took her arm, forcing her to stop and turn to face him. She saw the anger in his expression as his lips pressed into a thin line.

"How dare you humiliate me like that?" he muttered in a quiet voice laced with fury. She could smell the brandy on his breath.

She gave a bitter laugh. "How dare I? Who the hell do you think you are? I offered you my heart. I said I would give up everything to be with you. You led me to believe you felt the same way."

"I never promised you anything."

She stared back at him and shook her head sadly. "Karl, you are nothing more than a liar and a cheat. Just like most of the men I have ever known. You seduced me and encouraged me to make plans for a future you never intended to share. I despise you—"

He moved so quickly that the blow caught her by surprise. The back of his hand smashed into her cheek and jarred her neck. White sparks jumped before her eyes and she staggered, tasting blood in her mouth.

"You bastard . . ."

He froze, seemingly aghast at his loss of control. His expression twisted a moment before he shook his head. "Gerda . . . forgive me."

"Keep away from me!" she cried, retreating. She raised a gloved hand and stabbed a finger at him. "It's over. We're finished, you hear?"

"No, my love. It's not over." He advanced on her with a pained smile, arms wide to embrace her. "I'm so sorry. Forgive me."

"No! You come any closer and I'll scream blue murder. I

mean it. And when people come, I'll say you attacked me. Tried to molest me."

He paused in alarm. "You wouldn't."

"Try it and see," she said defiantly. "Then all Berlin will know what kind of a man you are."

"Please. Don't."

Gerda looked at him with contempt, then took a few paces back before turning and walking quickly in the direction of the nearby station at Papestrasse to take the most direct route home now that she was not with Dorner. Her heart was beating fast and her cheek smarted from the blow she had received. If it left a bruise, she was going to have to think of a way to explain it to her husband when she returned home. Not that he was averse to subjecting her to his own bruising treatment, she reflected bitterly.

There was no sound of anyone following her, no cry from her lover to ask her to stop and change her mind. With every step, her resentment at Dorner's lack of willingness to fight for her grew. Even as she had berated him, she had half hoped he would try to talk her round. In truth, she wanted to be with him. Only him. And she needed him to want her in return. Which was why she had tried to provoke his jealousy at the party.

She continued along the wide avenue that led towards the station, occasionally passing other pedestrians still abroad on this freezing night; dark figures, hunched into their coats, picked out against the dull loom of the snow and ice. As she neared the entrance to the station, she saw the red flare of a cigarette in the shadow of the arched gateway of a trader's yard. Instinctively she tried to give the smoker a wide berth. Then a husky voice addressed her.

"How much?"

She ignored him and quickened her pace. There was still nearly a hundred meters to go before she reached the station, and with a surge of panic, she realized there was no one else in sight on either side of the street. She cursed Dorner for not coming after her.

There was a faint cough from behind, and she glanced back and saw the dim glow of the cigarette tip as the man eased himself out of the shelter of the arch and began to follow her. She lengthened her stride, but when she was halfway to the station, she looked again and saw that he had closed in. Fear gripped her, and she broke into a run as she saw a man in a uniform emerge from the station's entrance.

"Hey!" she called out, waving her arm as she ran. "You there!"

The uniformed man stepped into the street to meet her. She could see he was a railway conductor.

"Miss? What's the matter with you?"

"There's a man." She pointed back down the sidewalk. But there was no one there, not even the telltale glow of the cigarette.

"What man?" asked the conductor.

"He was there. Following me."

"I can't see anyone." The conductor stared at her. "Are you sure, miss?"

"I . . ." Gerda breathed deeply. "Never mind. It doesn't matter."

"Don't worry, miss," he chuckled. "It's easily done on a dark night. People imagine all sorts of things. Believe me."

"I didn't imagine it," she snapped. "Excuse me."

She brushed past him into the station and made for the waiting room on the platform for the Anhalter-bound trains. The remains of a fire smoldered in the iron grate and the room was pleasantly warm. The only other occupants were a fat man in working clothes and a thin, frail-looking woman whom Gerda took to be his wife. They exchanged a brief nod, but no words. Every few moments, Gerda glanced out of the window onto the platform, but there was no sign of the man who had followed her.

After ten minutes, her train drew into the station and the three of them emerged from the waiting room. As the others boarded the second-to-last carriage, Gerda made for the rearmost and settled into a seat facing the back of the train. A few doors slammed, a whistle sounded and the train jerked into motion. As it clanked out of the station and into the night, passing through the blacked-out suburbs of Berlin, Gerda settled in her seat and lifted the edge of the carriage's blind to peer into the darkness. She was furious with Dorner, and vowed to win him back or else avenge her wounded pride.

There was a click and a blast of cold air before the carriage door closed again. She released the edge of the blind and turned to see that a man had entered the carriage and was approaching her. Her eyes widened in recognition. "You . . ."

Chapter One

20 December 1939

The couple, who appeared to be in their late forties, sat slumped in their chairs in front of the stove in the larger of the two rooms of their apartment. They had been dead for days, and the skin of their faces was white, with a dull marble sheen like pearl. Both were almost naked, stripped to a grimy vest and slip. The rest of their clothing was strewn around the plain wooden chairs. There were only ashes in the stove and the cast iron was icy to the touch. The air in the room had already been below freezing when the first policeman on the scene kicked the door open. It had become colder when the window had been hurriedly opened to disperse any toxic fumes that still lingered in the small apartment.

Sergeant Kittel stood beside the stove. Despite his buttoned-up greatcoat, gloves and muffler, he was cold, and stamped his boots to keep some warmth in his feet. He was impatient as well, and every few minutes he pulled out a pocket watch and glanced at the hands. The only sound in the room was the ticking of a clock on a narrow shelf beside the stove. The noises from the street were muted by the thick snow on the ground. He could hear the exchanges of the other residents of the apartment block on the stairs and landing outside the front door. With a sigh of steamy breath, he crossed to the opening leading into the narrow hall and passed through the apartment's door with the shattered splinters where the lock had once been. Two more policemen stood outside the entrance to the apartment, and beyond them Kittel could see a huddle of curious faces on the landing.

"Denicke! Clear those rubbernecking fools away! There is nothing to see here." He made to turn away and stopped. "No, wait. Keep the concierge back. The rest of them should go home and keep themselves warm."

The policeman nodded, but before he could carry out his orders, his superior spoke again. "Any sign of the criminal investigators yet?"

"No, sir."

"Hmm." Kittel growled irritably. He turned to the other uniformed policeman. "Get down to the entrance and keep an eye out. As soon as the Kripo officer gets here, bring him straight up. Before we all freeze to death."

As Denicke drew his truncheon and waved the small crowd back, his colleague squeezed past the people on the landing and made his way down the four flights of stairs to the ground floor. Kittel set his expression in a hard glare as he defied the other tenants to tarry on the landing, and was gratified to see that none dared meet his eye as they turned away and made their way back to their apartments. It was good to see them respond so meekly to authority. The power of the state must be unquestioned if victory in the war was to be assured.

Not like the last time, the sergeant reflected. He had served the last two years of the Great War before returning to the political chaos that had seized Berlin. Reds rioting on the streets, demanding revolution. Well, the soldiers returning from the front had soon put an end to that nonsense. He had been part of the armed gangs that had taken on the communists and clubbed and gunned them down to restore order to the capital. There would be no stab in the back this time. Besides, the new war was already as good as over. Poland had been crushed, and it was only a matter of time before France and Britain saw the futility of another conflict when the cause of it no longer existed. Poland had disappeared, swallowed up by Germany and her Russian ally. Though if the French and the British did decide to fight on, then victory for the Fatherland was far from certain.

Kittel shrugged dismissively and rubbed his hands together. Whatever course of action the governments of Europe decided, for now a state of war existed. It was the duty of every official in Germany to ensure that discipline was maintained.

As he returned to the living room, he looked over the humble dwelling. The apartment was typical of the kind inhabited by the poorer working families in the Pankow district. There was a living space with a tiny kitchen leading off. A bathroom with a toilet and tin tub. Two bedrooms. The larger had just enough space for two single beds, which were neatly made up. On the same shelf as the clock was a photograph in a silver frame of the couple, seated with a pair of young men in uniform standing behind them. All four wore expressions of formal solemnity typical of such family portraits.

For a moment the sergeant's heart softened as he spared a thought for the two soldiers who would soon receive a telegram informing them of their parents' death. Such was the irony of the time that they had gone to face the perils of bullet, shell and bomb and remained unscathed, while their kin at home had died.

The only other framed pictures in the apartment were of a simple log cabin set against a backdrop of snow-clad mountains, and the ubiquitous portrait of the Führer, hand on hip and inclined forward as he stared inscrutably out of the image.

Kittel heard a car drawing up in the street. He crossed to the open window and saw the black roof and hood of one of the police pool cars reserved for officers. The front passenger door swung out and a man in a dark gray coat and black felt hat eased himself onto the cleared sidewalk. He bent to say something to the driver, then closed the door and turned to look up at the apartment block, revealing a slender face. His gaze met that of the sergeant. The policeman waiting at the entrance approached, and the new arrival lowered his head to acknowledge the salute made to him. He was waved towards the entrance of the block and both men strode across the sidewalk and disappeared from view.

It took longer for the Kripo officer to climb the stairs than Kittel had anticipated, and he noticed as the criminal investigator crossed the landing and entered the apartment that he had a slight limp. His breathing was labored too. Like the other policemen, he was wearing a thick coat, scarf, hat and gloves, but there was a businesslike directness to his demeanor as he took out the chain lanyard from around his neck and presented his metal badge. One side depicted an eagle perched on a swastika and surrounded by a wreath of oak leaves. The reverse carried the word *Kriminalpolizei* and the bearer's identity number.

"Criminal Inspector Schenke, Pankow precinct," the new arrival announced, giving a curt nod. The sergeant responded in kind as he weighed the other man up. The inspector was wide-shouldered though his body, through the thick coat, seemed lean. His slender face could have belonged to a man aged anywhere between his mid twenties and forty.

"Sergeant Kittel, Heinesdorf station."

"You've picked a cold morning to call me out, Sergeant." Schenke smiled thinly, suggesting that he was not without humor. "But then with this weather, every morning is cold."

Winter had hit Berlin hard. The temperature had dropped below freezing a week earlier and continued to fall in the days that followed. The bitter weather had been accompanied by a severe blizzard that had covered the city in over twenty centimeters of snow. Already some of the newspapers were reporting that it was set to be one of the coldest winters for many decades. Bad at the best of times, thought Schenke, but with a war on, the hard winter added to the challenges of rationing, scarcity of coal and the blackout that consumed the city once the sun had set.

From late afternoon until the following dawn, the streets were swallowed up by the night, and Berliners were forced to grope their way to their destinations. Aside from the inconvenience, there was the danger of collision with vehicles, tripping on the curb or falling down stairs. The darkness, however, provided opportunities for some; prostitutes, for example, were less likely to draw the attention and opprobrium of the police or Hitler Youth patrols. It also allowed cover for more sinister activities. Robberies, assault and murders had increased significantly since the start of the war only four months earlier. Every night the capital became a dark and dangerous place, and those who ventured onto the streets glanced warily about them for fear of the violence that might strike at them from any alley or sheltered doorway.

"What do we have here? All I was told was that you have some bodies."

"Yes, sir. Two. Rudolf and Maria Oberg. Through there." Kittel stood aside to allow the inspector to enter the living room, then followed him inside. They took position either side of the stove and faced the corpses. Schenke looked from one to the other, then at the clothes on the floor and the rest of the small room.

"What information do you have so far?"

The sergeant took out his notebook and fumbled with his gloved fingers to open it before he spoke from his jottings.

"A neighbor came to the station yesterday to report that Oberg had not been at work for the last week. Both men are on the same shift at the Siemens plant. The neighbor's wife is the concierge. I have her waiting outside. She knocked on the door yesterday but got no response, so her husband came to see us. The station chief sent me and the boys out first thing this morning to follow up. When we didn't get any answer, we tried the door and found it locked. I gave the order to break in. We found the Obergs as you see them now."

Schenke leaned forward to inspect the bodies more closely. "And you decided to involve the Kripo? Because?"

Kittel raised an eyebrow and gestured towards the garments strewn over the floor. "If that ain't suspicious, then what is, sir? Who takes their clothes off in temperatures like this?"

"Quite. Was the window open when you entered the room?"

"No. It was off the latch but frozen in the frame. Needed a push to free it. My first thought was that they might have been overcome by fumes from the stove. There's been more than a few such deaths reported since winter started."

Schenke glanced at him. "But . . . ?"

"But their skin is mostly white, and there are signs of frostbite on the fingers and feet. If it had been fumes, there would be a red flush to their cheeks, sir."

"Quite so." The inspector squatted between the two chairs and examined the woman first. Her hair was dark and tied back in a bun, and she sat hunched, so that small rolls of skin formed under her jaw. Her eyes were closed and her expression was peaceful, as if she had fallen asleep. The husband, by contrast, sat drawn up, his thin arms clasped tightly around his bare knees. His face was contorted, lips drawn back in a grimace, eyes clenched shut. A fringe of gray hair ran around his crown, and there was a cut and a streak of dry blood at the back of his head.

"If it wasn't fumes, then what do you think happened here, Kittel?"

Kittel shifted uneasily.

Schenke could see the man's discomfort and had no wish to make it any harder for him to consider a difficult line of inquiry. It was a policeman's duty to think through all possibilities. "Spit it out, man."

"It could be a burglary. There are still some gypsies in Berlin, sir. And you know what they're like. Vermin. There's a local gang operating out of the old Siemens depot. We're constantly dealing with the thieving bastards. There have been many burglaries, and assaults, since the blackout started, sir."

"Very true," Schenke said. The Kripo had been instructed to help crack down on burglaries. The orders had come from Heydrich himself. The newly appointed head of the Reich Main Security Office was keen to prove to the people that the regime would enforce law and order efficiently and ruthlessly. "And you think that perhaps the burglars came across the couple, killed them and left them like this. Why do you think the victims have been stripped?"

"I wouldn't like to say, sir."

"No? If our burglars were not simply here for whatever pitiful possessions they could take from this apartment, and they had more sinister motives, you would expect the woman to be undressed, right? But not the husband."

Kittel nodded.

The inspector took off his hat and smoothed down his light brown hair. It was easier for Kittel to judge his age now—early thirties, he decided. His hair was not cropped short in the fashion of those who served in the army or the SS, but neatly cut to a conventional length. He had a broad brow that made his dark eyes seem as if they were deeper-set than they were. A narrow nose led to slightly downturned lips. He replaced his hat and gestured towards the Obergs. "It is not always the case that sex attackers just target the female, Sergeant. We must keep an open mind, eh?"

"If you say so, sir."

Schenke folded his arms and thought for a moment. "We have two dead bodies, in a state of undress, and this wound on the head of the man."

"Which might have been inflicted in a struggle with the gypsies, or whoever it was that did this."

"Possibly," Schenke conceded. "Though it's hardly fatal, and not even incapacitating. The scalp is torn, but there's almost no bruising. See?" He looked closely at the wound and then around the room, pointing to the floor beneath the shelf on which sat the clock and the silver-framed family portrait. "There's a few drops of blood there."

He stepped closer and examined the worn wooden edge at the corner of the shelf. A dark smudge drew his attention and he picked up a discarded shirt and rubbed the cloth on the wood. It came away with a dark red smear. "More blood."

He straightened up. "Let's see what light the concierge can throw on matters. Bring her in."

"Sir?" Kittel hesitated. "Bring a member of the public into a crime scene?"

"We haven't yet established that this is a crime scene. That might change depending upon what the concierge has to say."

As Kittel left the room, the inspector went to the window and examined the latch. It was old and worn and the lug was loose in the frame so it took three attempts before he managed to secure the window. Through the smeared glass he looked up at the gray sky, streaked with trails of smoke from the chimneys of those who still had stocks of coal to burn. Beneath the haze, the roofs and streets of the capital lay under a thick layer of snow that would have filled his heart with joy were it not for the war and the two bodies in the room behind him.

"Sir. Frau Glück."

Schenke moved away from the window and the light fell upon the bodies. The elderly woman raised a hand to her lips. "Sweet Jesus, save us!"

Schenke watched her reaction for a moment before he was satisfied her shock was natural. He stood behind the dead man as he addressed her. "I am afraid salvation is too late for some . . . You are the concierge of this building?"

She continued to stare at the corpses, eyes wide as she trembled. From cold or shock it was not possible for the inspector to decide. Most likely both, he surmised.

"Frau Glück?" He raised his voice a fraction and she tore her gaze away from the bodies and nodded.

"How well do you know the Obergs? As friends? Passing neighbors?"

She swallowed as she replied. "We stopped to talk from time to time. I keep a close eye on who comes and goes here. My husband is the block warden for this street. It's our business to keep an eye on people."

"Indeed." Schenke dealt with minor party officials regularly. They were a useful source of information. They were also nosy and inclined to use their limited influence to settle scores with neighbors who got on their wrong side. His instinctive dislike of such snoopers was fueled by his ongoing difficulties with his own block warden, a municipal engineer who had become a Nazi only two years ago and was doing his best to make up for the delay in joining through fervid devotion to the ideals of the party. Despite Schenke's distaste for the block warden system, he conceded that it had its uses as far as supplying the police with information. "I understand your husband worked with Oberg?"

"Yes . . . That is to say that Herr Oberg worked for my husband." She stiffened her back slightly. "He is the shift overseer, you know. That's why he noticed the absence of one of his men."

"And yet it took some days before he did anything about it. A delay that might have saved two lives."

She opened her mouth, ready to protest, and was met with a glare from the inspector's dark brown eyes. She looked down. "My husband is a busy man. He has responsibilities. He can't be expected to keep an eye on everyone."

"But that is *precisely* his responsibility as block warden." Schenke breathed in slowly and let the woman stew in her discomfort. "Let's hope Herr Glück takes better care of his flock in future. Did the Obergs have disagreements with neighbors? Or anyone else in the street? Anyone who might have borne a grudge?"

"Not that I know of. They kept to themselves most of the time. They moved into the block fifteen years ago with their sons. Such nice boys, I thought. Always polite and respectful. They'll be devastated."

"I imagine they will." Schenke clasped his hands behind his back. "That will be all for now. If there's anything else we need to ask you, we will contact you. Thank you for your cooperation, Frau Glück."

She looked at him with a mixture of surprise and disappointment, and was about to speak when he gave a curt nod towards the apartment's entrance. "You may go."

Sergeant Kittel waited until he heard her footsteps descending the stairs before he spoke. "Sir, surely there's more we can get out of that one?"

"What exactly? If anyone who looked suspicious had entered the building she'd have come straight out with it and told us. I know her type. She's nosy enough to know the business of everyone in the street. I am certain that she can't help us any further. Besides, there's been no crime here."

Kittel's bushy eyebrows shot up and he gestured towards the man's body. "Sir, if it wasn't the fumes that killed them, then what? Murder, I say. This is the work of some sick, degenerate pervert. That's why I put the call in to Kripo. That's why you're here." He continued with a faint sneer. "You're supposed to be the smart-arses. The ones who know better than the rest of us. If you can't see a crime when there's evidence of one right under your nose, then what good are you to the police force, and to the Reich?"

Schenke forced himself not to react. Most of the officers and men of the Kripo still regarded themselves as professionals who were above politics. It was an attitude that did not endear them to the many in the capital's police force who supported the party and its leader. Since they had come to power, the National Socialists had set about getting rid of those police officers who failed to embrace their ideology. But the Kripo's expertise and experience was hard-won, and its officers had proved more difficult to replace. That said, even the legendary abilities of their former commander, Dr. Bernard Weiss, had not been enough to save him. The fact that he was a Jew outweighed all his brilliance and the long list of successes he had enjoyed against the capital's criminals. Now Schenke found himself confronted by one of the party's supporters. The kind of man who sneered at intellectuals and took satisfaction in seeing their ideals crushed by the new regime. It would be best not to confront Kittel's politics. It would be better to simply pull rank.

"Sergeant, you forget yourself. I am your superior and you will respect that. I will not tolerate insubordination from any man. And I tell you now that no crime has been committed." He turned to the bodies. "You are correct that their deaths were not caused by fumes. But you are wrong in every other respect. There is no sign of burglary. Not one hint of any search for valuables. And one of the first things a thief would have taken is the photograph frame. No, not the Führer. That silver one next to the clock. There is no evidence of any assault."

Kittel snorted. "But the cut to the head . . ."

". . . is the result of a fall. No doubt caused when Herr Oberg was in a delirious state before his death. Perhaps when he was tearing his clothes off."

"Now you are talking utter nonsense, Inspector. What kind of person would take off their clothes in the middle of this freezing weather?"

"Someone who is dying from hypothermia." Schenke looked from one body to the other with pity in his expression. "They died from the cold. There's no fuel for the stove. It's likely they had burned the last of their coal some days before. Look at the window latch there; it's useless. I daresay it's been swinging open and shut for some time. It's probable that Oberg tried to secure the window when he was in a confused state thanks to the cold. Sometimes, not long before the end, the dying feel they are burning up and so they strip. Of course, it only hastens the end, as it did here. And if the temperature stays this low for much longer, we will be seeing more of these cases."

He drew himself up and nodded. "It was the cold, Sergeant. Not thieves, or gypsies. Just the cold. This is not a job for the Kripo. You'll have to write the report. And next time, I hope you'll think twice before you call us out."

He inclined his head in farewell and the policeman stepped back to let him pass, shaping to raise his arm. "Hail . . ."

But Schenke had already strode off, quickening his pace to avoid any exchange of the salute the party had introduced. It had always struck him as cheaply theatrical, like so many of the trappings of national socialism that strove to achieve drama and spectacle to excite their followers.

As he made his way down the stairs, he frowned. By the time he returned to his office at the precinct, over two hours would have been wasted. Time he could have spent dealing with the ongoing investigation into a ring of ration coupon forgers. All because the sergeant wanted a fresh excuse to target those gypsies who remained in the district.

At the bottom of the stairs, he passed the open door of the concierge's apartment. Frau Glück stood on the threshold. He touched the brim of his hat and stepped out into the bright street.

Even though the sky was overcast, the glare of the snow caused him to wrinkle his eyes. The driver had left the engine running, against fuel-saving regulations, in order to keep the car's heater going. Schenke slipped into the passenger seat without comment, grateful for the heat inside the vehicle. As the driver put the Opel into gear, the inspector took one last look at the gray facade of the apartment block. The concierge had emerged from her doorway to stand at the entrance, and their eyes met. He could not be sure, but he thought there was a touch of guilt in her expression. As well there should be. A terrible winter had come to Berlin. It was the duty of all the capital's inhabitants to look out for each other in the freezing days to come. If nothing else had been achieved in this pointless diversion, Schenke hoped that Frau Glück and her husband would take better care of their neighbors.

"Back to the precinct, sir?"

"Yes. And take it slowly. There's ice on the streets."

There was no sense in adding fresh names to the list of victims claimed by this harshest of winters, thought Schenke. No sense at all.

Chapter Two

The Kripo section at the Pankow precinct had a modest staff of less than ten men under Schenke's command, four of whom were still in training or serving out their probation period before they qualified. There were also two women, whose duties included dealing with children and vulnerable females involved in investigations. In normal circumstances there would have been another six investigators, but the exigencies of war had demanded the transfer of men away from peacetime duties. The section's offices were on the top floor of the precinct building, overlooking the yard containing garages, workshops, storerooms and a small barrack block. It was up three flights of stairs, and Schenke grimaced as he made the climb, favoring his bad leg. Although it was over six years since the motor-racing accident that had nearly killed him, his left knee was still stiff and painful, especially during the cold, damp winter months. He could walk without difficulty, but climbing stairs or any attempt to run more than a hundred meters caused a shooting pain in the joint. It was enough to render him unfit for military service.

That was a cause of shame to him, since many of his colleagues had been drafted into the forces to serve Germany in the recent war with Poland. With luck, peace would soon return to the continent, the men would resume their old occupations and Schenke would no longer have to be conscious of his failure to contribute to the Reich's war effort.

He paused at the top of the stairs, glanced down the corridor to make sure he was alone and bent over to massage the muscles around the knee, easing the stiffness and pain. Straightening, he made himself stride to the entrance of the Kripo's offices, and entered a room ten meters in length by four. Desks were arranged on either side, paired face-to-face. On the wall opposite the door was a line of windows, the glass covered in condensation and patches of ice on the inside. Notice boards hung along the side wall. Less than half his staff were at their desks, and they looked up as he entered. The rest were out on duty. In other branches of the police force they would have stood up for a superior officer, but the men and women belonging to the Kripo were plainclothes professionals and were content to eschew such formalities and get on with the job.

His second-in-command, Sergeant Hauser, a veteran policeman of nearly thirty years, turned his chair to face Schenke. He was sturdily built from his days boxing in the army, and his cropped hair looked like a sprinkling of pepper across the crown of his head.

"Got a new case for us, sir?"

Schenke shook his head. "Thankfully not, Hauser. Nothing suspicious. Almost a complete waste of time, in fact."

"Almost?"

"It gave me the chance to teach one of the uniformed boys not to waste our time."

Hauser smiled. There was always an edge to relations between criminal investigators and the beat police known as the Orpo.

Schenke took off his coat and folded it over his arm but

kept his hat and scarf in place. "Any news from the technical lab about the ration coupons we found at the Oskar warehouse?"

"Sure." Hauser turned to his desk and reached for a buff folder. "This came in while you were out. I've only had time to look at the summary. But it makes for interesting reading."

"Bring it through to my office. I'll have a look over some coffee." Schenke caught the eye of the most junior member of the section, a chubby youth with slicked-back blond hair. "Brandt!"

The young man stood up. "Sir?"

"Coffee for me and Hauser. Right away."

Brandt nodded and hurried out of the office towards the staff room at the end of the corridor.

"You always pick on the kid. Why not ask one of the girls?" Hauser muttered.

"He's fresh out of Charlottenberg and needs to pay his dues. Like you and I both did."

Schenke glanced towards the two desks where his female officers sat. Frieda Echs was in her mid forties and solidly built. She wore her brown hair in a short, almost manly cut. Opposite her sat Rosa Mayer, ten years younger, with blonde hair and the kind of finely structured face that made her look like a film star. Plenty of men in the precinct had tried to win her affection, but she had rebuffed any advances by saying she had a suitor who worked in Reichsführer Himmler's private office. Whether she was telling the truth or not, it served to ensure she was never troubled more than once by the same man.

"Besides," he continued, "Frieda and Rosa have earned their place in our little world here at Pankow. Until Brandt completes his probation, he makes the coffee."

Hauser shrugged his heavy shoulders and ran a large hand over his head. "That's not how it was back in the day."

"Then chalk up a win for progress, my friend. Let's have a look at this report."

Schenke led the way through the room to the glassed-in cubicle at the far end, nodding a greeting to the officers he passed along the way. A neat brass plate with his rank and name inscribed in a gothic style was screwed to the door. He opened it. There was a bookcase and a filing cabinet against the wall opposite the window; in between was his desk, a battered and worn-looking relic from the previous century. He had been offered a replacement when he took up the post, but had declined, preferring to keep the old one. It was large, solid and redolent of tradition and good service; somehow reassuring and imposing. Because of its size, there was barely enough room for the two chairs for visitors set to the right of the door.

Behind the desk, a portrait of the Führer in a gleaming black frame stared down the length of the section's office. Unlike the desk, it had not been a feature of the office during the time of Schenke's predecessor. It had been hung there shortly after Schenke's arrival, on the orders of the precinct commander, a corpulent man who had been appointed out of loyalty to the party rather than any proven competence. Schenke had left the picture in place and tried to ignore it, taking some pleasure at having his back turned to the Führer.

Pausing to hang his coat on a hook and slip off his leather gloves, he sat in his chair and waved Hauser to one of the others.

"So, what have the lab boys got for us?"

Hauser set the folder down and slid it across to his superior. Flipping the cover open, Schenke quickly read the summary, then leafed through the following pages. As he got to the end, there was a tap at the door and he looked up to see Brandt on the other side of the glass, a steaming mug in each hand.

"Come!"

The probationer frowned helplessly, until Hauser chuckled and turned the handle for him. Brandt flushed and set his burdens down before retreating, closing the door behind him.

"Initiative isn't his strong point," Hauser said. "Be a minor miracle if he ever qualifies."

"Indeed." Schenke reached for his coffee as he considered what he had just read. "It seems that our friend Leopold Kopinski has been more industrious than we thought. Those forged coupons we found at his place are from the same source as others turning up all across the city, according to the ink dye tests and analysis of the paper." He opened the folder and took out the samples, holding them up for close examination. There was a small perforated sheet of blue meat coupons and a purple one for sweets and nuts, the most prized of the coupons issued to the population of the capital. "They're good . . . very good."

He reached into his jacket and took out his ration book, setting some of his own coupons down beside the two sheets. "I'm not sure I'd be able to pick out the forgeries if I didn't know." He glanced at Hauser. "It's tempting to pocket a few and see if they work, eh?"

The sergeant grimaced. "Sure, if you want to risk being thrown into the cells at the Alex for a few months, or sent to the camps. That's what they did to a coupon forger the Karls-horst precinct took down. I don't fancy spending a winter like this in some flimsy hut. Mind you, his work looked like his kid had forged them with crayons. Kopinski's stuff is much better. Could fool almost anyone."

"Which brings us to the question of whether this is Kopinski's own work, or brought in from another Berlin gang. If it is his work, and he confesses to it, then we can nip this in the bud."

"We've got to find him first," Hauser responded. "He went to ground after the raid."

"He can't hide for long." Schenke took a sip from his mug and winced as he found the coffee still too hot to drink. "You know how it is. Someone will sell him out soon. For money, or because our Gestapo friends beat the truth out of them. Once we get our hands on him, we'll know how far these coupons have spread."

"And if we discover that he's not behind it?" Hauser queried. "Then it could be any of the gangs with the clout to forge coupons this good on a large scale. And what if the source isn't here in Berlin? What if it's one of the Hamburg gangs? If it isn't Kopinski, I'd say our problems are just beginning. Or, more precisely, they are just beginning for our esteemed department head. Oberführer Nebe is going to be given a tough time of it by Himmler."

The new order was keen to sweep away the ills of the era that had followed the end of the last war. Criminality was to be crushed wherever it appeared and the government would not tolerate being embarrassed by having its recently introduced rationing scheme undermined by forgeries. Kopinski's fate was already determined, whether he was the source of the coupons or not. There would be a swift, highly publicized trial, at which he would be found guilty of crimes against the German people. Since Germany was at war, a death sentence was inevitable in order to set an example to other criminals. And if the forged coupons were the work of someone else, then Reichsführer Himmler was going to demand that Nebe and his investigators find those responsible and put an end to the scandal. It would be wise to take some initiative early on, Schenke reflected.

"All right then, Hauser. I want you to get in touch with the district offices. Start with those closest to Berlin and work out in the direction of the other major cities. Ask the Kripo sections if they have come across any high-quality forgeries. If so, have them send us samples at once. At least it will give us some idea how big the problem is. Nebe will need to provide that kind of intelligence to Himmler as early as possible."

Hauser gave a wry smile. "And it'll do us no harm to have been the ones to furnish him with the details, eh?"

Schenke returned the smile. "It's about time the Pankow section got some credit for our work and stopped being treated like outcasts." He spoke with feeling and instantly regretted it.

There was an awkward pause as he watched Hauser closely, trying to read his response. Hauser was a member of the party, but had shown no desire to accept an SS rank as some had done. Especially as he served under a section commander who was not a Nazi. It was not that Schenke opposed the regime particularly. He was largely indifferent to it, as long as the Nazis did not interfere with his work directly. He had joined the Kripo after graduating from university in 1934. It had been an unusual choice for someone from a privileged background, albeit a minor aristocratic household, but he was passionate about the work and the moral clarity of pursuing those who traded in crime. Politicians would come and go, but there would always be criminals. At least that was what he used to believe.

Like so many Germans, he had regarded Hitler and his followers as posturing buffoons peddling obvious lies. Even as their influence spread, like mold in a petri dish, it was hard to take them seriously. Until it was too late. Ever since Hitler had become chancellor and assumed dictatorial powers, his party's hold on almost every aspect of life in Germany had been like some great constricting serpent forever tightening its coils. The police had been swept up along with the rest of Germany's institutions, and now the Kripo too was firmly under the control of the party. There was nothing Schenke could do about that. Perhaps the price of social order and the rebuilding of Germany in a bid to make the nation great again was the loss of freedom. But as long as they let him carry out his work, he felt able to claim some moral integrity for himself and his actions. He was a guardian of the true values of the service, even if others were not, and in the fullness of time he believed—he hoped—that the party's grip would weaken and Germany would revert to a less egregious form of government. Then he would no longer find himself troubled by his doubts.

That was a view he shared only with his closest friends and family. Here in the office, he kept his opinions guarded, even from Hauser, whom he respected as a fellow professional. Trust was a scarce commodity in Germany, and becoming ever more so with each passing day. Schenke had experienced neighbors informing on neighbors, even children informing on their own parents, and being lionized by the party for doing so. The only loyalty that was tolerated by the regime was that owed to the Führer, the party and the fatherland. Every other form of loyalty was suspect. Even Hauser, who he had served with for over four years, might be forced to choose between his party and his friends and comrades, like Schenke.

"You'd better put in those calls to the other districts."

"Yes, sir. Just as soon as I've had some lunch." Hauser stood up abruptly, opened the door and slipped out of the small office, picking up his coat and hat as he left for the canteen block.

Schenke exhaled a soft sigh of relief. His breath came out with a faint wisp of steam and he felt his body retreat into itself to fight the cold. Crossing to the radiator under the window, he touched it and found barely a trace of warmth. He opened the valve fully and stood against the scratched metal columns while the feeder pipes gurgled and the metal pinged as it expanded. He raised a cuff to the beads of ice on the window panes and cleared a small circle so that he could look out over the yard and the roofs of the houses and shops beyond. It had started to snow again, bright flecks swirling from the gray sky, adding more depth to the blanket already covering the roofs and streets and swiftly blotting out the cobbles that had been swept in the precinct courtyard below.

"Shit . . ." He muttered to himself as he recalled that he had a dinner invitation that evening at the Adlon hotel in the center of Berlin. He was not looking forward to it, despite the opportunity it offered to spend more time with Karin. They had been courting for over four months, having met at one of the department's receptions hosted by Nebe. It was typical of Berlin's social events—police officers, business leaders and lawyers jostling for the attention of senior party figures while white-jacketed waiters threaded their way through the throng balancing trays of drinks and snacks. Schenke usually left as early as was acceptable. It was a finely judged calculation, since being seen as a regular early leaver carried the risk of being judged a loner; or worse, one who was disdainful of such gatherings.

On that particular night, he had managed to edge towards the coat desk when Karin approached him, champagne glass in one hand. She was slim, in her late twenties, he guessed, and dressed in a sheer black dress sparkling with sequins. Her dark hair was cropped in a short bob, with a precise line across her forehead, like the film star Louise Brooks. After looking him up and down, she addressed him directly.

"You're the racing driver, aren't you?"

"Not anymore," he replied politely. "Merely a policeman these days. And I was only *a* racing driver, never *the* racing driver."

She smiled. "You are too modest. I used to be a follower of the Silver Arrows, and you were one of the best. Until . . ." She tilted her head to one side and pursed her lips gently.

"Until the accident on the Nürburgring circuit." Schenke completed the sentence for her.

"Yes, until then. I was there that day. You were set to win the race when it happened."

The memory rushed back into his mind. The exhilaration of speed and the prospect of winning. The roar of the engine and the jarring vibration of the track beneath the car. The instant shift to a kaleidoscopic rush of trees, sky, track—and then darkness. And afterwards, the agony, and the long months of slow recuperation. He forced the recollections from his thoughts as he responded in a dry tone.

"What can I say? Sometimes a man tries too hard to win. He takes risks and he fails."

"And sometimes a man succeeds." She gestured with her glass towards the portrait of the Führer hanging at the end of the salon. Schenke sensed she was judging his reaction, and he nodded without committing himself to a reply.

"Much as I would like to stay and discuss my motor-racing days, I fear I must leave. I have to start work early tomorrow. Excuse me." He made to turn towards the servant in charge of the coats, but she reached out and touched his shoulder.

"You haven't asked my name, Herr Schenke."

"Forgive me, Fräulein . . . ?"

"Karin Canaris." She smiled, full lips drawing back to reveal neat white teeth. "And now we are acquainted, I'd be grateful if you'd stay for one more drink."

It was more than one drink, Schenke reminded himself as he returned to his desk and pulled the folder closer. After that night, they began to see each other regularly. He was attracted by her striking looks and ready humor. It was true that she had recently shown a more needy side of her personality, but he had optimistically put that down to the depth of her feeling for him. He could sense himself being steered towards a more permanent relationship, and felt uneasy about the fact. It was true that Karin was well connected socially, something that might help his career. However, he considered that an unworthy motive for marriage, and while he was willing to meet her family, and risk her meeting his own, he was concerned this might add impetus to the relationship and ease its direction of travel from his grasp.

Tonight he was due to meet her uncle, who had taken charge of her upbringing after her father had shot himself during the economic crisis in the twenties. Her mother, a Russian émigré, had abandoned her and moved to Paris shortly afterwards. The uncle was a senior naval officer who commanded one of the intelligence organizations in Berlin. Schenke could imagine the type. Some Prussian aristocrat determined to look down his nose at his niece's suitor from a lower tier of society. It would be a difficult dinner, he feared.

The phone to the right of his desk rang shrilly, and he put thoughts of Karin aside and reached for the receiver.

"Inspector Schenke."

A woman's voice crackled. "It's the precinct switchboard, sir. I have a call for you."

"Who is it?"

"SS Oberführer Müller, sir."

Schenke felt his chest tighten. "Müller?"

"Yes, sir. Shall I connect you now, sir?"

Schenke took a calming breath. "Yes, of course. At once."

There was a faint click and then a clear, blunt voice addressed him. "Inspector Schenke?"

"Yes, sir."

"This is Oberführer Müller, head of Department Four at the Reich Main Security Office. I was appointed in September, so our paths may not have crossed yet. But I have been made aware of your reputation."

Schenke winced at the possible implications of that comment, and there was a pause at the other end of the line, as if the caller knew his choice of words might command anxiety and was content to have that effect.

"You have a good record, Schenke. Some fine police work. A credit to the Kripo."

"Thank you, sir." Schenke felt a rush of relief.

"Which is why I need to engage your services now. There has been an incident, a potentially delicate matter, and I require a reliable and discreet man to deal with it. You are that man, Schenke. I need you here at headquarters as soon as possible."

"Yes, sir."

"Very well. I will speak with you later."

The line went dead, but Schenke lingered to be certain his superior had concluded the call before he dialed the precinct's reception office.

"Have a car sent to the entrance for Inspector Schenke. Immediately, please."

"Yes, sir."

Schenke rose from his desk and slipped on his coat. His troubled mind was racing. What possible reason could there be for the head of the Gestapo to demand his immediate presence at their headquarters?

Chapter Three

It was shortly before noon by the time the pool car reached the ornate arched facade of the entrance to the Reich Main Security Office on Prinz-Albrecht-Strasse. On the drive south from the precinct into the heart of Berlin, Schenke had taken the time to review what he knew of Müller. Although he had never met the head of the Gestapo, he had seen him from a distance at parades and a handful of police conferences. Like any career officer with ambition, Schenke knew that it was important to be aware of the comings and goings of the senior ranks, and the changes they imposed on Germany's police and security services.

In the six years since the party had taken control of the state, they had remorselessly folded the police forces and their departments into a single hierarchy that answered to Heinrich Himmler. Unlike many of those presently in the senior ranks, Müller had been a professional policeman. He had a reputation for efficiency and an admirable work ethic. He demanded the same of those who worked for him and disciplined or dismissed those who failed to adopt his standards. Although he had been a member of the SS for a number of years, somehow he had managed to avoid becoming a member of the party until a few months ago. That had intrigued Schenke when he learned of it through the "mouth radio," as they called the professional gossip that went the rounds of the precincts. Müller, it seemed, was a policeman at heart, rather than a purely political animal, and that was of slight encouragement to Schenke as the car growled between banks of snow lining the edges of the roads.

There were fewer people than usual on the streets of the Mitte district at the heart of the capital. Winter had driven many indoors, where they tried to stay warm until the freezing weather receded. Those who were abroad wore heavy coats and hats as they picked their way along the icy sidewalks. There was less traffic since the war had come, bringing with it the rationing of fuel. Berlin had the feel of a city in hibernation, yearning for the passing of the winter season as well as a return to peace.

As the car drew up, Schenke opened the door and instructed the driver to wait for him outside, in the hope that the meeting would be brief.

"If I don't come back within the hour, I want you to return to the precinct and tell Hauser where I am."

"Yes, sir."

He turned towards the columned entrance, where two black-uniformed sentries were standing at ease. Climbing the steps, he passed through the double doors into the lofty hall beyond. Even inside, with extra stoves burning, the air was not much warmer than on the street, and the clerks were wearing coats as they sat at the desks on either side of the hall. At the far end was a staircase leading up to the wing of the building allocated to the Gestapo.

Schenke approached the reception desk, where a black-uniformed clerk stood up and snapped out a salute. Used to the less formal atmosphere of the precinct, Schenke hesitated before he responded in kind.

"Hail Hitler. I'm Inspector Schenke, here to see Oberführer Müller."

"Yes, sir."

"He sent for me."

"Yes, sir, I know. The Oberführer's aide has notified the front desk. You are to go directly to his office." He gestured towards the stairs. "First floor, turn right and continue to the end. I will inform his aide that you have arrived, sir."

The stairs led to a wide corridor with a high arched ceiling lit by large leaded windows on one side. A series of wooden benches were set beneath the windows, interspersed with gleaming black busts of the Führer on marble plinths. A handful of visitors sat or stood by the benches as they waited their turn to be seen. They glanced curiously at Schenke as he strode by, but no one attempted a greeting. The double door at the end of the corridor opened at his approach, and an aide waved him inside before closing the door behind them.

They stood in an anteroom larger than the entire space taken up by the Kripo section back at the precinct. The aide's desk was at least twice the size of Schenke's and was made of some finely polished dark wood. A bulky iron stove stood in the far corner and heated the room to a comfortable degree. At least a dozen chairs were arranged on one side, beneath the ubiquitous framed portrait of the nation's savior, looking down on the room from the oak-paneled wall.

"Inspector Schenke, may I take your coat, sir?"

He handed it to the aide, along with his hat, scarf and gloves.

The aide nodded to a door, ajar, opposite the desk. "The Oberführer is ready to see you, sir."

Schenke tugged the sleeves of his jacket to eliminate any creases and paced towards the door. His heart was beating more swiftly than usual. He could think of no reason for his summons to the Gestapo headquarters. It might have something to do with the investigation into the ration coupons. It could just as easily be to answer allegations about his loyalty to the regime made by some informer with a grudge. It was useless to speculate. He would know the reason soon enough.

Easing the door open and stepping into the red-carpeted interior, Schenke was met by an opulence he had not anticipated. The Oberführer's office was larger than the anteroom, and to the side of the door was a huge marble fireplace where coals glowed brightly and filled the room with warmth. The walls were paneled to half the height of the room and lined with framed pictures. Many featured Müller in the company of senior members of the party. The Oberführer himself sat behind a vast desk, bent over some paperwork. He looked up.

"Ah, Schenke, come over here. I won't be a moment."

Schenke did as he was told, only then realizing that there were no other chairs in the office, so that he was forced to stand in front of his superior. On the other side of the desk Müller continued to examine a list, which Schenke could see consisted of names. Some had a line drawn through them, others a tick next to them, while a few merited a brief comment. What the purpose of the list was, Schenke did not know, and he could not help wondering if it was something sinister or, given the time of year, merely a Christmas card list. Either was possible, but the fact that it was the head of the Gestapo dealing with it with quiet concentration betokened something ominous.

The Oberführer was forty years old, and below average height. His hair was clipped short and shaved above the ears, a look that was fashionable amongst party members. He wore the formal black uniform with the silver eagle on the left sleeve and his new party badge pinned through the lapel. As Schenke watched, he put a line through the last name on the list, signed the bottom of the sheet, turned it over and eased it to one side before capping his pen and looking up. His face was broad and the line of his mouth was wide, though the lips were thin, enhancing the sense of a flat line uncompromised by mirth or cruelty. His nose was long and wide, and beneath the large forehead a pair of steel-gray eyes bored into Schenke.

"I was expecting you earlier."

"I set off as soon as I got your call, sir. The roads were icy and my driver was obliged to take it more slowly than usual."

"Very well, you are here now." Müller eased himself back. "Before I tell you why, I'd like to know a little more about you. I read your file earlier and it makes for impressive reading. Second in your class on the officer course, two marks behind one Abraham Goldstein, alas no longer serving with us. Your probation assessments were excellent and one states that you were a model criminal investigator in every regard. You achieved good clearance rates and won early promotion to your present rank, where it is fair to say your fortunes seem to have languished. One would have thought that with your evident ability, not to mention a certain amount of residual fame arising from your motor-racing exploits, you would have achieved greater success."

"I do my job to the best of my ability, sir. I get results. That's success enough."

"And yet you only hold the rank of inspector in charge of a section in a minor precinct. I would expect a man with your record to be a rank or two higher at least." Müller stared into his eyes fixedly and it took Schenke some strength of will to hold his gaze. "Why do you think that is, Schenke?"

"It is not for me to say, sir. It is up to others to decide how competently I do my job and whether I am suitable material for promotion."

"Clearly they have decided you are not. I ask you a second time, why do you think that is?"

There was no mistaking the threat in his tone as he dared Schenke to deny him a response.

"I imagine it might have something to do with my not being a member of the party, sir."

"You imagine?" Müller arched an eyebrow. "I don't think there is any question of imagining it, Inspector. It is a given. Which naturally leads to the next question. Why have you not joined the party? And why have you not applied to join the SS like many of your colleagues have done?"

It was a question Schenke had prepared himself for long ago, when the party had first made clear its intention to take over the police forces and give them a new political purpose alongside their existing duties. He drew a calming breath before he gave his response. "Sir, I joined the police force to uphold the law and bring criminals to justice. I choose not to join the party as I feel it is my duty to focus my attention on my calling, rather than being distracted by political issues."

"Do you have political views, either way?"

It was a crude trap and Schenke hesitated before he replied. "The German people voted for the party. The party is the legally constituted government of the state. The state makes the law and it is the obligation of every police officer to enforce the law. That's how I see it, sir. And therefore I do not need to be a member of the party, nor do I deserve to be regarded with suspicion because I choose not to be a member."

"Your unswerving sense of loyalty to your profession and the state does you credit, Schenke, but I can't help wondering if that's the true reason behind your decision. I would be naïve to take your answer at face value. Wouldn't you agree?"

Schenke fought to keep his expression and bearing inscrutable as his mind raced to form a safe reply. "I would not presume to offer any such opinion regarding a senior officer, sir. As long as I do my job well, then I am content, and I am not concerned what others may think about my character."

Müller smiled slightly. "An answer worthy of any politician. And that is not a compliment. I think we understand one another, Inspector. As it happens, your political disengagement is one of the qualities that makes you most suitable for the task I have in mind. If you were a member of the party, it might well cloud your judgment. I need a good criminal investigator who will pursue the case without prejudice or hope of preferment."

He folded his hands together and rested his chin on them as he continued to stare at the man standing on the far side of the desk. "It's only fair to warn you that you will be dealing with persons of influence, some of whom have the power to make or break the career of a police officer. Particularly one of your lowly rank and lack of political connections. I will do what I can to shield you from such dangers, but my authority, such as it is, depends upon my being favored by Himmler and Heydrich. Especially Heydrich. I will not cross swords with him. Not on your behalf. Lesser party members and other officials I may be able to deal with. So be warned. Tread carefully as you go about your task."

Schenke felt an icy twinge at the back of his neck, despite the warmth in the room. "And what is the task, sir?"

"Something right up your alley. This morning the body of a woman was discovered by the tracks not far from Anhalter station. She appears to have been killed by a blow to the head, which crushed her skull. Her clothes were torn and there is evidence of assault. Her purse was not removed, nor her jewelry, so it doesn't appear that she was robbed. I want your office to lead the investigation."

"Why not leave it to the local Kripo section, sir?"

"There are certain complicating factors. The first policemen on the scene found her identity card. The victim's name is Gerda Korzeny. I doubt that name means anything to you, but she is the wife of one Gustav Korzeny, a senior party member and a lawyer. Bit of a backroom boy, but he serves an important role. He's the one who rewrites certain laws to make the party's actions legal. He makes it possible for the party to say that the law is what the party says it is. The same law that you are obliged to uphold, as you stated earlier. You see, Schenke, you are implicated in politics whether you choose to be or not. You may believe that you are standing above the stink of it, pinching your nose. But it only seems that way."

He inclined his head, daring his subordinate to disagree, then continued. "Korzeny was informed within a matter of hours. He demands that we catch the killer quickly. And that is why I sent for you."

"But sir, I am already involved in a number of cases. My section is taking the lead on a forgery case."

"Forgery?"

"Ration coupons, sir. They've been found across Berlin, and it may be that they are already in circulation in other cities."

"The investigation will be taken over by another section. I will assign them as soon as this interview is completed, and you can hand over all the paperwork. For now, you and your team have one task. Find the killer of Gerda Korzeny."

"I don't understand, sir. Any Kripo section could deal with the murder. But if the coupon forgery is not dealt with swiftly, it could undermine the morale of the public. It makes more sense to let me conclude that investigation and have someone else deal with the murder."

"I am sure it will make sense once you start to grapple with the niceties of the case. From what I understand, Frau Korzeny is—was—an interesting character."

"Sir?"

"You'll see for yourself." Müller reached for his pen and took another list from his in-tray as he spoke. "The Schöneberg precinct has taken charge of the initial investigation. You are to go there when you leave my office. I have already informed them that you and your team will be conducting the investigation and they are to afford you every cooperation. My aide will give you written authority to access any evidence you require, and to interview or question anyone you deem necessary in the pursuit of your investigation. You are to report your progress to my office. Do you have any questions?"

Schenke's mind was reeling with queries, but it was clear that nothing would sway the Oberführer from assigning the case to him. "Not at the moment, sir."

Müller's eyes glinted and his expression became stern and unbending. "Then find the killer. And do it as swiftly as you can. Dismissed."

Chapter Four

"So what's the story?" asked Hauptsturmführer Ritter, the acting precinct commander at Schöneberg. "Why does Gestapo Müller want your section to take the lead on this murder case?"

"Gestapo Müller?"

Ritter laughed. "That's what they're calling him. Seems there's some other SS general named Heinrich Müller and so Heydrich decided to give his new Gestapo lad a label to save confusion. So Gestapo Müller it is."

They were sitting at a side table in Ritter's office. Like the rest of the accommodation for the Kripo section at the precinct, it was spacious and comfortably furnished. Schenke could not help feeling a certain envy at his colleague's good fortune. The Kripo section head was a thin, almost gaunt man with close-cropped white hair and wire-rimmed glasses. He looked to be in his fifties, and Schenke guessed that he had reached the end of his career and faced the prospect of no further promotion once a new commander was appointed. But he was affable enough. A coaster, Schenke decided.

He had not quibbled when Schenke had handed over his letter of authority. Rather, there had been a relieved reaction, and Ritter had been almost friendly as they made their way to his office to discuss the preliminary details of the murder of Gerda Korzeny over coffee served in delicate china cups bearing the party's symbol. The fact that Ritter had taken the SS rank and wore the uniform warned Schenke that he must be careful not to make any indiscreet remarks.

"I haven't been given much information," he responded, and sipped his coffee. The flavor was acrid. Clearly not every luxury was afforded to the local Kripo section. "But what Müller did say was that the matter was sensitive. Therefore I think my selection for the task has more to do with my dispensability than my ability."

Ritter chuckled. "I fear you may be right. What do you know about Gerda Korzeny?"

"Nothing. Never heard the name before today. Müller told me she was married to a senior party official. And that she wasn't the usual party bigwig's wife. 'Interesting' was the word he used to describe her."

"I'll say." Ritter shook his head. "Frankly, I'm astonished that you aren't aware of her reputation. It's an open secret within the party and Berlin society. But then you aren't a member of the party, and your precinct is something of a suburb. Even so, you must have heard rumors."

"Sorry." Schenke shook his head. "The burden of being a provincial, I suppose."

"Ah, get away with you!" Ritter laughed. "I recognized your face at once. I have no doubt you were at the heart of the social scene back in your racing days, eh?"

Schenke smiled. "I enjoyed the parties."

"I bet you did. Dashing young fellow like yourself must have had a high time of it. So why did you give it all up?"

"The accident," Schenke prompted.

"Ah yes, I recall." Ritter drained his cup and set it down with a sharp rap. "Nasty business."

"I was in the hospital for five months. When I came out, I'd lost the appetite for speed."

"I imagine something like that might unnerve a man."

Schenke shot him a searching look. Was that an accusation? he wondered.

"Still," Ritter went on, "the racetrack's loss is the Kripo's gain. Not to mention mine, now that you're taking on the case."

"Speaking of which, what details do you have for me? All I got from Müller was the name and the location where the body was found, and that it was murder. Are you certain about that?"

"Positive." Ritter nodded emphatically. "Her head was smashed in with a heavy implement. A small axe or something like that. And it was clear that she had been attacked sexually."

"Oh?"

"She was naked from the waist down when we found her. A coat and skirt were bundled up nearby. The body and her belongings have been taken to the mortuary." He paused. "Damn shame. For all her faults, she was a fine-looking woman once. You might even have met her. I'm sure she would have been part of the same social crowd. Racing drivers, film stars and so on."

"Film stars? She was an actress?"

"Barely, if I'm honest. Bit of a leaden delivery, but she looked like a goddess up on the screen. She wasn't married then. Gerda Schnee."

Schenke's eyes widened. "Gerda Schnee!"

"You knew her, then?"

"Yes. I mean, I knew *of* her. I've seen some of her films.

One of the biggest stars back in the late twenties. But she wasn't at any of the parties I went to, as far as I recall."

"Blame that on her husband. He stopped her going out the moment they were married." Ritter shook his head. "Never knew why she settled for him. Dusty old lawyerly type like that. Word was that she was one of Josef Goebbels's mistresses and was blackmailing him so that she could still live in style after the film work dried up. He needed her made nice and respectable to save his reputation. So he got Korzeny to take the bullet for him. She behaved for a while, but then I guess marriage became a little dull and she looked for her entertainment outside of the home. Funny thing is, I've heard that Korzeny doted on her, despite all her affairs, and the humiliation she heaped on him."

"How has he taken it?"

"How do you think? The men who went to his home to break the news say he collapsed and bawled like a kid. He called me up within the hour, though. Shouting that she had been with another man last night, and that he must have been the killer and I'd better find him if I knew what was good for me."

Such threats were not helpful, thought Schenke, especially if they were backed up by political connections. "Has Korzeny been formally interviewed? Did he name the man his wife was meeting?"

"No. He put the phone down on me as soon as he'd given me my orders." Ritter sat back in his chair. "I thought I'd give you the pleasure of questioning him, since the case is yours now."

"Thank you," Schenke responded flatly.

"My pleasure, believe me." Ritter chuckled. "More coffee?"

The thought of another sip of the foul brew made Schenke wince. "No thank you. I think it's best that I get to work at once."

"I'll have the initial reports sent to your offices first thing tomorrow morning."

"No need for that. We'll operate from here. I'll have my section sent over later on."

"Here?" Ritter's brow wrinkled.

"Why not? This is the closest precinct to the crime scene. You'll need to allocate us some office space. Enough for ten of us. With desks."

"Out of the question! We've hardly enough space as it is," Ritter went on lamely.

Schenke took out the letter of authority he had tucked into his inner pocket. "My orders," he explained. "You can take it up with the Oberführer if you like."

He could sense the inner torment of the other man before Ritter let out a sigh of resignation. "I'll see what I can do."

"Good." Schenke pocketed the letter, glanced at his watch and then out of the office window. The sky was gloomy and threatened more snow. "It's nearly three o'clock. It'll be dark soon. I want to see the crime scene."

"Now? Isn't it a bit late for that? I can show you first thing in the morning, when you can see things clearly."

"Now would be best. Just as they taught us on the training course. The first hours are critical in gathering as much evidence as possible."

Ritter stiffened. "I never went on the course. I was transferred to the Kripo from the river police."

That explained a few things, Schenke mused. Ritter's advancement, limited as it was, was due to his party connections. An ideologically safe pair of hands appointed to replace some professional criminal investigator.

He used Ritter's telephone to put the call through to the Pankow precinct, alerting Hauser to the new investigation and asking him to round up the section and head to Schöneberg. Then he stood up and put on his coat. "Let's go."

* * *

It was dusk by the time they reached the siding where the body had been discovered, and the freezing air seemed suffused with a faint blue hue. There were already lights on in a number of windows, and some of those within were drawing their curtains to comply with the blackout restrictions. Soon Berlin would be swallowed up by the winter night and the blackout wardens would be patrolling the streets on the hunt for those who had failed to seal the light inside their homes. Stern warnings would be issued, or worse for repeat offenders: fines and a spell in prison. There would be other hunters on the street as well, Schenke reflected. People looking for black market traders; prostitutes and rent boys looking for customers, and men looking for them; as well as the usual pickpockets and muggers waiting to strike before vanishing into the darkness. And then there would be the rapists and the killers, like the man Schenke had been tasked to track down.

The driver parked next to another police car and a van in the depot behind the Anhalter station. The domed roof above the platforms towered into the gray sky and the whistles of trains and the rattle of carriages across sets of points was muted by the snow. Ritter and Schenke showed their badges to the railway policeman guarding the vehicles.

"This way," said Ritter as he led Schenke between two long lines of freight wagons, their footsteps crunching on the fresh layer of snow. When they emerged, Schenke saw a small group of men a short distance to one side of the main tracks leading into and out of the capital. Some of them were uniformed police, gathered about a roped-off area where plainclothes officers were examining the scene. There was an exchange of salutes as Ritter approached them, then he turned to indicate his companion.

"This is Criminal Inspector Schenke. His section has been assigned to take over the case from our precinct."

One of the plainclothesmen raised a hand. "We're being pulled off the case? Why?"

"Orders," Ritter replied tersely. "We've plenty of other business to be dealing with already. For now, we'll assist the inspector in any way that we can. Carry on."

The men exchanged puzzled looks, and some stared at Schenke before they turned back to their work. Two uniformed railway police stood to one side, cold and shivering as they rubbed their hands together and stamped their boots.

"They were the first men on the scene," Ritter explained.

"Good God, have they been here all day?"

"No. They've been on duty at Anhalter. I had them sent back here before we left the precinct, in case you wanted to speak to them."

Schenke nodded approvingly, then paused to take in his surroundings. They were on a patch of open ground close to where the line curved in towards the station. The nearest building, a long engine shed, was over a hundred meters away. There was little sign of life in the immediate area. Just a solitary figure, hunched over, trudging along a path that ran behind the nearest blocks of a working-class neighborhood. The roped-off area was in a slight dip, where it was possible to squat, or lie down, and not be seen.

The light was failing and it would soon be too dark to pick out much detail, so he turned and ducked under the rope. Inside the cordon, a series of small numbered stakes marked the location of clothing and other items that had been found scattered around the body.

"Have you got photographs yet?"

The question was addressed to Ritter, who nodded at one of the plainclothes officers inside the cordon. "Well, Leiman?"

The officer shook his head. "Nothing back from the lab, sir."

"A pity," Schenke muttered. "How was the body arranged when it was discovered?"

"You'd best ask them clowns." The detective pointed towards the railway police. "They'd moved her and gone over her possessions long before we arrived. Fucking amateurs. We've done what we can to record what evidence was left. They'd almost destroyed a trail of footprints leading into the hollow and over the tracks. We managed to get a few partial prints before the next fall of snow blanked everything out."

Schenke acknowledged this with a nod. "I may want to speak to you later, Leiman. Meanwhile, I'd better have a word with the clowns, while they can still remember to tie their own bootlaces, eh?"

"Good luck with that," the detective grunted. "Anyway, we're about done here, sir. We're losing the light, and I've logged all that we've got so far." He looked to Ritter. "Shall I send the manifest to you, sir? Or this gentleman?"

"Mark it for my attention," Schenke cut in. "And put it on my desk at the precinct."

"Your desk?"

"Once that's been allocated. Along with any other notes you've taken. Yours and the other officers'. Clear?"

"Yes, sir."

Schenke ducked back under the rope and went over to the two railway police officers. In the gathering gloom, he saw that both men were in their forties. One was so rotund that Schenke doubted whether he could even squeeze through a train door, let alone chase a felon down its aisles. His companion looked to be a fitter and tougher proposition for the petty criminals and vandals who occupied most of the railway police's attention.

"You were the first two police on the scene, right?"

"Yes, sir."

Schenke took out his notepad and removed his glove to get a precise grip on his pencil. "Names?"

"Altemann, sir," said the fat one. "He's Schmidt."

"Tell me what you know." Schenke focused his attention on Altemann.

"We were on the platform beat first thing this morning, sir. We'd just made the turnaround at number four when we heard a shout from down the tracks. It was one of them engine stokers. Yelling his head off and waving his arms around. When he got to us he was almost out of breath. Took a moment to get the facts out of him. Then he took us down here. We found the woman in that hollow, sir. Blood and clothing all over the place."

"How much detail did you get out of the stoker?"

"Just what I said, sir."

"But you took a statement from him, yes?"

Altemann glanced at his friend before he shook his head. "Poor man was too distressed, sir. Badly shaken. I sent him home then called the local precinct."

"You sent him home? The man who discovered the body. You just sent him home?" Schenke tried to contain his frustration and anger at the man's incompetence. "Tell me you have his name, at least."

Altemann opened his mouth, paused and then frowned. "Uh . . ."

"Gantz." His comrade spoke up. "Peter Gantz is his name."

"Do you have his address?"

"No, sir. But he'll be back on shift tomorrow. We can take his statement then if you like."

"I'd like that very much. See to it. Send me a copy as soon as it's typed up. And tell Gantz to make his whereabouts known in case we need to question him further."

Altemann frowned. "After we've taken his story? What's the point, sir?"

"To check that the story he tells me is consistent with the story he tells you. See?"

"Ah!" Altemann grinned. "Very clever, sir."

Schenke shot a look at the other policeman, who shook his head discreetly. "You take the statement, Schmidt."

"Yes, sir."

Schenke sighed inwardly and took another look around the snowy landscape of tracks, signal posts and freight wagons. It was growing dark and the details of the engine shed were dissolving into a featureless mass against the drab gray of the sky as the last of the lights in more distant buildings winked out in observation of the blackout. It added to the atmosphere of unfamiliarity and unease that came with the war. He felt a moment's longing for the winter holidays in Bavaria he had taken with his family as a child. He recalled with moving clarity trudging back through a village, trailing a sled. The air was crisp and the warm glow of lights in the mountain chalets spilled over snowy fields, promising the warmth of the hearth, hot drinks and companionship. The image faded as a whistle shrieked nearby and a freight train rumbled and hissed, dragging its clanking burden south in the direction of Tempelhof.

Ritter and his team had left the cordon and were trudging back towards the station.

Altemann coughed. "May we go, sir? They'll be needing us at the station to manage the commuters."

"A moment." Schenke looked towards the hollow. "There was a trail of footprints near the body, right?"

"Yes, sir. Two sets going one way, and one set leaving the crime scene and disappearing in the coal depot by the engine shed." Schmidt pointed at the end of the nearest of the freight wagons on the siding. "They entered the hollow from that direction. I followed the first set as far as I could. Stopped at one of the main lines. The snow was disturbed at that point. Might be where they came off one of the carriages."

"They jumped from a moving train?"

"Not necessarily, sir. Could have been stopped by a signal and they just stepped off."

"But you say the snow was disturbed."

"Yes, but there was no indication that someone had fallen and rolled. Like you'd expect them to if the train had been moving."

Schenke made a mental note. Schmidt was obviously the more shrewd of the two railway policemen. "Show me where the tracks led."

Schmidt took the lead, Schenke following. Altemann muttered under his breath before trailing behind them. The snow that had fallen during the day had obliterated any imprints on the ground, and Schmidt did his best to steer a course along the route he had traced that morning.

"They turned here, sir. Came across from the end of the other freight line and led from the main tracks."

"Have you got a flashlight?"

"Yes, sir." Schmidt fumbled in his pocket. "Here you are, sir."

Schenke took it and thumbed the switch. A bright beam lanced out across the snow, and he turned it on the end of the wagon and scanned the dull, grime-covered buffers and chains. Then the light fell on something of a different hue, a shred of gray cloth snagged on the head of a large rusty bolt at just above waist height.

Reaching into his pocket, he took out a small paper evidence envelope. He rested the torch on the footplate with the light pointed towards the bolt and carefully removed the small strip of cloth and tucked it into the envelope.

"Hey! You there! What the hell do you fools think you're doing? Put that bloody light out!"

They saw a portly figure surging towards them. Schenke pocketed the envelope and snapped the torch off, handing it back to Schmidt.

"I want your names. Wait until your shift commander hears of this. He'll have your bollocks for breakfast!"

There was just enough light for Schenke to make out the large sideburns and bristling moustache of the warden as he drew up, puffing for breath, in front of them. He swallowed, breathed deeply and thrust out a finger. "You fools. What if some French bomber saw that light, eh? Boom! Blown to bits. What do you think about that? And you two policemen. You should know better. Names, then."

"They're with me," said Schenke. He took out his badge and held it up. "Criminal Inspector Schenke."

The warden stepped up and strained to see the details on the badge, then eased back. "Kripo, eh?"

"That's right. We're investigating a body found by the tracks this morning. Official business. I needed the light to see what we were doing."

"Well, that's as may be. But there's a war on."

"I know. And so far not a single bomb has been dropped on Berlin. So I hardly think we're in danger of guiding any enemy planes to their targets."

"Even so, sir, there's no exceptions for blackout rules. Still, I'll let you off this once. It being official business and all." He wagged a finger. "No more warnings. I catch you using a light again, there'll be trouble."

He turned and stamped off through the snow. Schenke and the two policemen looked at each other and spontaneously chuckled.

"The Führer himself wouldn't dare cross that one," said Schenke. "Come on. It's cold. Let's get back to the vehicles. If I need to speak to either of you again, I'll send for you. Better a day in a warm precinct than doing your beat on a freezing platform."

"Amen to that!" Altemann clapped his hands as they trudged back along the side of the line of freight wagons.

The other car and the van had gone by the time they returned to the depot. Schenke bade a brief farewell to the policemen, then climbed into the pool car. The engine was running and the heater was turned up, so there was a warm fug inside.

"It's getting late. Let's go back to the precinct," said Ritter from the back seat.

Schenke shook his head. "First I want to see the body."

Chapter Five

The mortuary was a block away from the precinct, at the rear of a hospital. It had its own entrance so that bodies could be discreetly brought in or taken away for burial. As the car pulled up in the walled yard, Ritter leaned forward and tapped Schenke on the shoulder.

"Look here, this is your case now. Nothing to do with me any longer. I imagine you'll be here a while, so I'll get back to the precinct and make the arrangements to accommodate your section."

"Good. You can liaise with Sergeant Hauser when he arrives. Tell him I'll brief the team when I get there."

"Shall I send the car back for you?"

Schenke had already had enough of Ritter's grudging assistance and shook his head as he opened the door and climbed into the bitterly cold night air. "It's only a few minutes' walk. I'll manage."

"Good. Let's be off then, driver."

As soon as Schenke had closed the door the vehicle crunched over the fresh snow, the thin glow from the narrow slits covering the headlamps briefly sweeping round the brick walls and then out into the street. Schenke tugged his collar up and climbed the short ramp to the double doors of the mortuary. He pressed the button, and a muffled bell sounded within. After a brief delay, the door opened a crack and a thin-faced man peered out.

"Yes?"

"Criminal Inspector Schenke." He held up his identity badge. "I'm in charge of the Korzeny investigation. I've come to see the body."

The man opened the door for his visitor, then quickly closed it behind him. They were standing in a small lobby. To one side was a counter with a stool behind it. A newspaper lay open on the top and smoke curled from a cigarette balanced on the edge of an ashtray. Above was a notice board recording admission and removal of bodies, and opposite the entrance was another doorway leading into a corridor.

"The examiner's still working on that one, sir," the man explained, and gestured down the corridor towards a double door at the end. "He's in there."

Schenke strode along the corridor, passing a handful of offices and store cupboards on either side. The air was filled with a sickly chemical tang mixed with the more pleasant odor of floor polish. The doors at the end had frosted glass, and above them were spring hinges to make sure that they always remained closed. He eased the right-hand one open and stepped into a large tiled room, brightly lit. The single window, high on the far wall, was covered with a thick blackout curtain. One wall was lined with drawers, several of which were open. In one of them he could see a pair of splayed feet on a metal tray. The middle of the room was dominated by two large polished steel examination tables. On the nearest lay the body of a naked woman. Beside her stood a corpulent man with heavy-rimmed glasses. He wore a dull green gown with dark smears on the front.

He looked up from the body. "Police?"

Schenke held his badge up as he approached the table. "I'm Schenke from the Kripo. I'll be running the Korzeny investigation from now on."

The other man frowned. "I understood that was Ritter's responsibility."

"Not any longer. Orders from on high."

The man tilted his head, as if examining Schenke. He made to offer his hand, realized that it was smeared with blood and other fluids, and withdrew it. "Sorry, force of habit. I'm Dr. Muttling, the district medical examiner. So Ritter's working under you, or is he off the case?"

"He's been reassigned."

"Ah, very well." The hint of relief in Muttling's tone was obvious. "Let me introduce you to Gerda Korzeny. She is—was—famous at one time, you know. A film star no less."

"I remember her." Schenke stepped up to the table and looked down at the pale body lying in the glare of the overhead lights. Although there was bruising on her nose and around her face, the fine bones of her cheeks were intact. Her lips were slightly parted as her eyes stared at the ceiling. He frowned. At first glance her hair had looked dark, as if it was wet. Now that he stood over her he saw that the blonde hair that she had worn as an actress was now brown. He looked again at her face to make sure it was the same woman.

"Has her hair been dyed?"

"No. That's what I wondered when she was brought in. I've checked. That's her natural coloring." Muttling clicked his tongue. "Who knew that the celluloid sweetheart was a fake blonde?"

"It's news to me," Schenke admitted. He scrutinized the rest of her body. There were signs of bruising on her face, arms, shins and groin. "Looks like she put up a struggle before she was killed."

The examiner nodded. "Her attacker held her by the wrists at some stage. You can see the bruising from his fingers clearly. I'd say he was a strong man. There was blood in her nose, and bruising there." He leaned over and tapped the bridge of the nose lightly. "He might have muffled her cries. There's bruising to the cheek as well."

"It's likely she was only killed at the very end, then," said Schenke. "A blow to the head, I've been told."

"That's right." Muttling shuffled round to the end of the table and eased the hair on the top of her head to one side to reveal a deep wound, some ten centimeters in length. The scalp was torn, and fragments of bone stuck out like jagged fangs on either side of the dark cleft of congealed blood and brains. Schenke felt his stomach tighten.

"She was struck with considerable violence," the examiner continued in a matter-of-fact tone. "The murder weapon shattered her skull and penetrated as far as the thalamus. The nature of the damage tends to suggest the blow was delivered from above as she lay on the ground." He moved round and leaned over the body, miming a slow chopping movement. "Like so."

"Just the one blow?"

"That's all it took to kill her. There was no frenzied assault. Not at the end, at least."

Schenke sucked in a breath as he pictured her final moments, sprawled on her back in the freezing snow. The terror as her killer loomed over her and raised his weapon. "What did he use? A hatchet perhaps?"

Muttling shook his head. "The edges of the wound would be more regular. The impact smashed the top of her skull. I'd say it was likely to have been a heavy bar of some kind. And given what I said about the depth of the injury, the force needed to deal such a blow would require some strength. You'll be looking for a burly individual, Inspector."

"Or an enraged one."

"A single blow is all it took, remember. If our man was enraged, I'd expect there to have been more blows."

"That's true." Schenke shifted his gaze from the destruction wrought on Gerda Korzeny's head and looked over the rest of her body. "Was she raped?"

"Yes. You can see the bruising around the pubic area. And there are some lesions inside the vagina."

Schenke winced. His professional experience had taught him that there were many reasons why some men felt driven to commit sexual assaults. But it only mattered to him that they did it at all, and that he tracked them down and made them pay the price for their savagery. He thought of the fear and suffering that had occurred before Gerda's death. He felt a cold anger stirring in his heart as he resolved to find the man who had killed her. He turned towards the examiner. "Is there anything else you can tell me?"

"Not much. I think she must have been drinking; certainly her clothes smelled of spirits. And the lividity of some of the bruises suggests they were caused before last night. Possibly days before, if I had to make a reasoned estimate." He looked at the policeman warily as he repeated the words. "If I had to make an estimate."

"It's not in your report?"

"I haven't written up my notes yet . . ."

Schenke considered the implications, especially in the context of the unusual circumstances in which he had been given the case. "I want all your observations included in the report, Herr Doctor. Leave nothing out, is that understood?"

"Given that the earlier bruises have nothing to do with the circumstances of her death, I am reluctant to include reference to them for fear that it might confuse the investigation and implicate other, innocent parties."

Schenke approached the examiner and tapped him on the chest.

"Include everything, understand? I am in charge of the investigation. If anyone takes exception to my methods or my findings, then I will take full responsibility. Not you. Happy now?"

The examiner flushed with embarrassment, and then tried to make up for it with a display of professionalism. "I'll write my notes up before I leave here tonight. The report will be sent to the precinct first thing in the morning."

"Good," Schenke responded coldly. "I will expect it then. No later."

He backed off and took one last look at the broken, bruised body, pitiful in the cold pallor of the mortuary lights. It was hard to imagine it had once been a beautiful, graceful woman animated by wit and laughter and that ineffable sense of presence that film stars possessed. It felt to Schenke as if some small part of his world had been extinguished. Gerda Korzeny's death was notable, even against the backdrop of a war that had already claimed the lives of so many, and that would claim vastly more if the politicians of the great nations did not come to their senses and make peace. Only her ghost lived on in the films she had starred in.

He turned and strode away, barging the swing doors aside as he made for the entrance to the mortuary, quickening his pace in a bid to escape the stench of the place, even though he felt a painful twinge in his leg. The thin clerk glanced up from his newspaper, cigarette hanging from his lip, but before he could stir from his stool, Schenke had wrenched the door open and stepped outside, closing it loudly behind him.

The night air was icy and sharp, but he breathed it in to flush out his lungs. Then he hunched his head into the folds of his scarf and set off through the dark streets towards the precinct. As he walked, he thought through all he had learned in the last few hours. Gerda Korzeny's death was leading him into dark and dangerous territory, and he would have to tread very carefully.

* * *

Hauser had already arrived by the time Schenke entered the building. The sergeant was sitting on a bench in the entrance hall, and he smiled and stood up as he saw his superior.

"Nice digs they've got here, sir."

"This is just the shopfront. Wait until you see more of the place." Schenke forced a smile and expelled the scene at the mortuary from his mind. "Where are the rest of the section?"

"I left them to pack a few necessaries and warn their families they'd be late home tonight. They'll follow on in two of the pool cars. Shouldn't be long now."

"And how did Frau Hauser take it?"

The sergeant shrugged at the mention of his wife. "She married a policeman. She knows what that means. The job is no respecter of family life, even at this time of year. I was supposed to track down a carp for the boys to put in the bath tonight for Christmas. Guess that'll have to wait."

"I'm sorry."

"Not your fault, sir. Just orders." Hauser adopted his usual flat tone. "What have you found out so far?"

"I'll tell you on the way."

"Oh?" Hauser arched an eyebrow. "Where are we going?"

"To interview the husband. As soon as I have his address." Schenke glanced at his watch. It was 5.30. With luck, there would be time for him to speak to Korzeny and still make it to the Adlon in time for dinner with Karin and her uncle. "You find us a car while I speak to Ritter. And leave a note for Frieda to take charge and get our new office set up. I'll brief the section on what we know as soon as we've questioned Gustav Korzeny."

Ten minutes later, Schenke climbed into the passenger seat of a pool car and read out an address on a street in the fashionable neighborhood of Prenzlauer Berg. Hauser slid the stick into first gear and they pulled out of the yard, driving cautiously down the darkened street. The thin slits of the headlamp covers provided barely enough light to find their way, occasionally picking out huddled figures shuffling along the pavements or carefully crossing the road. As Hauser concentrated on the route ahead, Schenke briefed him on the details of his visit to the murder scene and the mortuary.

"There's more, though," he added in a cautious tone.

"I feared there would be," the sergeant growled. "Can't say I haven't been wondering why our section has been sent to deal with a murder on the other side of the city."

"It isn't about our section. It's about me," Schenke responded. "The orders came from Müller. He wants someone from outside the party to lead the investigation."

"Did he say why?"

"Didn't have to. It's obvious." Schenke sighed. "The party doesn't want this causing any internal friction between factions. And if there's any danger of damage to the party's reputation, then I can be dealt with without upsetting anyone."

"Then maybe you should have joined the party, sir. That's why I did. It's a useful insurance policy."

Schenke glanced at him quickly. It was a frank admission, and one he had never heard from Hauser before. "An insurance policy? Is that all it is to you?"

"Not just that, I suppose. The country took quite a beating after the last war. You were only a youngster when the Reds were trying to seize control. Bloody chaos on the streets. We needed order and heads needed to be cracked to get things under control. Only for those tossers in the Reichstag to start messing things up again. When the party, and the Führer, came along and promised to set things right and make Germany great again, I went along with that. Wasn't so happy with some of their ideas, but on balance, yes, why not the party? And then there's my future to think about. I've got a family. I started seeing some real fools and thugs getting promoted ahead of me just because they were party members. That's hard to take. It was simple to sign up. If it means putting an end to being overlooked for promotion, then I think it's worth it. As for the rest . . ." He raised a hand from the steering wheel with a dismissive gesture. "The uniforms, the theatrics, flags and funny salutes? That's for the mugs."

"I'd be careful who you say that in front of."

"I am being careful, sir. You're not a party member. If you were for the new order, then you'd have joined by now. I'd guess some might think you were against the party."

"What if it's just that I'm not interested in politics and politicians?"

"That might be true. But politicians are interested in you. That's the way things are now, sir. And you'll have to pick a side one day. Sooner rather than later. If you haven't already."

"Do you think I have?"

"I don't want to know. For my sake as well as yours. Just don't make it a problem between us."

It was a warning, Schenke realized. "I'll do my best not to cause trouble for you, or the rest of the section. I'll take responsibility if there are any political complications."

"That's all very well for you to say. The trouble is, you may not get to decide where the responsibility lies, nor how far it extends. Just be careful, sir."

"I will. Trust me."

"I have so far."

They crossed the dark flow of the Landwehr canal and continued north, passing along the edge of the Tiergarten, where a year earlier park lamps and Christmas lights had sparkled amongst the trees. Now the trees loomed dark against the dull gleam of the snow and it felt to Schenke as if they had slipped back to an earlier era of history. Ahead lay the intersection in front of the Brandenburg Gate, and it was only when they had passed through the gate and onto the tree-lined avenue beyond that any sense of normality returned. The sidewalks were filled with Christmas shoppers anxiously searching for those luxuries that were still not rationed. Here the blackout was enforced less stringently and shop windows glimmered with subdued lighting. A dimly lit cinema notice board announced the latest Emil Jannings motion picture, and a long line of people queued patiently for tickets.

Hauser drove across the island in the Spree and headed towards Prenzlauer Berg, where they stopped for directions before turning into an affluent street lined with large houses. Schenke ordered him to slow down and wound down the window, snapping the side lamp on and off as he checked the numbers.

"Ah, here we are. This one. Pull over."

Hauser eased alongside the curb, and they stepped out into the muffled quiet of the snow-swept street. There were drifts along the sidewalk, and the boughs of the trees were laden with ice and snow, clearly visible against the night sky, so that Schenke was reminded of a photographic negative, as if the world was the opposite of what it should be. A disquieting thought that he quickly pushed aside.

The gate was fastened by a simple iron bolt, which grated as Hauser slid it back. Their footsteps crunched softly on the short curved drive as they approached the three-story town house, and Hauser let out an appreciative whistle.

"So this is how film stars live. Very nice."

"Former film stars," said Schenke. "She hasn't made a film for nearly ten years."

"And she won't be making any more in a hurry," added Hauser.

When they reached the flight of steps leading up to the front door, Schenke took the lead and pulled the handle to announce their presence.

"Is Korzeny expecting us?" asked Hauser.

"No. I don't want to hear any prepared answers."

"Right . . ."

The faint clack of footsteps sounded from within, then there was a rattle of a heavy latch and one of the tall, gleaming doors swung inward to reveal a young servant in a neat black suit with a party badge on the lapel. "How may I help you, sirs?"

Chapter Six

Schenke raised the badge on his chain lanyard. "Kripo. We've come to see Herr Korzeny."

The servant frowned. "But the police were here earlier."

"The Kripo is now in charge of the investigation. We need to ask some questions."

"At this hour, sir? The master will be taking dinner shortly."

"I am sure you can keep it warm for him," said Hauser as he stepped across the threshold. "Take us to him. There's a good boy."

The servant tried to stand his ground. "Do you know who my master is?"

"I should hope so," said Hauser. "Otherwise we'd not be much good at our jobs. Let's not waste any more of his precious time. Take us to him, we'll have a nice chat and then we'll leave you in peace. Fair enough?" The sergeant was standing in the middle of the tiled entrance hall, and he opened his arms and leaned his head forward. "Well, which way do we go?"

The youth flinched. "Please follow me, gentlemen."

They filed through the inner door into a large hall illuminated by a chandelier that hung from a fixture in the ceiling far above and lit not just the hall but also the staircase that rose from the end towards galleries on either side. The servant led them to one side of the staircase, passing a finely crafted sideboard upon which rested a familiar bust, then paused outside a door and knocked twice, sharply.

"What is it?" a voice demanded.

"There are some more gentlemen from the police asking to speak to you, sir."

"Tell them to go away."

He shot the visitors an anxious look and was about to speak again when Schenke took pity. "We'll deal with it from here. You go and see to your master's dinner and make sure it isn't burned."

The youth scurried off towards a passageway leading off the back of the hall and Schenke entered the room. It was clearly Korzeny's study. A bookcase lined one wall, a fire glowed opposite, and in between was a large desk lit by a table lamp. A man in his late fifties sat in a leather chair. His gray hair was disheveled and he wore a thick dressing gown over a collarless shirt. In front of him sat an open photograph album and a bottle of brandy. He cupped a glass tumbler in his hands as he looked up angrily.

"Who the hell are you?"

"Inspector Schenke and Sergeant Hauser from the Kripo. We're here to talk about your wife's death."

Schenke saw the man wince. He took a sip from his tumbler and shook his head. "I don't want to speak to any more police today. Go. Please go . . ."

His reluctance was understandable, thought Schenke, who had dealt with grieving family members before. Nevertheless, it was vital to get as much information as quickly as possible. He rationalized it in terms of the improved prospect of a conviction weighed against the discomfort of a moment. He removed his hat and gloves and nodded at Hauser to do the same before he grasped one of the chairs beside the bookcase and dragged it across the carpet to the desk. The sergeant sat in another and readied his notebook and pencil. Korzeny watched them with a resigned air and took another slug of brandy before he closed the photograph album and eased it gently to one side.

"What more can I tell you, in addition to what I told the other policemen?"

"I haven't had the chance to talk to them," said Schenke. "I was only put in charge of the investigation a few hours ago, so I haven't much to go on yet. That's why it's important I speak to you now. I apologize for troubling you, but it is necessary if we are to catch the killer."

Korzeny sighed. "Very well, if it helps you find the bastard . . ."

Schenke laid his hat and gloves down beside the chair and undid the buttons of his coat.

"Can you tell me when you last saw Frau Korzeny?"

"After dinner yesterday."

"What time was that?"

"We eat at six o'clock. I prefer to dine early." Korzeny ran a hand wearily over his hair. "She left halfway through the meal. She said she was going to see a film with a friend and needed to get ready."

"Was there any reason for her to leave before she had finished dinner?"

"There was an argument. A heated exchange. The latest in a long line of arguments."

Schenke noted the lawyer's use of the passive voice. Professional habits die hard, he mused. At his side, Hauser's pencil moved quickly over the page.

"What was the cause?" he coaxed after a brief silence.

"The usual thing. Other men. I asked her who the friend was. She said it was the wife of one of Heydrich's aides."

"Did she give you a name?"

"Irma Bauer. But I knew she was lying. She was going to see a man. The man who killed her," he added through clenched teeth. "Killed my Gerda . . ."

His eyes glistened and his hands were trembling as he reached for the bottle and topped up his glass. Schenke saw that they needed to divert his focus away from his wife for the moment.

"Do you know the name of the man you think she was going to meet?"

Korzeny shook his head.

"And what about the other men?"

"Some I know about. Only some. I gave their names to your colleagues. Ask them. I'm too tired to recall them all again."

Schenke was minded to ask him to repeat them, but decided to keep the man's attention focused on the previous night. "What time did she leave the house?"

"Just after seven thirty, as I recall."

"Did she say when she would return?"

Korzeny smiled sadly. "She didn't say anything after I confronted her with her lies at dinner. She left the table, went to her room to change her dress. I didn't see her leave. Just heard the door close . . . like all the times before."

"I see. And how long did she usually stay out when this had happened in the past?"

Korzeny looked up with a pained expression. "Late. Sometimes she didn't return until the following day. I would demand to know where she had been. She never told me. Sometimes she even laughed in my face."

"Not an easy thing to take," Schenke commented. "You said you saw her after dinner . . ."

The other man froze for an instant and his gaze shifted. For a lawyer, he made a poor liar, thought Schenke.

"Yet, just now, you said you didn't see her leave."

"I . . . I must have been mistaken."

Schenke paused to let him continue, but Korzeny picked up his glass and took a gulp.

"Herr Korzeny, it would be better if you were completely honest. If you keep anything from us, or try to mislead us, we will find out. And next time we won't be so polite."

The lawyer stared at him, then drained his glass and set it down with a sharp tap. "All right. I followed her. As soon as she closed the front door, I took my coat and hat and left by the side door. She had not gone far and it was easy to keep her in sight from a safe distance."

"Where did she go?"

"To Memeler Strasse station. I went in after her and kept out of sight until she boarded the train. I got on the next carriage and kept an eye on her through the glass of the connecting doors."

"Did she meet anyone on the train?"

Korzeny shook his head. "She kept to herself. She changed lines at Friedrichstadt and I boarded the next carriage again and saw her join her lover." His lips pressed together for a moment in a bitter expression.

"What happened?" Schenke prompted.

"I thought about rushing through and confronting them there and then."

"Why didn't you?"

"I don't know . . . Perhaps I wanted to believe I was wrong, and there was another explanation."

Hauser glanced at his superior with a slight shake of the head.

"What then?"

"They got off at Innsbrucker Platz and I followed them into the Friedenau district until they entered a large house. When the door opened for them, I heard music and voices. There was a party going on."

"Did you get a good look at the man accompanying your wife?"

Korzeny shook his head. "He was wearing a greatcoat and a fur hat. I was not close enough to make out his face before the door closed."

"A pity. What next?"

"I stood in the doorway of a carriage house on the far side of the street. More guests arrived shortly afterwards. I waited for ten or fifteen minutes and then crossed the street to see if it was possible to see inside. There was a chink in the blackout curtains at the bottom of a window at the rear of the house. So I stopped there."

"And what did you see?"

"I was looking into a salon. It was crowded. Over a hundred people, I'd say. After a while, I saw Gerda by the fireplace. There were several men around her. They were drinking and laughing." The bitter expression returned to the lawyer's face and there was a dangerous glint in his eyes. "She kissed one of the men."

"Did you recognize him?"

"No."

"Could you see him clearly?"

"His back was to me. Then I heard a door opening and loud voices close by, so I turned and ran. Someone shouted after me. Demanded to know who I was. I ran until I was sure no one was following me. My first thought was to wait until she left and then to confront her, but it was so cold and I couldn't bear it any more. I came home. I decided I'd deal with her when she got back here."

"You came home?" Hauser looked up from his notepad. "What time was that?"

"No later than ten."

"Did anyone see you return?" asked Schenke. "Any of your servants?"

"No."

"What did you do next?"

"Nothing. I waited in this room for a while, then I went to bed. There was no point in waiting up. She had stayed out overnight before. I resolved to confront her in the morning, or whenever she came back. But she never did."

Schenke thought over what he had heard before he posed a question.

"Tell me, did your arguments ever become physical?"

Korzeny's eyes narrowed. "Do you mean was I ever violent?"

"Yes," Schenke replied.

"I was. Sometimes. I'm not proud to admit it."

Schenke recalled the medical examiner's comment about the bruising on the body. "Had you used any force recently?"

Korzeny's gaze dropped to the glass and he swirled it gently. "A few days ago. There was another argument. I wanted her . . . She said she was too tired. I . . . It didn't end well."

"Did you assault her sexually?"

There was a sharp intake of breath from the other side of the desk and then the lawyer shook his head vigorously. "It wasn't like that. I swear it. Maybe at first, but she didn't resist in the end. She was willing. After all, she was my wife. We had a duty to each other. A duty I was more willing to honor than she was," he concluded, his voice slurred.

Schenke noticed Hauser's grip tightening around the pencil. The sergeant kept his head down to conceal his response from Korzeny. Schenke had little doubt that his colleague would have been less restrained had they not been interviewing an influential member of the party.

"Did your wife have a gray scarf or shawl perhaps?" he continued.

Korzeny shook his head. "Not that I'm aware of. She didn't like the color. Why do you ask?"

Schenke was conscious of the evidence envelope in his coat pocket and decided not to give anything away to Korzeny at this stage of the investigation.

"I saw your wife in many films. She was a fine actress."

"Yes . . . yes, she was."

"But I had no idea she was not a natural blonde."

"Not many people did back then. Any more than they knew what her real name was."

"Oh?" Schenke exchanged a glance with Hauser. "Not Gerda Schnee, then?"

"Of course not." A look of amusement formed on Korzeny's face. "That was the name given to her by the studio. The name and the look. Before then she was Bertha Weissmann. From Rott, a village in Bavaria. UFA invented Gerda."

Schenke's mind was already racing. "Weissmann? Was she Jewish?"

"Her father was. She was mixed race of the first degree. Even so, she had a friend in the party who saw to it that she was granted Reich citizenship."

"Friend?"

Korzeny hesitated. "A powerful friend."

"Who was that?"

"It is best that you do not ask. In any case, I saw to it that she was not classified as a Jew before I married her."

Schenke could imagine that the well-connected lawyer would have taken such a precaution.

"How did you and Gerda meet?"

Korzeny took another gulp from his glass and was reaching for the bottle when Schenke leaned forward and moved it out of reach. "That's enough for now, Herr Korzeny. There are no answers at the bottom of any bottle."

"How dare you . . . Let me have that."

Schenke took the bottle and placed it on the floor beside

the desk. "You can have it when we leave. Tell me how you met."

Korzeny glowered at him for a moment before he slumped back in his chair with a creak of leather. "All right. We met at a film premiere in '35. It was her last film. UFA had just suspended her contract."

"Why was that?"

"Because of that swine Goebbels. He ordered the studio to dump her. He'd dropped her a few months earlier, after his wife discovered he was being unfaithful. Gerda swore she'd tell everyone about their affair. The party was about to pass the race laws at the time. You can imagine how embarrassing it would have been for Hitler to discover that one of his inner circle had been intimate with a woman of Jewish blood. So Goebbels had her records altered and told her she'd do well to keep her mouth shut if she knew what was good for her. It was about that time that I met her. At the party after the premiere. She was drunk and in a pitiful state . . . And quite beautiful."

He clasped his hands together. "I was a career man back then. I devoted my life to the law, and to the party. I had been married before, but my first wife died giving birth to a stillborn child. My work became my sole focus. Until I met Gerda at that wretched party. At first I took pity on her. She needed someone to look after her. To protect her. So I took her back to the flat she rented, and that's where it began. She was grateful, for a while at least, and I was flattered. What man wouldn't be? And the arrangement satisfied Goebbels. It kept her quiet. As for me? Well, I am sure I am not the only older man who has made the mistake of falling in love with a much younger woman and only succeeded in making a fool of himself. I imagine you find me as much a figure of fun as anyone else does. Go ahead, laugh."

Schenke shook his head. "I am not here to judge you. Just

to get information that will help us find your wife's killer. That's all that matters to us. Go on."

Korzeny gave him a searching look before he continued. "We were married here in Berlin. Many of my party comrades were there: Heydrich, Himmler, Goering . . . even that club-footed bastard Goebbels. I would like to think we were happy at first, even if she did not return my love in full. As it was, it was only a few months before she grew cold and started going out by herself in the evenings. She claimed she was seeing friends, but it was obvious what was going on."

"You had proof that she was having affairs?"

"A man knows, Inspector. Only a fool would not know that he was being cuckolded. I had been made to look foolish enough already. I had no desire to be made even more so. I told her to stop it. She laughed in my face. I told her she would regret it if she continued." He sniffed in contempt at himself. "She called my bluff. So I begged her. I threatened her. I even hit her. Then pleaded for forgiveness. But nothing worked. She knew I was too weak to throw her out, and she carried on seeing her men. I tell you, there is nothing more painful than a vivid imagination. There were times when I could not bear it, and I thought of taking my own life. And then someone took her life from me instead . . . She is gone. My Gerda is dead." His expression crumpled and he raised a hand to cover his face as his shoulders heaved.

Schenke had been trained not to be affected by displays of emotion. The instructor at Charlottenberg had introduced them to the new concept of sociopathology, which had been identified by an American academic to show how persuasive such individuals could be. On one occasion he had brought an inmate from a local prison into the lecture theater as a practical demonstration. Schenke had been surprised at the time by his failure to tell when the man had been lying. Since then he had encountered a handful of similar individuals. These days he did not assume that an emotional performance was anything more than that. Innocence and guilt were proven by evidence, not empathy and intuition. The latter were useful tools, to be sure, but they had to be cross-checked against other factors before they could be deemed of any use. He sat still and silent while Korzeny wept. It was possible the lawyer's grief was genuine. It was possible that the details he gave of his marriage and the circumstances of the previous evening were true, but at this stage of the investigation anything was possible.

At length Korzeny stopped crying and rubbed his face before looking across the desk self-consciously. "I apologize. That was unseemly."

Schenke said nothing, just stared back.

"Is there anything else I can help you with?" Korzeny asked.

"Just the obvious question. Can you think of anyone who might have wanted to harm your wife? Could it have been one of the men she was involved with?"

"Certainly. Like the man I saw her with. If not him then perhaps one of the others. Jealousy is a powerful motive."

"The same accusation could be made about you," Schenke said sharply, and watched closely for Korzeny's response.

The lawyer met his gaze. "Of course I was jealous. She was my wife. I loved her. And she was seeing other men . . . I have had quite enough of your questions tonight, Inspector. Please go now. Before I feel tempted to telephone your superior and complain about the manner of your questioning."

"You may complain, Herr Korzeny, but I should tell you that the normal chain of command is not being followed as far as this investigation goes."

"What do you mean?"

"My orders come from the top."

Korzeny's eyes widened a fraction, and Schenke could almost hear the lawyer's mind churning with anxiety. "Whose orders?"

"I am not at liberty to say." Schenke turned to Hauser. "We're done for now. Did you get everything, Hauser? Any points that need clearing up?"

Hauser made a show of flicking through the pages of his notebook before he shook his head. "It's all pretty clear to me, sir."

Schenke reached for his hat and gloves and stood up. "We'll call you if we need any further information. Meanwhile, I would advise you to remain in Berlin. Goodbye for now. We'll leave you to enjoy the brandy in peace."

As the two men reached the door, Korzeny cleared his throat. "Inspector Schenke."

He turned. "Sir?"

"This case will be over one day. Don't get too used to hiding behind another man's authority. You'll be back at your old desk, and I will still be here. And I will not forget our encounter."

Schenke shook his head and left the room, closing the door behind him. "Think he'll make good on that threat?" Hauser asked as they made their way to the entrance hall.

"Who knows? I'll worry about it when the time comes."

After the warmth of the study, the air outside was bitingly cold, and they hurried to the car. Hauser started the engine and turned the heater up, then tried to clear the windscreen with the cuff of his coat.

"Shit, it's frozen on the inside. Can't go anywhere for the moment, sir."

Schenke nodded and thought over the interview with Korzeny. "What did you think of his account?"

Hauser cupped his hands and blew into them. "The man's a fool. What did he think was going to happen if he married a woman like that? Hasn't he seen *The Blue Angel*? She was what? Nearly twenty years younger. And beautiful with it. He's a seedy old lawyer with money. A match made in Purgatory."

Schenke chuckled. "That's the Catholic in you speaking. But seriously, do you think he might be involved in her death?"

Hauser looked at him. "It's possible. Wouldn't be the first crime of passion. He admitted that he was capable of treating her rough."

"He did. And I saw the consequences on Frau Korzeny's body."

There was silence, save for the rumble of the engine and the whirr of the fan in the heater unit. Schenke squinted at the luminous marks on his wristwatch. "It's nearly quarter past seven. We have to get moving. Drop me at the Adlon on the way back to Schöneberg. I have to meet someone. I'll get a taxi from there and catch up with you at the precinct."

"Woman trouble?"

"Let's just say your wife is going to have to take her turn when it comes to cursing me. I should be dining with my girl right now."

"There's a war on, a killer on the loose and powerful men breathing down your neck, but you go and stand up a date. All I can say, sir, is that you know how to live dangerously."

Chapter Seven

The car drew up on the cobbled square outside the entrance to the Adlon Hotel and Schenke climbed out, nodding his thanks to Hauser before the latter drove off. Piles of snow had been cleared from the front of the Brandenburg Gate opposite the grand facade of the hotel. A doorman opened the door for him and he hurried inside, taking off his coat and hat as he strode towards the entrance of the dining salon and running a hand over his hair to smooth it down.

"I'm afraid I'm late," he apologized to the maître d'. "I had a table booked at seven in the name of Schenke, for three of us. I take it my guests have arrived?"

"Yes, sir. The gentleman arrived ten minutes ago. The lady was here on time and waited for half an hour before she left."

Schenke felt his heart sink into his guts at the thought of facing Karin's anger. First, though, he'd have to try to explain himself to her uncle.

"Shall I take your coat, sir? Unless you intend to depart as well."

Schenke felt himself flush with embarrassment and irritation. "I'll keep it with me, just in case."

"As you wish, sir." The maître d' closed the booking log and marched off through the arch leading into the hotel's dining hall, calling out over his shoulder, "This way, if you please."

Schenke moved briskly to catch up and entered a large, high-ceilinged room with a mirrored wall that made it appear twice its actual size. Christmas decorations looped overhead and met above a tall fir tree in the center of the room, festooned with ribbons and baubles. The air was filled with the light clink of cutlery on porcelain and muted conversation punctuated by laughter. Waiters in short jackets glided smoothly amongst the tables, bearing plates and bottles. Festive cheer seemed to fill the faces of the diners, save for the man in a naval officer's uniform sitting alone at a table in the far corner. He was tall and thin, with white hair and a long face, and his sharp blue eyes fixed on Schenke as the latter approached the table. He eased his chair back and stood.

"May I assume you are the man my niece and I were expecting to have dinner with?" he demanded with a frosty expression.

"Yes, sir. Horst Schenke."

Karin's uncle examined him silently before he extended his hand. "Admiral Canaris."

They shook hands and Canaris gestured towards the chair on the opposite side of the table. "Sit."

Schenke did as he was told and noted the two empty cocktail glasses and the crumpled napkin in front of the third place setting.

Canaris raised a hand. "Waiter! Over here." He turned his steely gaze towards Schenke. "What will you drink?"

Schenke was still consumed by anxiety over Karin's

leaving the hotel. He hoped she would understand once he had the chance to explain the reason for his late arrival. And he would rather not have to endure the company of her disapproving uncle any longer than necessary.

"I'm afraid I cannot stay. I came to apologize to you and Karin, but I am on duty. I have to get back to the precinct."

"It's a bit late to apologize to Karin now. You'd better make your excuses to me."

"But sir, I—"

"You will stay for one drink, Inspector. It is the least you can do considering how much offense you have already caused this evening."

Schenke nodded. "One drink then."

"A brandy for this man," Canaris instructed the waiter. "And I'll have a glass of water."

The waiter hurried off towards the bar. Canaris stared at Schenke. At length he smiled. "I won't be drinking. I have work to do later this evening. Like yourself, unexpected demands are made on my time."

"I can imagine. Karin told me that you work for military intelligence."

"Did she?" Canaris raised an eyebrow. "Well, there's no harm in you knowing that. In your line of work I imagine you could find out everything about me easily enough. There are no secrets kept from those at the Reich Main Security Office."

"I would not know about that. I'm just a criminal investigator."

"You are too modest. Karin has told me about your previous life as a racing driver."

"That was many years ago."

"Nevertheless, it brought you a degree of fame. It's what caused Karin to become interested in you, she told me."

Schenke felt his heart sink at the remark. He had never traded on his reputation as a rising star of the race circuit. It was a period of his life he had enjoyed at the time but no longer wished for. The crash and the long period in the hospital had seen to that. To hear that Karin had been attracted by an aspect of his identity that wasn't important to him diminished his regard for her affection a little.

"Do you know where she is now?"

"She left a message for me saying that she would return to her flat."

"Is she angry with me?"

"Not angry . . . Furious is the word I'd use."

Schenke noticed the humorous glint in the older man's eyes and smiled. "Damn, this is going to take some making up for."

"You understand my niece well, then."

The waiter returned with the drinks. Canaris waited until he had left them before continuing. "I'd suggest you call her as soon as you can and make your apologies. Karin has a fiery spirit, but she's an intelligent girl and knows a good man when she sees one. If I am any judge of her character, I would say she will forgive you. But I would not test her indulgence too far if you wish to form a closer relationship."

Schenke took a sip of brandy, enjoying the warm flow into his stomach. "I'll call her then."

"By the way, if you don't mind my asking, what is the reason for your failure to join us for dinner? Just in case I have to help fight your corner when I next see her."

It was a generous gesture, Schenke thought. He wondered how much he could, or should, divulge. It was a police matter and Müller had been clear that any aspect of the case that impinged on the reputation of the party was to be treated discreetly. But the death of Gerda Korzeny would make its way into the papers in the next day or so. In any case, given the nature of Canaris's line of work, it was likely that he would know the substantive details soon enough. There was little to be risked by giving him some basic information.

"A body was discovered last night. The wife of a senior member of the party. I was ordered to take charge of the investigation. I've been dealing with it most of the day. I came as soon as I could."

The admiral sipped his water. "Are you permitted to name the poor woman?"

"I don't see why not. Gerda Korzeny."

"Ah."

"You know her?"

"I know of her. I believe she was an actress some years back. Gerda Schnee."

Schenke nodded. "She was forced to give it up when the studio canceled her contract. After that, she married a lawyer working for the party."

Canaris was thoughtful. "Not the happiest of marriages, I have heard. It is said that she has had a number of affairs. I daresay her unfortunate death may have something to do with her previous behavior."

"That's one line of inquiry," Schenke admitted.

"Why have you, in particular, been called in to investigate this murder?"

Schenke turned the glass in his hand as he replied. "As far as I can tell at this stage, the party is concerned that the investigation may reflect badly on them. It's also possible that Frau Korzeny's murder might stir up trouble between different factions within the party. They needed an outsider and so I was called in. The truth is, I have no particular expertise in murder cases. I've handled my share of them, but I am no better or worse than most other Kripo officers."

"Sounds like you've landed on dangerous ground there, Inspector. Tread carefully."

"That's my intention."

They shared a smile before Canaris continued. "You say you're an outsider. Not a party member?"

"No."

"Do you mind if I ask why not?"

Schenke decided to stick with the same explanation he had offered Müller. "I don't see that it is relevant to the work I do."

"Sounds to me as though it has just become relevant. In the sense that your selection for this investigation was made based on the very issue of whether you were a member or not." Canaris waved a hand dismissively. "Do pardon me. My job is to understand why things happen. I find it hard to leave my work in the office sometimes. I am sure it is the same for you. We are both detectives of a kind."

It was a flattering comparison and Schenke was grateful that the admiral was inclined not to criticize him severely for missing the dinner appointment. Karin, on the other hand . . . He winced, glanced at his watch and drank some more brandy. "I'll have to go soon."

"A pity. I would have enjoyed the opportunity to become better acquainted with my niece's beau. Perhaps we can rearrange dinner for another night."

"That would be a pleasure, sir. If Karin ever forgives me."

Canaris chuckled. "From what she has said about you, I suspect she might."

"That's good to know."

Schenke's anxiety began to wane and the effects of the brandy on his empty stomach caused him to feel content and well disposed to the man opposite. And curious. He cleared his throat and leaned forward, lowering his voice to avoid being overheard. "Sir, might I ask you for some information in return?"

"In return?" Canaris cocked an eyebrow. "I had not realized that we had agreed to any kind of reciprocity of information . . . I'm joking. How can I help you?"

"You work for military intelligence, so you will be as well informed about the war as anyone."

"What do you want to ask me?" Canaris responded warily.

"Is there going to be peace? If not, will Germany win?"

Canaris laughed. "Do you know how many people have asked me that? If you gave me a mere pfennig for each time, why, I'd be as rich as Croesus. I simply don't know. It is a complex matter. There are no straightforward answers."

Schenke was a little shamed by the naivety of his question, and annoyed at the mocking response. "Very well, in your opinion, what are the chances of peace?"

"That's more like it." Canaris's expression became serious. When he spoke, it was in the same low tone as Schenke had used. "Military intelligence is not an exact science. We search for information, sift through reports and make connections, and try to read the intentions of our enemies. And our allies. We also try to mislead them. In normal circumstances, if such a concept has any worth, we are all part of a well-oiled machine. But we are not living in normal circumstances. Germany has a leader who believes he is destiny's child. Let us be clear, I am not saying that he is or he isn't. When such an individual has absolute power over a nation, the machinery of state is merely a tool of his vision. I have no insight into his intentions, so I cannot answer your question. I hope—only hope, mind you—that France and Britain can be coaxed into talking peace with the Führer. But I fear he will not be able to persuade them that any expression of his appetite to avoid war is genuine. Not after all that has passed. A man's word is only as good as the proof of his integrity. In which case, to answer your question, I believe that France and Britain will not give us peace."

Schenke looked round him at the cheery faces of the other people in the dining hall. In a few days it would be the first Christmas of the war. The season of goodwill to all men would ring hollow. How much more hollow would it be with every Christmas that followed as the war continued, as it had a generation earlier? He turned his gaze to Canaris. "Can we win?"

"All things are possible, Inspector. In the meantime, it is the duty of every German to serve the Reich to the best of his ability." He raised his glass. "A toast. Victory in war, and a successful resolution to your investigation."

Schenke raised his glass and then drained the contents. "I really must go." He stood up. "If you see her first, tell Karin I'm truly sorry to have missed our dinner together."

"I will. Be sure to call her as soon as you can, if you value her friendship."

Schenke nodded. "Good evening then, sir. I hope we'll meet again."

"So do I. Meanwhile, don't forget what I said. Tread carefully. Very carefully."

The taxi, one of the greatly reduced number still permitted to operate in the capital, dropped Schenke at the Schöneberg precinct shortly after nine o'clock. He was feeling guilty about the diversion to the Adlon, but there was some vindication in that Canaris had provided confirmation of Gerda Korzeny's affairs. He paid off the driver and climbed the stairs to the precinct's entrance. This late in the evening, most of the staff had long since departed for home, and only a single policeman manned the reception counter. He quickly stood to attention.

"Inspector Schenke?"

"That's me."

"I was told to expect you, sir. Sergeant Hauser and the others are waiting for you on the third floor. Top of the building."

Schenke nodded his acknowledgment and headed for the stairs. It had been a long day, and the cold and activity had made his bad leg ache. As he climbed each step, a shooting pain ran from his knee to his pelvis. By the time he reached the third floor, he was perspiring freely and had to pause a moment until the throbbing discomfort had eased enough to make walking tolerable. A door was open along the corridor, and he could hear voices raised in an angry exchange before Hauser shouted for quiet.

"He'll be here as soon as he can, so stop your bloody jabbering and get on with setting the office up. Off your arses, move!"

Ritter had provided them with a long, thin storeroom, one side of which sloped into the eaves. There were skylights overhead but no windows. As Schenke entered, two of his men were shifting boxes to the far end while others were setting up trestle tables and chairs. Frieda Echs and Rosa Mayer were sweeping dust and cobwebs away. Hauser stood with a broom in one hand. His expression relaxed as he saw Schenke enter and remove his hat.

"About time," he muttered as he approached the inspector. "There was a mutiny brewing here."

"So I heard from outside."

"How did it go with your lady, sir?"

Schenke related the details briefly, then glanced round. "Not the best of accommodation. I'll have to see what can be done about it in the morning. I don't think Ritter's too happy having us on his patch. Did he hand over the initial paperwork?"

Hauser pointed to a handful of folders lying on one of the tables. "The last of it will be ready in the morning, he reckoned."

"Let's hope so. Where's my office?"

Hauser nodded in the direction of the same table. "You're looking at it. I was told we just get this room."

"Shit . . . Well, let's see how Ritter responds when he gets a call from Gestapo Müller tomorrow."

Hauser grinned. "That's a telephone call I'd pay good money to listen in to."

Schenke took off his coat and, finding there was no stand nor even any hooks in the room, folded it and laid it beside the files. Then he joined the others in clearing away the clutter to the far end of the room and setting up the remaining tables. Soon there was enough space for his team to draw up their chairs around his makeshift desk. Before he started the briefing, he went to the door to look out into the corridor, but there was no sign of anyone else on the top floor. All the same, he closed the door before he sat down to address his section.

"I know this is not the best time to be given a murder case like this. But killers are no respecters of public holidays." He was pleased to see this opening comment raise a few grim smiles around the room. "It's going to be a tough Christmas, and the war isn't helping, with all the extra work the blackout is generating for the police. But we've been given our orders, and we must identify Gerda Korzeny's killer as quickly as possible and nail the bastard. That means there'll be a lot of legwork. I'll have lists of people I want interviewed ready for you first thing tomorrow.

"Our first task is to find out about Frau Korzeny. Who she knew, where she'd been in the last month. I want to know if her movements last night were part of a pattern, or a one-off. Either way, I need every detail of her last hours. She was a striking-looking woman. People are going to have noticed her. Brandt, you and Hauser can start at Anhalter. Speak to the staff there. Engine drivers, stokers, conductors, railway police, kiosk workers. Anyone who might have seen something. We need all this while memories are still fresh."

He lowered his voice. "There's something else you need to keep in mind while you go about the investigation. We were picked for this job because the higher-ups didn't want this to go to a team headed by a party member. That's why they chose me, and why you in turn are getting stuck with it."

He saw some of his team exchange wary looks, and he could understand their uneasiness at being put in this position.

"What that means is that we must keep the important details of the investigation to ourselves. If anyone asks you for information, you tell them to speak to me, and me alone. Is that clear? By the same token, if you come across anyone who clams up or fails to cooperate, then you tell them that our authority goes right to the top of the Reich Main Security Office. If that doesn't put the fear of God into them, nothing will. We've been given the big stick to wave around, so let's use it, but never forget that our masters are expecting results, quickly." He opened the main file and held up a picture of Gerda Korzeny taken from a society magazine. "I don't like the way we have been pressed into this any more than you do, but we're the Kripo, the finest department in the police service, and it's our duty to find the victim's killer and see that justice is done. For her husband, for her family and for Gerda Korzeny." He looked at each of them in turn. "I want your very best on this case."

He held her picture up for a moment longer and then placed it back in the file. "Right, that's all for tonight. I want you back here no later than seven tomorrow morning."

There were some groans and muttering and Hauser called out, "That'll do! You heard the inspector. Seven. Anyone turn up after that and I'll kick their arse all the way round the office."

The team filed out of the room until only Hauser and Schenke remained.

"What about you?" asked Hauser.

"I'll stay here and read through what we've got so far."

"You'll freeze."

"If it gets too cold up here, I'll take the work down to the messroom. I'll be fine."

"Want me to stay and help?"

Schenke shook his head. "Get back to your family."

"I was hoping you'd say that." Hauser reached for his coat and tapped a finger to his forehead. "See you in the morning, sir."

As the sergeant's footsteps echoed down the stairwell, Schenke crossed over to the only telephone in the room. He hesitated, then made the call to Karin's flat. A dull dial tone sounded for over a minute before he gave up and replaced the handset. Turning away, he dragged one of the tables underneath the brightest of the three bulbs lighting the storeroom. As a light wind moaned over the skylights, he pulled his coat around his shoulders, sat down, opened the first folder and began to read.

Chapter Eight

21 December

It was just after six in the morning when Schenke called Karin's number again. Even though she was not an early riser he needed to call her to make his apologies before turning his mind to the investigation. He had slept at his desk for no more than two hours during the night, and had risen to refresh himself and have a shave in the precinct's washroom. He had borrowed a razor, brush and shaving soap from one of the precinct's uniformed officers. There was no hot water, as the limited supplies of coal in the capital meant that boilers could only be used intermittently. He shivered as he moved the blade through the lather. Afterwards, fully dressed, he decided that he could not put the call off any longer.

There was a soft repetitive burr on the line, but no answer, and Schenke held on with a growing sense of hope that she had gone out early, or that she was refusing to answer the telephone, so that he could delay enduring her anger. He felt the tension ease from his body as he decided to end the call.

"Hello?" The line suddenly crackled into life. "Who is this?"

It was too late to hang up, and besides, it would be cowardly and ignoble to do so. Schenke sat erect. "It's me, Horst."

"Horst . . . you bastard."

"I—"

"Have you any idea how humiliated I felt?" The cold fury in her tone was unmistakable. "Sitting there in my new dress, waiting to introduce you to my uncle. After all the nice things I had told him about you. He must have thought me a complete fool, and you the latest in a long line of unsuitable men."

"Karin, I'm sorry."

"You'd better be. You will be. Sorry? You think that's good enough to put right the hurt you have caused me?"

"I had no choice. There's been a murder. My team had to deal with it. We have to move quickly if we are to have a chance of finding the killer."

"You could have called me and told me you had to cancel."

It was true. He had had plenty of opportunities. There was no excuse for it, but he thought he'd try anyway. "So much was happening. I'd hoped that I would be able to make it to the Adlon on time, but there was too much to do and no time to stop and think until it was too late."

"You mean you forgot?"

"No," he responded, and continued incautiously, "I just had priorities."

"Well, that's lovely." She gave a bitter laugh. "I thought I was supposed to be special to you?"

"You are! I swear it."

"If I was special, you would have called before I set off for the Adlon."

Schenke had known plenty of women before, but none as fine-looking and graceful as Karin. She was intelligent, too. In fact her only faults, to his mind, were the prickly sense of entitlement and her demand for his attention. Given her privileged upbringing, that was as understandable as it was regrettable. But he was sufficiently smitten to want to be with her in the long term. He had tried to be apologetic, but he was tired and his patience was limited, and now his voice hardened.

"Karin, I'm a policeman. A criminal investigator. We do not get to choose our hours of work. The thieves, forgers, rapists and murderers decide that for us. You knew what I did for a living before you chose to be with me. This sort of thing will happen. If you want us to stay together, you are going to have to accept it from time to time."

"Maybe I shouldn't have to. There are plenty of other men who'd be happy to be seen with me."

"I am sure there are. You've told me about them. And how none of them was suitable for you. How you'd almost given up hope before you found me."

There was silence as she dealt with having her own words used against her. "Don't go thinking you can take me for granted, Horst. I won't stand for that."

"I'm not. I know how lucky I am to have you, believe me. I swear that I will do my best not to let this happen again. In any case, I went to the Adlon as soon as I could to apologize. But you'd already left."

"Are you surprised? I'd had enough of being made to look a fool."

Schenke avoided reopening that grievance and steered the conversation in another direction. "I explained it all to your uncle."

"I know. He told me. He also said you have a difficult job to do and that I should be more understanding."

Schenke was taken aback. "He said that? Really?"

"Yes. Though I can't help wondering if all you men are in it together, conspiring against women. He told me that you impressed him, and that's not something I recall him saying about any of my boyfriends before."

Her tone was softening and Schenke was relieved that the worst was over. Now was the time to make a peace offering.

"It would be nice if we could arrange another dinner soon."

"We'll see. I'm not sure if I've forgiven you yet, Horst."

"Then let me take you somewhere special first. Just the two of us."

"I'd like that . . . Let me know what you decide and then I'll check my diary and see if I'm free."

Schenke could not help smiling at her attempt to twist the screw one last time. Then he felt a stab of anxiety. What if there were other men asking her out? What if she accepted an invitation from someone else to make him jealous and pay him back? He felt his anger rising. And what if she enjoyed that man's company more than his? It was purest paranoia to think along those lines, he told himself angrily. Karin's affections were directed towards him alone. He was sure of it . . . almost sure.

"I'll see what I can arrange." He glanced up at the clock and saw that it was nearly six thirty. "I'll have to go now. My team will be arriving soon. We've got a lot of work to do today."

"Must you go so soon?" Karin said, then continued quickly. "What's happening today then?"

Schenke realized that it was an attempt to prolong their conversation, and he too was reluctant to end the call now that Karin was won over again. There was nothing of detail that he was permitted to tell her, but there was no harm in discussing general police practice. "Routine procedures. We have to amass as much information as we can as soon as possible after the crime, while witnesses' memories are still fresh. It'll be interviews mostly, and going over the preliminary reports from the medical examiner and the technical lab. That sort of thing."

"Sounds complicated, my darling."

Schenke felt a warm glow in his chest. Darling. He was home free. "I'm hoping we get something significant soon. A name. An eyewitness, that's all it takes to find the culprit usually. Once we have our man, I'll apply for some leave. It would be nice to spend a few weeks together, away from Berlin."

"Sounds lovely," she said. "Give us a chance to get to know each other far better." There was a hidden promise in her voice and Schenke smiled. She could make a fine wife indeed, with her looks, sharp wit and appetite for new experiences. His thoughts slipped back to the previous evening. God willing neither of them would ever have to endure the emotional torment and betrayal of the Korzenys' marriage.

The comparison had come into his mind unbidden. Perhaps a reminder from his professional being that he needed to get back to work.

"I have to go now, my love."

He heard a faint intake of breath at the other end of the line, and then Karin spoke in the warm, honeyed drawl that he found so hard to resist. "Come back to me soon, Horst . . . I love you."

There was a soft click and the line went dead apart from a dull crackle and some clicks. Some sixth sense made Schenke keep the handset pressed to his ear as he strained to hear the noises coming from the receiver. They sounded random enough, and he thought himself a fool. After all, what eavesdropper would have found anything suspicious in their exchange?

Hauser was the first to arrive, as usual, and Schenke gave him the task of detailing the other men to work through the list of those who needed to be interviewed. More names would be added later, and the team would then have to go through the reports line by line to check for inconsistencies and conflicts. Schenke had compiled the list overnight after reading the preliminary reports and consulting the notes he had made and those Hauser had taken at the lawyer's home.

The envelope containing the strip of cloth was entrusted to Brandt to take to the Werderscher Markt laboratories for analysis. It was more than likely that the cloth had nothing to do with the murder, but it could not be discounted at this early stage.

Frieda and Rosa were assigned to comparing the known details with other murders in the precinct over the previous six months. If no similarities were discovered, then they were to extend the search back over previous years, and also further out to embrace other precincts in Berlin. It was a laborious and time-consuming task, Schenke knew from his early days in the Kripo. Logbooks had to be read through, and case files pulled from archives and the contents checked meticulously. But it was an important process and often turned up vital connections between cases. It required a considerable degree of concentration and recall of detail, and Frieda was one of the few members of his section that Schenke trusted with the job.

Once he had allocated the duties, Schenke prepared himself to put in a call to Müller. He made a list of headings regarding what was known so far, and what steps had been taken to further the investigation. When he capped his pen and put it down, the few lines looked painfully brief. Müller had made it clear that he wanted results swiftly. The trouble with murder investigations was that they often gave up their clues and leads slowly, and only after much hard work. But Schenke doubted that Müller would accept the realities within which the Kripo investigators operated. In recent years political contingencies, rather than evidence, had become the driving force behind a number of criminal investigations. Schenke had been fortunate not to have been drawn into such cases before. But now he was being made acutely aware of the creeping menace of political imperatives within the realm of daily police procedure.

Such matters had never been a consideration on the officer training course. Schenke and the other students had been trained in the procedures of criminal investigation and the law using scientific methods. The actions to be undertaken were stipulated in the manuals and reiterated through the practical experience of the instructors. The pursuit of evidence, in order to form a hypothesis, was an objective matter of analysis. But that had changed since the party had come to power. The police were still required to carry out their customary duties of keeping order and fighting crime. However, there was no mistaking the new reality. Like every organization in the Reich, they were ultimately the servants of the party rather than the guardians of law and justice. The law had become whatever the party said it was, and justice was irrelevant. It occurred to Schenke that this case was as much about the result that Müller required as it was about where the evidence led.

He reached for the receiver. There was a brief delay before the line clicked and a voice announced, "Switchboard."

"Connect me to the Reich Security Headquarters. State Security Police department."

"Yes, sir. A moment, please."

The line was connected and answered almost immediately by a man. "Gestapo. How may I serve you?"

The polite query belied the sinister reputation of the department and almost caused Schenke to smile. "I wish to speak to Oberführer Müller."

"What is your name, and the purpose of your call?"

"Criminal Inspector Schenke. The Oberführer is expecting a report from me."

"Hold, please."

There was a lengthy delay before a fresh voice spoke. "Inspector Schenke, what is it?" Müller's voice sounded even more brisk over the telephone than in person.

"Sir, I have called to report on the case."

"Well?"

Schenke went over the details of the crime scene, the preliminary examination of the corpse, the interview of Gerda's husband and what further steps he had ordered. Müller listened in silence until the end, and there was a pause before he spoke.

"Is that it?"

"Yes, sir."

"I had anticipated rather more."

"Sir, the investigation is a little over a day old. We have opened many lines of inquiry. I am confident we will garner a considerable amount of useful information over the coming days."

"I am not in the mood for excuses, Inspector. I want results and I want them quickly."

Tiredness and piqued professional pride pricked through Schenke's formal tone as he responded sharply. "I am conducting a murder inquiry, sir, not handing out parking tickets. There are protocols that must be applied in such a case."

"Don't take that attitude with me, Inspector," Müller shot back. "You Kripo types assume you're the only police officers worth a damn. You wouldn't be the first arrogant prick I've ground under the heel of my boot."

Schenke forced himself to answer calmly. "Herr Oberführer, if you do not have any faith in my ability to conduct this investigation according to your priorities, then may I humbly suggest you replace me and my team with another you consider to be more effective?"

"You'll continue the investigation. You don't wriggle out

of doing your duty that easily. And you'll produce results quickly. Those are my orders, Schenke. And I'll not tolerate your insubordinate attitude again, unless you wish to be sent to one of the police units hunting down those fools in Poland who are still trying to resist us. Do I make myself clear?"

"Perfectly, sir."

"Good. As it happens, I have some information for you that will help your investigation."

"Oh?"

"My department has the name of the man Gerda Korzeny was conducting an affair with at the time of her death. Do you have a pen handy?"

"Yes, sir."

"His name is Oberst Karl Dorner. His current accommodation is the officers' quarters on Flottwellstrasse. I suggest you speak to him yourself."

"Yes, I'll see to it," Schenke replied as he finished writing down the note. "May I ask how you came by this information?"

"All you need to know is that Dorner has been seen in the company of Gerda Korzeny on several occasions over the last month. They have shared intimacy. Report to me again tomorrow evening. Good day."

The line went dead before Schenke could respond, and he held the receiver to his ear a moment longer before placing it back on its cradle. He leaned back against the wooden frame of the chair. If what Müller had said was true, then Dorner was the most significant person of interest in the case. And the information had been handed to the Kripo just like that. How very fortunate, he mused. If Dorner proved to be the killer, then the case would be closed swiftly by the police, just as Müller required, without setting one party faction against another.

Now that Schenke had a name, it should be straightforward to find witnesses to confirm Gerda's relationship with the man. They must have been seen together. Unless they went to a friend's apartment or house for their trysts. But if that turned out to be the case, he suspected that Müller would be able to provide further information to lead the investigation in the right direction.

The idea was not comforting. This was not how a Kripo murder investigation should proceed. It was obvious Müller knew more than he had divulged. The Gestapo routinely ran surveillance on those it considered to be potential threats to the Reich. At the same time it strove to uncover compromising information that could be used to keep certain individuals beholden to the department. So which of them was under observation? Gerda, or Dorner? Perhaps both of them were being watched. Either way, Müller knew about them.

A further thought occurred to him. What if the Gestapo were listening in to his own telephone conversations? There had been those strange clicks on the line at the end of his conversation with Karin earlier. What if he was being followed? Was there anything he had said or done recently that might bring him to the attention of Müller and his agents? He wondered if he had been seen with Admiral Canaris. Though they had met for social reasons, it might arouse someone's suspicion. If he had not been on their watch list before this investigation, it was possible that he was now. What had he said to Karin earlier? He attempted to replay the exchange in his head to recall anything that might have caused either of them to provoke the Gestapo's interest. He strained to recall every word, every nuance. In the end he concluded that there was nothing that might concern anyone listening in to the conversation. All the same, he must ensure that he was guarded when he used the telephone in future.

This new aspect of the investigation was wearying, and very worrying indeed. Not for the first time, he cursed his bad fortune in being drawn into this dark world of the hidden machinations of the party.

He stood up and stretched his shoulders, then picked up his hat and coat.

"Frau Echs!"

She looked up from the open logbook on her desk. "Sir?"

"I'm going out. If Hauser gets back before me, tell him I may have a lead on the man Gerda was with on the night of her death. Get him to see what he can dig up on an Oberst Karl Dorner."

"Oberst Karl Dorner," she repeated as she took a note of the name. "Yes, sir."

Schenke nodded a farewell and left the storeroom. As he descended the stairs, he decided to take one of the uniformed policemen with him. He had no idea what Dorner was like, nor if he was complicit in Gerda's death. It would be safest to have a man to back him up.

Chapter Nine

The army officers' quarters were in an elegant hotel commandeered shortly before the war began to provide accommodation for the swelling numbers of military personnel required to serve in Berlin, or in transit on their way to join their units on campaign. From the street, the only indication of the hotel's new purpose was that the doorman had been replaced by a sentry in a greatcoat, shuffling his feet and rubbing his gloved hands as he tried to stay warm.

Alighting from the police car, Schenke raised his identity badge and he and the uniformed policeman were passed through the revolving door into the carpeted lobby. Several officers sat in the comfortable leather chairs arranged around low tables. The walls were painted a rich ocher, and a well-tended fire burned in a large iron grate under a brass canopy that radiated heat into the lobby.

Schenke looked around the cozy setting before approaching the reception desk, which was staffed by an elderly man in what he guessed was the livery of the original hotel.

"May I help you, sir?" The man smiled.

"I hope so. I'm looking for an Oberst Dorner. I was told he was staying here."

"Indeed he is, sir."

"Good. Then you can show me to his room."

The reception clerk's smile faded. "Might I ask who you are, sir?"

"Kripo." Schenke was weary and in no mood for the usual introduction. He flashed his badge.

"Kripo?" the clerk repeated. "Sir, the Liebmann Hotel is under military authority now. I'm not sure if I can help you."

Schenke leaned his elbows on the desk and glared at the man. "I am investigating a serious crime on the authority of Oberführer Müller of the Gestapo. You may have heard of him." He took Müller's letter out of his coat and held it up. "You can check my credentials if you like, but that would only waste more of my time. The Oberführer is impatient for results and won't take kindly to anyone hindering me in my duty."

The clerk gave an ingratiating nod. "Of course, sir. But I am afraid that Oberst Dorner is not in the hotel at the moment. Perhaps if you left your name and a note for him . . ."

"Where is he?"

"He left for work first thing this morning, sir. As he does every morning."

"How long has he been staying here?"

The clerk reached for a registration log and leafed back a couple of pages, then tapped his finger on an entry. "Since the start of September, sir."

"I see . . ." Plenty of time for Dorner to form a serious relationship with the victim, Schenke mused.

"Has the oberst ever brought a woman to the hotel?"

"No, sir."

"You seem very sure."

"It's the policy, sir. No women allowed beyond the lobby.

The army is strict on the matter. The oberst comes and goes by himself most of the time."

"Most of the time? Who else is with him on other occasions?"

"Army officers. I don't really know any more than that."

"And where does he work?"

"I don't know, sir. It's not my business to know. But you might try asking some of the officers in the lobby."

It was clear that the clerk was uncomfortable with being questioned and keen to deflect Schenke's attention.

"All right. But I haven't finished with you. Don't go anywhere."

He nodded at the policeman to keep an eye on the man, and then turned away from the counter and approached the seating area. He ran his gaze over the officers. Most were sitting alone, reading magazines or newspapers. Close to the fire, a group of three officers of field rank were talking quietly as they drank coffee and ate cake. Schenke took off his hat and strode over to them. Some of the other officers gave him curious looks as he passed but made no effort to engage him in conversation or offer a polite greeting.

"Excuse me, gentlemen." He forced a smile. "Would you spare me a moment?"

They looked up at him warily. One of them was a hauptmann; the others were majors, and the nearest of those spoke for the group. "Gestapo?"

Schenke shook his head. "Kripo."

He sensed an easing of tension in their expressions and sat down in a spare chair. "I'm hoping you might be able to help me. Do any of you know Oberst Dorner?"

They exchanged a look before the major answered. "Yes, Dorner's joined us for cards some nights. And we've shared a few rounds of drinks at the bar. What's your interest in him?"

It was a direct question and Schenke saw no harm in a straight reply. "I'm investigating a crime and the oberst's name came up as a possible witness. I need to ask him a few questions."

"Well, he's not here now," said the other major.

"I know. The clerk said that he was at work. Do you happen to know where that might be? It's important that I discover what he knows as soon as possible."

The first major scrutinized him briefly before he responded. "Since you're not Gestapo . . . Dorner's working with the Abwehr."

Schenke raised an eyebrow. "Military intelligence?"

"If you must use that oxymoron, then yes," the hauptmann said, then smiled. "Pardon my little joke. The truth is, Oberst Dorner is no fool. Which explains why he's so good at bridge. He's won at least two hundred marks off me alone."

The other officers chuckled and Schenke smiled with them, even as his mind was coolly noting every detail of their words and expressions. "I'm afraid all I have is his name. I don't suppose you could tell me which service arm he's with?"

"Cavalry. Not that it means much these days. Most of them want to join the armored units and charge the enemy from the safety of a tank."

Schenke doubted that a tank was as secure a proposition as the major implied. From the piping on his uniform, he identified the major as an artilleryman. A somewhat less perilous perspective from which to judge those who led the spearhead of the armored columns that had hurled themselves against the Polish army a few months earlier. Nonetheless, he needed to humor the man in order to see what further information he could extract.

"Do you know if Dorner has any friends I could talk to?"

"Why?" asked the hauptmann. "Is he in some kind of trouble?"

"No. It's a routine inquiry. The sort of questions we ask about almost everyone we deal with. Background detail, that's all. Any women in his life?"

The officers looked at each other and shook their heads before the artillery major pointedly reached for his coffee cup. "Sorry we can't be of any more help to you."

Schenke bridled at the curt dismissal but did not betray his reaction. He was used to the manner in which the officers of the military looked down on their civil counterparts. He stood up and nodded his thanks. "I'll leave you to it, gentlemen."

He returned to the reception desk.

"Stay here," he ordered the policeman. "If Dorner appears, detain him until I get back."

"Yes, sir."

Schenke gestured towards the keys hanging on the wooden rack behind the clerk. "I want to see the oberst's room. Now. Let's go."

The clerk opened a door on the third floor. It was a room overlooking the street in front of the hotel, Schenke noted as he oriented himself. The worn carpet that ran down the corridor also flowed into the room, and there was a faint smell of damp as the clerk switched on the lights and stepped aside for the policeman to enter. It was not just one room, but a small suite. Bedroom, bathroom and an adjoining living space with a modest table, two couches and a desk by the shuttered window. Some files were neatly piled to one side of the desk and a leather-bound notebook to the other.

"Do all officers of Dorner's rank get suites like this?"

"No, sir. Those in transit are allocated a single room.

Those who are stationed in Berlin get the better accommodation. The oberst was able to obtain special permission for one of our larger suites."

"Who gave the permission?"

"I don't know, sir. I would guess it came from the office he is working for. I could try to find out who signed the order, if you like."

"Yes. Do that."

The air in the room was cold.

"Is there no heating?" asked Schenke.

"Only from six to eight in the morning, and four until nine at night, sir."

"No wonder the officers like the lobby so much." Schenke turned to the clerk. "You can get back to reception. Let me have the key and I'll bring it down when I'm done here."

The man gave in under Schenke's implacable stare and handed over the key. "Yes, sir. If you need anything else . . ."

"I'll be sure to let you know."

He waited until the clerk had closed the door to the corridor before looking over the sitting room. It was kept tidy and Dorner's belongings were set out neatly. Crossing to the desk Schenke saw that the top folder in the pile was stamped with the eagle and swastika emblem above a handwritten notation: *Abwehr*. He was not sure if Müller's authority extended to reading through such files, but reasoned that if they were left in Dorner's room, there could not be much in them that constituted vital state secrets. He noted how the files were stacked so that he could replace them the same way, and opened the first.

There were several typed sheets detailing numbers of prisoners and quantities of matériel captured in Poland. Nothing of relevance to the murder investigation, he decided. The second folder had more of the same. As he picked up the third, he saw a photo that had been placed between the folders, out of sight. The woman had struck a dramatic pose as she looked over her shoulder towards the photographer. It must have been taken several years ago, and her hair was blonde, but there was no mistaking her identity: Gerda Korzeny. There was no signature on the front, and when he turned the photograph over, all that was on the reverse was the name and address of the studio that had produced the image. No message; no dedication to an admirer, as might be expected given her affair with Dorner.

The rest of the folders contained similar lists and numbers, with the only variation being the last, which detailed movements of Schupo battalions to Poland and the areas they were to be responsible for policing. Each area was defined in terms of size and population. Schenke glanced over it, then replaced the files as he had found them before he continued searching.

The leather notebook turned out to be a diary, with the sparest of entries noting meetings with various initials, K being the most numerous. The drawers of the desk yielded a blank notepad and a handful of envelopes. There were only a few books on the mantelpiece: a cheap mass-printed version of *My Struggle*, a guide to Berlin, and a battered copy of Guderian's polemic on armored warfare, dedicated by the author to his "dear friend and student, Karl" and signed with a flourish. Other than that, a handful of novels and collections of poetry.

The bathroom yielded no surprises. Dorner's wash kit was laid out in an orderly fashion and the towels were carefully folded on the rails. The bed in the next room was neatly made, and two spare uniforms and two civilian suits hung in the wardrobe. The drawers beneath contained socks and underwear and a spare pair of boots; another pair of shoes gleamed beside the wardrobe. Schenke looked under the bed. Close to the bedside table lay a pistol in its holster. He eased it out into the open. The holster was not army issue. It was the kind of arrangement used by police and security agencies to keep weapons out of sight. The pistol was a Walther P38, a common sidearm in the army and security forces. It was likely that a man of Dorner's rank would have no need to carry a weapon in Berlin, and even if he did, he would wear it on a waist belt. It was possible that this was an additional, unregistered weapon, and that was enough to excite Schenke's suspicion.

Replacing the holstered pistol, he opened the drawer of the bedside table. There was another picture lying inside. This one was surrounded by a plain black frame and depicted a thin woman with delicate features and dark hair, wearing a wedding dress. Beside her, holding her arm, was a young army officer, well built and with cropped blond hair and a wide, warm smile. At the bottom of the photograph was written: *Karl and Margarethe, 3 June 1928.*

"So you're married, my friend," Schenke muttered. "And it seems you were seeing Gerda on the side."

He closed the drawer. Even though he was tired and his leg ached, he resisted the temptation to sit down on the bed. He did not want to leave any clue that he had searched the room. He leaned against the wall as he contemplated Oberst Karl Dorner. The spartan neatness of his possessions in the suite indicated a soldier through and through. He had been sent to Berlin to work for military intelligence, and that spoke of a high degree of mental caliber. He had rugged good looks, which a uniform would enhance still further, and Schenke could imagine that he might easily catch the eye of a dissatisfied married woman. Since he was married himself, and if Müller's information was correct, then Dorner had a flexible moral code. But did that extend to murdering Gerda? It was possible. Perhaps they had argued. Perhaps she had wanted more from him and threatened to expose their affair. There were some army officers Schenke knew who guarded their reputations fiercely. Was Dorner such a man? Had he flown into a rage and killed his lover? If so, was that why he had left her body where it could be easily discovered? Had he panicked and abandoned the body near the tracks outside Anhalter in the middle of a bitter winter's night?

Something about this did not feel right to Schenke. If Dorner and Gerda were having an affair, he would have expected more evidence of it. Some love letters, or notes at least. Some personalized keepsakes, not just a blank picture. If Dorner was romantically involved with the victim, he was hiding it well. Perhaps he was simply unconcerned about the ephemera that genuine lovers liked to have to remind them of the object of their affections. Or he had disposed of such things to remove evidence linking him to the dead woman. But why keep the photograph?

He took a last look round the rooms and left the suite, locking it behind him. He handed the key in at the front desk and leaned towards the clerk.

"You are not to tell a soul that I have entered the oberst's room, understand?"

"Yes, sir."

"If the oberst asks you about my visit, you tell him I came looking for him and left after I had spoken to those officers in the lobby. That's all."

The clerk swallowed nervously. "Of course, sir."

Schenke fixed him with a warning stare and turned to leave, followed by the uniformed policeman.

Outside, the freezing air stung his exposed face, and he hurried across the cleared sidewalk, stepping over a knee-high berm of soot-stained snow. They climbed into the car, with Schenke taking the driving seat. He turned the engine on and rubbed his gloved hands as he recalled the location of the Abwehr headquarters. Karin had once pointed it out as they passed the building on a date, proudly telling him about her uncle, the rear admiral. It was a small world, he reflected. This connection between Dorner and his girlfriend's uncle was something of a coincidence. A small world indeed. Perhaps too small, he reflected as he put the car in gear and pulled out into the street.

Chapter Ten

The Abwehr offices were in the Bendlerblock building overlooking the Landwehr canal, which was now covered by a thick layer of ice and drifts of snow. An old man, bearded and hunched over, was pushing a baby carriage loaded with coal along the street. He moved to the canal side as Schenke approached, and lowered his head, perhaps to avoid the policeman's gaze as the car passed by.

There was a yard to the side of the building where a sentry waved Schenke in and directed him to a free parking space. He ordered the uniformed policeman to remain close to the car and entered a side door. The sentry asked to see his identity badge before he was allowed through to a reception room, where a naval clerk made a note of his name in the logbook before asking him the purpose of his visit. It was interesting to see that the Abwehr's security seemed to be more rigorous than that deployed at the Reich Security Headquarters. The Gestapo looked like amateurs compared to their colleagues at military intelligence. But then secrecy and discretion were not their forte. Quite the reverse. The influence of the Gestapo depended on persuading the general population that their every move was being watched. In fact, as Schenke knew, Müller's department was much smaller than most supposed. The fear the Gestapo provoked did most of their work for them.

"I'm here to speak to Oberst Dorner."

"Yes, sir." The clerk checked the day's manifest. "Is the oberst expecting you?"

"No."

He paused to scrutinize Schenke. "Sir, the oberst is a busy man. His schedule is full today. I suggest you contact his aide and arrange a meeting at a more convenient time."

"Now is convenient. Call his office and tell the oberst that Criminal Inspector Schenke wants to see him at once. Tell him we need to discuss Frau Korzeny."

"Sir, if you will just contact his aide—"

Weariness had all but eroded Schenke's patience and he slapped his hand down loudly on the desk. "Call him now, or I will charge you with obstructing a policeman in his duty. Believe me, the people I work for would punish you for more than that if I told them you had attempted to fob me off. Call him." He folded his arms as he glowered at the clerk.

"As you wish, sir. Please take a seat while I deal with the matter."

"I'm happy where I am."

The clerk picked up the receiver. "Switchboard? Connect me to Oberst Dorner's office." He drummed his fingers as he waited for the call to be answered. "Ah, reception desk here. I have a man who wants to speak to the oberst . . . Criminal Inspector Schenke . . . I'm sorry, sir, he wouldn't say. All he told me was that he must discuss . . ." The clerk looked up anxiously and Schenke mouthed the name. "Frau Korzeny, sir . . . Yes, I am sure that was it . . . Very well, sir. I'll let him know."

He replaced the receiver. "Oberst Dorner will see you, sir. He says you are to go up to his aide's office on the fifth floor. He'll join you there as soon as he has concluded some business. This way."

He led Schenke through a frosted glass door into a small hall where two elevators served the upper floors of the building. He slid the concertina grille back. The device gave slightly under their combined weight, and with a rattle and a jolt the elevator rose through the building. Through the grille Schenke caught glimpses of each landing they passed, where some of the Abwehr's staff passed by or stood in quiet conversation. At the top floor, the clerk pulled the lever to stop and dragged the grille aside.

"Here you are, sir. The oberst's aide is Sturmbannführer Schumacher. That's his door there. Third on the left."

The walls and doors of the corridor were painted in a light gray that lent the ambience a somber touch Schenke did not care for. Heating pipes and wiring coated with the same paint ran along both sides close to the ceiling, and he felt like he was in the bowels of a warship. There was no sign of movement, although he could hear muted voices from the aide's office. He paced along the herringbone-pattern wooden floor and knocked on the door the clerk had indicated.

Almost at once it was opened and a crop-haired SS officer greeted him with a smile. The scar high up on his forehead indicated that he had been a member of a student dueling society in his youth. He had the ruggedly handsome features of so many of the Prussian officer class. "Inspector Schenke? Do come in. I'm Sturmbannführer Schumacher, Oberst Dorner's aide. May I offer you some coffee? Or tea?"

He waved his guest into a generously proportioned office with a window facing the canal. One wall was taken up with shelves filled with newspapers, and a large table stood nearby with several small piles of paperwork on top. Two doors led off the room: a small one to the side of a map table, and a more substantial one with Dorner's nameplate opposite. There was a bureau and chair near the window, and smoke curled from an ashtray filled with cigarette butts. The Sturmbannführer exuded an odor of some male scent that competed with the tang of tobacco.

"A coffee would be welcome," said Schenke.

"Want anything in it?" Schumacher winked. "Shot of schnapps? Brandy?"

"Just the coffee, please."

He looked disappointed. "As you will." He indicated a chair at the end of the map table. "Have a seat while you wait."

"How long will the Oberst be?"

"Any minute." Schumacher smiled again and opened the smaller door, ducking his head round the side. "Could you make us a coffee? No, make that two."

He shut the door and sat across the table from Schenke. "There we are. Won't be a moment. I imagine you could use a hot drink. Bitter out, eh?"

"Yes. It is," Schenke replied flatly.

"At times like this, I count my blessings that I found my way to the Abwehr rather than shivering in some freezing, muddy trench." Schumacher reached into his side pocket and took out a cigarette case, flicking the spring catch and proffering it to the policeman. Schenke took one, and the Sturmbannführer leaned across the table and lit it, then sat back down with his own cigarette. He exhaled a swirl of smoke before he spoke again.

"You know, we don't often have the Kripo calling on us. In fact I don't ever recall seeing you fellows in here. Quite a novelty. May I ask what brings you to our humble den of conspiracy?"

Schenke arched an eyebrow. "Conspiracy?"

The other man laughed. "Oh, I know what people think bout military intelligence. All cloak-and-dagger stuff. Exotic Russian spies and knives wielded in the dark and so on. In reality, it's quite boring, as you can see. Just dusty maps and gleanings from foreign sources. Which is why I can't help being curious about the diversion from the normal routine that your visit constitutes." He leaned forward with a crafty smile. "Do tell."

Schenke drew deeply on his cigarette and relished the armth in his airways before he exhaled. "I am afraid I can't y. It's a matter between myself and the Oberst."

"Oh, how disappointing."

The smaller door opened and a woman in a coat entered ying a tray with china cups, a small jug and a steel pot. made to place it on the table but the Sturmbannführer his head. "Take it straight through. Our guest will ffee with the Oberst."

sir." She crossed the room and tapped on Dorner's without waiting for a reply. Schenke heard few quiet words with a deep-voiced man, d and returned to her own office.

e from her coat how miserly the building people are with the heating." Schumacher tut- stood up and crossed to his superior's door. "Are you ady for him, sir?"

"Send him in."

Schenke's first impression of Gerda's lover was that he had hardly changed from his appearance in the wedding photograph. Dorner stood and gave a formal bow of his head. "Inspector."

The tray stood before him on his desk, and he picked up the pot and poured the steaming brew neatly into the cups before glancing up. "Milk?"

"No thank you, sir."

"Do sit down, Schenke." He looked past the policema
"That will be all, Klaus. You might want to prepare the not
for the noon briefing. This won't take long."

That rather depends on what you say to me, thought
Schenke, and prepared himself not to be arbitrarily dismissed before he was ready.

As Dorner added some milk to his own cup, and two
heaped spoons of sugar, Schenke sat in front of the desk and
took in his surroundings. The room was neatly kept, just
the hotel room had been. It was smaller than the room ne
door. There was a window, opaque with moisture frozen
the outside. Although the walls were paneled to waist hei
with richly grained wood, the rest of them and the cei
were the same drab gray as the corridor. A framed pictu
Dorner's wife in hiking gear, laughing, stood on his
and papers and folders lay in three trays to one side.
sat down and fixed Schenke with bright blue eye
want to discuss Gerda Korzeny, it seems."

His expression was neutral, devoid of fe
mask, thought Schenke. It was impossible
anxious, or harboring any sentiment o
time, Schenke took out his notebook, open
his pen.

"I have been informed that you know her."

"That's right. We have met socially on a number of occ
sions since I was transferred to Berlin." Dorner sipped his
coffee. "What of it?"

"My source tells me that your acquaintance is not merely
social, Herr Oberst."

Dorner froze for an instant, and then took another sip before casually setting the cup and saucer down. "I was not
aware that my friendship with Frau Korzeny is a matter that
concerns the Kripo."

"You admit that you are having an affair then?"

"It's not a crime. I know how much the party likes to present Germany as some kind of shrine to moral values, but life goes on. The very man who is entrusted with spouting such propaganda is the worst hypocrite of them all. Gerda told me that herself, from past experience."

"I'm not here to discuss Reichsminister Goebbels, sir. I want to talk about you and Frau Korzeny."

"As you like. Ask away."

From his manner, it was possible that Dorner was not yet aware of her murder. That, or he was as much an actor as his lover had been in her day. It was necessary to frame the questions carefully.

"Is it true you saw her the night before last?"

"Yes. We had arranged to meet at a party at a house belonging to one of Gerda's friends in the film industry. Afterwards I walked her towards the station before I took a taxi back to the officers' quarters."

"Why didn't she return home in the taxi with you?"

"Because I told her I was coming here to finish some work."

"You lied to her. Why?"

"It had not been a good evening, Inspector. We had an argument. I needed to get away from her."

"What was the argument about?"

"She wanted to leave her husband and for me to leave my wife. I told her I would not do that. As far as I am concerned, we are good friends and we are having some fun. That is all. I have not made any promises to her that I am not prepared to keep." Dorner sniffed dismissively. "Gerda will sulk for a few days, but she'll come round. We have too much of a good thing to lose, and she knows it."

There was an arrogance to his assumption that stuck in Schenke's throat. He knew the type well from the social life that had come with the motor racing. At first it had been intoxicating to arrive from a modest background and mix with millionaires, movie stars and the bluest of aristocrats. Dorner seemed to be one of the latter, judging from his accent and bearing. The kind of man who regarded entitlement in all things as a birthright. Gerda had been a plaything for him. Nothing more.

Dorner picked up his cup. "She's in some kind of trouble, I take it? What has she done now?"

"Has she been in trouble before?" Schenke prompted.

"I would have thought you'd be in a position to know that," Dorner said. "She has been known to make a scene when she's in her cups. And that's often. There have been a few occasions when the police have taken her in for badmouthing the Führer or the party, and her husband has had to go down to the cells to get her out. Gerda is something of an embarrassment to him. Frankly, I feel sorry for Korzeny. He should never have married her." He shook his head and smiled thinly. "What has she done this time? Defaced one of Adolf's posters?"

"She's dead."

Schenke watched Dorner's face closely as he took in the news. At first there was no reaction. Then he laughed. "You're joking . . . Dead?"

"She was murdered."

His features changed into what looked like a genuine expression of shock. "No . . . it isn't possible. I saw her just the other night."

"So you have admitted," said Schenke. "You were with her the same night she was killed."

For the first time there was a glint of fear in Dorner's eyes, and he sat back in his chair and clasped his hands. "Are you suggesting I had something to do with it?"

Schenke did not reply. He knew the effectiveness of silence in such situations and let the man continue.

"Are you accusing me of being involved in her murder? Is that it?"

"Did you murder her?"

It was a blunt question, as favored by the Kripo's interrogation training course. Suspects tended to be wary of trick questions, and the direct approach often unsettled them. Dorner raised his eyebrows before his face flushed with anger.

"No. I did not . . . Have you asked her husband if he did it? Korzeny was not unwilling to use his fists from time to time."

"I am not here to talk about Korzeny. You claim that you did not murder his wife?"

"It is not a claim. It is the truth. I give you my word as a gentleman."

Schenke was not temperamentally disposed to take the word of anyone at face value, especially an aristocrat. In his experience they were as capable of being venal as the most common criminal. Even more so since they were inclined to consider themselves above the normal course of the law. He could not help observing that the man in front of him was more concerned with exculpating himself than grieving for his lost lover.

"Oberst Dorner, why don't you tell me about that night? In as much detail as you can. If you are innocent then it will help us to prove it, and to catch Frau Korzeny's killer." Schenke spoke evenly to help encourage the other man's co-operation. "It would be better for you to be open with me right now, rather than compel me to have you arrested and taken into the precinct for questioning. I imagine you would prefer to keep this matter as discreet as possible."

Dorner considered his response for a moment. "Tell me something. Why haven't I heard about Gerda's death before now? I would imagine the murder of a former film star would have found its way into the newspapers or onto the radio swiftly enough."

"The investigation is barely a day old, sir. The press will be given the story when we are ready." Schenke was not prepared to disclose Müller's role in the matter. "So, if you would tell me about the evening before last . . ."

The army officer paused to recollect the details. "I had arranged to meet Gerda at the Friedrichstadt station. She was late, so I was not as happy to see her as I might have been. She looked upset and said that she had had an argument with her husband. We took the train to Innsbrucker Platz. We could not find a taxi and walked to her friend's house instead."

"What was the address? And the friend's name?"

"Felixstrasse 282, in the Friedenau district. Marius Steiglitz. He's a scriptwriter. Works for the UFA."

"What time was that?"

"Just before nine, I think."

Schenke added the detail to his notes and indicated to Dorner to continue. "Tell me about the party."

"It was crowded and loud. Most of them seemed to be connected with the film industry, theater, those artistic types. Some writers and intellectuals and people from the sporting world. Preening dilettantes for the most part. Personally, I haven't much time for any of them, apart from those who are to do with sports. Besides them there were a handful of military types, and a few figures from the party."

"Did you and Frau Korzeny speak to any of them?"

"Oh, she rushed off to join her tribe as soon as we had drinks in our hands. Left me to talk to the few sane people in the place. I had too much to drink, and then I had more when I saw her flirting with some of the other men. That's when I thought, damn it. I've had enough. I decided it was over between us and needed to tell her as soon as possible. I grabbed her arm and told her we were leaving. She protested at first, but was too drunk to put up much of a struggle. We got our coats and left the party."

"What time was this?"

"I don't know . . . My mind wasn't very clear. Sometime after ten, I suppose. We argued as we walked away from the party. I told her our affair was over on the way. She was furious with me. Shouted abuse. I feared that she might attract attention. It wouldn't have done either of us any good if the police had been called to deal with it. She was becoming hysterical so I slapped her and told her to be quiet. Seemed to knock some sense into her. We parted before she walked off towards the station. I didn't look back."

There was a brief silence before Schenke responded. "You abandoned her on a dark street? That was the last you saw of her?"

Dorner nodded. "Good riddance, I thought at the time. But she's dead now. For what it's worth, I regret that. If I'd known she was in danger, I would have taken her back to her husband's home."

"Regret?" Schenke shook his head slowly. "Is that the best you can do? And what exactly do you regret, I wonder?"

"What are you suggesting?"

"Do you regret following her into the station, perhaps? Do you regret climbing on the same train? Do you regret killing her so that she could not expose your affair?"

Dorner raised his fist, then froze and forced himself to lean back in his chair as he took a deep breath. "I'm telling you the truth. I left her before we reached the station, like I told you. That's the last time I saw her. I'm saddened to know she's dead. She was a fine woman in most respects. When she wasn't drunk."

"If you didn't kill her, do you have any idea who might have wanted her dead?"

"Aside from that oaf of a husband? He has motive

enough. You should speak to him about it. And if not him, I'm sure there are plenty of other men she has humiliated and scorned in her time. Or tried to blackmail, like me. . . . I can't believe she's dead. . . . Who do you think would do such a thing?"

Schenke closed his notebook and capped his pen, and put them into his coat pocket. "At this stage it's hard to know. But we'll have a better idea very soon. You can be sure of that."

Dorner's gaze shifted towards the window. "You have to find the man who did it. He must pay for the crime. Gerda was a good woman, despite everything she did."

"I don't pass judgment on murder victims," said Schenke. "That's not my job. I just find their killers. That said, it would appear that Frau Korzeny made poor choices in terms of the men she chose as husband or lovers. Present company included."

"I said I would not leave my wife for her. That doesn't mean I had no affection for her. I did."

"Maybe so, but you seem to have difficulty expressing it, or showing grief."

"My grief is for me to deal with. On my own." Dorner stood up. "I've answered your questions. It's time for you to leave. I suggest you focus your attention on her husband. If anybody intended to do her harm, it was that grubby little lawyer. Good day to you, Inspector."

Schenke returned his glare with an unblinking stare, refusing to be cowed. He rose from his chair. "I have enough information for the present. If I have any further queries, I'll come and find you."

"We'll see." Dorner made to move around the desk, but Schenke raised his hand.

"I'll find my own way out."

Dorner returned to his seat and poured himself another

cup of coffee, refusing to look up at Schenke as he left the office. Outside, Sturmbannführer Schumacher looked up from the newspaper he was reading.

"Finished already?"

"For now."

"Oh?" Schumacher stubbed out his cigarette. "Until the next time, then. Shall I show you out?" He stood up and crossed to the door ahead of Schenke.

"No need, I can find my way back to the entrance."

"Ah, well now, you see, it's standing orders for visitors to be escorted."

"Is it?" Schenke observed him coolly. "An inspector from the Kripo is to be regarded as a security risk?"

"Not my doing, I'm afraid. Allow me."

He opened the door and ushered Schenke into the corridor. As they reached the elevators, a cage rose from beneath and slowed to a halt. A moment later, the door rattled open and a man in an admiral's uniform stepped out and stopped dead.

"Hello, my dear Inspector, this is a pleasant surprise." Canaris smiled and held out his hand. "What brings you here to our little nest of spies?"

"I am here on Kripo business, sir."

"Ah, I imagine it has something to do with that matter we discussed at dinner."

Schenke shaded with embarrassment at being reminded that he had spoken about sensitive information in even the most guarded manner. There was an awkward silence before Canaris patted him on the arm.

"I apologize. I shouldn't put you on the spot like that. Forgive me. Now tell me, have you patched things up with Karin yet?"

"Yes, sir."

"That's good. Very good. I'm sure we'll have another

chance to continue our acquaintance over dinner. I'll look forward to that. Must go. I have a meeting that can't wait."

They shook hands again and Canaris strode down the corridor as Schenke stepped into the elevator. The clerk rolled the door back and pushed the lever. Schumacher waved a farewell. Over his shoulder, Schenke glimpsed Canaris entering the aide's door, and then the cage dropped towards the ground floor.

Chapter Eleven

It was after two o'clock when Schenke returned to the Schöneberg precinct and climbed the stairs to the makeshift office at the top of the building. As he reached the second-floor landing, he saw Ritter approaching along the corridor whistling a Christmas carol. The tune cut out when he saw Schenke, and he forced a smile.

"Ah, my dear fellow. How is your investigation going?"

"It might be going a little better if my section had been given a proper office instead of a storeroom."

"That's all that was available." Ritter feigned a look of sympathy. "If I can arrange anything more comfortable, I'll let you know."

"That might be wise," Schenke responded. "I'll give you two days to come up with something before I refer the matter to my superior."

Ritter's expression hardened. "That sounds unpleasantly like a threat."

"Threat. Promise. Advice. Call it what you will. Just be sure there is a proper office available for us by Sunday."

"But that's Christmas Eve," Ritter protested. "Most of my staff will be getting ready for Christmas. It's not going to be possible."

"Then do it before then. That's my advice. But get it done."

Schenke did not wait for a response as he began to climb the last flight of stairs. He was angry with Ritter and did not want that to spill over into an open argument. It was never a good idea in a public place, where subordinates might witness it. His leg ached with each step and he winced.

As he entered the storeroom, he saw that Frieda and Rosa had coats, hats and gloves on as they sat at their tables, reading through recent case files. The room was freezing. He crossed to the only radiator and took off a glove to feel it. The painted iron was icy.

"What's happened to the heating?"

Frieda looked up from her work. "Went off shortly after you went out, sir. I sent Rosa down to let them know. The desk sergeant said he'd look into it. That's the last we heard."

Schenke glanced at Rosa and saw that she was shivering. He felt his temper rising.

"Take a break. Go down to the canteen and get something warm to eat. I should be done by then."

"Done, sir?"

"This nonsense has gone on long enough."

Schenke marched from the room and made his way downstairs, so immersed in fury that the ache in his leg was briefly forgotten. As he swept open the swinging door to the reception area, he saw the desk sergeant poring over an open newspaper, a steaming enamel mug resting close by. The room was spacious, but it was warmer than the storeroom, and Schenke's fury was building as he crossed to the desk. The sergeant sat up with an anxious expression as his superior approached.

"Can I help you, sir?"

"Yes, you damn well can. Get off your fat arse when you speak to me!"

The sergeant jumped from his stool. He stood at least a head shorter than the average man. Schenke glowered down at him.

"Are you the individual who was notified about the heating problem on the top floor by one of my section?"

"Yes, sir."

"And when was that?"

"A few hours ago, sir."

"So why hasn't anything been done about it?"

"I made a note for the maintenance team in the logbook, sir."

Schenke put his hands on the counter. "And?"

"It'll be seen to when maintenance get round to it, sir."

"When will that be?"

The sergeant shrugged. "The storerooms aren't a priority, sir. Could be any time."

Schenke swept the coffee mug from the counter, sending it sailing across to clatter off the wall below a framed picture of the Führer. Brown liquid sprayed over the counter and the newspaper and splattered the wall. "The storerooms are a priority now, dimwit! They're serving as an office. You want my section to freeze to death up there? Get your maintenance men upstairs and fix it."

"Can't do that, sir."

"What?"

"They've gone home, sir. Finished for Christmas. Won't be back at work until Wednesday."

Schenke was speechless, his jaw set and his lips compressed into a tight line as he gripped the counter. The sergeant read his expression and stood stiffly, looking over the inspector's shoulder. At length, Schenke relaxed his jaw and growled, "This is not acceptable."

Behind the sergeant there was a notice board with various

bits of paper and photos of undesirables to be on the lookout for. Beside it was a green-painted door. This opened, and a policeman emerged, grinning. The top two buttons of his tunic were undone and his demeanor implied that he had been drinking. He saw the inspector and shifted guiltily before nodding and hurrying towards the corridor leading to the toilets. Schenke strode round the counter and pushed open the door.

The loud conversation and laughter that met his ears faded as the policemen in the precinct's messroom turned to look at him. At least twenty of them, he estimated. The room was a good fifteen meters by five, brightly lit and heated by two large stoves fed by wood in wicker baskets. There were a number of long tables and benches and a few old upholstered couches. Most of the policemen held beer bottles, and some were eating from a bowl of boiled sausages.

"This will do nicely," Schenke muttered to himself as he took out Müller's letter of authority and held it up. "By order of Oberführer Müller of the Gestapo, I am commandeering this room. Take your belongings and get out immediately."

There was a stunned silence, and some of the men exchanged surprised looks, but no one moved. Schenke filled his lungs and roared, "Are you all fucking deaf? I gave you an order. If this room is not cleared within a minute, I'll have you on double shifts for the next month. Move!"

The prospect of a ruined Christmas did its work, and the men scrambled past Schenke and out into the reception area. When one of them reached for the bowl of sausages, Schenke snapped out his arm. "Leave it!"

He followed them out, shutting the door behind him. "This room is off limits until further notice."

"What'll we use instead?" a voice demanded.

"That's not my problem. Take it up with the precinct

commander. Now get out of here. Most of you could use a cold shower to sober up before you return home."

He waited for them to disperse before he made his way to the storeroom. As he entered, Frieda looked up, her hands gripping a steaming cup of coffee.

"Any luck, sir?"

"I've found us some new offices. Warm and close to the canteen. Let's pack up our papers and get out of this ice-box."

It did not take long for Ritter to respond to the complaints of his men. He entered the room and stood on the threshold in his uniform and gleaming boots. "What the hell do you think you're doing, ordering my men out of their mess? Who do you think you are, eh?"

Schenke put the file he was holding into a box and glanced round. "Since there is no heating in here, and none likely to be available until after Christmas, I've relocated us to the precinct's messroom."

"No! Out of the question. I—"

Schenke raised a hand to silence him. "In answer to your second question, I am the man with a letter of authority from Oberführer Müller. If you have a complaint, I suggest you take it up with Müller. I am sure he would be happy to explain the matter to you." He reached for the phone, lifted the receiver and offered it to Ritter. "Be my guest."

The other man was still breathing heavily in frustration. Schenke let him stew a while longer before replacing the receiver.

"I think it would be wise to have a word with your men. Tell them they can have their room back as soon as we have concluded our work here. That might persuade them to be a little more cooperative in helping us find the killer." He gestured towards the paperwork and boxes on the other tables. "And I'd be grateful if you'd send four of your men to help move this lot downstairs. I think that will be all, Herr Ritter. Thank you." He returned to packing the box in front of him. The door closed with a slam and he heard Ritter's footsteps pacing down the corridor.

Frieda met his eye and grinned. "Inspector, you're a real character sometimes."

"I play the part the situation demands." He smiled back. "Let's get these files packed, and go and enjoy the nice warm stoves they've been kind enough to provide for us."

"Now this is something of an improvement," said Hauser as he hung up his coat and looked round the room. "A regular home away from home you've found us, sir."

The files had been laid out on the mess tables assigned to the section's officers. Most of them were already at work, and the room was quiet. Schenke had one table to himself, close to the far stove, and sat in a leather chair. It was warm enough for him to take off his coat as he read through the first batch of interview notes from the men who had returned before Hauser. It was already dark outside and the blackout blinds had been pulled down; the overhead lights helped make the room feel even more warm and cozy.

"Get some coffee," said Schenke, "then you can make your report."

The sergeant returned with two mugs, one of which he set down in front of his superior.

"Thanks," Schenke said. "How did you make out down at the Anhalter?"

Hauser flipped open his notebook. "I spoke to as many of the staff as I could find who were on platform duty that night. I used one of Gerda Schnee's publicity pictures as well as the mortuary photograph. Thought it might help to trigger memories."

"Even though her hair was a different color."

"Inspector, not all of us are as superficial as single men. Some of us notice other features, such as eyes, lips, bone structure."

"Point taken. And I am not so single these days anyway."

Hauser cocked an eyebrow. "Oh yes? And how are things going with the delightful Karin?"

"We have our moments."

"Good ones mostly, I trust."

Schenke was not in the mood to talk about her and gestured towards the notebook. "You were saying?"

"I had no success. Which is surprising, as you'd imagine someone with Gerda's looks would be noticed. I also asked if anyone had been spotted acting suspiciously." He rolled his eyes. "You can imagine how that went. Almost every loiterer is now seen as an enemy agent, communist saboteur, gypsy pickpocket or Jewish pimp. I don't think we'll make any progress on that front."

"A pity." Schenke sipped his coffee. "We know that she never got as far as the Anhalter on the return journey. She came off the train before it reached the station. I had hoped someone might have seen her on a train or at another station."

"Why assume that she was on an inbound train? It's possible that she got to Anhalter and needed to go back towards Friedenau for some reason."

"Maybe, but for now, the last confirmed sighting we have of Gerda alive was outside the Innsbrucker Platz station. According to Oberst Dorner."

Schenke described the search of Dorner's quarters and the subsequent interview at the Abwehr offices.

"That's quite a break," Hauser mused. "Who would have

thought the Gestapo would be so helpful in pointing the finger at Dorner? A suspicious man might conclude that someone is playing with us, sir."

"Quite." Schenke met his gaze.

"What do you make of Dorner? Do you believe him?"

"No more than I believe Korzeny until I get evidence that supports either man's account. Dorner's already deceived his wife. He might have led his mistress to expect something he was never going to offer her. I see no reason to give him the benefit of the doubt. And then there's the small matter of the Gestapo's intervention. Very helpful, as you say. Too helpful . . ."

He turned to the reports that had already come in. "The medical examiner puts the time of death between ten in the evening and two in the morning, taking into account the temperature that night. He says the extreme cold makes it impossible to be more precise. But it helps narrow things down. The man who found the body—Gantz, the stoker—has been interviewed. He says he was late for his shift and taking a shortcut across the tracks when he found the body. As soon as he realized she was dead, he raised the alarm. That's all we have for now."

"Then the husband and the lover have to be our prime suspects."

Schenke nodded. "Looks that way. Though calling Dorner a lover is a bit wide of the mark. He was just using Gerda."

"No more than she was using him, I'd say."

"True, I suppose," Schenke conceded. "She wanted a way out of her marriage but Dorner wasn't going to help her. Indeed, he might have felt threatened by her and feared she would expose their relationship. Which gives us a motive for him. At the same time, Korzeny didn't want his wife to leave him, and his jealousy could turn violent. For now, I think we'd better put our efforts into Dorner and Korzeny."

"You want me to have them followed?"

"Yes. Put Brandt and Rosa onto it. She's good at tailing people."

Hauser sucked in a breath. "That's not going to be much fun in this cold."

"It's not supposed to be fun," Schenke replied tersely. "It's our job. Whatever the weather."

Hauser appeared taken aback by his superior's sour tone.

"I'm sorry," Schenke said. "I've got Müller breathing down my neck and we've not got much to offer him. Nothing more than he already suspects, at least. And I get the sense he's holding back more information."

"Damned Gestapo shouldn't be playing games with us," Hauser said. "We're supposed to be part of the same crew these days."

"That's what those at the top tell us, but the reality is always going to be that they're all building their own little empires. I get the feeling this case is part of that process. Frankly, I don't give a shit about party infighting. A woman's been murdered and we will find her killer. That's all we have to worry about."

Hauser shook his head. "You're wrong. We do have to give a shit about them. Otherwise this case is going to be the least of our worries. That applies to you particularly, sir. If things go badly, me and the rest of the section will be reassigned. You, on the other hand, will be made an example of. I'd be very careful if I were in your shoes. You're a good investigator, and we're lucky to have you as our section head. Don't go and mess things up for yourself, sir. Or you won't be the only one here to regret it."

It was the first time Hauser had been this open about his professional regard for his superior, and Schenke took a moment to feel a satisfied glow. It meant something to have his ability recognized by this hardened Kripo veteran. The pleasure was short-lived and replaced by guilt, given what he was putting off telling Hauser.

"I've got some bad news. For you and the others."

Hauser sighed heavily. "I knew this was coming. You're talking about the leave roster, aren't you?"

"Yes."

"So who is going to be saddled with losing their Christmas?"

"All of us."

Hauser closed his eyes. "Shit . . ."

"I've no choice. We're under pressure to get this case solved, and you know how crucial the first few days of an investigation are. I can't afford to have any of the team lose focus now. I'm sorry, but that's how it is. No leave until further notice."

"Have you told the others?"

"Not yet. But you can already imagine the happy mood when I do."

"This is not going to play well at home. For any of us with families."

"Can't be helped. I didn't choose this case. If I had my way, we'd still be picking our way through forged ration coupons back at the precinct and looking forward to the holiday. Fate plays its games, Hauser."

"Fair enough, sir. In which case, I've got a favor to ask."

"What's that?"

"You break it to the wife for me."

"Not on your life." Schenke waved his hand. "Now go and get your report written up and on my desk."

Hauser picked up his coffee and headed across the messroom to a spare bench by one of the tables. Schenke looked round the room at the others. There was none of the usual cynical banter and occasional laughter. They hunched over their work with a focused air and sat in silence as they shuffled papers and scribbled notes. It was going to be a tough Christmas for all Germans, he reflected. With the war seemingly stuck in a diplomatic stalemate, rationing restricting the seasonal luxuries, and worries about those serving in the forces, people's spirits had fallen. The party was doing its best to raise morale with stirring speeches and seasonal concerts being broadcast over the radio, interspersed with reassuring messages from soldiers from their positions along the frontier with France and their garrisons in Poland. Perhaps that was one of the reasons for holding back the news about the murder of a former public figure. No one wanted to read about that over their Christmas meal.

Frieda came towards him. "Sir, I've found something interesting."

"That's a carefully chosen word. Now I'm worried." Schenke forced a smile. "What have you got?"

"I've been checking the Schöneberg precinct's recent homicide reports. There's been a spate of murders since the blackout was imposed, as you'd expect. A fair few women amongst them. But our victim was the only one found close to the rail tracks. I cross-checked against other cases of deaths in the open. You know, accidents and so on. There have been more of those thanks to the blackout as well. People run over on the roads, tripping down stairs, falling from buses and trains. Then I came across a case of a woman found beside one of the lines leading into Anhalter." She paused to glance at her notes. "A nurse with a fractured skull. She was found ten days ago. It had been reported as an accidental death, falling from a carriage. It got me thinking . . ."

"That's what you're paid to do, Frieda," Schenke coaxed gently. "Carry on."

She looked reassured that he approved of her initiative. "I put some calls in to the other precincts with train lines that feed into the terminus, and there have been four other deaths attributed to accidents since the beginning of October. All of them with fatal head injuries. Could be coincidence, of course. But . . ."

Schenke felt a stab of doubt and anxiety prick the back of his neck as he considered what she had told him.

"Bring the nurse's file over here. Then get back on the telephone to those precincts. We want the full details of the deaths. Only those found close to railway tracks for now."

"Yes, sir." She made to turn away.

"Oh, and Frieda, that's good work."

"Yes, sir. Thank you."

Frieda brought the folder and Schenke opened it and began to read. There was a picture of a smiling round-faced woman in a plain black jacket and white blouse. Her name was Bertha Elsasser. Twenty years old. A nurse on a children's ward in a central Berlin hospital. She had been reported missing by her parents on 30 November and her body was found next to a stack of railway sleepers alongside the tracks two weeks later. As he looked at the mortuary photographs of her injuries, he felt a cold sensation seep into his gut. There was no denying the similarity of the fatal injury, even if her clothing had not been disturbed and no signs of sexual assault had been reported. If the other cases Frieda had identified showed similar injuries, then . . .

He was reluctant to continue the line of thought. If there was a clear link, then Gerda Korzeny's murder would be merely one of several such deaths. And the only reason that hers had been singled out for investigation was due to her place in society and the unmistakable signs of sexual assault. If it was the work of the same killer, had he been forced to abandon her body before he could disguise his handiwork as another accident? Or perhaps he had lost control when he killed her. Was there something about Gerda that had triggered his rage and betrayed his crime to the police?

Schenke clasped his hands together and rested his chin on them. If Frieda's hunch was right, they were going to be facing the far darker prospect that the killer had left a trail of victims across the capital and was even now planning further murders.

Chapter Twelve

The man sitting alone in a corner booth tapped his fingers on the table as he listened to the shrill of the trumpets and the catchy beat of the drums. He was dressed in a dark jacket with a black polo-neck sweater beneath. His hair, dark brown, was long enough to cover his ears and marked him out as one of the bohemian tendency. He would never be mistaken for a member of the party or one of the military, he thought.

In front of him, several of the youngsters were bent forward twisting their hips in time to the music and clicking their fingers. Beyond them, on the far side of the cellar, many more lined the bar, sitting on stools or leaning against the counter as they bobbed their heads rhythmically. Here and there red gleams swelled and faded in the gloom as customers drew on their cigarettes. The smoke-filled haze was a lurid hue thanks to the colored bulbs used to light the underground club.

Underground in both senses, he mused as he inhaled from his own cigarette and leaned back in the booth seat, stretching his legs. Most of the people in the cellar were young, part of the Swing Kids movement, which arranged clandestine gatherings to listen to their records and dance. The party had once merely frowned upon jazz and swing music, which originated from the United States. It had been banned from radio broadcasts years ago, and now it had been forbidden. Too decadent, they said. But that had not stopped young Berliners from pursuing their interest. Partly out of a genuine love of the music, and partly because anything that was forbidden was readily seized on by those who felt out of step with wider society.

The music blaring out of the gramophone came to an end and one of the young men, with hair that was longer than would be considered respectable by the party, lifted the arm and removed the disc. He slipped it back into its sleeve and then replaced it in the wooden case before rifling through the other records, looking for the next one to play. As they waited for more music to fill the cellar, the customers began to talk, and the cozy fug was filled with conversation and laughter.

The man swept his gaze along the people at the bar until it came to the woman standing at the end, slightly apart from the others and nodding self-consciously as if the music continued to play inside her head. She had arranged her mousy hair in a ponytail and wore a simple dark dress with a tasseled fringe. She had arrived ten minutes after he had settled in the booth and he had been watching her for over an hour. In all that time she had not spoken to anyone and she had not been approached. She had met his gaze on enough occasions for him to know that she was interested.

She looked to be in her late twenties; like him, she was one of the handful of older patrons of the club. It would be useful to find out how she had discovered its existence, he thought. The Swing Kids were tight-lipped about the location of such gatherings. He only knew of the Cellar Club because he'd followed someone here two months earlier. There were enough older customers for him not to stand out from the crowd. He had become accepted as a regular and was largely ignored by the youngsters as he blended in and became an unobtrusive fixture.

There was a crackle and the opening saxophone notes of the next record cut across the conversation. Those youngsters hovering in the center of the cellar began to dance again. The woman at the end of the bar stared across at him, then drained her glass and ordered another drink. When she had paid for it, she picked the glass up and made her way towards him. He felt his heartbeat quicken as he saw that she was even more attractive close to.

She stopped in front of his table and smiled shyly as she spoke. He could not make out what she said over the din of the music and the conversation echoing off the low ceiling. He cupped a hand to his ear as he mouthed, "I'm sorry."

As he'd anticipated, she took a step closer and leaned towards him as she raised her voice. "May I sit with you?"

"Please do. Be my guest."

He drew his legs in to make room for her to slip her feet under the table as she sat down on the far side of the booth. She set her drink down and offered him her hand.

"I'm Monika."

"Dieter," he responded. "Are you new here? I don't recall seeing you before."

"Yes. First time." She sipped her drink. "How about you?"

"I'm a regular. I love swing music. But it's hard to find anywhere you can hear it these days. You know how it is with the party telling us what we can and cannot like. But you have to play along. That's why I wear this." He briefly eased aside his scarf to reveal the gold-rimmed party badge beneath. "Stops people from asking where I'm going."

She looked shocked. "Are you a party member?"

"No chance." He raised his hand slightly in a mock salute. "You just have to pretend to like what they tell you to."

She laughed nervously at the gesture. "Oh, I know what you mean. Some people don't want us to enjoy ourselves anymore. Not unless we like Wagner."

He laughed, mirroring her. He knew from experience that this helped to sow the seeds of trust and attraction. He leaned a little closer. "So, Monika, how did you find out about this place?"

"My neighbor's daughter is part of the movement. We're good friends. She trusts me and she told me that there was a gathering tonight."

"Is she joining you?"

"No. She said she would, but then decided it was too cold." She shook her head. "So I came by myself."

"Kids these days, eh? Far too soft."

She turned to watch the dancers for a moment before speaking again. "To be honest, I was feeling quite awkward standing there alone."

"And you decided you might as well take pity on me and come over to keep me company?"

"Oh, that's not what I meant. I . . . I thought you looked nice."

He laughed again. "I was joking. Actually, I'd appreciate some company. I thought you looked nice too. I noticed you as soon as you came in."

"I saw you watching me," she said with relief. "I hoped you were interested. Took a couple of drinks before I plucked up enough courage to come over."

"I'm glad you did. Truly." He stubbed his cigarette out. "You're very pretty."

Her lips parted in a smile. "You think so? It's been a while since any man told me that."

"Not even your husband?" he asked gently.

She flinched.

"I'm sorry, I couldn't help noticing that mark on your finger."

She glanced down at her left hand and the pale mark on her third finger, and then covered it with her right. "It's not what you think."

"I'm not judging you. An attractive woman like you deserves to be complimented. That's all I meant. If I was your husband, I'd tell you every day."

He could see that she was pleased by his remark. "Thank you, Dieter."

He felt a thrill course through his veins as she used the name he had given. She was slipping into his power a little at a time. He held up his cigarette packet. "Would you like a smoke?"

"Thanks." She took one and he struck a match, the brief flare illuminating her face with a lurid orange glow. As he held it towards her, she cupped a hand around his to steady it, leaned her head forward and touched the tip of her cigarette to the wavering yellow tongue. Her cheeks sank as she drew on the cigarette, and the tip glowed brightly. She exhaled a swirling cloud of smoke and regarded him, taking his measure.

"My husband was killed in the first week of the war. That's why I'm not wearing my ring."

"I'm sorry to hear that," he said in a sincere tone. "It was insensitive of me to point it out."

"It's all right." She shrugged. "It's what happens in war. That's what I tell myself. He was a good man, I suppose. I should feel bad about his death, and bad about being here tonight so soon afterwards . . ."

"But?" he prompted.

"It was never a love match. We married because we had to."

"Shotgun wedding?"

"Something like that. But there was no child in the end." She inhaled deeply and breathed out another plume of smoke. "I'm alone. I wanted company. And here I am. How about you?"

He shook his head. "Never married. Too busy studying. Then, once I qualified, too busy working. That's how I ended up here. Looking for someone. Looking for company."

"Where do you work, Dieter?"

He had his answer ready. "Siemens. In accounting. Not the most exciting job, but it pays well enough."

They were silent as they listened to the music. When the record came to an end, she turned to him. "It's getting late and I've got to get home. It's been nice to meet you."

"And you. I'd like to see you again, if I may."

"Of course. Me too."

They stared at each other, then he laughed and she could not help doing the same. She stubbed out her cigarette. "Come on, you can walk me to the station."

"Are you sure?" he asked.

She drained her drink and stood up. A little unsteadily, he noted. They crossed the cellar and approached the girl looking after the coats and hats. She paid them little attention as she fetched their things, looking past them towards the dancers. Even so, he kept his head down so that their eyes would not meet and she would not get a good look at him. He felt safer once his fur hat was in place and he had pulled up the collar of his thick winter coat.

Monika, if that was really her name, had a worn beige coat with a fur lapel and collar, and a black felt hat. She led the way as they climbed the stairs to the back entrance of what had once been a vintner's warehouse, abandoned and closed up for many years before it had become an illicit club. A curtain covered the door, a single grimy red bulb hanging in front of it, and the watchman, a burly, dark-skinned easterner with narrow eyes, eased it aside then drew back a thin shutter and glanced out into the yard. Satisfied that there was no one watching, he slid back the heavy iron bolt, swung the door open and waved them outside.

After the warmth of the cellar, the icy air felt like it was burning their lungs.

"Sweet Jesus," Monika muttered. "Will it ever get any warmer?"

"Here, this might help," he said, putting his arm around her shoulder and pulling her closer. He felt her body tense before she relaxed against him.

They fell into step as they walked out of the yard into the street. It ran through an old commercial district of warehouses and yards before joining a main road lined with dark blocks of workers' apartments. As they made for the Papestrasse station, they passed other people, dark shapes against the gray of the snow and ice on the sidewalk, but he was confident that there was no chance of anyone recognizing them.

"Oh!"

She lurched as her foot slipped and he reacted instantly, tightening his grip and holding her upright.

"Thanks," she said. "If you hadn't been so quick, and strong, I'd have fallen."

"Then I wouldn't have been much good at looking after you," he replied, his teeth gleaming in the darkness.

He stopped them a short distance from the entrance to the station. It was best that he did not seem too eager at this stage. He needed her to take the initiative in order to win her trust enough to close the trap. "I guess this is where we say goodbye. For now. Perhaps you'll come back to the cellar one night?"

She looked up into his face, dimly visible in the starlight and gloom of the snowy street. "Must we part? I like you."

She stroked his cheek. "Come back with me. It's a cold night. I'll make us some coffee. The real thing."

He whistled appreciatively. "How could I refuse real coffee?"

She slid her hand round his arm and drew him towards the station. "Come on. We need to catch the last train. Two stops, a short walk and then coffee!"

Inside the station, he bought two tickets and they climbed the steps to the platform. There was only one other person there, at least twenty meters away. They went into the waiting room and stood in front of the embers dying in the grate. There was no light in the room thanks to the blackout, only the cozy glow around the last few coals. Without warning, she turned and took his face in her hands, kissing him softly on the lips. He slid his hands behind her back in a loose embrace.

She released him and looked down. "Sorry. Couldn't resist any longer."

"I'm not sorry. I was hoping we'd do something like that."

They kissed again. Longer this time. He could smell her hair and the sweet odor of a cheap scent. The moment would come soon. He could feel it, and his body tingled with anticipation. She felt the tremor.

"You're cold." She rubbed his back gently. "Poor thing."

A whistle blew, and there was a deep panting of steam and the heavy rattle of carriages as a train pulled up on the opposite platform. The engine hissed while a handful of doors opened and slammed shut. The train moved off amid a swirling cloud of steam and the station was quiet again. She looked at the clock above the fire.

"Ours should be here any minute now."

Sure enough, there came the sound of another train approaching, and they left the waiting room to meet it. A huge mass lumbered out of the darkness and clanked along the tracks amid another hiss of steam. As the locomotive passed by, he caught a glimpse of the stoker's face, rosy and sweating in the glow of the open firebox as he shoveled more coal into the flames. Then the tender passed, before the first of the carriages, blinds drawn to conceal the weak glow of the electric bulbs inside. The train stopped and a guard stepped down at the rear.

The man helped Monika into the coach, both of them briefly caught in the glare of the interior light before the door closed. The guard blew his whistle and climbed aboard and the train lurched into motion. There was not much time, the man calculated. Two stops, she'd said. He turned to her and kissed her again, hard this time. She tried to push him away. "Not in here."

He held her tightly with one hand while the other fumbled with the buttons of her coat.

She jerked her head back. "Dieter! Don't."

"Dieter?" He laughed coldly and slapped her hard, knocking her hat off.

She stared at him with a mixture of anger and fear. "What are you doing?"

As he ripped at the coat, pulling it apart, buttons fell onto the floor of the compartment. He flicked the folds aside to reveal her dress and thrust a hand between her thighs. She cried out. He slapped her again, harder this time.

"Make any more noise, and I'll hurt you. Badly." The calm facade of the man in the cellar had gone, and now his lips twisted into a feral snarl and his eyes blazed.

"Please . . . don't."

"Shut your mouth. Keep it shut." He raised a fist. "Or else."

She nodded and closed her eyes, clenching them tightly as his hands tore at her clothing, snatching off her shoes and ripping off her stockings and underwear. He wrenched the top of her dress down and his teeth closed round her breast. Pinning her down with one hand, he undid his belt with the other and eased his trousers down. She felt the coarse pressure of his hairy thighs pushing hers apart. She began to pray, her lips moving silently.

When he was spent, he pulled himself up, chest heaving from his savage exertion. She lay before him, her lipstick smudged over her jaw and cheeks, hair spread across the thinly cushioned seat of the compartment.

"Get your clothes on," he ordered.

As he pulled his trousers up and fastened his belt, she reached for her underwear with shaking hands and put it back on, before pulling her dress up and arranging the straps over her shoulder. He saw that she had forgotten her stockings and was crying. His right hand had slipped into the pocket of his coat and his fingers gripped the short iron bar he kept in a special pocket stitched into the lining.

"Do your coat up."

She pulled it around herself and fastened the remaining buttons.

"Now wipe your face. It's a mess. Make yourself respectable, damn you!"

She took out a handkerchief from her pocket and wiped off the lipstick. He let her continue until it was erased. "That'll do. Put your hat on."

She did as she was told, lips quivering. "Dieter, let me go. Please."

He yanked her to her feet and swung her round so that she was facing the door, her back to him. As he steered her towards it, he slid the bar out of his pocket. He turned the handle and thrust the door open. Steam and cold air rushed into the compartment as the train rattled along the tracks. Beyond her he could see a snowy bank dropping down to the rear of some apartment blocks. The train lurched, already slowing as it approached the next station. She took a half-step towards the door and he clutched her collar in his fist.

"No you don't!"

She opened her mouth and screamed. He raised the bar in his right hand and smashed it down onto the crown of her felt hat. He heard the soft crunch as her skull caved in, and her scream gave way to an explosive gasp. He hit her again, more savagely, and blood spurted from beneath the edge of the hat. Her legs began to fold under her, and he laid the bar down on the seat and used both hands to hold her steady. Then, bracing himself, he launched her out of the door with a violent thrust. She fell, limbs flailing lifelessly, and landed in a deep drift with a burst of snow. Then she was gone, lost in the dark, and he closed the door.

Picking up the iron bar, he worked it back into its pocket and glanced round the compartment. The only sign that she had been there was the splatter of blood by the door. As the train slowed, he picked up the stockings and bent to wipe it up as best he could, until only a faint smear remained. Nothing that would excite any interest. He balled up the stockings and put them into his pocket.

Shortly afterwards, the train halted in the Anhalter station, and he smoothed his coat and adjusted his cap before he opened the door and stepped out. His boots crunched on the snow as he strode towards the exit, head hunched in his collar. There was a porter inside the ticket office. He looked up hopefully at the passenger's approach, saw there was no baggage and touched a finger to his hat in greeting.

"Cold night, sir."

"Bitterly cold."

"Be some poor buggers freezing to death tonight, I'd say."

"I hope not. Good evening to you."

He left the station and set off in the direction of his home in the city. It was a walk of over five kilometers, but he did not care. How many had it been now? Seven, including tonight. And still no sign that anyone had linked his victims in any way. Why would they, when the blackout already reaped such a heavy toll? Set that against the backdrop of a nation at war, and who would notice a handful of deaths amongst the tens of thousands of lives lost? Mere straws in a haystack of carnage and misery. He smiled. If he was careful, he could continue his work as long as the war continued.

Provided he was careful.

His smile faded and he shook his head with regret. It would not be safe to return to the Cellar Club. It was a pity. He liked the atmosphere there. He liked the music and the sinuous moves of the young people as they danced. The latest victim would be found sometime in the next few days, and her picture might appear in a newspaper. If anyone at the club recognized her, they might be able to connect her with him. Better he stayed away from the place.

He knew that it would not be long before he struck again. There would be more killing soon. Very soon.

Chapter Thirteen

22 December

Schenke gripped the wheel tightly with one hand, changing down a gear as he accelerated through the corner of the Nürburgring track, passing through the slipstream of the Italian car in front of him and then slipping ahead of it. He felt his heart surge. A place on the podium was his if he could hold onto his position. As he completed the turn and the straight opened up ahead of him, he eased down the accelerator and waited until the W25's engine reached the required pitch for the change-up. The gearshift moved slickly and the rev counter dropped back as the silver Mercedes-Benz pulled away from the Italian. Fifty meters ahead he could see the wheels and tail fin of the Frenchman, just behind his own teammate.

The cars were speeding down towards the spectator stands, and on either side, beyond the wooden barrier, the crowds were waving their arms and German flags in delirium as the Silver Arrows roared by. Schenke's excitement was accompanied by pride. Pride in his skill, pride in the quality of the car he was driving, pride in the dedication of his team. But most of all, pride in his country. Germany was clawing its way out of the chaos and bloodshed that had followed its defeat in the war. Very soon, she would once again take her rightful place at the high table of great nations.

He was conscious of the stands, packed with spectators, rushing past on either side but he kept his eyes focused on the car ahead. The whine of the engine was like an anthem to his ears, resonating power and the promise of great things. The vibrations passing through the fabric of the vehicle were the tensed sinews of a wild animal chasing down its prey. He could see the next corner approaching fast; the leading car was already braking to prepare for the turn. Too soon, Schenke thought, as the French driver was forced to brake too. Then he saw his teammate accelerate again and realized his intention: to force a slowing of the pace to permit Schenke to make up some ground. It was not very sporting, but such things were mere details when all that mattered was winning. He smiled grimly and held his speed to the last possible moment before braking ahead of the corner. This was a double bend that exited in a looping curve before the next straight.

He dropped two gears and followed the Frenchman round as fast as he dared, gaining several meters until the rear of the Bugatti loomed large just ahead of him. Coming out of the first corner, he tried to cut inside, but his rival read the move and closed him off. They roared round into the second curve, and this time Schenke feinted towards the inside, then, as soon as the Bugatti began to cut across, swung to the outside and thrust the accelerator down. He drew alongside, then ahead of the Bugatti as they held their lines in the long curve leading to the straight.

The W25's engine coughed and lost power for a critical moment. The Bugatti drew ahead and edged across the track in front of him, just as the Mercedes-Benz's engine picked up again in a shrill mechanical roar. The car jolted forwards and Schenke could see the danger of collision. He applied pressure to the steering wheel to pull to one side.

But it was too late.

The front right wheel ran forward between the tire of the Bugatti and the fin at the rear. There was a savage jolt and the Bugatti swerved, jerking the W25 to the side. Schenke felt the steering wheel buck in his hands, and then the car swung to the left and tipped over. He saw a whirl of blue sky, clouds, trees, grass. His ears were filled with the whine of the engine, the tortured crash of tearing metal and the sound of his own screaming . . .

He leapt forward in his bed, bedclothes flying, and snapped into a crouch, arms raised to protect his head as he cried out in alarm and terror. His heart pounded in his chest and his eyes were clenched as sweat coursed from his clammy skin. For what seemed a long time he hovered between foggy consciousness and the awful vivid clarity of his nightmare. Gradually the real world firmed up around him and reason drove the shimmering images back into the shadows. He opened his eyes and breathed deeply. Around him, the bedroom was dark, the wardrobe and dresser just discernible against the striped wallpaper.

He reached for his watch. The luminous hands told him it was 4:30. An hour to go before the alarm clock went off. He fastened the watch to his wrist, then pulled the covers up and stared at the ceiling, not trusting himself to sleep again in case the nightmare returned.

He thought he had imagined the sound of the doorbell. Then it buzzed again and he threw back the covers. The air was cold and he shuffled his feet into slippers and turned the light on. The glare of the single bulb was painful as he stepped out into the corridor that ran through his apartment.

There was another buzz. Who the hell . . . ? He rubbed his face vigorously, then slipped the chain and turned the key, opening the door cautiously. Outside on the landing stood his neighbor, Kuhle, a municipal engineer and also the party's block warden. He wore a dressing gown, thinning gray hair stirred into a wild tangle, and regarded Schenke with suspicion.

"What is it?" Schenke said wearily.

"Are you all right, Herr Inspector?"

"Am I all right? I'm fine. Why do you ask?"

"I heard shouting from your apartment. And not just me. Frau Kestler from the floor below was woken by it as well. She called me and asked me to look into it." Kuhle craned his neck to try and peer past Schenke into the apartment. "What's going on?"

"Nothing. I had a bad dream. Nothing more."

"Perhaps I should come in and just check?"

"There's nothing to check. I told you, it was a dream. I apologize if it woke you and Frau Kestler."

The two men stood in silent confrontation before Kuhle cleared his throat. "I think it would be best if I looked round your apartment."

"And I think it would be best if you went back to bed and left me alone."

"That's no way to speak to a block warden. Even if you are a police officer. You should show more respect for party officials."

"I have every respect for the party," Schenke responded in a more cordial tone. "However, I am tired, as I am sure you are. I have a busy day ahead and need to get back to sleep. Thank you for your concern, Kuhle. I bid you good-night." He bowed his head as he closed the door and slipped the lock.

Once he had heard the sound of footsteps crossing the landing and a door closing, he put on his overcoat and went to the small kitchen at the far end of the apartment. He lit the gas stove to warm the room and sparingly measured a few spoons of coffee into his percolator. When it was ready and sputtering steam, he poured the dark brew into a mug and sat down, cupping his hands around it as he turned his thoughts to the investigation.

Frieda's discovery had unnerved him. What if Gerda's death proved to be the latest in a spree of such murders? The picture would be clearer once the files came through from the other precincts and he could compare them against each other. He hoped that Frieda was wrong, and that the spate of accidents was just that and nothing more sinister. But already he was beginning to imagine how tempting it might be for a predator to take advantage of wartime conditions to kill and kill again. From that point of view it seemed conceivable that there were more such killers stalking Berlin's streets undetected. If it became public knowledge, there would be an outcry that would shake the regime to its core. What was the point of Germany waging war on the nation's frontier when it could not protect its citizens in the heart of its capital city?

He drank some coffee. There was something else that concerned him. The investigation into Gerda's death was no simple murder inquiry. It was being steered by elements within the party. He was tired and struggling to concentrate and it took him a moment to clear his head and think it through. It was likely that Gerda's film career had been cut short by allegations that she had Jewish blood. That would have caused considerable embarrassment to Goebbels, amongst others, and might have jeopardized his place at Hitler's court. So she was offered the legal immunity afforded by changing her racial records and the financial security of a marriage to one of Goebbels's followers, Korzeny, to keep her quiet. But Gerda had needs of the flesh and continued to enjoy a string of affairs. Such behavior was sure to become public, news one day, a scandal the next, and she might be tempted to drag Goebbels down with her. A way of preventing that was to have her silenced. Permanently.

In which case, her death might be seen as an opportunity by Goebbels' rivals to blackmail the propaganda minister or even destroy him and his faction. The order to take on the investigation into Gerda's murder might have come from Müller, but Schenke was in little doubt that it originated from a higher authority. Heydrich perhaps, or even Himmler. The latter's ambition was there for all to see. He might play the part of loyal servant of the Führer, but at the same time he was clearing the way to be his master's successor. And if he could arrange for a third party to be instrumental in bringing down an opponent, he could avoid accusations of plotting against his rivals.

That might be why Schenke had been chosen for the job. He was not a party member and could not be accused of partiality. Even if he was fed clues by Müller, there was no record of them, and it would be his word against Müller's if the investigation was ever called into question.

"All very clever," he muttered sourly. If he failed to solve the case, he would be branded an incompetent failure. If he succeeded, there was a chance that the culprit might escape justice and be blackmailed into serving Müller and his superiors, while Schenke was warned to keep his mouth shut and returned to routine duties. Hauser had been right. They were being played. Unpalatable as that prospect was, his duty was clear and must be unclouded by conjecture about the motives of those with a stake in the case. Gerda Korzeny had been brutally murdered. For whatever reason, it had fallen to Schenke to find her killer.

But other factors had emerged in the last two days that now concerned him. It was a peculiar coincidence that Gerda's most recent lover happened to be an officer working at the Abwehr, and that Karin's uncle also worked for military intelligence. Indeed, he ran the department. Was it possible that Schenke was being played from another angle? Was Karin part of the conspiracy? It seemed a little far-fetched to think that she had deliberately attached herself to him some months before, unless the murder had been planned well in advance . . .

He went over the details of the period he had been dating her and found it hard to believe she was using him. Not for the purposes of any conspiracy, at least. And given that she was something of a difficult personality, it was hard to believe that her behavior was intended to win him over. He would have expected a more consistently flattering and seductive approach if that was the case.

Besides, he loved her. When she looked at him and smiled, he felt his heart surge with an instinctive need for her. He knew she could have had her pick of men in Berlin, but she had chosen him and he felt humbled by that. If only she were less inclined to loose talk. He had tried to warn her of the consequences at first, but she had laughed it off, and he feared for her.

It was possible that Admiral Canaris was involved somehow, and was using his niece to try and get information from Schenke. After all, Karin's message informing him that her uncle would be joining them for the dinner appointment at the Adlon had reached him the morning after the murder. Had Canaris already been informed about Gerda's death? Had he hoped to inveigle information about the case out of Schenke?

These tangled threads of speculation were beginning to make his head ache. The kitchen was warm, and he thought he could smell fumes. An image of the Oberg couple, dead in front of their stove, entered his mind, and even though they had died from the cold, he turned off the gas burners and took his mug to the living room, where he turned on a reading lamp and sat on the couch with his knees drawn up under his coat. He sipped his coffee steadily.

There was something about Dorner's attitude that troubled him. The intelligence officer did not strike him as a natural lothario. He was handsome and cut an impressive figure, yet he had shown little emotional reaction to Gerda's death. And what of that fortuitous encounter with Canaris after the interview with Dorner? The admiral had mentioned the investigation and been keen to arrange another dinner.

"Oh God." Schenke drained the mug and cradled his head in his hands as he groaned. "Why did I have to be involved? Why did this have to happen to me?"

He recalled the battered body of Gerda Korzeny in the mortuary and felt ashamed of his self-indulgence.

"Pull yourself together," he hissed angrily. His officer's commission, in a plain black frame, hung in pride of place above the mantelpiece. "Do your job, Schenke. Just do your job."

An hour later, showered, shaved and dressed, he felt alert and ready to continue the investigation in earnest once more. He crossed to the small bathroom window and raised the blackout blind. It was still dark outside, but the snow and the dull glow of the stars made it easy to discern the details of the area around his apartment block. On the far side of the street was a small park, the dark tracery of branches stark against the snow. There was a bandstand close to the street with benches arranged around the stage. A figure was sitting there, facing the apartment block. As Schenke watched, a tiny red spark flared and revealed the brim of a man's hat. He took a step back from the window, in case he was seen. Then he laughed at himself. This case was making him jump at shadows.

The phone in the living room rang, and he turned towards the sound, glad of the diversion. Who would call him at this time? It was too early for Karin. She rarely rose before sunrise, even outside the darker winter months.

He picked up the receiver. "Schenke."

"Sir, it's Hauser."

"You're at work already?"

"After the grief Helga gave me when I told her about losing my Christmas leave? You bet. I barely escaped from my apartment alive."

"Ah . . ."

"Anyway, you need to hear this. I just had a call from the railway police. They've found another body. Right by the track heading in the direction of the Anhalter station."

Chapter Fourteen

For the first time in a week, the dawn brought a clear blue sky and the morning sun shone brightly, giving a fine, crisp edge to every detail caught by its light. High above, a pair of warplanes left neat white contrails in their wake as they cruised across the capital. A fighter patrol, Schenke guessed, ordered into the air to reassure the people of Berlin that the Luftwaffe was vigilant. The icicles hanging from the telegraph poles glinted like diamond-encrusted ornaments. The snow was a brilliant white. Thin trails of smoke rising from chimneys in the nearest tenement blocks and the dark traces of rails and the grimy sides of locomotives and rolling stock were a stark contrast to the virgin hue of winter.

A fine morning indeed, thought Schenke, but bloody cold. The morning radio broadcast had forecast that the temperature would not rise above minus ten that day. At least there would be no further snowfall. There was a practical consideration to Schenke's gratitude for that as he picked his way across the strip of open ground below the embankment. It meant that the police would be able to examine the body and its surroundings without worrying about any clues being covered by fresh snow.

He sank nearly to his knees with every pace and it was slow going. He could see Hauser on top of the embankment along with several railway policemen. The latter were standing around chatting, their steamy breath and cigarette smoke wreathing the air around them. There was no need for so many, he thought. There was no crowd of onlookers to keep back. Indeed, those men were the onlookers, no doubt pleased to have a break from their usual routine. Fortunately, Hauser was already waving them away a short distance in the direction of the station to keep the crime scene as uncontaminated as possible.

Schenke reached the foot of the embankment and started to climb the steep slope, grimacing at the effort and pain it took to make the short ascent, almost doubled over in order to avoid slipping. It would not do to compromise the dignity of an inspector of the Kripo by tumbling over and rolling to the bottom. He was badly out of breath when he reached the top and exchanged a brief nod of greeting with Hauser.

"Where is she?"

"This way." Hauser led the way along the tracks until they came to some brambles weighed down by snow. Sprawled in the twisted vegetation lay the body of a woman. She wore a light brown coat with a fur collar. A dark hat hung nearby, caught on a thorny twig. The skin on her face and bare legs was white, frozen. Her head was twisted to the side, and Schenke could see the strands of a ponytail splayed out. That was useful, he mused. Very few younger women wore their hair that way these days. It would help people to remember her when they traced her movements. She had a pretty face. Not beautiful, but pleasing in a homely way.

He wondered if there was a husband or children waiting at home, concerned about her absence. Someone would have to tell them, and their small domestic world would collapse.

Sometimes it took courage, and not a little self-loathing, for Schenke to question grieving families. Afterwards, there was always the hardened resolve to bring them justice, along with a weary acknowledgment that often the perpetrator was never found, and further salt would be rubbed into their life-long wounds.

"Do we know her name?"

"Yes, sir." Hauser reached into his pocket and pulled out an identity card. "Monika Bronheim. It was in her purse, along with over a hundred marks."

"The killer didn't take it," said Schenke as he tilted the brim of his hat back and squatted beside the body. "He's smart. He left her purse so it looked like an accident. Nor did he want to be caught with any obvious evidence. And he's not concerned about money either, otherwise he'd have kept the cash and the identity card to sell on. A man of some means, I'd say."

"Just like the purse and jewelry left at the scene of Gerda Korzeny's murder. You're assuming this is the same man, then?" Hauser whistled. "Bit early for that, isn't it?"

Schenke looked up at him, squinting in the bright light. "And you're assuming that it isn't him? And this death isn't murder?"

"I thought criminal investigators were paid to make deductions based on evidence, sir."

Schenke lowered his gaze to the body and saw that the woman's forehead was misshapen. There was a distinct bulge high on the forehead and one of the eye sockets had dropped a fraction. Dried blood matted her hair. He took out a pencil and used the point to ease some clumps to one side, revealing shattered fragments of bone poking through the flesh. "Looks like murder to me. Killed with a violent blow from a blunt instrument. Same as Korzeny. Of course, we won't know for certain until the medical examiner completes his report, but—"

"All right. For argument's sake, could it have been an accident? Could she have just opened the door by mistake and fallen out? It has happened before."

"It's always possible, but from the look of the wound, I'd say it was too similar to Korzeny's to be a coincidence. I'd bet this is the work of the same person."

Hauser looked closely at the shattered skull. "You'd have to give me exceptionally good odds for me to take any bet, Inspector. Fair enough, let's say the same man killed both of them. And what if Frieda turns up more deaths like this? What if we look at the evidence again and conclude that the same man is responsible for all of them? Can you imagine how well that's going to go down if the story gets out? Sure, Müller will try and clamp down on it for fear of alarming the public, but word gets round. You know how effective the mouth radio can be. There's bound to be some reaction."

Their eyes met and Schenke responded quietly, "What of it?"

Hauser glanced over his shoulder. Brandt was standing ten paces away, watching them. The sergeant lowered his voice to make sure he was not overheard. "What I'm saying, sir, is that we won't be thanked if there is a reaction. Since you're in a betting mood, I'd put good money on some prick at the Reich Main Security Office hauling us over the coals for it."

"Then what are you suggesting we do about it?"

"Just saying let's not be too quick to link this with Korzeny's murder. And let's not tell anyone outside the section just yet that we think there may be a connection to the cases Frieda has found. Not until we have more proof."

The idea did not sit well with Schenke. In a murder case like this one, it was often useful to put some information in front of the public to help locate witnesses and encourage informants. If they did as Hauser suggested, they might miss a vital lead. On the other hand, the sergeant was right. They would not be thanked for alarming the public. There was enough anxiety thanks to the war, and a rising tide of criminality amongst those taking advantage of the stretched resources of the state's security apparatus. The party had long boasted that it would protect the people and stamp out crime. It would be challenging to defend such a pledge if women feared to leave their homes during the hours of darkness. The party would not look kindly on those who undermined its promises.

Pride and professionalism warred with pragmatism and self-preservation in Schenke's heart before a new thought resolved the issue, for the present.

"There is some advantage to be had if our killer thinks the police have not yet picked up his trail." It was a sop to salve a troubled conscience, and looking at Hauser's expression, he could see that his sergeant realized that all too clearly. Yet it suited him as well.

"Just for now." Hauser nodded. "Until we have enough proof to prove a firm connection. I think it's for the best, sir."

Schenke rose stiffly and indicated the area around the body. "Better get started."

They made a methodical sweep of the scene, discovering nothing in the disturbed snow, and then went over the clothing on the body.

"Were there any tracks left in the snow when she was found?"

Hauser shook his head. "I asked. There was nothing. She was spotted by the driver of a passing freight train just before dawn. He reported it as soon as he reached the depot."

"And since there was no snow last night to cover any footprints, she must have fallen, or been thrown, from a train."

"Looks that way," Hauser agreed.

"I wonder what kind of person Frau Bronheim was," Schenke mused.

"Street girl, maybe?"

"What makes you say that?"

"No stockings. And no wedding ring."

"Is that all it takes these days for a woman to be called that?"

"There are far more of them on the street since the blackout began. It's an easy way to make money, especially now that rationing is driving many to use the black market and prices are always on the up. And she was out on her own, late in the evening. Perhaps she picked the wrong punter to go with?"

"Equally, she could be a single woman enjoying an evening with friends."

"Dressed like that?"

"Even dressed like that. Besides, her killer might have left some of her clothing in the carriage. It's a reichsmark to a pfennig that we'll find evidence of a sexual assault. Just like Gerda Korzeny. Better have someone ask the rail police and see if anything has been found on the late trains."

"I'll get Brandt on it. That's something even he can handle."

"Good. After that, he can go to Monika's address and see if there's any family there. But I don't want him breaking the news yet. We need some idea of who she was, if she worked, where she worked. Who her friends were."

"I'll tell him, but are you sure he's up to it? Being a probationer and all."

"I'd say his probation is about to come to an end."

"Your funeral, sir."

"There's another possibility," said Schenke. "What if our man kept the stockings?"

"As a trophy?" Hauser scratched his chin. "Could be. Was there any clothing missing from Gerda's body?"

Schenke tried to recall the detail of the crime scene report. "Nothing I can recall. I'll check when I get back to the precinct. But it might not be clothing. He might keep different things, if he is a collector."

"Can't say I'm happy with the direction this is leading, sir. If he is taking trophies, then he'll be wanting more of them. That's what collectors do."

"I know. So we'd better do our damnedest to find him before he kills again." Schenke pulled his hat down and rubbed his gloved hands. "Have the body taken to the mortuary at Schöneberg."

Hauser nodded towards the railway police. "I'll get those bastards to carry it. Ain't going to be an easy job."

"Good. I'll leave you to it and get back to our nice warm office."

Hauser pulled up the collar of his coat. "Rank hath its privileges."

"Not when you've got to report to the head of the Gestapo it doesn't . . ."

"What developments have there been?" Müller demanded without preamble the moment the call was connected and he picked up the receiver.

Schenke had prepared himself to deliver his report. He decided that it would be best to be equally direct to his superior. "Sir, I have reason to believe that the killer of Gerda Korzeny has killed again. A body was discovered not far from where we found the first one. Cause of death was the same, a blow to the head."

"Was there evidence of sexual assault?"

"I believe so, sir."

"Why?"

"It's possible some items of clothing are missing, sir. We'll know more once the medical examiner gives me his preliminary report."

"And if he confirms rape then it will only add urgency to the need to find and stop the murderer."

"There's a further issue, sir . . ."

"Spit it out, man!"

"One of my team was going over recent murder reports looking for similarities, in case our man might have killed before. It's a long shot, but routine procedure."

"You don't need to lecture me on routine procedure, Schenke. Did you find anything?"

Schenke looked at his notebook. "Nothing amongst the murder reports, sir. But when the search was extended to deaths from head injuries, we came up with a number of reports of women who were assumed to have died in accidents. We've called the files in and we'll go over the records to see if any of these might have links to the work of Gerda Korzeny's killer."

"A number of reports? How many exactly?"

"Five, sir. So far."

"You expect to find more?"

"The accidents were just on this line, sir. I've given orders to extend the inquiry to other precincts, starting with those closest to Schöneberg. If we find nothing, then the killer may be confining his attacks to the area around the rail lines leading into the Anhalter station. If, on the other hand, we find reports of similar deaths, we might be looking at a wider series of murders."

Müller was silent long enough for Schenke to wonder if he had been cut off.

"Sir?"

"I'm still here. Listen to me, Schenke. We cannot afford

to have any loose mouths repeating what you just told me. Who else knows about this?"

"Just the people in my section, sir."

"Then keep it that way. That's an order."

"Yes, sir."

"If this gets out to the general public, I will hold you personally responsible. Is that clear?"

"Yes, sir."

"I hope so, Schenke. There is more at stake here than you can imagine. You had better not fail me."

"I will do my duty, sir."

"Damn right you will. And to make sure of it, I am going to assign one of my staff to your section to keep an eye on proceedings."

"Sir?" Schenke felt his heart sink. The last thing he wanted was to carry out the investigation under the gaze of one of Müller's henchmen.

"You heard me. I'll find a man and send him over. You will make certain that he is apprised of every aspect of the case from now on. If I find that you are holding anything back, there will be consequences. You will find this killer, and you will do it quickly, and you will not rest until it is done. Clear?"

"Yes, sir."

"Then get on with it!"

The line clicked and went dead. Schenke sighed in frustration and lowered his receiver onto the cradle. The prospect of a Gestapo man joining the close-knit Kripo section was not going to be welcomed. The team would need to be warned as soon as everyone was present. While he waited for them, he cleared the messroom notice board of the existing schedules and party directives and pinned up the available images and diagrams of the crime scenes, as well as the names of the women who might also have been victims.

Hauser, the last of them to arrive, entered the room just before eleven o'clock and nodded a greeting. "Medical examiner says he can send us his report this afternoon."

"Good. Get yourself a coffee."

When Hauser was seated, mug in hand, Schenke stood by the board. "All right, settle down." He waited until they had gathered around the board and he had their attention. "This is how things stand as a result of this morning's discovery. We're looking at the possibility of a multiple killer. Moreover, Gerda Korzeny is not likely to be his first kill, if Frieda's hunch is correct." He nodded towards her. "Good work, by the way."

She smiled back and he continued. "Given that Gerda was killed close to the freight yard, and the latest victim, Monika Bronheim, on the same line, and those who are presently recorded as accident victims on the same line again, and none of them more than a few stops away from Anhalter, it looks like our killer has established a clearly defined hunting ground. That helps us. As long as we don't let him know that we've identified a pattern." He paused. "Frieda has broadened her search, and if we start getting similar cases from farther afield, it means our killer might have cast his net more widely. We'll know soon enough, once the files arrive and we get the chance to look over them. In the meantime, I'll brief the railway police to increase their presence on evening trains in and out of the Anhalter."

He stepped up to the board and tapped Gerda Korzeny's crime scene photograph. "So far we have no witnesses who say they saw her in the company of a man once she reached the Papestrasse station. She was spotted getting on a train bound for the Anhalter. That's the last time she was seen before being discovered here." He indicated the map and stuck a pin in the location. "Monika Bronheim was found here."

Another pin was inserted to mark the place, and then more as he consulted his notes. "These are where those recorded as accidental deaths were found . . ." When all were in place he pointed one out. "This was the first body found, less than a kilometer along the track from Frau Bronheim. That was on the first of October."

Hauser leaned forward. "If that's right, and it is the same murdering bastard, then he's killed several women in less than three months."

"That we know of. There could be more."

Some of the team glanced at each other in surprise. None of them, as far as Schenke knew, had ever worked on a case of this potential scale. He let them reflect before he continued. "If we can connect these cases, we will need to be careful. I don't want anything I have said repeated outside this room." He looked round at them. "I mean it. Not a word. Not to anyone. We can't afford for this to get out and cause panic. This board is for our eyes alone. You will not discuss the case with other officers. If word does get out, I will find the person responsible and ram my fist so far down their throat they'll choke on my elbow. If they survive that, I will make sure they are sent to join a police outpost in the farthest-flung Polish village I can find."

He could see from their faces that they grasped the gravity of the matter.

"First thing we need to do is find out more about Monika Bronheim." He turned to Brandt. "What did you get for us?"

The young man opened his notebook. "She's married. Or was. Her husband was killed while serving with the army in Poland. No children. Parents live in Mariendorf. No siblings. The block warden's wife told me she had a job in one of the department stores in Kreuzberg. She has some female friends, and some male." He looked up. "That might be gossip. I got the impression the block warden's wife didn't like or approve of Bronheim. She kept asking me why the police were interested in her and what she'd done. I didn't say anything about her being killed."

"Quite right," said Schenke. "We keep all the details to ourselves for now. Thank you, Brandt. We'll need to do the same for any of the other names that Frieda turns up as possible victims. We know our killer is using the Anhalter line to try and pass the murders off as accidental deaths. As for the women, there may be some characteristic they all share, or maybe a link to a workplace, or something social. Whatever it is, we have to find it. As soon as Frieda has the details, she'll assign one of you to each of the women. I want you to go to their homes, their neighborhoods. Speak to family, friends, the people they know. Find out what their movements were, who they spent time with. We need all the information we can get."

He pointed to the crime scene picture of Gerda, a stark image of her body and clothes against the white of the snow.

"We don't know how many our man may have killed, but we do know that unless we find him and stop him, there will be more like Korzeny. It's our duty to see it doesn't happen. I know it's Christmas. I know we'd rather be with our families at this time of year, but we are police officers first and foremost and we don't get to choose when the other side commit crimes. And if we hunt this bastard down and save lives, then as far as I'm concerned, that's worth losing any Christmas for."

He let his words sink in. Some of the team, like Hauser and Frieda, were seasoned professionals who knew what they needed to do, but there were others, like Brandt, for whom this was their first murder investigation and who would be tested by it. His words were for them mainly, yet it was worth clearly stating in front of them all what he expected in the days to come.

"One other thing. There's a new man joining the team. He's been assigned to us from the Gestapo."

There were groans, and someone swore softly. Schenke raised his hands. "That's enough. We don't have any choice. He's being sent to liaise between the two departments, so he may be of use to us." That was stretching the truth, but it would not be helpful to share the real reason with the rest of the team. "I know some of you have reservations about our colleagues in the Gestapo."

"Not half!" Frieda said. She was about to elaborate but Schenke shot her a warning look and she closed her mouth.

"Look, I'd rather we were left to get on with the investigation by ourselves, but we've no option. What matters is that we cooperate with him and show him how professionals do the job. What I will say is that I don't want any of you sharing information with him without clearing it with me. It's important we don't give him a reason to interfere with our way of doing things. Understood?"

"Mushroom treatment?" asked Hauser.

"Not quite. We don't need to keep him in the dark. Just well enough informed that he doesn't cause a problem. And we don't feed him shit. Because if he discovers that's what we're up to, you can be sure he will repay the gesture in kind. Treat him like a green probationer. No offense, Brandt."

The young man gave a dismissive shrug.

"Any questions?"

Frieda raised her hand. "Will our guest be losing his Christmas as well, sir?"

"Yes, if I have anything to do with it. Now, if that's all?"

The others were silent.

"Thank you." Schenke nodded. "Dismissed. Now get some warm food inside you before Frieda gives you your instructions. It's cold out there."

They dispersed, some heading back to their tables while

others made for the canteen. As they passed through the door, Schenke saw a man in a long dark coat standing in the reception hall. He caught Hauser's eye and nodded. "I think that might be our man."

Hauser glanced in the direction indicated. "Wonder if he heard any of that?"

"Too late to worry now. Go and see. If he is Gestapo, tell him I'm in the middle of something and I'll see him when I'm done."

Hauser gave a sly smile. "And are you in the middle of something?"

"Yes. Going to get some coffee and something to eat. Then I need to make a phone call. Might as well put our friend in his place while I'm at it."

"You know, sir, party man as I am, and between you and me, the one thing I really can't stand is someone who plays at being a policeman. The dark hats and coats? You'd think they'd watched too many detective movies."

"You may be right. But sometimes those who model themselves on hard cases, real or fictional, turn out to be more dangerous in the flesh." Schenke stared at the man until the door closed. "We keep a close eye on him, Hauser."

"Yes, sir."

"Despite what I said to the others, he's here to spy on us, not to help us. We give him enough to keep Müller satisfied. Nothing more."

Chapter Fifteen

"Dinner at six? At the Adlon. That would be lovely." Karin's voice was seductive. "I am free tonight. I daresay I can persuade my uncle as well. He likes fine dining, and he's formed a good impression of you. One thing, though, Horst." Her voice became serious. "You'd better not let me down this time."

"I won't. I promise."

"I hope you're right. How are things going with your investigation? I've heard rumors that Gerda Korzeny has been murdered. Is that the case you are working on?"

"Where did you hear that? Who told you?" Schenke demanded.

"Like I said, just rumors. I heard it from more than one source. Some things don't remain a secret for very long in Berlin."

Schenke sighed irritably before he replied, not willing to go into detail. "We're making some progress. Following up a few leads. But it's only been a couple of days. Most arrests for murders happen within a day or two. After that, the odds against finding the killer lengthen with every day that passes. I hope we make some significant progress before Christmas. That would be the best gift I could ask for."

He meant it as a joke to lighten the tone of the conversation, but Karin's voice remained serious.

"You're an unusual man, Horst. Some people say that you're strange."

"Which people? I want names and addresses."

She laughed, and he felt a warm flush in his heart at the sound. He needed a shot of normality to relieve the stress of this investigation, and was looking forward to the dinner date. It would be good to see Karin again for the first time in nearly a week. Besides, he needed to speak with her uncle. It would be pleasure with a little business thrown in. He cleared his throat.

"Sorry, that's an old Kripo joke."

"Really? I wonder how many people still laugh at it these days."

Schenke sensed a quiver of anxiety clutch the back of his neck at her indiscretion. There was no telling if the line was being tapped. He felt compelled to try and warn her that someone might be listening in.

"It's just a joke, Karin. Between friends, nothing more. Let's talk about something else."

"Let's not. Why shouldn't I say what I think? The party doesn't control our minds. Not yet, at least."

Not for want of trying, thought Schenke. It had seized control of most of the means of disseminating thought. More worrying still, it had changed the curriculum in schools, indoctrinated children and turned some against their parents. He was aware of many cases where members of the Hitler Youth had denounced their parents for expressing "un-German" sentiments. And the year Hitler had seized power, he had witnessed one of the occasions when students at Berlin's university had burned a small mountain of books judged to be decadent or contrary to the new spirit of the nation. That night had shaken him. Before, he had been ambivalent about the party's ambitions for Germany. But the sight of books, and all the learning they contained, perishing in the flames while youths bathed in the lurid red glow of the pyre, chanting in glee, had filled his heart with a sick despair.

"Horst?"

He was suddenly aware that his mind had been drifting and he had not responded to her comment. Quickly he reviewed what she had said and cleared his throat.

"I don't think it's my place to comment on such things. I am a policeman. I do my duty and carry out my orders. I'm not interested in politics. I'd rather live in a world without it."

"There is no such place, Horst. Wherever people live, there is always politics. What matters is which side you take."

She had gone too far, he decided. This conversation had to end swiftly, before she put them at any further risk.

"Karin, much as I'd love to continue discussing such matters, I have plenty of work I need to deal with."

"Oh." The hurt in her voice was unmistakable, and so was the cold anger that followed. "Then I must not keep you from it. I'll see you at dinner."

"Yes."

"Make sure that I do, Horst. Goodbye."

She hung up before he could respond with any softening endearment. For a moment he stared at the receiver, as if she might come back on the line with some peace offering, but there was just a dull crackle and a click, and he put it back on its cradle. Around him the other members of his section were concentrating on their work and not looking in his direction, but he suspected that some had overheard the exchange. There was no helping that now. He had to hope their loyalty to him exceeded any temptation to be suspicious about his views of the party. For some years he had taken care not to express his views in public, and only did so sparingly in private. Even Hauser was not privy to the full depth of his feelings about the party, and the direction in which it was dragging Germany.

Five of the men were clustered about Frieda's desk as she briefed them on the information she had gleaned about the supposedly accidental deaths. One by one they took the sheets of information she had prepared for them and left the office. Hauser was hunched over a bench eating a sausage in a seeded roll, a change from the rye bread sandwiches his wife prepared for him every day, and Schenke guessed that the sergeant had not yet been forgiven for ruining the family Christmas.

He yawned and finished his coffee. There was no putting it off any longer. He rose from his desk and walked unhurriedly to the door of the messroom. As he passed Hauser, they exchanged a weary look.

"If you can manage it, sir, get the bastard to piss off back to where he came from."

"I'll be sure to pass on your good wishes."

"I'd rather you didn't."

Opening the door, Schenke could see Müller's agent sitting on the bench opposite. He was still wearing his black felt hat, and his leather coat was buttoned up as he sat erect, legs crossed and gloved hands resting in his lap. As soon as he saw Schenke, he stood up and saluted.

"Inspector Schenke? I recognize you from the picture in your file." His lips lifted in a forced smile.

So your opening words are a gentle threat, thought Schenke. He hesitated long enough to indicate his disdain and then shook the man's hand.

"And you are?"

"Forgive me, sir. I am Liebwitz. Scharführer Otto Liebwitz." He removed one of his gloves and fished inside his coat, taking out a folded slip of paper. "My orders, sir."

Flipping it open, Schenke scanned the few terse lines under the Gestapo letterhead. "Müller says that you are here to help with the investigation and that I am to afford you every cooperation."

"That is what the Oberführer told me, sir." Liebwitz removed his hat to reveal fine white hair above a large forehead. He appeared to be in his mid twenties. His brown eyes seemed to exaggerate the pallor of his thin face, which was almost delicate-featured. His accent was not local and hinted at a Bavarian upbringing. Schenke tried not to dislike him at first sight.

"I see. What is your background?"

"Sir?"

"Police, or via the SS or SD? You're too young to have been one of Rohm's crowd."

"I'm from the SS, sir. I was a direct appointment from Heidelberg University two years ago."

It was difficult for Schenke to hide his surprise. Why would the Gestapo recruit an academic to their ranks? More to the point, why would a student from such a highly regarded institution want to join them?

"That's an unusual entry route. What were you studying at Heidelberg?"

"Theology, sir. I completed my doctorate the year before last. I wasn't having much luck finding a lecturing vacancy."

That did not surprise Schenke. Many academics were still quietly opposing the new order. After the removal of Jewish lecturers and the sacking of the more outspoken, the rest had ceased to be vocal in public but continued their resistance by more subtle means. Denying a party member a teaching post was one of them.

"So how did you end up in the Gestapo?"

"I was approached by someone who knows Heydrich. He said there were posts in the security services open to men of high caliber and that he would arrange an interview for me."

"High caliber? Is that how you would describe yourself?" Schenke asked wryly.

Liebwitz thought a moment, then responded without a trace of self-consciousness. "Yes, sir. I was top of my class at university. Heydrich said I would be perfect for the Gestapo and appointed me the next day. I've been there ever since."

"And what is your function there, if I may ask?"

"Data analysis, sir."

"Data analysis? What the hell is that?"

Liebwitz blinked. "It is what it sounds like, sir. I look at intelligence reports of public attitudes and correlate them with other data, such as cinema attendance, and search for patterns that indicate shifts in public sentiment, which I then report to my superiors." He spoke almost entirely in a monotone and kept his eyes fixed on Schenke all the time. It was a little unnerving, the inspector decided.

"And they pay you for that?"

"Well, yes, sir." Liebwitz frowned. "Of course they do. It's my job."

"And do you work with other people? On this data analysis of yours?"

"No, sir. I work by myself. I have always preferred to."

"I can imagine. Life and soul of the party at university, were you?"

"Sir?"

"Never mind. What training have you had? Training that's relevant to police work?"

"None, sir. But I expect it is similar to what I already do. If not, then I can learn the necessary skills quickly. I have an ability to absorb knowledge. And I am a crack shot."

"Glad to hear it."

Liebwitz was tall, almost the same height as Schenke, but looked to be of light build beneath his coat. It was hard to know what to make of him. He might be very intelligent, but he seemed to lack self-awareness and any kind of spontaneity. There was a mechanical stiffness that exuded from his every movement and utterance. Schenke was put in mind of one of the drone workers from Fritz Lang's *Metropolis*. It occurred to him that Müller might have sent the young man to join the section simply because he could not stand his presence, rather than because he would be a useful spy. But it was best not to make such a judgment yet, Schenke mused. Better to watch him a while before deciding if he constituted a threat.

"You'd better come through then and meet my team."

Schenke led the way into the messroom and coughed. "Men, and ladies! A moment, please. This is Scharführer Liebwitz of the Gestapo. He will be serving with us for the present." He gestured towards Hauser. "This is Sergeant Hauser, my second-in-command. The ladies over there are Frieda Echs and Rosa Mayer. The youngster is Brandt. The other lads are Schmidt, Persinger, Baumer, Zimmermann, and the handsome one there, preening himself in front of Rosa yet again, is Hoffer."

Liebwitz bowed his head sharply in acknowledgment, and then glanced briefly at each person in turn, but he made no comment, nor did he attempt any kind of greeting. Neither did the team members, who merely regarded him curiously.

"Well, that was short and sweet," said Schenke. "Back to work. Liebwitz, take that table at the back of the room. You can hang your hat and coat behind it."

"I will keep my coat on. I feel the cold. And it is cold in here." The young man paused. "No more than twelve degrees."

"Suit yourself." Schenke made to turn back to his own desk.

"What do you want me to do, sir?"

"Do?"

"Yes, sir. To assist with the investigation."

"Nothing, for now. Stay here in the office and watch and learn. You'll start to pick it up soon enough."

"Oberführer Müller ordered me to stay with you, sir. To go where you go and keep you under observation."

"Did he now?"

"Yes, sir."

Schenke tried to hide his irritation. "Thank you for letting me know. I'll make sure I keep you by my side. I am sure you could be useful if we get in a tight spot."

"Tight spot?"

"Danger."

"Yes, sir. I will be. I came top of my class in marksmanship in the Gestapo induction course. And unarmed combat."

Schenke looked at him as if seeing him for the first time. "Unarmed combat? You?"

"Do you wish me to demonstrate?"

"Not now, Liebwitz. If your skills are ever needed, I am sure you will acquit yourself well, with those credentials. Now, if you will excuse me, I have some reports to read. Make yourself comfortable in the meantime."

"Yes, sir."

As Schenke returned to his chair, the new arrival looked round the room, taking in the details, and then went to the table indicated and sat down, in the same erect posture that Schenke had observed in the reception hall. Hauser crammed the last of his meal into his mouth and chewed vigorously before he swallowed. He came over to speak to Schenke.

"He's a real live wire, that one. Going to be fun having him lurking at our shoulders."

"Maybe." Schenke reflected on what the Gestapo man had said about himself. "But he may be of some use to us."

"Really? Trained by the Kripo, was he?"

"No," Schenke conceded. "But he has other skills. We'll see. Meanwhile, I'm happy for him to watch and learn the trade. But what I said earlier still goes. No one is to give him any details on the case without letting me know first. Whatever else he is, Liebwitz is Gestapo. He's Müller's man, not ours."

Hauser glanced over at him. "He looks like an idiot."

"If what he said to me is true, then that's the last thing he is. Awkward maybe, and a bit eccentric in the way that very intelligent people can be, but not an idiot. Whether he has any common sense or not is something we'll find out."

"Want me to take him under my wing, sir? Keep him off your back?""

"No dice." Schenke shook his head. "He's got orders to stick close to me. And I suspect he's the kind of man who follows his orders literally."

Once Frieda had dispatched the men to investigate the accident victims, she and Rosa turned their attention to tracking down any more suspicious deaths. For the rest of the afternoon they called one precinct after another, locating the clerk in charge of files and requesting them to be sent over to Schöneberg. Meanwhile, Hauser and Schenke read through the files that had already turned up and made notes. It was hard to concentrate under the gaze of Liebwitz, and in the end, to give the man something to keep him occupied, Schenke instructed him to read the medical examiner's report on Gerda. He watched as the Gestapo man bent over the file and studied each page closely.

"Sure he's not simple?" asked Hauser. "He has the look of the slow kid in the class."

"Just concentrate on your own work," said Schenke. "There's a good boy."

Late in the afternoon, after darkness had fallen, the inspector gave the order for work to end for the day. As his section collected their coats and hats, Liebwitz approached him.

"What time should I be here tomorrow, sir?"

"We start early. Be here by seven."

"Yes, sir." Liebwitz nodded. "Is there any way I can be of use to the investigation?"

"Yes. Be here by seven. Goodnight."

Hauser was the last to leave, and gave a quick wave before he closed the door behind him. For a moment Schenke enjoyed the still and the quiet. He returned to his chair, put his feet on the table and folded his arms behind his head as he went over the investigation. He was as certain as he could be that the murders of Gerda and Monika were the work of the same man. From the initial findings it was probable that some of the deaths recorded as accidental could also be attributed to the same killer. When the complete case files turned up with medical examiner reports, he was certain the link would be established. That would mean that a murderer was hunting women under the cover of the blackout.

He tried to put himself in the killer's shoes, using the information they had gathered so far. It was possible that the man had killed before the war began. Before the blackout was imposed. If so, they would need to check cases from back then too, to see if there were similar murders or accidents on the books. He could not recall any such cases. It was more likely, to Schenke's mind, that the killer was someone who had fantasized about attacking women but had been put off by the risks under peacetime conditions. For such an individual, the war would have been a boon. A license to act.

He would have been wary to begin with. He might not have intended to kill his first victim. It might have been incidental. To stop her crying out in panic, or for help. He might have been shocked by what he had done. But then shock gave way to a sense of urgency as he contrived to make the death look like an accident. He might have gone home shaken, vowing never to repeat the exercise, never to give in to his dark appetite again. And then, as the days passed, and there was no hue and cry, and the death was passed off as an accident, he might have felt the growing urge to strike again. To be prepared to kill from the outset and cover his tracks as before. Each kill would convince him of his superiority over the police, who failed to see the deaths for what they were.

What if the killer picked the kind of women the police were not inclined to make certain assumptions about? It was no secret that many in the service regarded prostitutes as being responsible for their own vulnerability to sexual attackers. Too often Schenke had heard his colleagues say that such women had it to coming to them. These cases tended to be conducted with far less sensitivity and diligence. Yet on the other hand, the same police officers were inclined to impute foul play to the death of a prostitute, while considering the death of a woman they regarded as respectable as an accident, given the same set of circumstances. Gerda's death had been different. There had been no attempt to disguise it as an accident. What had happened that night? Schenke wondered. Had she escaped, and the killer had been forced to give chase before striking her down?

He stood up, stretching his shoulders. Glancing at the clock on the wall, he saw that it was just after five. There was enough time to wash and shave in the washing block before he took a car to the Adlon for dinner. It was a fine place to eat, and this time it would go as planned. Besides, there was nothing quite as public as meeting there, and if he was being watched, then the fact of his choosing the Adlon would make it appear he had nothing to hide. When one of his dinner companions was head of the Abwehr, that was no small consideration. This time Schenke would be on his guard. There was more to Canaris than he had first thought, and some sixth sense told him that the admiral knew more about the investigation into Gerda's death than he had yet revealed.

Chapter Sixteen

Karin was wearing a shimmering blue dress. Silk, Schenke guessed as he threaded his way through the dining salon towards the table. He felt a stab of disappointment as he saw that she was alone. No Canaris then. It seemed that he would have to find a different way to track down and subtly question the admiral.

Karin looked up and smiled brightly as she caught sight of him. He felt a warm thrill as he smiled back. Her fine blonde hair had been arranged in plaits pinned up like a wreath, exposing her graceful neck. Although she wore no lipstick, her lips had a natural rosy color, and her bright blue eyes sparkled beneath finely plucked eyebrows. She was beautiful, he thought, as he always did when they met for a date. And he was conscious that other eyes feasted on her, no doubt wondering what she saw in the unremarkable man in a drab suit who accompanied her. Let them wonder, he decided. He did not feel any need to justify himself to those inclined to superficial observation.

"You're a few minutes early," Karin said as he leaned to kiss her on the cheek she presented.

"And so are you, my love."

"I've been here since five o'clock. Had a drink in the bar with some of the crowd."

Schenke sat opposite her at the small table, set for three. "Your uncle won't be joining us, I take it?"

"He will, a bit later."

"Ah, that'll be nice." He reached a hand across the table and took hers. "In the meantime, it'll be good to have you to myself."

"It feels like ages." She made a face. "You men seem to have hardly any time for us women any longer."

"War will do that. Anyway, I don't want to talk about my work. What have you been up to?"

She lowered her gaze as she thought for a moment. "Today I went to the Reich museum of German art for a reception for a new series of sculptures. Boring. Yesterday I was at a performance of Julefest carols in the morning. You may not have heard—the party are busy rewriting the lyrics of traditional carols." She rolled her eyes. "In the afternoon, I went shopping with the girls. That was a bit of a disaster."

"How so?"

"There's less and less in the department stores every day. It's almost impossible to find anything nice for your Christmas present. At least we were able to get coffee and cake at Reinhold's on the Kurfürstendamm. Otherwise I would have fainted away with exhaustion."

Schenke could not help laughing.

Karin frowned. "What's so funny?"

"Nothing really. It's just that with everything going on—the war, the murder case—here's you and your friends doing the usual rounds as you have always done. I find it quite reassuring."

"You patronizing pig," she said, then smiled to show she was teasing. She affected an air of moral indignation. "As it happens, I do know there is a war on. I cannot find a decent

French perfume for love or money. Tell me, darling, just how is a girl to cope? If only the Führer would come to his senses and put an end to this pointless fighting."

She was talking too loudly and Schenke glanced round at the nearest diners. Most were too caught up in their own loud conversations to pay Karin any attention. But at one table nearby, two overweight men in brown party uniforms glared across at her, and Schenke made an apologetic face and squeezed her hand.

"Please, keep it down."

"What?" She looked hurt. "I was only having a little joke."

"There's a time and a place for all that." Schenke gave a nod in the direction of the two men and lowered his voice. "Not in front of their kind, eh?"

Karin glanced at them and shrugged. "As you wish. But I would have thought their kind could do with a little levity to divert them from their tiresome earnestness."

His expression became deadly serious. "For God's sake, Karin. Be careful. There's a limit to how far your uncle can protect you, even if he is the head of the Abwehr."

Her shoulders slumped. "I'm sorry, but I find them so . . . wearying. It's like the country has been taken over by the kind of people who underperformed at school and refuse to read anything more complicated than the headlines of the gutter press. Anyway, enough of them. Let's not think about it."

"Let's not," he agreed.

"What shall we do for Christmas? You could come to my uncle's house. He's planning some big family parties over Christmas and New Year. Or we could spend it at your apartment. Just the two of us, snuggled up on the couch in front of the fire." She paused and stroked the palm of his hand with her fingertips. "That would be lovely. I'm sure my uncle wouldn't miss us too badly."

A twinge of guilt tightened in Schenke's gut and he took a deep breath.

"What's wrong?" she demanded.

"About Christmas . . . I'm not sure how much free time I will have. This case is getting more complicated than I anticipated. I've already told my team that we may be working through the holiday. You can imagine how popular that made me."

"I can imagine it very easily . . ." Her fingertips stopped moving and her hand stiffened.

He suddenly felt more tired than ever. "My love, believe me when I say that I would do everything in my power for us to spend Christmas together. But I am being put under pressure by my superiors to find the killer. They demand a result; I'm doing my best to achieve that. Not least because I want to be with you for Christmas. Please understand."

"Horst, if I didn't know better, I'd think you were trying to avoid me. Is that it?"

"No!" He stared at her earnestly. "Don't think that for one moment. Trust me, I want to be with you for as long as I can be."

She scrutinized him closely. "Do you know, that's the first time you have spoken to me in such terms. Do you really see us being together in the future? Long-term?"

The words had gushed out of Schenke and could not be taken back. In truth, he could think of no one he would prefer to be with than Karin. But, equally, he knew that his career would always be something that came between them. Something she would have to recognize and accept. Just as he had to accept that she was part of a social world he cared little for. When they were alone, she was less frivolous, more perceptive than the persona she presented to others. More intelligent and more passionate about the issues she cared about. Like her disapproval of the party and how it was transforming Germany. Views he shared and entrusted only to her.

"I'd like us to be together," he responded.

She was silent for a moment, keeping her eyes fixed on his. "For the long term?"

There it was. The question. How should he answer her? How could a person commit to something permanent when the very nature of life was so contingent? Particularly in wartime, which so acutely bent and reshaped people's sense of themselves. And wasn't his job a kind of war in itself? A constant struggle against all manner of immorality and inhumanity. It had changed him, he knew. He was not the young man who had joined the Kripo several years before. He was not the same gilded youth who had been an idealist at university and a daring celebrity on the racetrack. Injury and experience of the darkest corners of the human soul had changed him irrevocably. All that remained of his idealism was a desire to root out what little portion of evil crossed his path, in the full knowledge that any success he had was no more than a scintilla of goodness against the dark, corrupted sickness that thrived in the shadows of every society.

Knowing that, how could he offer himself to a woman with as much promise as Karin? How could he, in all good conscience, ask that she share what he knew about the world? It seemed wrong. Even if life was fleeting and uncertain, every beam of light that shone amid the greater darkness must be cherished, however desperate and fatalistic he might feel.

He looked up and saw the flicker of hope in her expression, and could not bring himself to snuff it out. "Yes, I'd like that."

They stared at each other for a beat before her face creased into an excited smile. She half rose, craning her neck to reach him, and kissed him on the lips. As she sat back down, one of the party officials at the nearby table sniffed with derision and addressed his companion.

"Such behavior. And at the Adlon of all places."

Karin rounded on him. "Show a little consideration for the happiness of others. Or has the party forbidden that too?"

The man's fat face wrinkled with indignation and he turned to Schenke. "You would do well to take your woman in hand. Before she does something unwise."

"She is her own woman and answerable to her conscience," Schenke responded. "And I will let no man tell me to dictate to her what she should do." His expression was glowering, his tone low and threatening. "You've finished your meal. I suggest you leave."

"You arrogant whelp! Do you know who you are talking to?"

"Why? Have you forgotten?"

Schenke felt Karin squeeze his hand and she nodded towards the entrance. Her uncle was striding towards them. He smiled a greeting and bent to kiss Karin. As he straightened, he became aware of the tense atmosphere between the two tables.

"Is there some problem here? Ah, I know you, don't I?" He turned to the two party members, who took in his uniform and the decorations displayed on his jacket, as well as the gold party badge that the Führer himself had bestowed on him.

"No, Admiral. No problem." The party man rose to his feet and gestured to his companion to do likewise. "We have an urgent appointment. We're leaving."

"Oh?" Canaris raised an eyebrow. "What a shame. It would have been nice to resume our acquaintance."

The two men muttered their farewells and hurried away.

"Who were those two oafs?" Karin asked as her uncle sat down.

"I have no idea. Never met them before, but there's no

better way of unnerving someone than pretending you have, or you know of them, particularly if you happen to run the Abwehr."

He turned to Schenke. "Good to see you again, Inspector. Or would you prefer Horst?"

Schenke hesitated, unsure of the other man's expression. "As you like."

"Good. Then let's not discuss business. Frankly, it would be a rare pleasure to put all that aside."

Karin looked from one to the other. "Is there something I'm missing here?"

Canaris smiled. "Only that I had the good fortune to bump into Horst at the Abwehr yesterday."

She turned to Schenke and raised an eyebrow. "Oh? And what were you doing there, darling?"

The endearment was somewhat undercut by the cool tone of the question, and Schenke stirred uncomfortably as he replied. "Just a routine interview."

"He came to question one of my officers, Oberst Dorner. I am sure you remember him."

"Karl Dorner?" Karin smiled. "How could I forget? Quite a charmer, and a wonderful dancer. For a Prussian." She turned her gaze to Schenke. "What's he been up to?"

"I really can't discuss it. Not at the moment."

Canaris chuckled. "Under orders not to, eh? Well, good for you. Then let me be the one to tell you, my dear Karin, and relieve poor Horst of his difficulty. It's no great secret that Dorner was having an affair with the late Gerda Korzeny. Which is why it was necessary for Horst to interview him. Purely as a matter of procedure, of course. Isn't that right?" He fixed his penetrating gaze on Schenke.

"That's right, Admiral."

Karin's eyes widened and she raised a hand to her lips. "No! Well, that is something. Though now you tell me, I can't say that I'm surprised. Karl has an eye for the ladies.

And from what I've heard, Gerda had an appetite for male company. So do you think he did it, Horst? Do you think he is a lady-killer, so to speak?"

Schenke did not care for the lighthearted tone of her query. In his mind's eye he saw Gerda's shattered skull against the gleaming steel of the medical examiner's slab, and there was no room for any levity in his heart. He replied quietly. "I will not discuss this, Karin. Let's not talk about it anymore."

"Horst is right," said Canaris. "We're here to enjoy dinner and good company." He turned and raised a hand to catch the eye of a waiter. "Menus here, please. And bring us a bottle of Latour."

"My apologies, sir. There is no more Latour in the cellar."

"A pity. How about the Magritte?"

"Again, my apologies, sir. Our supply of fine French wines has been disrupted. May I suggest the Weissburgunder Pinot Blanc? It is almost as good."

A moment later, the admiral was savoring the aroma of the wine with closed eyes as the waiter stood at his shoulder, notepad at the ready. Canaris took a sip and smiled. "Perfectly adequate. Now, what shall we eat?"

They opened the menus. Schenke rarely concerned himself with fine foods. Even so, he felt his stomach stir as he read through the extensive choices.

"I'll have the venison," Canaris announced.

The waiter made an apologetic face. "Venison is unavailable tonight, sir. As is the lobster, the salmon and some cuts of beef. And there's no asparagus."

Canaris's expression darkened. "Then half of this menu is unavailable. So why hasn't it been updated? Explain yourself, man, or I'll send for the manager."

The waiter looked over his shoulder nervously before he bent forward and responded quietly. "The management told us we need to carry on as before. It would not look good if we offered a more limited menu, sir. It would not sit well with the Adlon's clientele."

"I can tell you, it does not sit well with me to discover that half the options on the menu do not exist. Nor am I particularly pleased to discover that the choice of wines is similarly limited."

"There is a war on, sir," the waiter responded lamely.

Canaris patted his chest. "I do not think someone wearing this uniform needs to have that fact pointed out to him."

"No, sir. My apologies. The truth is, the Adlon is struggling to find supplies of many items now that we can no longer source them from France and England. Confidentially, I can tell you that many of the whisky and brandy bottles behind the bar contain cold tea. To help keep up appearances, you understand, sir."

Canaris sighed. "Very well, we'll have the pâté, then the entrecôte. If that is acceptable to my companions."

Schenke and Karin nodded and returned the menus to the waiter, along with the required ration coupons, then the admiral dismissed him with a curt wave of the hand.

"One hopes that our enemies come to their senses swiftly and put an end to this nonsense," Canaris grumbled. "It's pointless to continue now that Poland has fallen. If only they would believe that peace is possible with Germany."

"And do *you* believe that?" asked Karin. "Under our present leadership?"

"I think you know my views on that matter. I just obey orders, my dear. The same as Horst here. You'd have to ask a politician. Now, tell me, what was the cause of your little confrontation with our two friends on the next table?"

"Politics," she replied bluntly.

"I see. Moving on to safer ground, what else is new in your life?"

"I have been trying to push Horst to marry me."

For the first time since they had met, Schenke saw Canaris express genuine surprise. He squirmed with embarrassment and cleared his throat. "We were talking about our future together, sir. But we didn't get much further than that before we became embroiled in a brief spat with those men on the other table."

Canaris looked at them both. "A word of advice. We live in uncertain times. Take what pleasure you can from this world at every opportunity."

The meal was eaten in a convivial atmosphere. After the main course had been cleared away, Karin excused herself and headed towards the washrooms.

"She's a fine woman," Canaris commented. "You are a lucky fellow, Horst. She will make a good wife one day. With her connections, just the kind who will help a man advance his career."

"As long as she understands what she can and cannot say in public."

"Quite . . . And I daresay your own connections might serve you well."

"I'm not sure what you mean, sir."

"You do not think I would let my niece become close to any man without me knowing something about their background."

Schenke turned the stem of his glass between his thumb and forefinger. "You've been investigating me."

"Let's just say it is my business to know the business of others. I understand that your family name is von Schenke. And that your father is Otto Graf von Schenke. Which leads me to wonder why you would have adopted a vulgarization of the name. Are you ashamed of your aristocratic lineage?"

The question touched on Schenke's politics, and the cause he had briefly espoused as a student. "Not ashamed. But there is no place for such things in the modern world. I shortened my name to fit in with my colleagues when I joined the Kripo. That's all there is to it."

"If you say so."

There was a pause before Schenke spoke again. "Tell me, Admiral. It was no coincidence that you bumped into me at the Abwehr after I had interviewed Dorner."

Canaris regarded him steadily. "Of course it was not a coincidence. I take a very close interest in the activities of those I command."

"So you would be in a position to tell me if there was more to Dorner's involvement with Gerda Korzeny than merely an affair of the heart."

"I would."

"And?"

"I do not think that Oberst Dorner was responsible for the murder of the Korzeny woman."

"From what I could tell, he didn't seem to have much emotional attachment to her."

"Is that a crime?"

"No. But it does suggest other possibilities." Schenke emptied his glass. "For example, it occurs to me that Dorner might have cultivated the relationship as an intelligence-gathering exercise with regard to one of the party's factions. And that he might have been acting on your orders."

Canaris pursed his lips. "You could assume that."

"Is it true?"

He picked up the wine bottle. "Your glass is empty." He refilled Schenke's glass, then sat back and folded his hands. "Inspector, you must understand that a man in my position does not always have the luxury of operating in an open and above-board manner. At times I am even obliged to carry out my work in ways that are legally questionable."

"Including murder?"

Canaris smiled. "You are barking up the wrong tree in this instance."

"But murder would be an option in other situations?"

The admiral was still, his expression unreadable. "I couldn't comment. And I would be remiss in my duty in looking after the best interests of Karin's beau if I failed to warn you not to press me on this matter."

"Are you threatening me?"

"Such an ugly word. Consider it advice from one who would prefer to be your friend. Karin is coming back. Let's leave it there." He glanced at his wristwatch. "In fact, I still have some work to do tonight."

He stood up and kissed his niece on the cheek.

"You're leaving?"

"The burdens of command, my dear. You have a good night. Have them put the cost of the meal on my account. Until the next time, Horst."

Schenke stood and bowed his head in farewell. "Until next time, Admiral."

As Canaris walked away, Karin sat down and took Schenke's hand. "Alone again at last. Let's finish this bottle and go back to your flat. We can discuss the engagement in a more intimate setting."

Schenke nodded, but his gaze was fixed on Canaris. As the admiral reached the entrance to the dining room, he turned to glance back, and there was no mistaking the cold, challenging look in his eyes.

Chapter Seventeen

He leaned against the side of the kiosk outside the Brandenburg Gate U-Bahn station at the top of Unter den Linden. A cold wind blew through the columns of the gate and caused the red banners hanging from the entablature to flap like the wings of some giant bird of prey. Though it was a cold night, the boulevard was filled with enough people that he would not draw attention to himself as he kept a close watch on the entrance to the Adlon hotel opposite. An awning stretched out across the sidewalk towards the taxi rank, and two doormen in double-breasted coats stood ready to help the hotel's customers to and from the doors giving on to the lobby.

Over two hours ago, he had followed Schenke from the Schöneberg precinct, tailing him to the station and boarding the same carriage before settling a few seats behind, from where he could keep an eye on the inspector over the heads of the other passengers. It had been easy to discover which precinct was conducting the investigation into Gerda Korzeny's murder. He had posed as a beggar as he sat opposite the entrance, swathed in a thick quilt, squatting next to an old cap into which he had placed a handful of coins. He had identified Schenke when the inspector had left the precinct, and had allowed him to gain twenty paces along the street before abandoning the quilt, snatching up his cap and setting off after him.

Half an hour after leaving the precinct, Schenke entered the Adlon and his tail settled against the kiosk to wait. As the minutes ticked by, the cold seeped through his coat and into his body, and the only comfort he could take was from the warmth of the cigarette smoke he drew into his lungs as he kept watch. He paid close attention to people coming and going, and moved round the kiosk whenever a policeman approached along the boulevard.

Just after eight o'clock, a figure in a navy uniform came out of the hotel and stood for a moment while a doorman ushered a taxi forward and opened the door. As the light from the hotel fell on the officer's face, the man beside the kiosk recognized him and edged back instinctively. A moment later the admiral had ducked into the taxi and the vehicle pulled away and headed down Unter den Linden.

The man resumed his observation of the hotel, hands clasped to keep his fingers from becoming numb. More customers arrived and departed over the next twenty minutes, and then he saw a couple emerge from the doors. A tall, elegant woman with blonde hair visible beneath her fur hat, and Schenke. The inspector was holding his hat in his hand and he kissed the woman before he eased it onto his head. Hand in hand, the couple began to cross the boulevard.

The man moved to the far side of the kiosk as they approached and descended the stairs into the U-Bahn station. He waited for their heads to drop out of sight before he followed them, keeping far enough back so they would not be aware of him, still less suspicious. Passing through the ticket barrier, they went to the northbound platform, and he followed them aboard the first train to pull into the station. There were not many other passengers in the carriage and he sat several seats behind them. Schenke and his woman paid little attention to anyone else as they sat and talked for a few minutes. She leaned her head on his shoulder and he lifted his arm, drew her closer and kissed her hair.

It amused him to watch them absorbed in their happiness, oblivious to the presence of a killer a short distance away. The same killer that Schenke was hunting so assiduously and so far without result. It was tempting to let the inspector know he had sat close to his prey without any idea of his proximity. It would torment him, and that thought filled the man with delight. But for now, it was more important to know where Schenke lived and determine his vulnerabilities.

As the train pulled into Pankow, the couple stirred and stood up. They disembarked and he followed them out of the station, keeping his distance as he watched them walk arm in arm along the street. They made their way into a smart residential area with the kind of apartment buildings favored by professional working people. He stopped as they climbed a short flight of steps leading to the doors of a block in the middle of a street lined with bare trees. Once they had disappeared inside he stood on the sidewalk opposite and stared up at the building. Shortly afterwards, a dull outline of light appeared around one of the windows.

He smiled. "Found you," he whispered.

Now that he had located the lair of the enemy, several courses of action were available to him. If the investigation made progress and posed a threat, he could always eliminate Schenke. Better still, he could eliminate his girlfriend. That might be as effective as killing the inspector, and certainly more gratifying.

He drew in a sharp breath. That was something to be saved for another day. Tonight he had other matters to deal with.

* * *

He stared at his reflection in the mirror on the front of the wardrobe, illuminated by the light bulb hanging above the mirror. The blackout blind behind him had been drawn some hours before. The uniform coat he had stolen from the washroom in the Anhalter station fitted him well, and he would easily pass for the real thing, especially in the gloom of the railway lighting. Taking the cap from the dresser, he placed it on his head and adjusted it so that the brim was low and helped to conceal his features. He tucked some strands of hair neatly behind his ears to make himself look more like an official. The beauty of this disguise was that he knew people would focus more on the uniform itself rather than the person wearing it. Equally useful, people had an inherent tendency to trust a man in uniform, and do as he directed. The ruse had served him well so far.

Tugging the cuffs down, he took a final look at himself in the mirror and turned to glance at the clock beside his bed. Nearly ten o'clock. The last of the evening commuters would have gone home by now and only the late trains would be running, with many compartments empty. And he had the advantage of the uniform.

He left the bedroom and made his way to the rack by the door. There was a lightweight coat there, a size too big, and he put it on over the uniform, then stuffed the cap into a side bag, replacing it with a fur hat. Now he would look like any other civilian on the streets. It would be the work of a moment to remove the outer coat and hat and put on the cap, and he would be transformed. Later, after it was all over, he would resume his initial clothing to return to the apartment. He felt pleased with himself. So far the arrangement had worked perfectly.

It was getting late now, yet as he opened the door to step out of the apartment, he felt no tiredness. Quite the opposite. His muscles were taut, his senses sharpened to an acute pitch, and his mind was more alert than it was during the day. He felt more alive than ever.

Don't be a fool, a voice chided him from the back of his mind. *Don't be so impressed by yourself that you make mistakes.*

"Be careful," he muttered as he walked down the stairs to the entrance hall and opened the door. It was bitingly cold, and he turned his collar up and shoved his gloved hands in his pockets as he walked to the end of the street, heading in the direction of the Anhalter station. There were only a few vehicles moving slowly along what had once been a busy thoroughfare, but there were more people here than he had seen in a while, including groups of youngsters drinking from shared bottles and shouting down any Hitler Youth patrols who dared to confront them about their lack of sobriety. With Christmas only days away, and with a state of war hanging over the nation, it was hardly surprising that people were determined to do what they could to lighten the mood. Each in his own way, the man thought with a smile as he felt the reassuring weight of the iron bar against his thigh. Tonight he was making for the suburbs of Mariendorf where he would find his next victim.

If there were more policemen keeping watch on the passengers and loiterers under the towering barrel roof of the Anhalter station, he did not notice them. He bought a third-class ticket on the first train departing in the direction of Mariendorf and climbed into one of the public carriages with its narrow wooden seats. A moment later, a whistle blew and the train lurched into motion, and slowly pulled away into the night.

He had been sitting in the corner of the Mariendorf station café for half an hour. People came and went, some stopping for a drink or a snack from the limited menu chalked up on the board behind the counter. Some were in noisy groups, ordering a round of Glühwein before venturing back out into the freezing night. Others came singly, waiting for friends, their expressions lighting up as they waved a greeting. Only a handful were alone, and of these, he focused his attention on the women.

Then she came into the bar. He did not notice her at first, because her clothes were plain and a knitted wool cap covered her head down to the eyebrows. When she took the cap off to reveal her gleaming dark hair, the widow's peak above her large, sensitive eyes, and her fine bone structure, he felt a tingling at the back of his neck. He made no move and watched her unobtrusively as she approached the counter, ordered a coffee and a pastry and sat down at the back of the café, away from the windows and the entrance. She sipped her coffee and picked at the pastry, savoring every mouthful and making it last. At one point, a loud group of students came in and one of the men stopped at her table and gestured for her to join them. She shook her head, made some excuse, and the student shrugged, affected a deep bow and rejoined his friends.

By the time the clock on the wall chimed eleven, the clientele of the café had thinned out and she rose to leave, pulling her cap back on. He stood up and left the café ahead of her, positioning himself to the side of a nearby kiosk with a clear view of the entrance. There were few people on either platform, so there was no danger of losing sight of her. She walked towards the waiting room on the Anhalter platform and glanced through the window but did not enter. Instead, she continued a short distance and stood in the angle between the station wall and one of the iron trusses that supported the roof.

She was avoiding company, he realized. She had even declined the prospect of a warm fire in the waiting room in order to be alone. He could see her hugging herself as she waited for the train heading towards the center of Berlin. Was she nursing the breakup of a romance? he wondered. Had she lost someone close recently? Or was she, like him, an outsider, doing her best not to attract attention? Whatever the reason, it made his job easier.

A signal clanged farther down the track and a soft ringing hiss came from the rails. Glancing round, he saw the dim glow of a shielded light drift into sight as the train rounded a distant corner. He heard the rhythmic escape of steam and the whistle as the driver announced his approach. The door to the station office opened and a guard emerged, small flag in one hand. He looked both ways along the platform and coughed to clear his throat before he called out.

"Last train to the Anhalter station! Last train approaching!"

Those waiting on the platform shuffled forward, heads turned as the train emerged from the night like some dark monster bellowing steam and smoke, threatening to consume all in its path. With a squeal of brakes and a deep exhaling hiss, it stopped alongside the platform. A single door opened, and a man with a briefcase alighted and strode towards the station's entrance.

"All aboard!" the guard cried, and the handful of people on the platform entered the carriages and slammed the doors behind them. The woman hung back a moment and then hurried to get aboard the rearmost carriage; the man jumped into the one ahead of it as the guard blew the whistle to signal the train's departure.

The carriage jolted as the train edged out of the station and into the night. The man stood feet apart to brace himself against the uneven motion. There was only one other person in the carriage, a bespectacled soldier in a greatcoat, his kit bag resting on the seat beside him. He glanced up, then returned his attention to the book he was reading.

The man moved towards the door at the rear of the carriage. He opened it and stepped into the small sheltered space between the two coaches, closing the door behind him. The clank and clatter of the wheels filled his ears as he hurriedly took off his side bag, removed his coat and hat, donned the cap and shoved the other items into the bag. Making sure that the strap of the bag did not cover the party badge, he drew a calming breath and opened the door into the rear carriage. As he stepped inside, he slipped the lock to stop anyone else entering.

As he had hoped, she was the only passenger there. Whereas most people would have chosen a carriage closer to the front, so that they would be near the exit when they reached the terminus, this woman had decided to hang back to remain alone. He slung his bag behind him and made his way towards her, noticing that she glanced at him once and then looked away.

"Good evening, miss." He spoke in a Berlin accent. "Can I see your ticket, please?"

"Yes. Yes, of course. Just a moment." She rummaged in her pocket, frowned, and tried the other side. Then the first again. "I can't seem to find it . . . I swear I put it in this pocket." She looked up. "I'm terribly sorry."

He made himself frown disapprovingly. "Traveling without a valid ticket is an offense, miss."

"I know. I know. I swear to you I have the ticket somewhere. Just give me a moment."

She stood up and searched her pockets again, and he could not help feeling impressed by her attempt to play the innocent. Giving up on her coat, she opened a worn leather handbag and rifled through the contents.

"I can't think where it's gone."

"Miss, if you can't find the ticket, then I'll have to take you in when we reach the Anhalter station."

She looked up with a frightened expression. "No. Look, let me buy a replacement from you."

He shook his head. "Regulations, miss. If we catch someone fare-dodging, they have to be questioned and charged with an offense."

"But I've done nothing wrong. I've just lost the ticket, I swear."

"We'll have to see about that. May I have a look at your identity papers?" He held out his left hand as his right slid into his pocket and felt for the end of the iron bar.

"My papers?"

"Yes, miss."

She reached into her handbag and hesitated for an instant as if making a choice, then pulled out a creased, folded card. He took it, thumbed it open and held it up so he could see it clearly by the light of the nearest bulb. The photograph looked like her, despite a different hairstyle and fuller features. But it could easily be someone else, or it could be a forgery. Which might explain her behavior.

He read the details, then held the card to one side of her face as he addressed her. "Magda Buchmann?"

She nodded.

"It says here that you live in Dahlem. What are you doing so far from home?"

"Visiting relatives. I spent the evening with my aunt and uncle. Now I'm going home."

That was almost certainly a lie, he thought. It was time to move things on. He was conscious of the proximity of the next station. Taking off his cap, he scratched his head.

"I don't believe you. I don't think this card is genuine and I don't think your name is Magda Buchmann. I'm going to have to arrest you."

"No. Please, don't!" she begged, and he saw the desperation in her eyes. "Please."

He paused for a beat and nodded slowly as he returned the card. "Very well. If I do something for you, you can do something for me. Do you understand? Now take that coat off."

She froze.

"I said take that coat off."

She shook her head. "No."

"TAKE IT OFF!"

"I don't want to. I'm cold."

He lashed out and slapped her hard across the face, and a lock of hair fell over her eyes. She shook it aside and stared at him in horror.

"Are you deaf, you bitch? I told you to take it off."

He did not wait for a response, but thrust her back so she collapsed on the seat, then fell on top of her, his hands tearing at her coat. The worn cloth parted and he felt for the material of her dress, wrenching the hem up and tugging her underwear aside. As he clawed for the buttons on the front of his trousers, he could feel her hot breath on his cheek and raised himself for a better view of her face. Her eyes were wide and her mouth hung open, revealing neat white teeth.

"This is going to hurt, bitch!" he snarled.

"NO!" she screamed, and thrust her torso up, trying to dislodge him. He worked his penis out of his trousers and against the inside of her thigh. She recoiled. At the same time, her left hand came up, clenched like a claw, and she scratched at his eyes. Her other hand felt for her handbag.

He cried out, enraged, and snatched at her hand, clenching it in a powerful grip, crushing her fingers.

"Bastard!" she spat through gritted teeth. Her hand came out of the handbag and something shimmered, cold and glinting. She slammed it into his side and he felt a searing pain as the blade cut through cloth, flesh and muscle and ground against a rib. She struck again as he rolled away, jaw gaping in surprise.

"What? What's this?" He slumped to his knees and reached for his side, feeling warm blood soaking through the cloth. "Fucking bitch . . . Stabbed me! I'm going to kill you . . ."

Before he could recover, she leaped up, dodging past him, and sprinted down the aisle, abandoning her hat and handbag. He clambered to his feet and raced after her.

"Help! Help me!" she screamed as she ran.

He was gaining on her, enraged by the pain in his side and fury that he had been defied by his prey. She reached the door, dropping the knife as her fingers worked frantically at the catch. Glancing over her shoulder, she shrieked again for help, seeing his twisted features and bared teeth as he raced towards her. The catch slipped back, and she twisted the handle and wrenched the door open. The wind tore at her open coat as she snatched at the handle of the next carriage and threw open the door. To her right she saw the emergency chain, and she hurled herself towards it, fingers closing on the links as she wrenched it down.

She felt a savage blow as the man crashed against her and carried them down onto the floor between the seats. The impact drove the air from her lungs in an explosive gasp. She lay dazed as he rained blows on her, striking her head and chest. Around them the carriage jolted and rattled in protest as the locomotive's driver applied the brakes.

"Hey! Hey, you there!" a man's voice shouted from nearby. "What the hell are you doing? Get off her!"

The blows stopped and she felt the pressure on her body ease as her attacker scrambled to his feet and stood over her. There was a blur of movement, and then he was brandishing a sturdy length of iron and roaring, "Stay back!"

She groaned, and with what seemed an immense effort sat up and shuffled back against the edge of thc seat.

"Get away from the woman!"

She could see a man in a soldier's uniform two meters away from her attacker. He stood in a crouch, hands raised and bunched into fists. Her attacker surged forward and swung his bar viciously, but the soldier easily avoided it, though his glasses fell to the ground as he sprang back. He reached to the belt at his side and ripped a bayonet from its scabbard, aiming the point at the other man's face.

"Drop the bar and get back! Do it, or I'll gut you."

The carriage jolted again as the heavy iron wheels struggled for purchase on the icy tracks. The two men and the woman lurched towards the front of the train before a shrill squeal sounded from the brakes. Taking advantage of the moment, the attacker lashed out with the bar and caught the soldier high on his left arm. The soldier struck back with his bayonet, tearing through the cloth of the other man's coat but not cutting through to the flesh. The carriage lurched again and they fell apart as the train slid to a halt and the rattles and groans gave way to silence.

The attacker paused. He glanced at the woman, eyes wide, nostrils flaring as his lips parted in a ferocious snarl. He was almost insensible with rage and a desire to beat her to a bloody pulp. But there was no time for that. The soldier was shaping to strike him again, even as his left arm hung uselessly at his side. The attacker let out a feral roar of frustration, then threw himself towards the door at the side of the carriage. The handle was frozen, and he had to drop the iron bar so that he could work it free with both hands. At last the door swung open and slammed back against the side of the carriage. A shower of ice crystals and snowflakes swirled in as he hesitated briefly, glancing at the slope of the embankment below him.

The carriage jolted again and there was a blur of movement as the door swung back savagely against him and pinned the breast of his jacket against the frame. He felt a jerk as his lapel caught on something, then tore off as he thrust the door back and leaped out. He just had time to brace his knees, then powder snow exploded all around him and the impetus carried him on down the slope, rolling and slithering. Behind him, the soldier was shouting for help from the passengers in the other carriages.

Once he reached the bottom of the embankment, he scrambled to his feet, breathing hard. His side throbbed painfully and he clamped a hand to the wound as he struggled through the snow towards the dark mass of the nearest building. Glancing back, he saw two figures scrambling down the embankment in pursuit.

"Shit . . ." He gasped through gritted teeth and increased his pace. There was a long heap of snow that had been cleared from the road behind the buildings, and he rolled over the top of it and made for a narrow alley between two adjacent tenement blocks. As soon as he was out of sight, he slung off the side bag and took out his other coat and hat, hurriedly putting them on. He sucked in a calming breath and continued through the alley and swiftly into the street beyond, turning and turning again until he had put some distance and a different direction between himself and any pursuers.

Chapter Eighteen

23 December

Schenke woke in the middle of the night and went to the toilet. As he washed his hands, he paused to look at himself in the mirror and saw that he was gaunt and exhausted-looking. He filled the sink with cold water and plunged his face in, forcing himself to keep it there as he counted to sixty. The icy water stung, but he could feel his senses getting sharper with every moment of immersion. He raised his head with a rush of spray and gasped for air. Reaching for a towel, he dabbed himself down and pulled out the plug before returning to bed.

A single light glowed in the hall and provided enough illumination in the bedroom to make out the shape of Karin curled under two quilts and a blanket. He eased himself beneath the covers and into the warmth around her. As he pressed against her, she let out a low moan and snuggled her back against him, muttering something indistinct. He kissed her neck and wrapped an arm around her protectively.

Closing his eyes, he tried to order his thoughts about the investigation. His discussion with Canaris the night before had complicated matters. There was more to Gerda's death than the admiral was prepared to reveal. And yet if her murder was linked to the other deaths Frieda had identified, then that raised the question of whether there was a more serious conspiracy being played out. Conversely, it might be that Gerda was a victim chosen at random by the killer and her death had nothing to do with the infighting between party factions. In some ways that was a more worrying possibility. If the identity of the killer was not known within the party, he might be even harder to track down.

Schenke was suddenly struck by fear for Karin's safety. For a moment he was tormented by images of her being stalked in some dark street or on a train rattling through the night. He could not bear the thought of losing her and enfolded her more tightly still.

She stirred, and mumbled. "Horst, are you all right, my love?"

"Yes," he lied. "Just getting comfortable. Go back to sleep."

"Mmmm."

He remained still until her breathing had settled into an easy, regular rhythm, then eased himself onto his back, opening his eyes and staring at the ceiling. He had hoped to think things through and clear his head so he might get some more sleep. At length his heavy eyelids closed again and he drifted off.

Three hours later, at quarter to five, the alarm clock rang. He reached over and turned it off as Karin stirred and then huddled further into the covers. He went to wash, shave and dress, then ate a quick breakfast of rye bread and honey with coffee before returning to the bedroom. Karin was still asleep, and he sat on the edge of the bed and leaned over to kiss her on the forehead.

"Take care, my love," he whispered in her ear, then rose up and went into the hall to collect his coat and hat.

* * *

He was not the first to reach the section's new office at Schöneberg. Liebwitz was already sitting at the end of one of the tables in front of the coat hooks, where his leather coat and hat hung neatly. The Gestapo man rose and saluted.

"Hail Hitler."

Schenke paused on the threshold and nodded back mutely before he closed the door behind him.

"Good morning, Liebwitz. You're up early."

"I am always at work by this time, Inspector."

"Really? How diligent of you. Please feel free to stop standing at attention."

"Yes, sir." Liebwitz made an effort to loosen his posture.

"For God's sake, man, sit down and relax."

"Yes, sir. May I ask what your plan of action is today?"

"Indeed," Schenke replied. "You may ask."

He paused briefly to enjoy the puzzled look on Liebwitz's face then made his way to his table and saw a folded note on top of his paperwork. It was from Ritter, and he read it twice to be sure before muttering, "Shit . . ."

The door of the office opened and Rosa and Frieda entered. They were wearing bulky coats and fur hats and nodded a greeting to him as they made for the rack of hooks close to the stove. He held up the piece of paper. "There was another attack last night, but this time he was frightened off. And the victim is here in the building." He stood up. "Frieda, get a notepad and come with me. Rosa, you inform Hauser what's happened the moment he arrives. Tell him to get hold of any reports on the incident. I want to know the full details as soon as we come back to the office."

"Yes, sir."

"Meanwhile, I want the background reports on the accident victims on my desk."

"Yes, sir."

Liebwitz raised a hand. "Sir?"

"What is it?"

"My orders are to accompany you on this investigation. Wherever you go. I should attend the interview when you speak to any witnesses."

Schenke grimaced and silently cursed the man for arriving at the office so early. The Gestapo agent's orders from Müller were unambiguous and it would only cause trouble to order him to remain in the office. A more subtle tactic was required. "I need someone to take shorthand when I speak with the victim. That's all. Too many of us may well unnerve her. So unless you have shorthand . . ."

"I have been trained in shorthand, sir."

"Is that true?" Schenke demanded.

Liebwitz looked surprised. "Of course it's true. Why would I say so if it wasn't?"

"Why indeed? Very well. Get a notebook and come with me. You take charge here, Frieda. Update Hauser the moment he arrives."

He led the way upstairs to Ritter's office and knocked sharply on the door before opening it without waiting for a reply. Ritter was at his desk, still wearing his coat, writing notes on a document in front of him. He frowned at the interruption until he saw the paper in Schenke's hand.

"What happened?" Schenke demanded as he stood over the desk. Liebwitz remained by the door.

Ritter set down his pen and leaned back. "There was an incident on a late train heading towards the Anhalter station. A railway police officer, or a man posing as a railway police officer, attacked a woman. She was able to raise the alarm and fight him off before a soldier on leave intervened. Her attacker managed to escape when the train stopped. He was pursued as far as the nearest buildings but disappeared into the streets. The woman claims that she wounded him with a knife."

"Wounded," said Schenke. "That's good. We can put the

word out to doctors and hospitals to report treating anyone with stab wounds. What about the woman? She's here?"

"I've got her in a cell downstairs. There's a doctor seeing to her injuries at the moment. First one we could find at this hour."

"Why is she in a cell?"

"She tried to run last night when the railway police turned up. Just turned and ran down the train. She didn't get very far. I had her taken into protective custody and put somewhere safe once we got her back to the precinct. She's given a statement. I'll have it typed up for you as soon as my secretary gets in."

"Good. And the soldier?"

"He's in an office down the corridor. I had one of the night shift get him something to eat and drink, but he's not happy about being held. He took a blow on the arm from the attacker but nothing seems to be broken. I told the doctor to check on him once he's finished with the woman. Wants to get back to his family as soon as possible and I've had to threaten him with a day or two in the cells to keep him quiet."

"And what of the crime scene? Has it been secured?"

"Of course," Ritter responded tersely. "The carriages have been moved to a siding. After a somewhat frank exchange of views with the official in charge of the line's rolling stock. The place where the train stopped and the assailant fled is under guard until the Kripo arrive and take over. I'm assuming this is related to your case. If not, we'll take it off your hands when the time comes."

Schenke was pleased. Clearly the exposure of Ritter's incompetence at the first murder scene had prompted him to act with professionalism this time. "We'll start with the soldier. Where can I find him?"

"Down the corridor. Three doors on from my office. Brace yourself, though, he's a charmer."

Outside the room indicated, Schenke peered through the small glass window in the door as he addressed Liebwitz. "When we go in, I'll do the talking. Your job is to take notes. Clear?"

"Yes, sir."

"Good."

He opened the door. The soldier was sitting hunched over a table with an empty plate to one side. He still wore his overcoat, and the dawn light streaming through the window glinted off his glasses as he looked up.

"About bloody time," he snorted. "Been sitting here for hours. Can I go home to my family now?"

"Not quite yet." Schenke made himself smile. "But I won't keep you long. I'm Criminal Inspector Schenke. My colleague is from the Gestapo."

The soldier's eyes focused on Liebwitz for a moment and then he turned his attention back to Schenke. "I've given a statement already. Why do I need to speak to you?"

"It's possible the attack you witnessed is related to another case. That's what we're here to talk about. I'd like your account in person. Besides, I understand you were injured. We can't let you go before your arm is looked at by the doctor. He'll be with us shortly."

"My arm's fine. It was just numb for a bit. I don't need a doctor."

"All the same, we'd be happier if he examined you just to be sure. We'd be remiss if we let you walk out of here with a serious injury."

Schenke pulled up a chair and sat opposite the soldier, indicating to Liebwitz to take his place beside him. When both were settled and the Gestapo man had taken out his notebook and readied his pen, the inspector folded his hands. "Let's begin. What's your name and rank?"

"I've already told everything to the other lot."

"Now I'd like you to tell me."

"Look, sir, I'm a soldier on leave. I've got ten days to spend with the family before I have to go back to my regiment. You have no right to keep me here any longer."

"That's not true," said Schenke. "All branches of the military are subordinate to the authority of the Reich Main Security Office and subject to summary punishment should individuals fail to comply with General Order 6, Appendix C, Section 22. Which means I can order you to do as I say, and if you object then I will charge you with insubordination. Which also means, amongst other consequences, that your leave will be spent in a cell and you will not see your family." He let his words sink in. "Let's start again, shall we? Name and rank."

"Peter Krämer, sir. Gefreiter, 75th Infantry Regiment."

Liebwitz began to make notes as Schenke continued. "Now, tell us what happened last night."

Krämer folded his arms, wincing as he bent the left one. "Like I said, I'm on leave. My family live in Pankow. I was taking a train up from the south. It was delayed several times and I had to change and was lucky to catch the last service into Berlin. I was the only one in the carriage, until we got to the last station, before the attack."

"That would be shortly after eleven, right?"

"If you say so. I wasn't paying attention to the time. Anyway, a man got on."

"Did you get a good look at him?"

"Not then. Far as I was concerned, he was just a civvy. He had a fur hat and dark coat and a side bag. That's all I saw. Other than that he was tall and seemed well built. He looked my way, then turned towards the rear carriage as the train started moving. I carried on reading. I saw him go through the door." He paused to recollect what had happened next, then resumed. "It was a few minutes later when I heard something that sounded like a scream. I wasn't sure whether it was just some noise coming from the train, so I didn't give it much thought. Then the door leading to the rear carriage flies open, and this woman comes through in a panic. Right behind her there's the man, one of them railway cops, chasing her. She grabs the alarm chain just before he knocks her down—"

"Wait a moment," Schenke interrupted. "A railway policeman? A different man to the first one you saw?"

"No. Same man. Had to be. Same build. I could see that he had brown hair this time, with his cap on. Besides, I checked the last carriage later and there was no sign of the civvy."

"All right, go on."

"I heard her crying out and I went down there as fast as I could to help her. I saw him on top of her, beating her. I told him to stop. When he got up to face me, he took out a crowbar and started swinging at me. That's when I drew the bayonet, to defend myself, you understand?"

"Of course."

"It all happened pretty quickly. He hit my arm, I got one in on him."

"You injured him?"

"I might have done. The bayonet tore his coat. The train was lurching about and then it stopped. Soon as it did, he opened the door and jumped. I called out, to get attention. There were some other people on the train, farther up. A couple of them went after him, but he was quick and had a good start. They had no chance of catching him. Last I saw, he was heading towards the nearest buildings."

"Why didn't you go after him? You were closest."

Krämer winced uncertainly. "My arm was hurting like hell, and there was the woman. She looked in a bad way. It seemed like she needed help first."

"Did you get a good look at him when you went to help the woman?"

"Not really. He knocked my glasses off." He tapped the

rim of the pair he was wearing. "Luckily I always carry a spare pair in my kit bag. All I can tell you is he had light brown hair. Blue eyes, or gray. Square jaw . . . That's about it. Like I say, it all happened quickly." He looked across the table at Schenke. "There's nothing more. Can I go now?"

"Not yet. There's a doctor coming to examine you. You'll wait for him. That's an order. Meanwhile, you'll give your address to the desk officer downstairs before you leave. In case we need to speak to you again."

Schenke glanced round at Liebwitz. "You got everything?"

The Gestapo man flicked over his notes and nodded. Schenke stood up.

"Thanks for your assistance, Krämer. You have a good Christmas with your family, all right?"

"Yes, sir. I'll do my best."

He led the way out of the room and closed the door behind them. They moved a short distance along the corridor so that they would not be overheard by the soldier. Liebwitz was the first to speak.

"I do have one question, sir."

"Yes?"

"I wasn't aware of General Order 6, Appendix C, Section 22, sir. I'll have to make sure I read up on that as soon as I can. My apologies."

"Save your breath. There isn't any such regulation. I made it up to keep Krämer from playing the barrack-room lawyer."

"You lied?"

"It gets the job done from time to time. It's a damned shame he wasn't able to give us a more detailed description of the attacker. Still, we've got some good solid leads to go on. We know his MO, we know something about his appearance and we know he's been injured. That's helpful. Very helpful." He turned towards the stairs and gestured to Liebwitz to follow him. "We need to speak to the woman. If our man is responsible for Gerda Korzeny's death, and the others, then she's very lucky."

"I don't think being assaulted and nearly murdered can be considered fortunate, sir."

"Point taken. But she survived. Better than that, she managed to fight back and wound the bastard. That takes some guts." Schenke paused a moment. "She must have got a good look at her attacker. If anyone can give us some useful leads, it's going to be her. Someone who has the presence of mind to do what she did is going to be interesting to meet. Very interesting indeed . . ."

Chapter Nineteen

The doctor was still examining the woman when Schenke and Liebwitz entered the cell. The room was long and narrow, with a wooden bed frame, a thin mattress and a blanket at the far end. Above, there was a small barred window at street level. Snow was piled up to half the height of the dirty glass panes, and the main source of illumination was the bulb behind a wire grille on the ceiling. By its glow, Schenke could see the doctor leaning over the woman as she lay on the bed. The air in the room felt cold and damp, and the walls glistened with condensation. The only warmth came from a single heating pipe running through the cell above head height.

The doctor looked up, his trembling hand holding a bloodstained swab of cotton.

"How is she?" Schenke demanded.

"See for yourself."

Schenke led his companion to the side of the bed. The woman lay on her back on a stretcher, still dressed in her coat, staring up at the three men nervously. Her face was bruised and swollen and there were stitches in the puckered skin of a cut on her cheek and another on her forehead. The doctor put the swab down.

"As you can see, she was badly beaten. There are no bones broken or any signs of internal injuries, as far as I can see from a superficial examination. From the way she's been wincing I'd say there's some bruising on her ribs on the left side. Whoever did this could easily have inflicted fatal injuries if he'd carried on with the beating."

"Has she said anything?" asked Liebwitz. "Has she identified her attacker?"

"She's not said a word to me. I have asked her name, but she didn't reply."

"What about her identity card? Her ration book?"

"I don't know about those. There was a small bag on the stretcher when she was brought in, but that was taken away by a policeman. You might try looking into it."

"Thanks for the tip," Schenke responded drily. He saw that the woman was shivering. "We need to get her out of this room. Why on earth are you treating her in here anyway?"

"That's what I was ordered to do. You think we'd be in this icebox if I had anything to do with it?"

"Then let's move her."

"On whose authority?"

"Mine. Is there anything more you need to do for her?"

"She's cold and probably still in shock. Keep her warm, get a hot drink inside her, and when you release her, she should go to a pharmacy and get something for the pain. And I'd say she's not to return to work for a week at least."

Schenke nodded. "All right, we'll see to it. You can go now. Thanks."

The doctor raised an eyebrow at the curt dismissal, then shrugged and packed up his large leather bag and left the room. Liebwitz pointed to the stretcher handles.

"Should we carry her up?"

"She can walk. If she's fit enough to attempt an escape, she's fit enough to make her way up to the section office. We'll question her there." He looked at the woman. "On your feet, please, miss."

She shifted and winced, touching her side.

"Slowly does it," suggested Schenke, offering his hand. She took it and swung her legs over the side of the bed until she was sitting on the edge. She breathed deeply and coughed, her face screwing up in pain. When the fit had passed, Schenke nodded to his companion. "Give me some help here."

He slipped his right hand round her back and eased her up onto her feet. Liebwitz supported her from the other side and they made their way out of the dank cell and up the stairs to ground level. As they entered the office, Schenke saw that most of the team had arrived and were drinking and smoking as they waited for the morning briefing. They all rose to their feet as the trio entered, and eyed the woman speculatively.

"Is this the one who got away?" asked Hauser.

Schenke nodded. "Get her something to drink. Chocolate if they have it. With plenty of sugar."

Hauser hurried off. Schenke settled the woman in the chair nearest to the stove, added some more coal and closed the hatch. He then looked at the others. "Make your reports to Frieda and Rosa. And give me some space over here so we can talk."

He turned to Liebwitz. "I want you to find that handbag. Ask Ritter for it. If he doesn't have it, tell him I want it tracked down and brought to me the instant it's located."

"Yes, sir." Liebwitz gave a nod of acknowledgment and strode away.

When the Gestapo man was out of earshot, Schenke pulled up a stool and sat down across from the woman. He took out a cigarette and lit it, drawing a few puffs. He offered one to the woman, but she shook her head.

"You look like you could use one."

She remained silent.

"Look, I'll find out who you are soon enough. So why not spare me the work and just tell me, eh? I don't know why you're being so uncooperative. You were attacked by a man who might have killed you. Don't you want to see him caught? Don't you want to prevent him from doing that to some other woman?"

She looked at him for a moment before she muttered, "Magda. My name is Magda Buchmann."

"Magda," Schenke responded warmly. "That's nice. My name's Horst. I'd like to say it's a pleasure to meet you, but these are hardly ideal circumstances, I'm afraid."

Her lips lifted in a slight, brief smile in response to his informality. "No."

"I mean what I said, Magda. That man could have killed you. We have to catch him before it happens again. We need your help to find him and stop him. Will you help us, Magda?"

She nodded. "I'll do what I can."

"Thank you."

Hauser returned with a steaming mug and a paper bag and set them down in front of her.

"Chocolate. That'll put some color back into your cheeks. And there's some biscuits in the bag. My wife baked them last night. They're good." He patted his stomach. "I should know."

She looked grateful, but Schenke noticed a slight stillness as she spotted the party badge on Hauser's lapel. Then she cleared her throat. "Thank you."

"You're welcome."

Schenke looked at his sergeant. "I was going to wait for Liebwitz to return with her bag, but you can take the notes."

"Yes, sir." Hauser pulled up a chair and sat to one side. He took out his notebook and a pencil.

Schenke leaned forward and looked her in the eyes. "Magda, what happened last night? Start from the beginning. Why had you gone out in the first place?"

"Do I have to answer your questions now? Can't I rest a while? I feel so sore and I'm still confused about the details."

"We have to get as much information from you as possible, while it's still fresh in your mind. Lives may depend on it. So come on, help us."

She gave a deep sigh and looked down at the floor as she began. "I was supposed to be meeting a friend. We had agreed to have a meal and go and see a movie. I took a train down to Mariendorf to meet him in the station café, but he never turned up. I waited for a while before I realized he had decided to stand me up. I was angry and felt humiliated. But still I waited until it was almost time for the last train heading back to the Anhalter. I remember leaving the café and going to stand on the platform until the train arrived."

"In this cold?" asked Hauser. "Why not the waiting room? It must have been freezing."

"It was. But I didn't want to be with people. Didn't want them to see how upset I was."

"Where do you live?" queried Schenke.

There was a hesitation before she replied. "I rent a room in a friend's apartment."

"What's the address?" asked Hauser.

She looked to Schenke. "Do I have to say? My friend is not supposed to let rooms to others. Her landlord would throw her out if he discovered I was living there."

"Magda, this a serious matter. You could have been murdered. We need your address so we can contact you if we catch the man who attacked you. You'll have to identify him, and act as a witness when he goes on trial. We'll do our best not to embarrass your friend."

"I will be moving soon. I need to be closer to work.

There's no point in me telling you where I live now. I'll let you know my new address as soon as I can." She looked at him earnestly. "I promise."

"We need it now, Magda."

Her shoulders sank. "Apartment 4b, 84 Zubrigge Strasse, Dahlem."

Hauser made a note. "And your friend's name?"

"Eva Fogler."

"Thank you," said Schenke. "Now, you were saying that you were waiting on the platform for the train. Was there anyone else there? Apart from those in the waiting room?"

"A few."

"Did any of them stand out in any way?"

Magda shook her head. "I wasn't paying them any mind. I was trying to stay warm."

Hauser clicked his tongue. "And that's what waiting rooms are for . . ."

Schenke glanced at his colleague before returning his attention to the woman. "What happened then?"

"When I heard the train approaching, I moved towards the edge of the platform, along with the others."

"Were any of them in uniform?"

"Not as far as I recall."

"So the man who attacked you may have been on the train already."

"I suppose so. Anyway, I got into the last carriage as soon as it stopped."

"Why that carriage?"

"For the same reason as I didn't go into the waiting room. I wanted to be on my own. I settled down and the train started moving. I was looking forward to getting home and going to sleep. That's when the railway policeman entered the carriage." Schenke noticed that her hands were trembling. "He asked me for my ticket. But I couldn't find it, and that's when he attacked me. Forced me down and started tearing at my clothes. As he was doing . . . that, I reached for my bag. I had a knife in it."

"You carry a knife in your bag?" asked Hauser.

"For safety."

"And yet you were out alone, chose an empty carriage. Wouldn't it have been safer to stay where there were plenty of people around? Some might argue that you were asking for trouble."

"I suppose so," she conceded. "But I thought I'd be all right if I had something to protect me, just in case."

"What happened next?" asked Schenke.

"I stabbed him. As hard as I could. He shouted and rolled off me. I ran for the next carriage."

"Where's the knife now?" asked Schenke. "Did you keep it?"

She shook her head. "I don't know. I think I must have dropped it at some point. I can't remember."

Schenke turned to Hauser. "We'll need to have the carriage searched for the knife. Make a note." He nodded to Magda to go on.

"He was on his feet and chasing after me quicker than I thought possible. I'd only just made it through to the next carriage when he caught me. I saw the emergency chain and grabbed it. Then he hit me, hard. I remember going down on the floor, then more blows." Her head sank and she was silent for a few seconds before continuing in a quiet voice, barely more than a whisper. "There was a moment when I felt calm, when I was sure I was about to die. Then . . . then I was dizzy. I can't recall it very clearly. There was another man, a soldier. They struggled and then there was a blast of cold air and the attacker was gone. After that, shouting, and more people. I closed my eyes and curled up to make it all go away. Then I was brought here . . ."

"Magda, do you recall what the man looked like? Can you describe him for us?"

She breathed in deeply. "I don't think I'll ever forget him. He had a cap on, so I couldn't see much of his hair. A few strands. Brown. Eyes like steel and a face like those you see on the party posters."

Hauser frowned. "What do you mean?"

"All those soldiers and workers who look like statues. Statues sculpted by second-rate headstone masons," she added with such contempt that Schenke could not help a quick smile. There was more to her than he had first thought. It was a rare moment of revelation, and she glanced anxiously at both policemen. "What I mean to say is, he had one of those bold faces. Like an athlete. He was strong as well. And tall."

"That's good. We'll sit you down with one of our artists later on. If we get a good likeness, it'll be a great help to our investigation."

"And will I be allowed to leave?"

"I should think so. As long as we know where to find you when we need you again."

The door to the office opened as Liebwitz returned. He was holding a bag in his hand and raised it for them to see as he approached. "Ritter's people had it, sir. They weren't going to give it up until I said I'd phone Oberführer Müller. That made them more cooperative."

"I bet." Schenke took the bag. "Have you looked through it?"

"No, sir. Your orders were to bring the bag to you. Nothing else."

As literal as ever, Schenke thought. It was reassuring to know where they stood with Liebwitz. His manner might infuriate his colleagues at the Gestapo, but it made it far easier for those at the Kripo to tolerate his presence knowing they didn't have to look over their shoulders all the time.

Magda held out her hand. "Can I have my bag, please?"

"In a moment. Once I've searched it."

"But it's my personal property. You have no right to it."

"Technically, it is material evidence from the scene of a crime. I could keep it here at the station as long as I want." He put his hand over it. "Is there any reason why you are so anxious about me taking a look?"

She gave him a strained look and shook her head.

"Very well."

The bag was perhaps twenty centimeters square and made of black leather. Once no doubt it had been polished to a gleam, but now it was worn and battered and the leather was starting to crack. It was finely crafted, with neat stitching and what seemed to be a silver clasp. Schenke twisted the clasp and peered inside. He saw the identity card and took it out. The name matched, and the photograph seemed a passable likeness.

Hauser leaned over to have a look. "You've lost a fair amount of weight there, Magda. You almost look like another person."

She shrugged. "There's a war on. Rationing and strained nerves will do that to a person. As will being nearly beaten to death."

Schenke scrutinized the document more closely. "Looks genuine."

"Want me to have it checked?" asked Hauser.

"I hope that won't be necessary." Schenke took out the other contents and laid them in a row beside the bag. "Keys, brush, compact mirror, lipstick, ration book and coupons . . ."

He felt something in the lining of the bag. He ran his fingers over the shape, oblong and thin, and came to a slit in the lining. He held it open and took out another identity card.

Magda sat still, her expression frozen, while Hauser and Liebwitz examined the card. Schenke glanced at her.

"Can you tell me why you have Johanna Kasper's identity card in your possession?"

"I found it a few days ago, in the street. I was going to hand it in to the police. I swear."

"Why hide it in the lining?"

"It wasn't hidden. It must have slid in there."

Schenke examined the lining. It was possible. But unlikely.

"It slid in there," Hauser repeated. "I doubt that. Then there's the interesting resemblance you bear to Johanna Kasper. That's something of a coincidence. Someone might think that one of these identity cards is a fake. Someone else, with a more suspicious nature, might think both of them are fake. What do you say, Magda? Or are you Johanna? Or someone else entirely?"

Her bottom lip was trembling now. "I'm the victim here. Why are you treating me like this?"

Schenke intervened. "We're trying to establish who you really are. As things stand, there's a possibility that the attack on you is not the only crime we may have to deal with."

"You bastard . . ." She looked at the three policemen and continued in a choked voice, "You're all bastards. All you Nazis . . ."

Schenke felt around in the bag to see if there was anything else. His fingers brushed over another object in an internal pocket. He eased it free and saw that it was yet another identity card. He was about to comment when he saw a bold yellow J on the left-hand side.

Chapter Twenty

Schenke's hand froze, still inside the bag and out of sight of Hauser and Liebwitz. He looked up at the woman. She met his gaze with a pleading expression and the slightest shake of her head. He hesitated, his mind racing. Her dark hair and features made it almost certain that this was her real identity card, and the others were fakes, used to conceal her racial origins. With them she would be able to use trains and trams, have access to all the shops and eating places that other Berliners could use. Moreover, she would not be subject to the continual harassment that was reserved for Jews. If he revealed the card now, in the company of two members of the party, their treatment of her might be counterproductive. Why should she cooperate with the police when that might make her life more difficult? It would be better to win her trust rather than risk losing her assistance for the sake of prosecuting her for using false identity cards. That was a matter for another time.

He let the card slip from his fingers and withdrew his hand. He replaced the contents of the bag, except for the identity card in Johanna Kasper's name. "We'll keep this one for now. If it's genuine, we'll return it to its owner."

Hauser shot him a surprised look, but said nothing. Liebwitz stared at the handbag for a moment and then opened his mouth to speak, but Schenke got in first.

"Liebwitz, find out who the precinct uses to do witness drawings and bring them here."

"Yes, sir." He strode out of the office as Schenke turned to his sergeant.

"Hauser, I want you to take some of the team to the crime scene."

"Which one? The carriage, or the place where the attacker jumped out?"

"Both. You take Baumer and Persinger and go over the carriage. Hoffer and Brandt, when he turns up, can search the railway embankment. They can take Liebwitz with them, since he has an eye for detail. Once he's got hold of the artist. I'll join you later."

"Later?"

"After I've finished questioning Magda."

"Shouldn't I be in on that, sir, taking notes?"

"I can handle it. And we need those crime scenes swept."

Hauser nodded. "As you wish, sir."

"And send Rosa over here."

The sergeant closed his notebook and stood up. He glanced at Magda, then shook his head at his superior and walked off.

Schenke waited until he was out of earshot before he spoke again in an undertone. "Let's find out who you really are."

He reached into the bag and took out the Jewish identity card, opening it behind the bag where only he could see it. The photo was unmistakably of the woman sitting in front of him; her name was given as Ruth Frankel, twenty-six years of age and born in Rosenthal. As Rosa approached, he replaced the card and handed the bag back to Magda—whose true identity had been revealed as Ruth—before standing up.

"We're continuing the questioning somewhere quieter, where we won't be disturbed. Rosa, I'm assigning you to Miss Buchmann. She is a key witness in the investigation. You're to keep watch on her and see to her needs while she is in our custody."

"Yes, sir."

"Good, let's go."

They made their way to the top of the building and entered the room that Ritter had initially assigned to them. There were still some tables and chairs there, and Schenke indicated that Ruth should sit.

"Rosa, I want you to wait outside and make sure no one disturbs us, for any reason. Clear?"

"Yes, sir."

He closed the door and leaned against it as he regarded Ruth. She looked exhausted, and sat with her shoulders slumped as she stared back at him. The stitches, bruises and swelling gave her a slightly lopsided appearance, which was a pity, he thought, since she looked pretty in the photograph used for the identity card. She swallowed nervously.

"What are you going to do with me? Hand me over to the Gestapo?"

"Not if I can help it. I'm not interested in whether you have forged identity cards, or the fact that you're a Jew. My priority is finding the man who attacked you."

"Why? Why would anyone care if a Jew gets beaten up?"

"Because I don't think you're the first one he's attacked. He's killed more than one woman. You're lucky to be alive."

She gestured to her face. "You think this is lucky? You think I'm fortunate to be a Jew?"

"Fair point. I can't do anything about that. But I can try to make sure that women are kept safe from murderers, regardless of whether they are Aryan or Jewish. And you can help me. In exchange, I will make sure that you are not prosecuted for possessing false identity papers. That's why I sent the others away and brought you up here. They might not be so willing to offer you a deal."

She looked at him shrewdly. "You'll return the identity cards to me if I cooperate?"

He shook his head. "I'll destroy them."

"No! They cost me almost everything of value that I had. I need them."

"Just be thankful I'm offering to overlook them and let you go free," Schenke countered. "If someone else had caught you with those, you'd still be in that cell. And tomorrow, you'd be in court. Luckily it was me that discovered your secret. You help me and I'll help you. That's the deal."

"I want my cards back," she insisted. "I had to give up my mother's wedding ring and my father's gold watch for them. That's all they left me when they got out."

"Got out? Of Germany?"

She nodded. "They were on the last ship to leave for the United States. I stayed to look after my grandmother. I was supposed to join them after she died. But then the war came."

"Why did they leave you their valuables?"

"Why do you think?" she responded bitterly. "Nearly everything else was confiscated. They hid what they could from the authorities and gave them to me to help provide for my needs while I remained here."

"I see." Schenke was quiet for a moment, and then he crossed the room and sat on the edge of a table close to her. "Look, I'm a policeman, not a politician. I don't make the laws that govern Germany. It's simply my duty to uphold them. For what it's worth, I have no personal grievance against Jews. I know it's hard for you."

"And how would you know that?"

"I read newspapers. I listen to the radio. I talk to people."

She shook her head. "Nazi newspapers. Nazi radio stations. And I daresay you and most of those you know are Nazi party members."

"Not everyone in Germany is the same. I'm sure you've discovered that for yourself. Some people hate Jews. Some don't. I don't have feelings either way."

"How convenient for you." She scrutinized him briefly before she spoke again. "I am a German too. Or I was, until even our nationality was taken from us. You know that a great wrong is being done, don't you? There will be a reckoning one day, and then what will matter is which side you were on. Those who didn't oppose the party will be regarded with as much disdain as those who supported it."

"Who knows when that day will come? I'll put it to you one last time. Will you help us? Yes or no?"

"If I say no, then I'll be put on a train and sent east."

"That's not for me to decide."

She ignored his evasion. "You'd do that to me? Then what choice do I have? And what will you give me in return? My life?"

"Some might think that's enough. I will let you go free. I will not take any action over the fake identity cards. If your assistance helps us catch the man I am after, I'll see what else I can do to help you. On condition that you never speak of any deal we may agree between us." He paused to let her consider. "Now, will you cooperate?"

She nodded.

"Good. I'll keep calling you Magda, and I won't tell anyone else on my team about your real name for now."

Her relief was palpable, and her thin shoulders slumped.

"I'll also be keeping you in custody until the investigation is over or I have no further need to hold you."

"But you said you'd let me go after I gave a description of the attacker!"

"That was before I found out you are a Jew. Even though we have a deal, that does not mean I trust you to come back when I need your help again. I daresay the address you gave us is false, and the address on your real identity card may be out of date. I know the authorities are confiscating property owned by Jews. Until the killer is caught, you will be in my care. I will make sure you have a bed and food, and a change of clothes, and that you are protected. If you try and run, I'll make damn sure that you are hunted down and prosecuted for using fake identity cards. Do you understand?"

"Clearly," she responded.

"I'll take you to an interview room for now. When the artist arrives, give him all the detail you can recall. I want a picture of the man so we can circulate it to every precinct, every railway station. Someone will recognize him."

"I hope so, Inspector." She shivered.

They left the office and Schenke indicated to Rosa to follow them. He ushered Ruth into a small room farther along the corridor and saw that the stove was unlit. "I'll get some heat in here."

"Thank you."

They looked at each other in silence, then Schenke stepped outside and closed the door behind him. Rosa was waiting a short distance along the corridor.

"She's in your care. Don't let her leave the room. Don't let anyone in there, without my permission. If she needs the toilet, or anything to eat and drink, you go with her and don't let her out of your sight. And then you bring her straight back here."

"Yes, sir."

Schenke returned to his desk. He picked up his hat and coat and ordered a car to be prepared for him. Leaving the precinct, he saw that the overcast was getting darker. More snow was coming. He prayed that it wouldn't start falling before his men could search the crime scene.

"We've moved the carriages to the siding, over there." The depot master pointed across the yard's tracks to two carriages standing apart from the rest of the rolling stock. A pair of railway policemen were walking around the outside, no doubt trying to keep warm. "Your lads are already going over the inside."

"Good." Schenke nodded. "And where's the place the train stopped when the emergency chain was pulled?"

"Just over a kilometer down the line. You going to walk there?"

"Sure."

"Then don't forget to take the left track when you reach the points. That's the line that goes through Papestrasse in the direction of Mariendorf. There were some Kripo types making for it earlier on and there should be some more police on the spot."

"There better be," Schenke responded. The investigation could do without anyone disturbing the scene, or the killer returning to retrieve evidence while there was no one about.

A path had been cleared through the snow between the tracks, and he made his way over to the carriages. He showed his identity badge to the railway policemen and climbed the narrow steps at the end of the nearest carriage. Opening the door, he was struck by how cold it was. The blackout blinds had been raised and rime ran across the windows in feathery crystal patterns. The only other person in the carriage was Baumer, hunched over between two seats close by. He looked up as Schenke closed the door, and tapped a finger to the brim of his hat in a casual salute.

"What have you got?" asked Schenke as he made his way over to his colleague.

Baumer gestured towards the floor, where there were dark stains and smears. "There's blood. And there's this . . ." He stepped aside to reveal a knife lying on one of the seats. It was one of the spring-loaded weapons popular with Berlin's crime gangs, Schenke noted. A slender blade, fifteen centimeters long, with a marginally longer handle cross-scored to give a good grip. There was more blood on the blade and the handle.

"Has anyone picked it up?"

Baumer grunted. "One of the railway cops. It was on the floor between the seats. He held it up for me to see with a nice big smile on his face, like I should give him a treat. Luckily he was wearing gloves. I shouted at the fool to put it down. Hasn't been touched since."

"Good. Anything else?"

Baumer stepped into the aisle and pointed to the door leading to the other carriage. "There are more traces of blood going that way, and some on the door."

"All right. Keep looking. If there's nothing else, bag the knife and write up your notes."

Schenke moved carefully along the carriage, keeping clear of the traces of dry blood while scrutinizing the other seats in case there was any further evidence. At the door, he turned the handle using the tips of his gloved fingers and stepped through to the second carriage, where Hauser and Persinger were at work.

"Nice of you to join us," Hauser greeted him, straightening up and rubbing the small of his back. "Looks like our friend Magda was telling the truth, as far as I can tell. The emergency chain's been pulled. There's blood down here on the floor, and signs of scuff marks. We found the soldier's glasses under a seat. One of the lenses is cracked, but I daresay he'll be glad to have them back. Best of all, we found this." He used his handkerchief to hold up an iron bar. "It was on the seat by the door. I think we'll be able to match it to the injuries on the two victims we know about. And if there's a link to any of those deaths put down to accidents, then our killer has been a busy man."

Schenke's attention was on the door, above the seat where the bar had been found. He leaned towards a loose screw in the frame. There were a few strands of thread there, and a fragment of cloth caught around the head of the screw.

"What's that you have there?" asked Hauser.

"Look . . ." Schenke pointed. "Might be nothing. Might be that the attacker caught his coat as he jumped. Get it bagged."

"Yes, sir."

"Anything else here?"

Hauser shook his head.

"Then let's go and see what we've got at the place where he landed. Persinger, you take the evidence bags back to the precinct."

"Yes, sir."

Schenke led the way to the front of the carriage and opened the door to climb down. He and Hauser started out along the tracks, stepping from sleeper to sleeper as they followed the footsteps of the policemen who had set out earlier. Above, the sun was discernible as a faint disc amid the gray haze covering the sky, and Schenke feared that there might be a fresh fall of snow at any time.

He increased his pace as they reached the points and continued along the tracks that led to the left. They curved gently between some trees, in whose bare branches crows perched, calling out with raucous cries as they spied the two men toiling below. Beyond the trees the track emerged onto an embankment, and Schenke could see a small group of men a short distance ahead. A uniformed officer stood to one side, while the others were bent over the disturbed snow of the embankment.

Liebwitz was standing at the top. He saluted Schenke as he and Hauser approached.

"Anything to report?" asked Schenke.

"Not much of any help, sir. It was clear where the man landed and rolled over. Just there." He pointed to an impression in the snow at the top of the embankment. "You can see the route he took to the bottom and across the open ground to those buildings. The other tracks to the side are from the men who pursued him a short distance. We've been searching through the snow along the line he took."

"Who asked you?" demanded Hauser. "This is the Kripo's business. You're supposed to be an observer. I put Hoffer in charge."

"I outrank Hoffer," Liebwitz replied.

"Not when you're on Kripo's turf. Here you do things our way."

"With respect, Sergeant Hauser, I outrank Hoffer in any context."

Schenke raised a hand to forestall any further exchange. "Let's get on with it, while we still have the chance. If there's any more snow, we'll have to wait until it stops and start the search again. We'll work from the bottom. Five-meter intervals up from Brandt. Let's go."

With the railway policeman looking on in smug bemusement, Schenke and the others crouched over the disturbed snow of the embankment and began to sweep it aside with their fingertips, looking for anything the killer might have dropped. The light was steadily fading and a light breeze picked up, adding to the chill. Schenke was not pleased by the Gestapo man's playing on his rank. While it was true that he was Hoffer's superior, it was also the case that he had not been trained to conduct criminal investigations, or how to handle a search of a crime scene.

After half an hour, Schenke had covered half of his allotted stretch and he looked to where Brandt was sweeping the snow.

"Careful there, Brandt! Slowly does it, or you may miss something."

"Yes, sir. Sorry."

"Sir!" Hoffer suddenly rose, holding a strip of cloth between his fingertips.

"I'm coming."

Schenke backed away a couple of paces and descended parallel to the killer's tracks. Hauser did the same, and they joined Hoffer as he held up his find. On closer inspection, Schenke saw that it was a woollen fragment from a uniform overcoat. There was a jagged cut down one side and a frayed, torn section at the end. Thanks to the subzero temperature, the cloth was quite dry.

"Looks like it was caught on something," Hoffer suggested, and Hauser glanced at his superior.

"That loose screw by the door. It's from his coat . . ."

Hoffer grinned. "Do you want to know what the best bit is?"

Schenke was tired and in no mood for games. "Well?"

Hoffer turned the torn cloth over to reveal a section of lapel, in the middle of which gleamed a party member badge. There was a gold band running round the edge of it, and Schenke could not help smiling too as he and Hauser inspected the find more closely.

"Bloody wonderful, eh?" Hauser chuckled. "Once we get the number off the back, we'll have the bastard's name. We'll find out where he lives and that'll be that."

Schenke took the strip of cloth from Hoffer and held it up for examination, using the tip of a gloved finger to tease the badge round. The fastening pin had snapped and it was caught in the cloth by the short length that remained. Other than the twisted stub of metal, the base of the broken pin, the reverse of the badge was blank, save for some scratches.

"The bastard has filed the serial number off," Hauser growled.

"Shit . . . Let's hope the lab boys can recover something."

Hoffer frowned. "How will they do that, sir?"

"You should have paid more attention during training," Schenke responded in a reproachful tone. "Seems the killer knows as little about acid etching as you do."

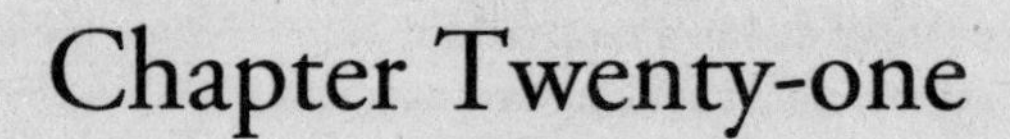

Chapter Twenty-one

It was two o'clock in the afternoon by the time Schenke returned to the car with Hauser and Liebwitz. Hauser took the wheel and Schenke sat with the Gestapo man in the rear as they set off for the Schöneberg precinct. The evidence gathered from the crime scene had set Schenke's mind racing as he pieced together the details of the investigation. They now had two eyewitnesses, though the soldier's testimony would be weaker in court, thanks to the loss of his glasses. They had a fragment of the killer's coat. They had a sample of his blood. They had his iron bar, and hopefully that would yield some fingerprints, or at least be identified as the weapon that had killed Gerda Korzeny and Monika Bronheim. It was also likely to be the same weapon responsible for the deaths that had previously been regarded as accidents. Then there was the fact that the woman being held at the precinct had stabbed her assailant. If the wound was serious and he went to a hospital, or a doctor's surgery, there would be a record of it.

Most significantly, they had found the party badge. An ordinary party badge would have been a cause of less excitement, since there were so many of them. But those with the gold trim were less common, because they were only distributed to the most long-standing and loyal of members, and each was numbered. They were not the kind of item that was easily misplaced, or lost. Those who possessed them guarded them jealously. If the acid etching revealed even a partial number then they would have a list of names of men to be brought in for questioning.

For the first time in days, the heavy weight of expectation and exhaustion was lifted from Schenke's shoulders and he was eager to press on. "I think we're closing in on him."

Hauser nodded. "With any luck we'll have the bastard in a cell in time for Christmas. And we'll notch up another feather in our cap."

"I'm not sure that works." Liebwitz frowned. "The mixed metaphor, I mean."

Schenke turned to him in surprise, and then both he and Hauser laughed good-humoredly. They had little affection for the pedantic Gestapo man, but they were in too much of a good mood to let his dour presence ruin their optimism.

"Did I say something funny?" Liebwitz asked.

Schenke shook his head and turned to look out of the side window. It was thick with condensation, so he wiped it with his glove. Out in the street, pedestrians were hunched down in an effort to keep warm. He caught a glimpse of a figure sitting in the shelter of an arched alcove clutching a sign that read: *War veteran. Please help*. The sight took the edge off his good humor. Against the scale of death another war entailed, what was the true worth of the work he and his colleagues undertook? Why the concern over a handful of deaths in Berlin when so many tens of thousands had died in Poland? A few deaths was a crime, a multitude merely a statistic, as someone had once said, more or less. And yet it mattered. War was the abnormality. The upholding of the law was the pillar that supported any notion of what was normal and enduring. It was the foundation of civilization itself. He was comforted by the thought of being a guardian of civilization, even in what he, and many others, had come to regard as an uncivilized age. Wars came and went, but the laws of civilization endured, thanks to the efforts of men like himself.

The warm feeling faded as his thoughts turned back to the veteran. The mangled victims of the previous war had been a common sight on the streets of Berlin. Now they would have to compete with a new generation of men maimed and crippled in the service of the fatherland.

Pushing the dark prospect from his mind, Schenke made plans for what needed to be done. "Hauser, when we get back, I want you to take the badge to the Kripo labs and see if they can recover the number. If we can get that, we can match it to a name. Start with the party headquarters. If anyone tries to stall you, you can tell them you are enquiring under the authority of the head of the Gestapo."

"I'll enjoy that."

"Don't push it too far. Just do it if the need arises."

Liebwitz coughed. "Wouldn't it be better if I took on the task, sir? With me being a bona fide member of the Gestapo."

Schenke hesitated before he answered. There was some value in the suggestion, yet Liebwitz's first loyalty was to the Gestapo, not the Kripo. If his superiors were playing some kind of deep game, then their man could not be trusted with such a critical line of inquiry. Yet what could he say that would not offend Liebwitz's professionalism?

"No, I have something more important for you. I need help going over the files relating to the other deaths. We need to check the medical examiners' reports. You have an excellent eye for detail. You may see something I might miss."

"Yes, sir." Liebwitz nodded. "That's true."

Schenke met Hauser's sidelong gaze in the mirror and saw him roll his eyes with theatrical emphasis.

Back at the Schöneberg precinct, Frieda hurried to Schenke with an anxious expression.

"What's happened?" he demanded.

"It's Oberführer Müller, sir. He's telephoned twice since you left. He wants you to call him at once."

Schenke cursed under his breath, then turned to Hauser. "You know what you have to do. Get on with it. Find that name, whatever it takes."

"Yes, sir." Hauser made for his table as Schenke turned to Liebwitz. "Get those files on the women's deaths. Go over them and look for any similarities to the known murders and the attack on Magda Buchmann. We need to establish a credible link to those for when the case goes to court. I don't want there to be holes in our evidence that the defense will exploit to save the neck of our killer."

"I will do my best, sir."

"I'm counting on it. Now go."

As the Gestapo man followed Frieda to the files piled on her table, Schenke paced thoughtfully to his chair and sat down. He took off his hat and flattened his hair against the crown of his head before he sighed and reached for the handset.

"Connect me to Oberführer Müller at the Reich Main Security Office."

He heard the switchboard operator making the request to her counterpart at the Gestapo switchboard, and a moment later the tone sounded twice before there was a click.

"Müller."

"Sir, it's Inspector Schenke."

"Schenke? Where the devil have you been? I've been trying to track you down all day. I want your report. Any closer to resolving the matter?"

Schenke outlined the latest developments. Müller listened without interrupting, and there was a pause after the inspector finished speaking.

"I see," Müller said eventually. "A party badge, you say?"

"Yes, sir."

"Any chance that it's a forgery, given that this man was posing as a railway policeman in the first place?"

"The badge appears to be genuine, sir. In the meantime, we'll see how far we can get with recovering the serial number. If we have that, we have our man."

"It may be that the badge was stolen, or perhaps lost by its owner and found by this killer."

"That's possible," Schenke conceded. "But we'll still need to question the badge holder and check his movements against what we know of the killer's. That will confirm things one way or the other."

"Indeed . . . Look here, Schenke, if the killer is a party member, you will let me know first, and no one in your team is to breathe a word about it without my express authorization. We can't be having the party's reputation damaged to the smallest degree now that there is a war on. The whole of Germany must unite behind our leaders and the party if we are to prevail. Do I make myself clear?"

"Yes, sir . . ."

"No need to take that tone with me. This is about what is best for the fatherland. Neither you nor I have the right to undermine that. It is our duty to do what we can to support the Führer and the party, whatever that takes."

"I understand, sir."

"Be sure that you do, Schenke. By the way, your reticence to join the party and apply for SS rank has been noted."

Schenke felt a cold prickle on his neck. "My loyalty to Germany is absolute, sir."

"I am glad to hear it. Now, you say there are witnesses who saw this man?"

"Yes, sir. His intended victim, and a soldier. However, the soldier's glasses were knocked off at the start of the struggle. The woman had a much better chance to identify her attacker. We're holding her at the precinct. She's with an artist at the moment and we'll have a likeness before the day is out."

"How reliable do you think she is?"

Schenke considered the question for a moment. There was no questioning Ruth's sharpness of mind, but the difficulty would be that any testimony she gave would be colored by her racial background. A defense lawyer would be sure to raise it to discredit her. He realized that it would be better for Müller to know now, rather than risk his angry response later. Even though he had told Ruth that he would hide her real identity, to continue to do so would place them both in jeopardy when the truth came out.

He cleared his throat. "Sir, there's something you need to know about the woman. I found a Jewish identity card on her when we brought her in after the attack. I haven't told anyone else here in case that predisposed them against her. I needed to ensure her full cooperation."

"A Jewess?" Müller breathed in sharply enough for Schenke to hear the soft hiss down the line. "How can we trust the word of a Jew? Especially if she saw that her attacker was wearing a party badge. You know what their kind are like. Inveterate liars and schemers, the lot of them. You might as well trust a pack of rats."

"She has not given me any cause to believe that she is lying, sir."

"Of course not. They're too crafty for that. Be on your

guard, Schenke. Don't trust a word she says unless you can verify it from other sources."

"Yes, sir."

"Still . . . there may be some way we can play this to our advantage."

"How so?"

"I think it's time we put the story in the newspapers. We'll tell them about Gerda Korzeny and the other murder, but downplay the possible links to other attacks for the moment. No sense in feeding the public a story that might frighten them. Let's tell the press that police are close to identifying the killer of the Korzeny woman, and that you have an eyewitness to a subsequent attack. You release her name, and the fact that she is a Jew, and then put her back on the street. You tell the journalists that you are confident the killer will be caught within a matter of days. Tell them that he has left a trail of clues behind him and that he is clearly someone of low intelligence. Let's try and provoke him into some action that exposes him. If you have a sketch of the man, then you let them have that as well, and offer a reward for anyone assisting the police in tracking him down." He paused. "And of course, no mention is to be made of the badge, or any implication that a party member is involved. Do you have all that?"

"Yes, sir . . ." Schenke steeled himself.

Miller detected the shift in tone at once. "But?"

"What is the point of involving the press? It might well serve to drive the man into hiding. That will only make our job harder."

"Look, he knows that you are on to him now. He knows that you have a witness. In all likelihood, he knows that you have the party badge, and if it does belong to him then he fears that you already know his name. Chances are he is in hiding. In which case we need the help of the public to find him."

"I understand, but if we give the name of the witness, aren't we putting her in danger?"

"Of course we are! I thought you Kripo types were supposed to be intelligent? We might as well use her as bait and try and lure the man from cover. It's a long shot, but worth a try."

"And what if he has some way of tracking her down?"

"So what? One Jew more or less is no concern of mine. Might as well make the bait more enticing; give the press a photograph of her as well. If he really is a party member, he's not going to take too kindly to being caught by the Kripo thanks to the help of some Jew."

Schenke could feel the anger welling up inside him. "There's something I am still struggling to understand, sir. At first we thought we were dealing with one murder. Gerda Korzeny. We had no idea about any other deaths. Why is the party so interested in her murder?"

"I suppose there's no harm in letting you know. You've probably worked out most of the details for yourself by now. Gerda Korzeny was involved with Goebbels a few years ago. He has always had a passion for film stars. The Führer does not approve of this. But imagine how much less he might approve if it was discovered that the Reichsminister's former girlfriend had Jewish blood, and that Goebbels had conspired to cover that up. That knowledge was a very useful card dealt to the Reich Security Main Office. We could use it to protect the reputation of the propaganda minister, or to destroy him if the need arises."

"You're talking about blackmail."

"Call it what you like. It's intelligence at the end of the day, ready to be used as seems best. When the Korzeny woman was murdered, it seemed to my superiors that someone had decided to remove her in order to protect Goebbels's reputation, perhaps to undermine our hold over him. If you can track down her killer, we might end up with a new card to play, when the time is right. Proof of murder is a powerful tool in persuading someone to serve your interests.

"No doubt you think it is a sordid little scheme. That is why you are a policeman and not a politician. But a time will come, Schenke, when you can no longer hide behind your police badge. You will have to choose where your first loyalty lies. Moreover, you will have to choose which faction you serve within the party. Will you be one of Goebbels's men? Or one of ours? Or will you opt for some other master, such as Goering or Canaris? My advice is to choose wisely. Himmler is not the kind of man who tolerates any kind of betrayal by those who serve in the Reich Main Security Office. Serve him and the party loyally, and you will do well. Do we understand one another?"

Schenke was silent for a beat, considering the implications of all that he had been told. There was little scope for any pretense that a man could stand apart from the ambitions and actions of the party with impunity. Almost every aspect of life in Germany was in their iron grip, and they asked of the people one simple question: are you for us or against us? There was no place for open political debate. A slim majority of the people had voted for a coalition of Nazis and conservatives some years earlier, and the party had seized on that mandate and ruthlessly exploited it to ensure there would never be a chance to reverse the decision. Politics was dead. Only conspiracy remained to those who opposed the regime. For everyone else, it was simply a matter of accommodation, and therefore survival. He drew a deep breath and replied calmly, "Yes, sir."

"Then I suggest you get on with it. If you move quickly, the story can be on the front page of tomorrow's newspapers. I will inform the propaganda ministry and I'm certain they will not demur. It'll provide a nice distraction from news about the war. I suggest you brief your team as soon as you can. I'll arrange for some reporters to meet with you later this afternoon. Good day, Inspector."

There was a click and the line went dead. Schenke lowered the receiver and held his head in his hands. Then he sat up and called Hauser over.

"We need to get the team together. There are going to be some developments in the investigation that aren't going to be to our liking."

"Oh?"

"Müller's throwing a spanner in our works. I want everyone here in the office within the hour. Find a uniformed man to keep an eye on the witness while we're talking. And send Brandt out for some coffee. It's going to be a long afternoon."

Chapter Twenty-two

"Quiet!" Schenke ordered, raising his hands to silence the angry comments from the others. "I know it's not how we usually do things, but we have no choice. I have my orders. News of the investigation will be in the papers tomorrow morning. I'll be speaking to the reporters after this briefing. I don't want anyone else to speak to them. Not one word. I'll do what I can to restrict the information I give them. We want to encourage the public to help us find the killer, but not give him too much detail about our work." He paused to look round the room. "I don't say this lightly, but I am confident that this section is one of the Kripo's finest. We've got a record to be proud of and we'll carry on doing what we do best. We will find this bastard and he will pay for what he has done. No matter who tries to interfere in the investigation."

He avoided meeting Liebwitz's gaze as he made the final comment, but Hauser and some of the others shot hostile glances at the Gestapo man. Schenke turned towards the pinboard and went over what had been found at the scene of the latest attack before he summed up.

"So, we have eyewitnesses, we have the murder weapon, we have the attacker's blood, a shred of his coat and a party badge. Rosa?"

"Sir?"

"Has the artist finished his sketch?"

The policewoman nodded. "It's been photographed. The first prints will be ready by four o'clock."

"Was Magda confident about the likeness?"

"She reckons it's good, sir."

"Fine. We'll make sure the reporters have copies. If they put it in the papers, our man will find it hard to show his face in public. Let's hope it spurs someone who knows him to make the connection and report it to the police."

Schenke turned to Hauser. "Sergeant, what's the latest on that party badge?"

Hauser stood up. "It looks like the real thing, according to the technical boys. They're doing alloy tests to check it against the production runs. But that'll take a few days yet."

"What about the serial number?"

"They managed to get the first three digits, 894. There was one, or possibly two further digits but the acid etching couldn't define them. Soon as I had their report, I contacted the party. But they gave me the runaround right from the start." He shrugged his heavy shoulders. "The record office said they would not release the information without written authorization."

"Did you tell them we are acting on Müller's orders?"

"Yes, sir. That cut no ice. They want it in writing from him directly."

"Damn. I'll speak to him as soon as I can. Hopefully a personal call from the head of the Gestapo will grease the wheels of the party's bureaucracy."

Hauser grinned at the prospect. "They'll be shitting themselves in an effort to give us what we want."

"As soon as you get the name and an address, let me

know. We'll pay our friend a visit and see if he's at home. If it is our man, Christmas drinks are on me."

There were smiles and stamping of feet in approval, until Liebwitz stood up and the noise abated.

"Inspector, what if it isn't our man?"

"Then we carry on with other lines of inquiry. That's how we do things in the Kripo. But we get the evidence and we get our man in the end. We don't have the luxury of operating with the expediency favored by the Gestapo, as I understand it."

Liebwitz thought a moment. "The department's methods are not always quite as scientific as I would like, it's true, sir."

Coming from a Gestapo man, that was something of an admission, Schenke realized, and he warmed to Liebwitz by some slight degree. "We may make a policeman of you yet . . . Which brings us to the files dealing with the other deaths. Where are we with that?"

Liebwitz consulted his notes. "There are clear similarities across the medical examiners' reports with those relating to the two murders we know about, sir. The fatal injuries of the accident victims could easily have been caused by blows struck by an iron bar. I called two of the medical examiners to confirm the details and they agreed it was possible."

"Good work." Schenke pointed to Frieda next. "What about the background checks? What information have our boys given you?"

"There's no obvious pattern amongst the victims, sir. The women came from a variety of backgrounds. They tended to be on the young side. Gerda was the exception, although she may have looked younger in poor light. You know how difficult it can be to tell with some movie stars. Most of the victims were unmarried, or recently widowed thanks to the war. I imagine that's why they were free to go out of an evening. It's possible some of them were on the game, but none of their families admitted it, and the neighbors didn't think it was likely. I don't think our killer chose them at his leisure. It's more likely they were victims of opportunity, sir. Or at least some of them were."

Schenke drew the threads of the investigation together. "What we have is a killer who uses the blackout to cover his attacks. He chooses women who are on their own, or at least waits until they are, then follows them onto a late-running train that he knows will be nearly empty. He approaches them in the uniform of a railway policeman, knowing that they are not likely to perceive him as a threat. He attacks them, rapes them and then strikes them with that iron bar to kill them before throwing the bodies from the train. He leaves the train possibly still in disguise, though it's more likely he changes out of the uniform so as not to draw attention to himself from any legitimate railway police or workers."

"Why take the risk of killing them on a train?" asked Frieda. "Surely he'd do better to lure them somewhere quiet, or follow them back to their homes. He'd have more time to do what he wanted, and less chance of being caught in the act."

"Maybe, but that way there would be no chance of having the authorities categorize the deaths as accidental. Besides, throwing them from the train saves him the job of disposing of the bodies. And if snow falls overnight, the victim may go undiscovered for a considerable length of time, and we'd have lost much of the crime scene evidence. That's assuming someone was suspicious enough to argue that they might not have died as a result of an accident. Particularly if the killer ensures that he varies his hunting ground from time to time, moving between areas covered by different precincts. He knows something about the turf each precinct is responsible for."

Hauser nodded. "If that's the case, then we have to consider the possibility that he might be one of us; someone in the police. Or perhaps a retired cop."

"It's possible," Schenke accepted. "But I don't want to share that thought with the press. Not yet. There's going to be enough alarm at the prospect of a killer at large. We don't want to compound that by making the public too afraid to approach us. Meanwhile, I want someone to go over police personnel records. See if there are any cases of dismissal relating to attacks on women. Brandt!"

The probationer raised a hand. "Sir?"

"That'll be your job. According to the eyewitness, our man is in his thirties, so look for cases of dismissal up to the age of forty-five just to be sure."

"Yes, sir."

There was a rap on the door, and one of the uniformed officers from the precinct stepped in.

"What is it?" Schenke demanded, unhappy at the interruption.

The man approached and held out a folder. "The artist's sketch, sir."

The room stirred with anticipation as Schenke took the folder and dismissed the policeman. He opened the flimsy card cover and picked up the sheet of paper inside.

Although Ruth had described the man before, this visual representation provided more detail. The artist had done a good job, rendering the face with clear, bold strokes and shading it to give a sense of the bone structure. The hair was always the most difficult thing to depict, given how its shape could be determined by factors such as exposure to rain, physical exertion or formal styling. Even changing a part could make a person look different. In this case, the man's hair was uncommonly long, almost covering his ears, and the pencil had given it a tone somewhat darker than the brown Ruth had described.

As for the rest, the brow was broad and bold. The eyes

were set evenly apart and were drawn with a neutral expression that belied Ruth's memory of them as being steely. A well-defined nose, with what looked to be a slight swelling halfway down, stretched to a wide jaw and full lips. As Ruth had said, it was a face that reflected the idealized Germanic features that appeared on propaganda posters.

Schenke held the sketch up against the pinboard and secured it with a drawing pin. The others moved closer to examine the image.

"He's a handsome brute," Rosa announced.

"So that's your type then?" Persinger chuckled. "Always wondered what kind of man stoked your fires. Now we know. He's a looker all right."

"That's enough!" Schenke snapped.

They fell silent.

"This is our man." He tapped the sketch. "Once we get hold of copies, I want each of you to take one and keep it with you during the investigation. Between us and the press, someone will recognize this face. Tomorrow is Christmas Eve. It'll be the last time plenty of people are on the streets before the holiday. It's up to us to make sure the hours we have left count. The killer is using the railways, so we'll start there.

"Schmidt, Persinger, Baumer, Hoffer, I want you to get down to the Anhalter station and show that sketch to all members of staff you can find. Then move down the line and do the same at every station between the terminus and Mariendorf.

"Hauser, you take the rest and go to the bars, clubs and cafés around each of the stations. He's got to be picking his victims up somewhere he can watch them and make sure that they'll be taking a train. If I had to guess, I'd say he was using the cafés inside the stations, or those close by.

"Rosa, I want you to check the suspect's image against the files here at the precinct. Who knows, he may already have crossed the path of the local police at some point. After that, you start calling the hospitals and doctors we haven't yet approached to check for any treatment of stab wounds in the last day.

"Frieda, you get the dullest job, I'm afraid. I want you to put the call out to the other precincts with train lines running through their turf. Start with those you found who have reported fatal accidents. Tell them what we know of the killer's MO, and that the local police need to be on the lookout for him once we can send copies of the picture through. Same goes for the railway police right across the Berlin network."

"That's a lot of phone calls, sir."

"True, but on the bright side, you get to do them from the warmth of this office. We need to know how wide-ranging our killer is. It might be that he's hunting only on the lines to the south of Berlin. I hope to God that is the case and there aren't scores of other victims out there. If he is just using the southern lines, he may shift to other hunting grounds now that he knows we're on his trail."

"And what if he goes to ground because of that?" asked Hauser. "What if he waits until things go quiet, then resumes his killing? What if he stops using rail lines?"

"That's all possible," Schenke admitted. "But he likes the blackout; he feels comfortable using it as cover. And he likes the long winter nights. My guess is he'll want to make the most of the opportunity that the winter gives him. Right, you all know what you've got to do. Go to it, and let's hope we get a result."

"Sir." Liebwitz raised his hand. "What duty do you have for me?"

"Müller might refuse to give me written permission to access the party member records, in which case I'll need you to go to party headquarters and get the information for us, even if that means leaving my side for a few hours."

Liebwitz frowned. "Why should they let me have access rather than you or your men, sir?"

Schenke stared at him. "Surely you cannot be so obtuse that you don't grasp that the Gestapo get to go where the humble members of the Kripo are not allowed to tread? Give them some story that sounds convincing."

"Story?"

"Look, tell them that you're conducting a routine background search on an applicant who wants to join the Gestapo. That sounds innocuous enough."

"Ah, a lie, then." Liebwitz considered this. "You're quite right, sir. It does sound innocent enough."

Schenke sighed. "You're surprised that a mere Kripo inspector could have thought that through all by himself?"

"Not at all, sir. I have the utmost respect for the Kripo."

"Then you'd better go and deal with it, in case Müller refuses me."

"Yes, sir. At once."

As the Gestapo man went to fetch his hat and coat, Hauser watched him speculatively. "I'm still not quite sure if he's stupid, or just lacking in common sense. Either way, I am almost certain his mother dropped him on his head once too often."

"As long as he does his job, I'm happy."

"But what exactly is his job, as far as we're concerned? I don't trust him."

"As it happens, I think *I am* starting to trust him. Or rather, to trust *in* him. I think there's less to him than meets the eye. He may be Gestapo, dark hat and leather coat and all, but I don't think there's much guile there. None that I've seen, at any rate. Müller may have unwittingly done us a favor in sending Liebwitz to watch us."

"If you say so, sir. Better get the lads to work."

The sergeant called on his men to grab their coats.

Schenke watched them go, talking noisily as they left the office. Once the door had closed behind them only Frieda and Rosa remained, bent over their desks as they concentrated on their duties. Schenke steeled himself for another conversation with Müller.

An hour later, the first of the reporters arrived at the precinct. Schenke gave orders to keep him in the reception until the rest of them turned up. He was in a troubled mood. Müller had refused to provide the written authority needed to satisfy the party's personnel office. At the same time, he had demanded to know the numbers revealed on the back of the badge. When Schenke had demurred, as was proper with details arising from the Kripo investigations, Müller had ordered him to provide the information, and he had had no choice but to do so. The only hope now was that Liebwitz would succeed in gaining access where the Kripo had failed.

While he waited for the rest of the reporters to arrive, he called Karin's flat, but there was no reply. He tried his own apartment, and after a few rings she picked up.

"Haven't you got better places to be?" he asked.

"I have, but it's cold outside, and your apartment is lovely and warm. I decided to stay in bed and read. You have some interesting books in your study. I had no idea you were a follower of Kierkegaard."

"I find that *Fear and Trembling* has a certain currency these days."

"And some of the other titles provide an interesting insight into your values."

"Such as?"

"Husserl, Freud, Engels, to name a few."

Schenke felt a mixture of mild irritation and concern at the thought of Karin sitting in his study running her fingers across the spines of his books.

"A Kripo inspector needs to keep his mind exercised, my love."

"And it's not just the philosophy. There's a well-worn collection of expressionist prints. Then there's the music. Mahler? I wonder what the Führer would make of your influences?"

He was relieved that her voice had a gentle teasing tone as she spoke. He cleared his throat before he responded, and wondered if anyone was listening in to their conversation. "I am sure there is nothing there that would provoke any real concern."

"Perhaps not individually, but as a whole, it paints an interesting picture."

"Only in your imagination. All it would say to me is that you are invading the privacy of a man with eclectic intellectual pursuits. Anyway, we can discuss such things at our leisure later on."

"Good, so you will be coming home tonight."

"I think the Reich can spare me. Do you want to go out?"

There was a pause before she replied, in a silky voice. "No. I want to stay in, with you. Preferably in bed. Would you like me to prepare something for us to eat?"

"That would be nice."

"What time will you be back?"

"By eight o'clock, I hope. If it's any later, I'll let you know. It might be best to prepare something cold."

When she spoke again, her tone was less intimate. "I see. I'll have to go out and buy some supplies. You have so little in your kitchen cupboards."

He had a mental image of her walking down a dark street with a bag of shopping in each hand, and felt a stab of concern for her safety. "Be careful."

"Careful? What do you mean?"

"Keep to where there are people and don't go out after it gets dark."

"Why?"

"Just do it for me, Karin. With all that's going on here, I'd be happier knowing you were safe."

"I understand. I'll see you later, darling."

There was a knock at the door and Schenke signaled to Frieda to answer it.

"I have to go now. I'll see you around eight."

"I look forward to it . . . I love you, my Horst."

He felt his heart flush with pleasure. He lowered his voice as he replied. "I love you too."

There was a pause. Neither of them spoke, and Schenke took the chance to replace the receiver.

"Sir." Frieda gestured towards the reception area. "The rest of the reporters have arrived."

"Good. Have we got the prints yet?"

"Yes, sir."

"I don't want the press nosing about the precinct. You know how light-fingered they can be. I'll speak to them in the reception hall. With luck, they won't like the cold and we can keep this as short as possible."

Chapter Twenty-three

Despite it being a murder case, there were fewer reporters than Schenke had hoped. The desk sergeant handed him a clipboard and he glanced over the names and the newspapers they represented. They stood in a loose arc around him, notebooks at the ready. There were two photographers with them, casually smoking as they held back and waited their turn.

"You know how this works, gentlemen. I'll give you the overview and then you can ask questions. I'll answer anything that does not jeopardize the case or any potential court proceedings. Everything else goes. All clear?"

They nodded.

"Good." He drew a breath and organized his thoughts before he began. "I am Criminal Inspector Horst Schenke, leading the investigation, and—"

"Horst Schenke?" one of the reporters interrupted. "*The* Horst Schenke?"

Schenke turned to the man, a thickset individual in his forties with a thin trimmed moustache. The other reporters looked on expectantly.

"Pardon?"

"Horst Schenke the racing driver?" the reporter continued with a grin. "I thought I knew your face. I'm Greiser, from the *People's Observer*. So what are you doing in the police force? It's an honor to meet you, sir. I was a big fan of the Silver Arrows, like most of us who followed motor racing."

Schenke forced a smile. "Look, my racing career ended years ago. I'd be happy to talk about that another time, Greiser, but it's important that we get on with the briefing. There could be lives at stake. We are here to discuss a police matter and nothing else. Is that clear?"

The reporter nodded and Schenke resumed. "As you may already know, this is a murder investigation. Three days ago, a body was found close to the rolling stock depot outside the Anhalter station. The female victim had been subjected to a sexual assault and a violent attack before she died from her injuries. Her name was Gerda Korzeny. My unit was assigned to the investigation the following morning. Since then another woman's body has been found, with similar injuries and also showing evidence of sexual assault. Her name was Monika Bronheim. We believe the two cases are linked and that the same individual committed both murders. Last night, a third attack took place. In this instance, the woman concerned was able to fight off her attacker and escape to find help. Although she sustained injuries in the assault, she provided a good description of her assailant and the police have a sketch of the man we are looking for. That, and copies of photographs of the victims, will be provided to you. It is possible that these two murders and the attack are linked to a number of other incidents that are also being investigated by my officers."

He paused as they finished writing and looked up, pencils poised. "You will no doubt appreciate how concerned we are to find this man before he has the chance to strike again.

What I can tell you is that we think he is using the uniform of a railway policeman to approach his victims and win their trust before he attacks. I can also tell you that the woman who survived the attack managed to stab her assailant in the side with a knife. Given the amount of blood that was discovered at the scene, it is possible that he may have sought medical treatment for the wound. We would ask you to make sure you mention this in your reports. I also want you to ask your readers if they have any information about a man with such an injury. They can report anything suspicious to their nearest precinct, and tell them to pass it on to my section here at Schöneberg."

"Will there be a reward?" one of the other reporters asked. "For information leading to an arrest?"

Schenke shook his head. "No reward has been authorized at this stage."

"Pity. The readers love that. Gets them worked up and on the lookout."

"This time they'll just have to get worked up and on the lookout for altruistic reasons."

"Good luck with that," said another reporter.

"Name?"

"Reissman, from *The Attack*. Like my colleague said, you'll have a better chance of getting information if you offer a reward. Even a modest amount will do the trick."

"I will pass on your suggestion to my superior. I am sure he will give serious consideration to the advice of the gentlemen of the press, amongst all his other duties."

Reissman had heavy, poorly shaved jowls and they trembled as he spoke. "No need to take that tone, sir. Just trying to be helpful. We want this killer caught just as much as anyone else."

"Really? I'd be willing to bet that the longer he continues killing, the more copies of your newspapers you will sell."

"If he continues killing, the public have a right to read the story. And if you catch him, then they'll want to follow the trial."

"And either way, you'll sell more newspapers, eh?"

Reissman shrugged. "I daresay."

"Let's make sure we assist each other as much as possible, gentlemen. If I help you sell more papers, then you make sure you give the readers the details I pass on to you. There are few enough police as it is, so I need the eyes and ears of the public to help us find this man. And you are going to coax your readers into action. That's what you're good at." Schenke raised a finger in warning. "That said, I don't want you indulging in groundless speculation. If any of you start trying to pin this on foreign workers, Jews or communists, without evidence from me to back up such a claim, you will not be allowed to attend any further Kripo briefings."

"What about the name of the woman in the latest attack?" asked Greiser.

Schenke tensed as he made ready to reply. He was not comfortable with Müller's decision, but he had been given his orders. "Ruth Frankel."

The reporters scribbled in their notebooks. Reissman was the first to comment. "Sounds like a Jewish name, sir."

"The victim is Jewish," Schenke confirmed.

The reporter bristled. "You're taking the word of a Jew?"

His newspaper, *The Attack*, was owned by Goebbels, who used it to vent his spleen about those the party had decided were not worthy of being members of the master race. Schenke regarded the newspaper with contempt. Reissman's tone was what he expected from one of Goebbels's reporters.

"I'm taking the word of a victim and eyewitness."

"But she's a Jew."

"That's irrelevant."

"Irrelevant?" Reissman's eyes bulged. "Everyone knows

the Jews are scheming liars. Why should anyone trust this woman?"

"If she can help me find the killer, I'll trust her. Same as I would any witness. And if she can help prevent the deaths of any more Aryan women, I'd hope you and your readers would think that a good thing."

"Of course it's a good thing! I'm saying that you should be on your guard when you deal with her, sir. In the general run of things no good comes from trusting a Jew." Reissman saw the cold expression on the inspector's face and added, "Just offering you some friendly advice, sir."

"I think I can handle any danger she might pose. Thank you for your concern." Schenke glanced round the other reporters. "Any more questions?"

Greiser raised his hand. "One thing. Do the police have plans to increase their vigilance on the railways until the killer is caught?"

"That's one for my superiors," Schenke replied. "I'm only handling the investigation. Any more? No? Then I'll let you have those photographs."

He opened the folder Frieda had prepared for him. "This is the first victim, Gerda Korzeny."

The reporters crowded round to take their copies. Lustig held his up and whistled. "Our killer sure picks them. She looks like a movie star."

"She was a movie star, you fool," Reissman responded. "That's Gerda Schnee. I'm sure of it."

"That was her name," Schenke confirmed. "Before she married."

"Who's the husband? Some film producer? Steel magnate? Press baron?" Reissman tucked the print into his notebook and readied his pencil. "Bet he has a fancy title."

"Afraid not. Gustav Korzeny is a lawyer. He works for the party."

Greiser clicked his tongue. "Those party bigwigs get all the best lookers. Still, I bet she does okay out of it."

"Not anymore," Schenke pointed out. "She's dead. Murdered. Don't forget that when you're writing this up. Treat the dead with respect. At the end of the day, she's like any other woman unfortunate enough to cross the path of a killer."

"Is the husband a suspect?" asked one of the other reporters, a broad-faced man with small wire-framed glasses.

"Not at the moment," Schenke replied. "We have not identified any suspects yet." He handed out the second batch of prints to the reporters. "This is Monika Bronheim." It was an enlargement of the photograph on her identity card, and she looked pasty and slightly out of focus. The reporters took the images without comment, gave them a cursory glance and waited for him to continue.

"I appreciate that Gerda Korzeny is the headline, but don't forget that Monika is also a victim. Make sure she gets a mention. It may prompt someone who saw her on the night, or who knows something useful. She may not have been a movie star, but her family have as much right to see justice done as Gerda Korzeny's do. I have some crime scene pictures here as well. I'd like you to use them. Again, it might give us some leads if people recognize the settings."

The reporters took the photographs eagerly, clearly hoping for something sensational, but Schenke had selected long shots that revealed the context around the body, rather than darker, more salacious close-ups of the victims.

"And lastly, we have the sketch of the man we're looking for in connection with the attack on Ruth Frankel. He is almost certainly the man who carried out the other murders we know about, and further deaths we are still looking into. It's vital that you get this in front of your readers."

The reporters examined the prints taken from the sketch. Again Reissman spoke first. "If your artist has done a good job and he really looks like this, I'd say the Kripo's job is going to be easy. There aren't too many men in Berlin with such fine features and that hairstyle."

"Let's hope it's accurate, then," said Schenke. "And let's hope our man is as conspicuous as he seems. Right, you've got what you need. If there are any further developments in the case, I will let you know. Meanwhile, I'd be grateful if you pressed your editors to get this on the front page. I want this face staring out of every news kiosk in Berlin."

"What about the Jew woman?" asked Reissman. "Can we use her picture?"

Schenke felt his guts tighten in disgust. It did not sit right with his conscience and yet he had no choice but to obey his superior to use the woman as bait. "If you must. We're finished here. You've got the story and the pictures. Go and write your reports and make sure they get into the morning editions. Even a delay of a day may cost us another life." He nodded curtly. "Good afternoon, gentlemen."

He stood for a moment watching them file out of the precinct, uncomfortable with what he had been obliged to do. A more difficult discussion was still to be had, and he braced himself for it as he headed towards the interview room.

"You did what?" Ruth Frankel glared at him. "You gave them my name? But you said you wouldn't. My God . . . Everyone will know about me now." She clenched her fingers on the edge of the table. "You bastard. You're all bastards. What do you think will become of me when the story gets out?"

"I don't know," Schenke replied. "We have all the information we need from you for now. You are free to leave the precinct. If we require anything else, we'll send for you."

"I thought I was supposed to remain here in your custody."

"The situation has changed. I have new orders concerning you. I'm to let you go until we speak to you again."

"If I'm still alive, you mean. I'm no fool, Inspector. I know why you have given out my name. You want the killer to try and find me. That's what this is about, isn't it?"

She was more quick-witted than he had supposed.

"You will be watched." Schenke tried to sound reassuring. "If the killer tries to attack you again, help will be close by. You'll be safe."

"Safe!" She laughed bitterly. "You might as well have painted a target on my coat."

There was nothing he could say to counter her accusation. But he vowed to himself that he would do his best to protect her, as far as a loose interpretation of Müller's orders allowed.

"Is the address you provided really where you live?"

She did not answer immediately, confirming his suspicions. "No."

"So what's your actual address?"

"I don't have one."

"Are you saying you live on the streets? In this weather?"

"No. I stay with friends of my family for a few days at a time, then move on."

"Sounds like you're on the run."

She looked up sharply. "That's how you have made us live. My family were forced to give up their apartment. When my parents were allowed to leave Germany, I stayed with my uncle and aunt and was tasked with looking after my grandmother. They already had several members of the family sheltering with them. In the end, they had to ask me to leave to make way for my cousin and her child. I've been moving from one place to the next ever since."

"How long for?"

"Nine months."

"And how do you survive? Do you work?"

"At Siemens." She smiled sardonically. "And if we work really hard, they even pay us from time to time, though barely enough to get by on. As a policeman, I'm sure you know how it goes. Jews are only allowed to buy food at certain times of the day, and only after everyone else has taken the best of what's available. It was hard enough before the war started."

Schenke was indeed aware of the restrictions placed on Jews, but he had not given it much thought until now. "Where are you staying at the moment?"

"I can't tell you."

"Why not?"

"I don't want to get anyone into trouble with the police."

"Look." Schenke spoke patiently. "I am not interested in what goes on where you are staying. I need to know where to find you. That's all."

"I'm not having one of you follow me back there. I won't trust you with other people's lives."

"So where will you go?" Schenke challenged her. "Do you think you can sleep rough? You wouldn't last the night. You'd freeze to death."

"I'll manage," she replied.

"No, you won't . . ."

"What choice do I have? I've survived so far."

Schenke felt a mixture of frustration and pity, along with a stab of guilt over her predicament. He could understand her reluctance to reveal where she was currently living. There might be others of her kind there, some hiding from the authorities, trying to disappear into the streets of the city and avoid the increasingly severe regulations governing the lives of Jews. He had heard whispered rumors that the resettlement camps in the east were not the peaceful havens promised by the party. Many Jews had chosen to go into hiding rather than risk being sent there. It was possible that Ruth Frankel was trying to protect some of these fugitives.

Maybe she was one herself. In which case, she was breaking the law and it was his duty to denounce her to the Gestapo.

Even as he thought it, the notion repelled him. Besides, he needed her for this investigation. She was the only one who had seen the killer's face clearly. Schenke needed to make sure she was kept safe for long enough to identify her attacker in court. But what could he do? Keep her in protective custody so that she would not have to sleep on the streets? That would mean locking her up in a freezing cell that was not much better than being forced outside. She should be somewhere only he knew about. His apartment was too obvious; besides, Karin was there and might object. Worse, it would place Karin at risk as well. There was another possibility. Some people he trusted as if they were his own family.

"Ruth, you need to stay safe and warm for a few nights. I think I know of a suitable place, but we have to get your story straight before we go there."

Her eyes narrowed fractionally. "Why should I trust you again? You betrayed me to the press."

"I had no choice. I had my orders."

"I wonder how long that excuse is going to endure in Germany. You are fortunate that you can make your own choices, Inspector. Choice is a rare luxury for me, but for you choice is always there. You could have kept my name out of the newspapers."

"If I had defied my superior, he could easily have swept me aside and put another man in my place to carry out his orders. At least you can be sure I will do what I can to keep you safe."

"I don't feel confident that I can trust you."

Schenke sighed wearily. "Look. I have some friends. Good people. They have a large, comfortable house where you could be looked after away from the eyes of prying neighbors. If I take you to them and ask for their help, I am sure they will give it. But I cannot tell them the truth, for their own safety. I'll need to lie to them. And I'll need you to go along with the lie. Are you willing to do that?"

She gave him a long, thoughtful look. "I'll do what I have to, in order to survive. I'll lie for you. There's nothing else I can do. I don't know you well enough to trust you yet. You may be an honest man. A good man. I don't know. All I do know is that I am forced to put my life in your hands. But I don't like it . . ."

Chapter Twenty-four

"Wait here," Schenke instructed as he climbed out of the passenger seat. Ruth pulled her coat more tightly about her shoulders and hunched down in the rear behind Brandt, who was at the wheel. The probationer was on night duty in case there were any new developments. Despite the car's heater being on full during the drive up from Schöneberg, it had failed to raise the temperature inside to more than a few degrees above freezing.

As they had set off, Schenke had explained his plan to her briefly. After that, there had been little conversation. He could understand her reluctance to give anything away to a police officer, and knew that if he attempted to establish a better relationship, it was bound to be seen as some kind of trick. They had sat in uncomfortable silence for most of the journey across the city.

He ducked down to address Brandt. "Make sure she stays in the car and doesn't try to run off."

"Yes, sir." Brandt nodded.

"Where would I run to?" Ruth peered out of the window

at the avenue stretching ahead and behind them. The bare limbs of elm trees lined the route, along which were gated entrances to the villas that made up the affluent neighborhood. "I don't even know where we are."

"Tegel." Schenke paused. "I used to live here when I moved to Berlin."

"On this street?" She gave him an appraising look. "Your family's rich, then?"

"It's not my family. A good friend. I'll be back in a moment."

He closed the door and turned to the familiar pair of iron gates set into large stone pillars. Each gate carried a design of an H within a wreath of oak leaves. He raised the large latch, eased one of the gates open and passed through. The curved drive had not been cleared of snow for days and it crunched under his shoes as he paced towards the balustrade leading up to the reception door. The house rose above him, tall windows shuttered against the winter on each of the three stories. A dull gleam lined some of the downstairs windows, including the parlor, where he knew Count Anton Harstein and his wife would be sitting by their fire, reading for an hour before dinner was served.

He climbed the stairs to the portico and tapped his toes against the base of one of the pillars to dislodge the snow from his shoes. Then he pulled the handle to one side to announce his presence. He heard the muffled sound of a bell within, followed by a lengthy silence, broken by the low sweep of a light breeze and the chuffing of a train in the distance. Then the clatter of a sliding bolt and the turn of the handle, and the door opened. A wedge of light fell across the steps and spilled over the driveway towards the small pond and fountain in the middle of the garden. The light lit up Schenke's face.

"Why, it's young Master Horst," said the thin figure in a

plain black jacket and trousers. His lined face, illuminated from the side, creased into a warm smile as he beckoned Schenke to enter. “Come in, sir. Out of the cold.”

Schenke stepped over the threshold and the servant shut the door behind him. “May I take your coat and hat, sir?”

“No. I won’t be staying long, Wilhelm.”

“Ah, that’s a pity. It’s been some months since we last saw you, sir. That dinner before the master’s son left to join his regiment.”

“I remember.”

Paul Harstein had been called up in preparation for the invasion of Poland. No one had been told the true purpose of the mobilization at the time. It had been a fine meal, a last gathering of family and close friends, with Paul proudly wearing his officer’s uniform. Horst had felt a touch of envy at the time. Thanks to the racing accident, he would never be able to serve in the military.

“Is Count Harstein at home? I saw the light in the parlor.”

“Yes, sir. Will you require refreshments? I can have Klara make you a hot snack.”

“Thank you, but no. This won’t take long.”

“Very well, sir. I’ll be in the kitchen if you need anything.” The elderly retainer bowed and turned to make his way across the black and white tiles to the small door under the staircase that led to the servants’ quarters.

Schenke crossed to the parlor. As he entered, warm air enfolded him. The room was spacious, with bookcases on both sides of a large fireplace, where blazing logs crackled and hissed behind a wire screen. Light from a modest chandelier provided enough illumination to read by comfortably. The other walls were lined with portraits of family ancestors and a handful of landscapes featuring mountains and castles, minor works from the previous century painted by Caspar David Friedrich.

Anton Harstein had hardly changed since the days when he had financed the racing team. He had recognized Schenke's potential from the start, and the two had become friends. He had welcomed Schenke into his house and treated him as part of the family for the three years he had raced with the Silver Arrows. After the accident and the months in the hospital, Schenke had decided not to return to the sport, and he had found his own accommodation when he joined the police. But he had remained good friends with the Harsteins and knew that he could trust them.

Countess Harstein spotted him in the doorway and snapped her book shut with a surprised gasp, rising from her seat to hurry over and embrace him. "My darling Horst. What a lovely surprise."

He kissed her on the forehead. "How are you, Astrid?"

"All the better for seeing you. Come over by the fire where I can get a proper look at you."

She held him at arm's length and looked him up and down. "You are thin. And tired. They're working you too hard."

He brushed off her concern with a casual snort and turned to her husband. The count had risen stiffly from his chair and smiled from beneath the unfashionably bushy moustache that ran across his cheeks to merge with his sideburns.

"And how are you, sir?"

"In good health, lad. To what do we owe this pleasure?" he asked brusquely. "It's been a few months since we last saw you."

"I know. I'm sorry."

"Ah, I imagine our friends in the party are keeping you busy. Well, they'd know all about criminal activity."

Schenke's smile faded. "I'd be careful about saying such things."

"What? Is a man not allowed to make a joke anymore?

Not even in the privacy of his own home, and to those he regards as his family?" He affected a look of horror. "I hope you won't arrest me, Inspector."

It was the kind of ribbing that Harstein had always enjoyed at his expense, ever since Schenke had announced his intention of joining the police. It might be presented as lighthearted, but there was no concealing the old man's disappointment that his protégé had given up on his racing career.

"I won't. But another policeman might," Schenke admonished him.

"Pah! Some people are too easily offended these days. It's a poor show. Poor show indeed. A sign of the times. Ah, but you're not here to mourn the passing of better times." The count's expression became serious. "Better times indeed . . ."

"Have you heard anything from Paul?"

"I have," Harstein replied. "One letter. Filled with the kind of tall tales told by young officers, as you'd expect. I'm sure he's having a ball and doing his duty for the fatherland, as every man should." He patted his guest on the shoulder. "Whatever form that duty takes."

"I do my bit," Schenke agreed.

"He'll be home soon enough, now that the fighting in Poland has come to an end."

"The war isn't over yet," said his wife. "The danger has not passed."

"Pfft. You worry too much. I'm sure he'll be fine."

"I hope so." She caught Schenke's eyes. "One great war in a lifetime is more than enough."

The count lightly slapped the side of his head. "What am I thinking? I haven't offered you a drink. Will you join us for dinner?"

"I can't. I have to leave again very soon. But first I have a favor to ask."

Harstein's smile faded. "My boy, if it's money, I'm not sure how much help we can be. We've already lost most of the staff. Only Wilhelm and his wife are left. It's been some time since I was able to cover the costs of the racing team."

"I'm not asking for money, sir."

"Ah, good. How can we help, then?"

"I have someone in a car outside the house. She needs a place to stay for a few days. Somewhere she can be safe and looked after. I was hoping you would let her stay here."

The countess frowned. "But who is she, dear?"

"Is she in trouble?" Harstein demanded. "Has she been thrown out by her family?"

"No. It's nothing like that. She's an important witness. At the moment she has nowhere safe to go and needs shelter. Can you help her? It will only be for a short time."

Harstein bristled. "Well, I don't know that—"

"Of course we can help," his wife interrupted. "No Christian soul could turn away a girl in need at this time of year, and in this weather. What's her name?"

"Johanna Kasper."

Harstein arched an eyebrow. "I take it that's not her real name."

Schenke had anticipated this reaction and had a cover story ready. Ruth had told him of others like her who had used it to find temporary accommodation in Berlin. "She's a quarter Jewish, on her father's side. Her mother's family are quite respectable. I'm sure you will find her unobtrusive and grateful. In any case, there's more than enough spare room in this house." He looked from one to the other. "What do you say? Will you help?"

The elderly couple exchanged a glance. The count spoke first. "There are certain people who would not be happy to know we had sheltered her, even if she is of mixed blood. Is it lawful for us to do so?"

"It is lawful for Jewish descent of the second degree, sir," Schenke replied deliberately, feeling a pang of guilt at his dissembling.

"I see. Then there is no risk attached to this favor."

"No legal risk, sir. My concern is to keep her concealed from a person being hunted by the police. Her life is in danger."

"And you bring her here, to us, and place us in danger too?"

"Only myself and my driver know that she is here. There is no risk I can conceive of. She will be safe, and so will you. I give you my word."

Harstein nodded slowly. "Very well . . ."

"We'd be delighted to help her," the countess said. "Now, don't let the poor girl get any colder. Go and bring her in here at once."

"Thank you." Schenke kissed her on the cheek.

"Well, if it's necessary, then I agree," Harstein added.

Schenke hurried outside and opened the car door. "They'll do it. I've told them that you're a quarter Jewish. I'm not sure they truly believe it, but just keep up the pretense."

She climbed out and took his arm as they followed his tracks back up the driveway. "How does it make you feel to lie to your friends about me?"

"I'd rather not, but I suppose I can comfort myself with the thought that it's as much about protecting them as it is about keeping you safe. If they are ever questioned about sheltering you, they can truthfully claim that they did not know they were harboring a Jew."

"And you think that will save them?" Ruth shook her head pityingly. "One thing I have learned is that there are no limits to what the party is prepared to do to serve its ends. Take my people. One attack on us after another, and then a law is rushed through to make it legal. Do you think the

Harsteins will be safe under such a regime? Do you think you are?"

Schenke shook his head. "I'm a policeman. I am on the right side of the law."

"For now . . ."

The Harsteins were waiting for them in the hall and greeted Ruth politely before the countess rang for Wilhelm and instructed him to prepare some soup for the guest.

"She can stay in your old room, Horst. There's no heating in the guest wing and the furniture is covered with dust sheets. We only keep a few rooms ready these days."

He nodded. "I'll show her up, then I must go."

Leading the way up the wide oak staircase Schenke briefly recalled the first Christmas he had spent here. He and Paul had had too much to drink and used trays as sleds to race down the stairs, and had been roundly scolded by Wilhelm for doing so. He smiled at the memory and a longing for the simpler pleasures of youth made his heart ache.

At the top of the stairs, he turned towards the family wing, where the rooms were arranged each side of the corridor. He indicated a door.

"This was my room when I came to stay."

"From what the countess said, it still is."

The comment felt overly personal to Schenke, and his expression hardened as he opened the door, beckoned her inside and flicked the brass light switch. The bulbs in the small chandelier gleamed into life and lit the room with a warm glow. There was the bed he remembered, with its large bolster and thick quilt. The walnut wardrobe and the desk by the window. Pictures of racing cars lined the walls, and over the fireplace was a framed photograph of him sitting in the cockpit of the racing car in which he had crashed a few weeks after the picture was taken.

Ruth's eyes scanned the room and stopped at the image. She stepped closer to it.

"That's you, isn't it? I wondered why your face was familiar."

"You follow motor racing?"

"Not closely. My uncle was a huge fan of the Silver Arrows." She turned to him. "I saw you race once. From a distance. We were guests in my uncle's box at the stadium. His firm used it to entertain business clients."

Not for the first time, Schenke felt the strange distance between the Germany of that time and the nation that had been forced into being by the party. Ruth Frankel's family had been part of society back then. As had his own family before the terrible destruction of the country's finances by the madness of uncontrolled inflation. They had that in common then. Fate had dealt both of them a losing hand. But while the Schenkes had lost only their wealth, the Frankels had lost almost everything. Even their status within the human race had been stripped by the party, which now classified them as something less than human.

"You are a man of surprises, Inspector Schenke," she said quietly as she gazed at the photograph. "Not quite the usual policeman, I think."

"You're wrong. I am a criminal investigator right down to the bone," he responded harshly. "You are a witness to a murder investigation, nothing more. I suggest you don't make yourself too comfortable here. You are not a houseguest, or a friend of the family. This is strictly a police matter. When we've caught the killer and he's been tried and convicted, then you're on your own again. Is that clear?"

She returned his stare with a cold expression. "Perfectly."

"Good. I'll be in touch. Meanwhile, don't leave the house for any reason."

"Yes, sir."

He felt a twinge of irritation at her sarcasm, and felt the urge to snap at her, but restrained himself. He was exhausted and struggling to think straight, let alone retain much semblance of a professional veneer. He needed to go to his apartment, have a quiet meal with Karin and get some sleep. Why was he lingering here?

He nodded curtly, turned away and strode out of the room and down the stairs. A quick kiss on the countess's cheek, a shake of Harstein's hand and a muttered promise to try and see them more often, and then he was outside in the cold, and the sharpness of the air on his bare skin and in his lungs brought him back to a state of alertness.

Climbing into the car, he sat for a moment struggling to concentrate.

Brandt coughed lightly. "Where to, sir?"

"Drop me at my apartment on your way back to the precinct. Keep awake in case the phone rings. You can rest for a few hours when the rest of the team arrives in the morning."

"Yes, sir." There was surliness in the younger man's voice.

"This is what you signed up for, Brandt," Schenke said sharply. "If you don't like it, there's always the army. Is that what you want?"

"No, sir. I always wanted to be a cop. Nothing else."

"Good, then you'd better get used to the long hours. Let's go."

As Brandt shifted into first and eased away from the curb, Schenke took a last glance at the house, up towards the wing where his old room was. A faint gleam outlined the shutters and he felt better now that he knew his witness was safely hidden from her attacker. If nothing else, it was a brief respite from the harsh rules and regulations that the party had created to make the lives of Berlin's Jews as bitter as possible.

Chapter Twenty-five

The first thing Schenke noticed when he returned to his apartment was the warmth. It enveloped him the moment he stepped through the door. He frowned. The concierge had been ordered by the block warden to limit the use of the building's boiler to early morning and evenings only. Schenke had a small fireplace in the living room, but that was not nearly effective enough to produce this much heat. He removed his hat and coat and hung them on the stand beside the door as he called out. "Karin?"

"Just a moment!" came the reply, and she emerged from the kitchen. Her hair was held back by a clip and she wore one of his cardigans over her blouse and some close-cut trousers. The cardigan was baggy on her, and the thick socks on her feet were equally oversized. But the ad hoc ensemble of her clothing and his only seemed to make her more attractive, and he felt a rush of affection fill his heart.

She half slipped and half skipped over the polished wooden floor in the corridor and folded her arms around him, raising her face to kiss him. Her lips were soft and hot against his and he held her close for a moment until she pushed him back gently.

"I've got something on the stove!"

She turned and hurried back into the kitchen, and he followed at a more measured pace, smiling at his good fortune to have such a fine woman in his life. He caught the rich, meaty aroma as he approached the door, and entered to see her standing in front of the cooker stirring something in a small pan with a wooden spoon. She looked over her shoulder and smiled. "Sauce is nearly done. I've got the rest keeping warm in the oven. Your timing's good."

He stood behind her and rested his hands on her shoulders, then gently kissed the back of her neck. She flinched at the touch of his lips, but only from pleasure, and reached a hand up and touched his cheek as she let out a soft moan. Abruptly she withdrew her hand and turned towards him.

"There'll be time for that later. Let's eat first, then we'll have a hot bath together."

"Bath? But there's no hot water until the morning."

"Isn't there?" Karin smiled mischievously. "I think you're in for a surprise then."

"What do you mean?" Schenke cocked his head to one side. "Wait. The heating is on full *and* there's hot water? What have you been up to?"

"I had a quiet word with the concierge. I explained that you've been working so hard these last few days and needed some creature comforts. I may have mentioned that you were under the direct command of the head of the Gestapo. After that, she was very helpful."

"I'm sure." Schenke sighed. "Karin, my love, that's the kind of thing that might come back to haunt me. If word got back to Müller that I'd abused my position to win petty privileges . . ."

"There is nothing petty about a hot bath in the middle of a freezing winter. Besides, how is Müller going to find out?"

"You'd be surprised how much information reaches the ears of the Gestapo."

She was serious for a moment. "No. I don't believe I would be surprised anymore. Something strange happened to me today. I had a coffee with a friend this afternoon and I noticed a man was watching me across the room. He looked away as soon as our eyes met, each time. I saw him again as I was walking to the station to catch the train to Pankow."

Schenke felt a cold ache of fear in his guts. "Did you get a good look at him?"

She thought briefly and then shook her head. "No. He was too far away to make out any useful details. Could have been in his thirties or forties. That's the best I can recall. Do you think it's possible that it was him? The killer?"

"I don't know." He saw the fear in her expression. "I doubt it. Just a coincidence. When the story gets out, I dare-say every woman in Berlin will be looking over her shoul-der. That's no bad thing, even if the party doesn't like it. Try not to worry."

They stared at each other for a beat, then she turned back to the cooker and stirred the sauce vigorously. "You get the plates out of the oven. Be careful, they'll be hot."

He picked up the towel he used to dry the cutlery and felt a moment's shame that it hadn't been washed for a while and was stained and grimy.

"Yes, I noticed that," she commented without looking up. "This apartment is in sore need of a woman's care. You've been living on your own too long, I'd say."

"Nonsense," Schenke responded as he eased the oven door open, wincing as a blast of hot air struck his face. "I have a charwoman who comes in every week to clean and do the laundry."

"Really? Either you're not paying her enough, or she's blind and decrepit."

"As it happens, she's a ravishing blonde. A music student who is working to help pay for her studies."

Karin's eyes narrowed. "You're teasing me."

"And you're jumping to conclusions. You need to go on a Kripo training course to knock that out of you."

"As long as that's all they knock out of me."

Schenke felt a familiar weary disappointment at her comment. "All we do is investigate crimes, Karin. That's all. We don't beat people up. We don't smash newspaper offices to pieces, nor do we burn down synagogues. We do our best to bring criminals to justice, whatever else may happen around us."

She smiled. "I know. I'm sorry, that was a cheap crack. Anyway, see what I prepared for dinner."

He reached into the oven and took out two plates with metal covers over them. He lifted one of the covers and his eyes gleamed as he saw the thick steak resting alongside glazed roasted vegetables. He could feel his appetite swelling as his nose filled with the aroma.

"I haven't seen a steak like that for over a month. Where did you get it?"

"I could tell you that I saved my ration coupons, but that wouldn't be honest. I have a friend who has a friend who supplies some of the more select eating establishments in Berlin. The kind that don't pay much attention to rationing."

"The black market, you mean?" Schenke sucked in a breath through his teeth. "You need to be careful."

"Maybe I do. But we have something of a moral quandary here, Inspector Schenke. Do you eat this fine piece of meat, or do you uphold the iron self-discipline of the criminal investigation department and turn me in at the nearest precinct? Well?"

He paused as if in deliberation before replying. "On reflection, and in the interests of not wasting police time, I suggest that we eat the evidence and don't mention this grievous breach of the law again. Agreed?" He looked at her.

"Agreed." She nodded. "Now, let's eat."

In the apartment's modest dining room, three candles were burning in a candelabra Schenke usually kept in the hall. Places had been set on either side, and a bottle of red wine stood between two glasses.

"Very romantic." He smiled gratefully. "I hope this continues in the direction I think it's taking."

"Don't leap to conclusions, my love."

Karin poured creamy peppered sauce over the steaks and placed a plate in front of each chair, and they sat down. Schenke filled their glasses, and Karin raised hers in a toast.

"To a peaceful Christmas and a peace treaty in the new year."

"I'll drink to that."

They began to eat, the pleasure of fine food ensuring a silence between them as they savored the rich flavor of the steak. After a while, they began discussing the events of their day. Karin had spent the morning shopping for Christmas presents. Schenke felt guilty. There had been no time for him to go shopping. He would have to find something before it was too late. A gift suitable for a woman with fine taste. A gift that would indicate how much she meant to him.

"What about you, my darling?" she asked. "Any progress?"

He recounted the details they had released to the press and Müller's order to release the name of his witness.

"Isn't that unusual? Not to mention dangerous for her?"

"Absolutely," Schenke replied. "But he feels that it might lure the killer out. If he is a party member he might have contacts that allowed him to trace the address she gave us, even if she is not really living there. We have the building under observation. Frankly, I think it's a fool's errand. If the killer has a grain of sense, he'll steer clear. In any case, I have taken the witness somewhere she'll be safe for a few days. A friend's house."

"And how do they feel about harboring a Jew?"

"I told them she was of mixed race."

Karin looked at him directly. "You lied to them."

"Half lied."

She rolled her eyes. "You are wasted on the police. With such a talent for dissembling, you should have been a lawyer."

"Who would wish such a fate on any man of integrity?"

"Seriously, are you any closer to catching the killer?"

He finished the last forkful of his dinner as he considered the question. "I think so. The sketch will be in the morning papers. As will the details about his wound. Someone will recognize him and hopefully report it before he can strike again. If we make an arrest, and the witness identifies him, I'm sure we have enough evidence to send him to the guillotine."

He dabbed his mouth and pushed his plate to one side. "Any dessert?"

"Sorry, but no. However, there is something else I have prepared for you. Wait here."

She rose from the table and headed down the corridor towards the bathroom. Schenke heard the sound of water being run, and then a swirling in the bath before she called out to him. "Ready!" He drained his wineglass and went to join her.

Schenke liked his creature comforts, and the bathroom had been one of the main reasons why he had chosen this apartment. There was a shower as well as a bath; the latter was an old enameled example of sufficient dimensions that he could lie in it full length, with the water covering his body. As he entered the room, he saw that Karin was sitting at one end of the bath. She gave him a coquettish smile.

"Will you join me?"

Schenke regarded the soft profile of her body. "Why not?"

He took off his clothes and folded them on the bathroom chair before stepping into the bath. The water was still hot, but just about tolerable. He eased himself down slowly, teeth gritted, and let out a long satisfied sigh as the water closed over him.

They both shuffled down, being careful not to spill any water, and positioned their feet either side of the other's torso, resting their heads against opposite ends of the bath.

"Now tell me that doesn't feel good," she challenged him.

"Bliss . . ." he murmured happily.

They lay still for a moment, the only sound an occasional drip from the hot tap. Schenke closed his eyes and breathed deeply.

"I hope you won't be too tired later on," she said.

"I think I'll manage."

There was another pause. "I must say, I found the contents of your bookshelves fascinating."

"So you said. I like to read what interests me."

"That's fine, until you no longer can. You can't be blind to the party's direction of travel. They won't be satisfied until they have determined precisely what we can read, what we can think, what we can feel."

"You exaggerate, Karin. That is an impossible goal."

"Maybe, but *they* don't seem to realize that. And they certainly don't act as if they think their ambition is futile."

"Then they're fools," Schenke replied, and realized he had spoken aloud what he had only thought in private for some time. He regarded her warily for an instant, and felt guilty for doing so. It was unworthy of him to suspect her.

And yet who could one trust absolutely in such times as this?

She had seen the subtle change in his expression and smiled sadly. "I know what you're thinking. I can understand your caution, my darling. But what if I said something that meant I had to put my trust in you? For example, what if I said I regard the party as an abomination? What if I said that Hitler and his cronies are little more than gangsters and their ideology the kind of strutting stupidity that appeals to the baser instincts of the German people?"

Schenke said nothing, then cleared his throat. "Is that the kind of thing you might say?"

She flicked some water in his face in exasperation. "I'm being serious, Horst. I'm trusting you with what I really believe."

"That's what concerns me."

"And what are you going to do about it?"

"Nothing. I shall pretend you never said it at all."

"Why?"

"Because that is dangerous talk. If anyone overheard you, you would be placing yourself in grave danger. Even if your uncle is head of the Abwehr."

"Who could overhear me?" She gestured round at the bathroom walls. "We're alone in here."

"That's true. But still."

"You see? They've even got you thinking that walls have ears. How long before you and everyone else in Germany no longer dares to utter any opinion that runs counter to the line set out by the party? Can you not see the danger in that?"

"Of course I can. But Hitler and his people are like every other regime. They come and go if you wait long enough. And the world moves on."

She shook her head. "I wish I could believe that. Besides, every day they remain in power, more people are arrested and disappear. More of our soldiers die in this needless war. More of what few liberties remain are stripped away. Surely we should not just sit by and watch it happen?"

He was getting very uncomfortable with the direction of the conversation. "What do you suggest we do about it, Karin?"

She regarded him without expression for a while before she spoke again. "The right thing to do is to oppose the party. And to persuade others to do the same. I have been pushing my uncle in that direction for many months now. It was hard work at first, but then he read the reports coming back from Poland. Do you have any idea what has been happening there? Our soldiers have been ordered to round up and murder every person who commands the following and respect of the Polish people. Army officers, politicians, academics, lawyers, civil servants, mayors, even senior police officers. Some of our soldiers have questioned their orders, but have been told the Führer compels them to do it. How can any civilized person condone that? It is simply unconscionable, my uncle says. Those of us who oppose the party are building the movement one person at a time. You could join us, Horst. I think I know you well enough to see that."

"You're wrong. I refuse to get involved in politics. I am given my orders and I carry them out."

"Would you do anything the party told you to? Could you justify that?"

"No," he replied quietly. "I could not. And when the time comes for my conscience to be tested, I hope I will do the right thing. In the meantime, there will always be crime, and even if I can't change the way Germany is headed, I can protect people from crooks, rapists and murderers. That is a moral thing to do, I think. It is something that will always need to be done, whatever regime is in charge of Germany." He eased himself up and reached for a towel. "The water's getting cold. Let's go to bed. I don't want to talk about such things anymore."

They held each other close in bed and all thought of the wider world was pushed to one side as they made love. Later, Schenke lay on his back staring at the ceiling. Karin's head was on his shoulder, her arm across his chest and one leg drawn up over his thigh. She breathed easily as she slept. But rest did not come to him.

He was perturbed by their earlier discussion. Karin's beliefs were dangerous. To her, and to him if their relationship continued. Even if he had a great deal of sympathy for her opposition to the regime, what realistic prospect was there of overcoming the ruthless machinery of state that the party wielded without mercy? None at all, was his brutally honest assessment. The moment anyone openly criticized the regime, they were beaten down and dragged off to a camp. All that remained was to conspire in small groups scattered across Germany, too few and too weak to make a difference. He was reminded of the secretive Christian sects in Roman times who lived under the shadow of the crosses onto which those who were discovered were nailed and left to die. A chilling warning to those who dared to defy the emperor and his regime. It was hopeless to think of resisting the ambitions of the party. And to that extent, he realized they had already defeated him.

He tried to push such thoughts away by concentrating on the murder investigation. Come the morrow, the killer's face would be known across the city. Surely he would not be able to evade detection for long. Particularly in the depths of the harshest winter in living memory. The cold and the need for food would drive him into the open at some point. Unless he chose to risk holing up somewhere until he froze or starved to death. If and when he did emerge, Schenke would be waiting. And the killer would face justice for the women he had murdered.

Yet what was the point of devoting himself to the capture of one criminal when the whole of Germany and the hapless people of Poland were falling victim to a regime run by criminals who defined legality as whatever they wanted it to be? When bullies, thugs, thieves and murderers like those who controlled the party committed crimes on such a monumental scale, the work carried out diligently by Schenke and men like him seemed like little more than an absurdist response to a brutal world.

What, then, was the point of being a policeman when criminals ruled? It was a troubling question, and one for which he could find no answer, no matter what he had said to Karin earlier. And what would he do when the party ordered him to become a criminal like them? What could he do? The choice was stark. Do the right thing and suffer the consequences, or do their bidding and sell his soul to a cause his heart and mind told him represented the opposite of all the values he regarded as civilized.

"I'm damned," he whispered in the darkness. "We're all truly damned."

Chapter Twenty-six

The clock on the office mantelpiece had chimed ten o'clock when the door opened and the orderly entered carrying a pile of newspapers. He raised his eyebrows in surprise to find one of his superiors still at work so late.

The officer's jacket hung on the back of his chair as he sat, collar unbuttoned, hunched over some paperwork. A gas heater hissed in the corner of the room, turned up full so that the room was warm and comfortable. He lowered his pen and stretched his shoulders.

"What is it?"

"Tomorrow morning's editions of the Berlin papers, sir. Just in."

He gestured to the edge of the desk. "Leave them there."

The orderly did as he was told, closing the door behind him on the way out.

The officer rolled his head wearily and felt the crack of a joint in his spine. Stretching his shoulders, he winced at the pain in his side. It was still tender, and he cursed his misfortune in encountering a woman who went armed with a knife. The wild bitch might have done more damage had the blade not been deflected off a rib. As it was, he had been forced to dispose of his bloodstained clothes. That was when he'd realized he had lost the gold party badge. It must have come off in the struggle. Or when he had rolled down the embankment. Either way, it was gone. He was anxious that it might be found by the police. Not that it would help them much, since he had filed off the serial number even before his first kill.

His thoughts turned back to his wound as it began to throb again. It was fortunate that the doctor he had chosen to treat it did not question the name he gave. The blade had glanced off a rib and not penetrated far. After cleaning the gash, the doctor had stitched it up and covered it with a dressing, then taken the cash payment and a small bonus for not making any record of the treatment. The officer had walked away resolving never to set eyes on the doctor again. Unless he needed to be silenced.

He completed his last correction on the document in front of him and placed the report in the tray for the typist to collect, then stretched his shoulders again and reached for the newspapers. Unfolding the first, the *People's Observer*, he glanced over the lead story about the awarding of medals to war heroes, then froze as he saw a sketch alongside a small feature at the bottom of the front page. A cold terror coursed through his body. The image was about twice the size of those used in identity cards, and though it was only a drawing, it was a rough likeness of him, except for one detail.

He read the headline—*Eyewitness aiding police in hunt for Korzeny killer*—then hurriedly scanned the article, his guts slowly tightening. The article was short and the details were spare and mostly known to him already; the name of the lead investigator and the precinct handling the investigation, the possibility that the death might be linked to other murders, and the contact details for any readers who might be able to offer information to help track down the killer.

But there was more. The report gave the name of the eyewitness and the fact that she was a Jew.

He recalled her face from the encounter on the train, and the pain after she stuck her blade into him. "Filthy little Jewish bitch," he muttered through gritted teeth.

He felt rage surge through his body, and yet had there been anyone else in the room, all they would have seen was his cold expression as his gaze focused on the newspaper. He had long ago mastered the art of revealing to others only what he chose to. His victims had seen his real nature, and then merely for a moment before their deaths. The only living souls who were aware of the monster in him were the bespectacled soldier he had knocked down in the next carriage, and this Jew. Strangely, there was no mention of the soldier acting as a witness. Which left the woman. She must be found and silenced before she could do any more damage. Fortunately, there was one aspect of the sketch that would not help the police in tracking him down. Not that they were responsible for the mistake, any more than the Jew was. He smiled at this confirmation of his superior mind. If Germans were the master race, then he was one of its finest specimens. To remain that way he must act swiftly. And he must cover his tracks carefully.

He crossed the room to the bookshelves on the far wall and took out the directory listing the numbers of the state's various departments. He worked his way through the police listings until he found the direct number for the criminal investigation section at the Schöneberg precinct. It was different from the contact number given in the newspaper. That was good, he calculated. If he called the direct number, it would enhance the credibility of the deception he planned. In addition, he could not risk any request for an operator to connect him, even if one was still on duty so late. Making a note of the number, he replaced the directory, then opened the door and glanced in both directions along the corridor outside. There was no sign of movement and no sound. He was alone.

Closing the door, he returned to his desk and sat down, breathing calmly to settle his nerves. He picked up the receiver and dialed the number. There was a dull burr before the intermittent buzz as the telephone rang at the other end of the line. No one answered. He let it ring for a while longer before he replaced the receiver. Surely there had to be someone on duty to answer the precinct's phone, even at this late hour. He picked up the receiver and dialed again. This time there was an answer within the first few rings.

"Schöneberg police," a voice announced wearily.

"Ah, good. I was on the point of giving up. This is the second time I have tried calling you. Where were you?"

"Who's speaking?"

The officer had his story ready and replied at once. "Hauptsturmführer Bremer of the Reich Main Security Office. And you are?"

He could almost sense the policeman's alarm at being on the telephone to a superior, and one from the SS into the bargain.

"Sergeant Gruber, sir. I am sorry, sir. I was . . . dealing with a drunk at the front desk."

It was clearly a lie, but he let it pass. "Gruber, you say?"

"Yes, sir."

"I'll overlook your tardiness this time. I'd advise you to make sure you stand by the phone when on duty in future."

"Yes, sir. Of course, sir."

"Gruber, it has come to my attention that you had a Jew woman at your precinct earlier today by the name of Ruth Frankel. She is wanted for questioning by our department. I will come over to the precinct shortly to take her into custody. I'd be grateful if you'd have her ready and waiting in reception for when I arrive with the paperwork."

"Yes, sir, but—"

"But what?"

"She is no longer being held here, sir."

"What's that? What do you mean? I was assured she was there."

"She was, sir. But the Kripo took her into their custody and removed her from the precinct."

There was a moment before he could respond. "Where was she taken, Gruber? Tell me."

"I don't know, sir."

"How can you not know? Are you in the habit of releasing enemies of the Reich? This is an outrage. I will hold you personally responsible."

"Sir, wait," the policeman pleaded. "There's a Kripo officer still on duty. Do you want to speak to him? I can bring him to the phone for you."

"He will have to do. What's his name?"

"Brandt, sir."

"Go and find him. And be quick about it."

The policeman set the receiver down sharply before he hurried off to do his superior's bidding. The officer considered the implications of the woman's removal from the precinct. By the time he heard the faint rap of approaching footsteps in the earpiece, he was ready.

"Brandt speaking, sir."

"This is Hauptsturmführer Bremer from the Reich Main Security Office. I was informed that you have a Jewess at the precinct, only to be told that the Kripo have taken her into their custody and removed her from her cell. Well?"

"That's true, sir. Yes."

"A simple yes would have sufficed, Brandt."

"Yes, sir."

"I have orders to take her for questioning by the Gestapo. I need to know where she is."

"I think I should check with my superior first, sir."

"Your superior being Inspector Schenke, correct?"

"Yes, sir."

"I outrank Schenke and I am giving you a direct order. You will tell me where Frankel was taken at once. Otherwise it will be you I take in for questioning by the Gestapo, for obstructing us in our duties. Clear?"

"Yes, sir. The Jewess is an eyewitness in a murder case, sir. She was due to be released from protective custody earlier today, but the inspector decided it would not be safe to let her return home. He took her somewhere he said would be safer for her."

"Where exactly?"

There was a pause before Brandt responded. "I should call the inspector, sir. Or it might be better if you contacted him yourself."

"I am not going to waste precious hours tracking down your inspector. What I can do is report you for failing to cooperate with the Gestapo and for refusing to obey the orders of a superior. And that will not go well for you, Brandt, you can be certain of that. Now, let's not waste any more time, nor test my patience any further. What happened to Frankel? Where is she?"

"Sir, I don't think it is proper for me to tell you where she is. You should speak to the inspector. He's the one who—"

"Shut up, Brandt!" the officer shouted. "Shut up! Do you know what you are? You are an insignificant little shit stain! Do you have any idea who you are dealing with? No, you do not! I have had better men than you arrested and beaten to a pulp for causing me less inconvenience. Do you hear me?"

"Y-yes, sir."

"Then do as I damn well order and don't give me any more of your bullshit if you want to keep enough teeth to eat your Christmas dinner. Do I make myself clear?"

"Yes, sir. The inspector had me drive himself and the witness to a house in Tegel. He went inside for a moment and then came out to fetch Frankel. When he returned to the car he ordered me to drop him at his apartment and return to the precinct. That's all I know, sir," Brandt concluded in a plaintive tone.

"And what was this address?"

"I can't recall, sir. Honestly. It was a large house with a gated drive. There was a large H design on the gates."

"What street was it on? You must recall the address, man!"

"Yes, sir. It was . . . Tirpitzstrasse, in Tegel. Yes, I'm sure of it."

The officer made a note. "Good. That will have to do, Brandt. Since it's too late to do anything about the matter now, I will contact your inspector in the morning to make the necessary arrangements. In future, I suggest that you answer your superiors more directly when they ask you a question. Otherwise I doubt you will proceed any further in your career. If you proceed at all."

"Should I call the inspector to let him know, sir?"

He took a deep breath to control his disquiet and forced himself to continue in the same intolerant tone. "You must take some perverse pleasure in making your superiors angry, Brandt. I would imagine that the inspector will feel the same way about being disturbed late at night as I do about having you waste my time."

He hung up, satisfied with his performance. He would have made a fine actor. Not as handsome as some, but every bit as convincing as Emil Jannings. Time was short. He needed to act on the information now. Brandt might wait until the next morning to tell Schenke about the telephone call. But there was a possibility that after some agonized reflection he'd call the inspector's apartment to relate what had happened.

The officer went to the small cupboard where his coat and peaked cap hung. They concealed a small shelf containing a locked briefcase. He pulled on a cardigan before putting on the coat, then took his pistol from the holster and tucked it in his side pocket. He looked at the briefcase, wondering if he should take the wig. There was no need for it tonight. Not for what he had in mind. He closed the cupboard door and left the office.

Signing out one of the pool cars, he drove out of the underground car park and emerged onto the street. It had been cleared after the most recent fall of snow and he was able to accelerate smoothly as he headed west towards Tegel. His plan was simple. He would enter the house described by Brandt, find the Frankel woman, and shoot her dead where she lay in bed.

Chapter Twenty-seven

24 December

He reached Tirpitzstrasse just after midnight and drove on to park in the next street. Stepping out, he pulled on his cap and raised his collar, both to keep him warm and to conceal his features, before making his way down the tree-lined avenue that Brandt had identified. There were many grand houses with drives, their gates adorned with eagles, bears and coats of arms, but only one with the letter H worked into the design.

He stood close to one of the pillars and peered at a plaque with the embossed letters faintly visible in the loom of snow: Harstein. It was a familiar name, and a moment later he recalled the link to Horst Schenke. He leaned round to stare through the iron rods of the gate towards the house. The driveway curved gently towards the garden at the front, where the water from a small fountain had frozen in a smooth mass that gleamed dully in the starlight. Beyond lay the house itself, a dark shape that rose up against the night sky. The only light that showed from within was a glimmer around the shutters of a downstairs room and a faint glow from two of the rooms upstairs.

As he watched, one of the upstairs lights was extinguished. There were no cars in the driveway; only a thin line of footsteps in the snow leading from the gate to the entrance portico. There would not be many people inside, he calculated, and fewer still awake at this hour. Though some clearly were. Ruth Frankel was likely to be staying in either the servants' quarters or one of the guest rooms, depending on the status accorded to her by her hosts. He hoped it was the latter, since household servants often shared a room.

He glanced round and reassured himself that he was alone and unobserved, then approached the large iron latch that secured the gate and raised it slowly so there was only the faintest rasp of metal on metal. Easing the gate open to squeeze through, he closed it behind him with the latch resting against the outside of the bracket to ensure that he could make a swift exit if he needed to. He proceeded up the driveway using the existing tracks in case the Kripo duty officer alerted his superior and the police came to the house while he was inside.

He wondered if he should knock boldly on the front door and try and pass himself off as part of the investigation. But there was a danger that his bluff might be called, giving the woman time to hide or escape. It would be better if he could find a way into the house without those inside being aware. As he approached the portico, he saw that a path had been cleared around the side of the house, perhaps for deliveries of groceries or coal. He crossed the snow to where the path ran along the base of the front wall and under the window where a sliver of light shone from beneath the shutter.

He stopped to peer through the narrow gap between the bottom of the shutter and the worn, flaking window frame. Beyond lay a large room with bookcases. The glow of a fire came from a grate with chairs either side. Facing the window was an elderly man reading a book. Opposite him sat a woman, her gray hair arranged in a bun. As the intruder watched, she rose stiffly and walked to the old man, kissing him on the forehead. There was a brief exchange of words before she left the room and closed the door. The old man returned his attention to the book.

The intruder eased himself up and continued following the path to the corner of the building and around the side. Mounds of snow-laden shrubs and bushes spread out across the garden, with a tall brick wall marking the boundary between this villa and the next. Along the side of the house there was another door; he tested the handle gently, but it was locked. Moving to the rear, he found the metal door of the coal chute and considered using it to gain entry. But being covered in coal dust after he left the scene might lead to questions being asked. He continued searching until he found a low window close to the ground a short distance beyond. There were two panes in a frame large enough for him to wriggle through. It was likely that the window provided light for the cellar.

Taking out his pistol, he spread his spare hand on the lower pane of glass to absorb some of the shock of the impact, then held the barrel and aimed the butt. He struck with a sudden, savage blow and there was a sharp crash and the tinkle of glass falling to the floor inside. Pocketing the weapon, he reached a hand inside, taking care not to snag his glove on the jagged edges, and felt for the catch. He slid it open and pushed the window up, then paused, listening for any sound of movement or voices that indicated that the alarm had been raised, but the house remained still and silent. He eased himself through the opening feetfirst. The window frame was at head height, so he dropped a short distance, landing softly with his knees bent.

His heart was beating quickly and his senses were strained to their limit. It was not fear that he felt, but excitement and exultation, the same sensations he experienced when stalking his victims. He would put an end to the prey that had eluded and wounded him. The physical pain she had caused him was one thing. The injury to his pride at being defied by a weaker woman, and a Jew at that, was intolerable.

He reached into his pocket and took out a small torch, thumbing the switch. A narrow beam lanced out and he swept it around the cellar. The low ceiling curved above a long space that seemed to run from the back to the front of the house. The walls were lined with wine racks, mostly empty, and shelves. There were a number of travel chests and large boxes filled with toys and old clothes. Halfway along the wall a flight of steps led up to the ground floor. He tested his weight on the first riser. It creaked, but not enough to worry him, and he climbed the steps towards the door at the top.

The round brass knob moved easily and he drew the door towards him, covering the narrow beam of the flashlight with his other hand. He was looking out onto a corridor, off the entrance hall. A lamp with a weak bulb provided enough light to see by, so he turned the torch off and put it back in his pocket. Taking out his Walther pistol, he stepped into the corridor, ears straining for any sound. All was still.

Then he heard a muffled cough and turned quickly. There was a faint glow coming from the bottom of a door along the corridor. He realized it was the same room he had peered into from outside. Checking that the safety catch on the Walther was locked, he took a deep, calming breath and approached the door. He grasped the handle, twisted it and pushed. In front of him he could see the chair by the fire where the elderly man had been sitting, but now it was empty.

"What the devil?"

He spun towards the voice and saw a man in a thick cardigan in the act of slotting a book onto a shelf. At almost the same time, Harstein turned towards him, lifting the book to throw it as he opened his mouth to raise the alarm.

"Don't!" the intruder hissed, pointing the pistol at the

other man's chest. "Make a sound and you'll die, followed by everyone else in the house."

The old man froze, lowered the book and placed it on the edge of a shelf. "Who the hell are you?"

"Quiet. Go and sit down in your chair." The intruder wagged his pistol towards the fireplace. "Do it."

Harstein did as he was ordered.

"That's better. Now cross your legs and place your hands on the arms of the chair."

"Why are you—"

"Shut your mouth and do exactly as I say if you don't want to die."

The intruder approached the chair, tightened his grip on the pistol and smashed the butt hard against Harstein's head. It jerked to one side and the old man let out a groan. He took off his right glove and thrust it into Harstein's mouth. The latter's eyes opened wide and he raised his hands to try to remove the improvised gag.

"Leave it." The intruder moved round in front of the chair and raised the pistol threateningly. "Or else."

The old man lowered his hands and placed them back on the armrests.

"Now listen to me. I am going to ask you some questions. If you want to live, you will answer me truthfully. If you lie, trust me, I'll know, and I will kill you. If you try to remove the glove, I will kill you. If you try to raise the alarm in any way, I'll kill you. Nod if you understand."

Harstein nodded slowly, his eyes fixed on the intruder. A trickle of blood rolled down his cheek.

"I need you to understand that I am not bluffing. So . . ." The intruder swapped the pistol to his left hand and slammed a powerful punch into the old man's guts. He lurched in the chair and hunched forward groaning.

The intruder raised a finger to his lips. "Shh. Not so much noise."

Another blow to the guts, then a powerful hook to the cheek and another to the jaw before he took his glove out of Harstein's mouth. "So, questions."

The quiet of the room was broken by the faint hiss from a log in the grate and the labored breathing of the old man.

"How many others in the house? Besides you and your wife."

Harstein answered softly. "Two. My housekeeper and his wife."

"What did I say about lying? I'll give you another chance. Let's try again. How many?"

"Three."

"Who's the third one?"

"A woman. A guest."

"A guest?" he repeated. "Since when have good Germans admitted dirty, stinking Jews into their homes as guests?"

He saw the alarm in the old man's eyes.

"I know about her. Now tell me where she is. I'm only interested in her. Tell me and I'll let you and the others live."

"You give me your word you'll not harm us? Or the girl."

"You ask for my word?" The intruder shook his head incredulously. "I haven't time to waste on questions of honor. Tell me where I can find her."

The old man hesitated for a beat and then sighed in despair. "Upstairs. Take the corridor to the right. Second door on the left."

"Thank you."

"What will you do with her?"

"What I should have done the first time I encountered her. Now stay where you are and don't make a sound."

The intruder moved towards the fireplace and picked up a heavy iron poker. He stood behind Harstein's chair and stared down at the old man's head.

"Do you really put so much faith in what someone says?"

"A man is only as good as his word," Harstein responded calmly.

"By now you must understand how this ends. I am afraid I cannot allow you to give the police any details about me. So . . ."

He raised the poker to strike. At the last instant, the old man made to turn, but he never saw the blow that killed him. The impact shattered his skull, and blood, fragments of bone and brain matter exploded into the air. The second blow caved the skull in. The intruder let the poker drop to the carpet. He stared at the spasming body for a few seconds before it slumped into stillness, then turned away.

Replacing the glove on his hand, he picked up the poker before moving towards the door. "It's time to settle the account, you Jewish bitch," he growled. "But there are some other members of the household I need to attend to before we spend a little time together . . ."

Chapter Twenty-eight

Tired as she was, sleep did not come easily to Ruth Frankel. She was in a strange house, whose owners had been told a lie about her racial identity. Even if they had accepted Inspector Schenke's explanation, they must surely harbor suspicions about her. Despite the need for sleep, she had left a small table lamp switched on in case she had to stir quickly and dress. Her clothes hung over the back of a chair at the small desk against the far wall, and she lay in her slip under the thick quilt. Her gaze shifted from the molded ceiling rose and moved over the details of the room. The framed images of racing cars, the small wardrobe, the bookcase filled with bound volumes of motor-racing magazines . . .

Her thoughts switched back to the count and his wife. They had treated her kindly, if not warmly, though that was to be expected. She was not a family friend, nor an invited guest. Merely a stranger being taken in as a favor to Inspector Schenke. As such, she determined that she would try and be unobtrusive. They had asked her to remain in her room as much as possible to avoid the two servants, who would be curious about the visitor turning up after dark. Harstein had decided to tell them that she was the daughter of a distant relative.

They seemed like an amiable couple, thought Ruth. Not haughty and cold like some of the Junker families she had encountered back in the days when Jews were tolerated by German society. Her father had been a respected and successful partner in a legal firm and had mixed with the wealthiest and most powerful people in Berlin. All that had changed when the party's rapid rise had encouraged the forward-looking to choose sides, and many of those had cut their ties with their Jewish friends and thrown in their lot with the Nazis.

Once the party had seized power, the full weight of the state had been brought to bear against Jewish interests. Her father had been forced to sell his share in the business for a pittance, before being forbidden to take on any Aryan clients. The family had had to give up their fine apartment on Wilhelmstrasse and move into smaller accommodation. They had begun the process of applying for permission to leave the country, but by then the party had decided to treat the Jews as hostages and only allowed them to quit Germany after ransoming nearly everything they possessed. The last twist of the knife was denying Ruth permission to leave until her parents paid the requisite fee after they had reached America.

The Nazis were little better than a bunch of gangsters, she concluded bitterly. They used threats and violence to keep people in line and swaggered about as bullies did when they knew their victims were so cowed they dared not raise a word in protest. Their dark and fearful influence had penetrated the soul of Germany so deeply that she could see no prospect of change or salvation. Even hope itself seemed to wither in the poisonous atmosphere of Berlin. What hope was there to be had when the German army had crushed Poland within a matter of weeks and might do the same to France and her British ally?

In such a world, to be a Jew was little better than to be one of the rats that the party liked to depict in their anti-Semitic propaganda films, scurrying for shelter as grim-faced fanatics with clubs rained down deadly blows. She shuddered at the thought and shrank down a little further beneath the quilt.

A faint crack and tinkle of glass sounded from somewhere outside the window. Or had the sound come from inside the house? She felt a cold tremor ripple down her spine and lay still, breathing lightly as she listened. There was no further sound. Perhaps it was one of the servants. A dropped tray, broken glasses, or maybe a bowl. There were myriad possibilities, but none of them put her mind at rest.

She sat up on the edge of the bed. She was not sure what to do. Much as she wanted to find out what had caused the noise, it would look unseemly, not to mention suspicious, to be found wandering around the house by her hosts or one of the staff. The prospect of being forced to leave this comfortable haven filled her with dread.

"Damn . . ." she muttered, and snapped on the main bedside light before she began to dress quickly in the cold air. She put on her coat to add another layer of warmth, then picked up her shoes and tiptoed to the door. There was a squeal of protest from the hinges, and she gritted her teeth anxiously and paused before easing the door open a fraction of a centimeter at a time until there was enough space to slip out of the room.

It was dark in the corridor, with only the faintest glimmer of light cast through the door behind her and from somewhere at the bottom of the stairs. She reached the staircase and peered down into the hall, then froze as she saw the figure of a man emerging from the gloom. There was something about the way he moved that caused her to draw back. He paused at the bottom of the stairs and looked around, and she saw the dull shape of the pistol in one hand, the poker in the other. She could make out the cap on his head, the runes on his collar and the pattern of the epaulets on the shoulders of his coat.

Her heart began to beat quickly and she hardly dared breathe as he moved towards the entrance to the servants' quarters to one side of the stairs and passed out of sight.

She gasped, her mind racing. There was an intruder in the house wearing an SS uniform. Despite that, she was certain he could not be here on legitimate business at such a late hour. Moreover, the SS and the Gestapo were inclined to make their raids at dawn and with a loud hammering at the door. This man was something else. Something more sinister.

What should she do? The others had to be warned. Her hosts had placed her in the family wing, which meant that their own bedroom must be close by. She approached the first door and opened it. The bed was empty. Crossing to the other side of the corridor, she tried another room. There was a large four-poster with a canopy, the kind of furniture that would have seemed more at home in a castle rather than this suburban villa. A soft, guttural snoring came from the bed.

Ruth saw that the countess was sleeping alone. She pulled the quilt back and shook the old woman's shoulder.

"Frau Harstein, wake up," she whispered urgently. "Wake up!"

The countess snorted and tried to shake off the hand on her shoulder.

"Wake up, I said." Ruth shook her again. Harder this time.

"What . . . what is it?" the countess mumbled. Her body

suddenly stiffened as she saw the dark shape looming over her, and she shuffled up in the bed. "Who is that? What is the meaning of this?" she demanded.

"Shh! It's me, Johanna."

"What on earth are you doing in my room?"

"Quiet. There's a man in the house. He's got a gun."

"A man? A robber?"

"I don't know. He's in uniform."

"Where's my husband?"

"I didn't see him. I didn't hear him either. I think we're in danger. We have to hide, or get out of here at once." Ruth tugged at her hand. "Please get up."

The other woman climbed stiffly out of the bed and put on her slippers before wrapping a shawl over her quilted nightdress.

"Is there a telephone upstairs?" Ruth asked. "We need help."

"Yes . . . yes, there is one in an alcove by the guest wing."

"I'll go."

"No, wait. It's not easy to find. I'd better go." The countess moved towards the door, then stopped. "You need to hide, girl."

"Hide? Where?"

"Go to the end of the corridor; there's a small hatch over a dumbwaiter. You can use that to get down to the kitchen. Wait there. If there's any sign of trouble, use the kitchen door to get outside and go for help." She stepped back and took Ruth's hand. "Don't stop for anything. Understand?"

Hurrying along the corridor, Ruth found the hatch and slid it to one side to reveal a dark space. She reached in and felt around with her hands. There was enough room for her to huddle inside. She climbed in, closed the hatch and groped around until she found the thick cables that controlled the ascent and descent of the dumbwaiter. She pulled on one and the small cage lurched up a fraction. Switching to the other, she eased it up and the dumbwaiter began to sink towards the kitchen.

At the top of the staircase, the countess glanced down into the hall. There was the sound of a brief commotion. A voice began to cry out in surprise and was abruptly silenced. She flinched back from the polished wooden rail and turned to hurry to the end of the corridor leading to the guest wing. A short distance along was the telephone provided for the family's guests. She picked up the receiver with trembling fingers and dialed the number for the operator. Her heart was beating wildly as she heard the line begin to purr at the exchange. There was a torturously long delay, and then a click.

"Tegel exchange. How can I help you?"

"I need the police." The old woman spoke quickly. "There's an intruder in our house."

"Police? Which precinct, madam?"

"Tegel. Get me the police there. Hurry."

"Connecting now."

There were more clicks from the receiver before it began to purr again. She heard a creak from the staircase and glanced round. In the glow of the light from the hall, she saw a dull shadow moving up the wall at the top of the stairs.

"Dear God," she whispered as she clutched the receiver to her ear, willing someone to speak. The shadow loomed larger, and she saw the peaked cap and shoulders of a uniformed man.

"Tegel precinct," a voice said clearly in her ear.

"There's an intruder in my house," she blurted out. "Thirty-four Tirpitzstrasse. Get someone over here at once." She called out the first name that came into her mind. "Call Inspector Schenke. For pity's sake!"

"Just a moment . . . Now what was the address again?"

The shadow had disappeared as the man turned to climb

the last steps to the landing, and now he loomed up, silhouetted against the dim light behind him. In one hand he held a pistol, in the other an iron bar—a fire poker, she realized. She could see something dark dripping from the end of it.

"Your address, madam? Was that thirty-four Tirpitzstrasse?"

She tried to speak, but her throat seemed constricted and she could only manage a gasp as the figure came towards her and spoke in a low voice.

"Put that down. Now."

She didn't respond, so he pocketed the pistol and took the receiver from her, holding the poker to warn her as he spoke calmly.

"Is that the police? . . . No, that won't be necessary. I'm afraid my wife is a woman with an overactive imagination. There's no trouble here . . . No, I assure you all's well. There's no need to . . . Oh, very well. But you'll be wasting your time."

He replaced the receiver and stood over the old lady. "That wasn't very helpful of you, was it? Now tell me, where's the girl? Still in her room?"

"Girl?" She shook her head. "What girl?"

"If that's how you want to play it, then I'll find her by myself."

He swung the poker in a powerful arc before it smashed into the side of the countess's head. She collapsed amid the loose folds of her nightdress, blood rapidly pooling from the matted tangle of gray hair. He spared her a glance before stepping around her body to begin searching the guest rooms.

As the dumbwaiter bumped gently against the buffer bars in the kitchen, Ruth climbed out and put her shoes on. She needed to be ready to run at a moment's notice. The kitchen was brightly illuminated by two overhead lights, and she glanced round at the counters and the twin cookers, with pans hanging from hooks on a rail above. The shelves of the large dressers on the opposite wall were filled with plates and bowls and racks of cutlery. On the far side of the large wooden table that dominated the center of the room was a steel sink and draining board with a pile of dirty plates and pots to one side and a handful of others on the drying rack. The tap was running and steam curled up from the sink. She noticed that the outflow was blocked by vegetable matter. The sink was overflowing, water running down the side and onto the tiled floor. Already it was flooding around the far end of the table. Crimson tendrils curled out within the slowly expanding puddle.

She swallowed and walked round the table. The family's housekeeper was lying on his front, arms splayed out. The back of his head had been crushed and blood oozed into the red halo surrounding his upper body. His sleeves were rolled up, and she realized that he must have been washing dishes when his attacker struck him. Close by she saw the body of a woman in an apron curled on her side amid shattered shards of crockery. The handle of a carving knife stuck out from under her chin and the point had pierced the top of her skull.

She glanced around, cold with fear, recalling that the countess had gone to call the police. Who else had the intruder butchered? Who was still left alive? There was no other sound apart from the running water. Harstein must have been downstairs, in which case he must be dead too. Ruth feared that it was only her left now, and she had to fight off a wave of paralyzing fear at the prospect. She could not face the killer. Even if she armed herself with a cleaver, he had a gun. She must get out of the house and escape.

Rushing to the kitchen door, she grasped the handle and turned it, but the door was locked. She rattled it frantically, then stopped dead, realizing that she was making too much noise.

"The key," she hissed through gritted teeth, and turned back to the housekeeper's body. Leaning down, she braced herself and searched his pockets. There was nothing in the trousers, and she patted at his waistcoat, feeling for something solid in the material. She stood up holding a metal ring with several keys hanging from it and returned to the door. The first two did not fit and the third seemed to go in freely but then refused to turn. As she fumbled for the next one, she heard footsteps passing through the room overhead.

"Come on, come on," she muttered as she thrust the key clumsily at the lock. This time it turned easily and the weathered door unlocked with a soft click. She withdrew the key and tugged the door open. It came towards her swiftly on well-oiled hinges and hit her hard on the chest. She reeled backwards, struggling to keep her balance, and her arm flailed and caught a jar of preserved fruit on a shelf. It toppled, and she could only watch helplessly as it plummeted towards the tiles and exploded deafeningly in shards of glass and syrupy juice. Upstairs, the footsteps stopped, then pounded back across the ceiling. She recovered her balance and stepped out into the freezing darkness, hauling the door back into its frame behind her and locking it.

There was a small flight of steps with a covered fuel bin for the cookers to the side. Inside, bags of coal and empty sacks lay piled. A few paces from the bottom of the steps was a cleared pathway leading round the villa. She was tempted to run, but knew that she was unlikely to outpace her pursuer. The image of the dead man in the kitchen came back to her vividly. She was not going to die like that.

The handle behind her rattled and there was a dull thud against the inside of the door. She started in terror and hurried down the steps, keeping close to the edge, and then paced over the snow to the cleared path. At once she backed up, placing her feet in the tracks she had just left until she had returned to the stairs. Taking a wide stride, she edged round them into the fuel shelter and hunched beside the coal sacks, hurriedly covering herself with the empty bags until she could just see over the top of them.

An instant later, there was a splintering crash as the lock shattered and the door burst open. She heard labored breathing as the man rushed down the steps. She saw his back, bathed in the light from the kitchen, as he followed the tracks to the path and stopped. She could not see the pistol, but the poker was in his clenched fist as he looked one way along the path and then the other.

"Bitch . . ." he growled. "Fucking bitch."

There was no mistaking that voice and she felt a bolt of icy terror pierce her body as she sat motionless, not even breathing as she stared out from under the sacks. He cupped a hand to his mouth. "I'll find you! You hear? You can't hide from me, wherever you run. Don't think the police can protect you. No one can! And when I find you, I will fuck you every possible way before I cut you to pieces. You hear me, you Jewish bitch? I will find you!" He hurled the poker into the garden and turned to stride away along the path leading towards the front of the house and the street beyond.

Ruth waited until he was out of sight, and hesitated a moment longer, steeling her nerves. Then, sweeping the empty sacks aside, she emerged from the fuel bin and tiptoed down the steps and along the path. At the corner of the building, she paused and peered round. He was twenty or so paces ahead of her, heading towards the gate. Once he had disappeared through it, she emerged from cover and ran down the driveway, pulling the gate open and sticking her head out. He was making his way along the sidewalk towards the end of the street. She followed cautiously, doing her best to keep close to the trees lining the street so that she could duck out of sight if he looked back. But he made no effort to do so as he increased his pace, crossed the road and turned right at the intersection.

Ruth continued to follow him at a safe distance as he made his way down the next street and approached a parked car. He stopped by the driver's door, swung it open and climbed in. She moved closer as she heard the engine turn over. The car failed to start, and there was a pause before he tried the ignition again. She was no more than ten paces away and could see some stenciled lettering on the rear of the vehicle. It was hard to make it out, so she crept closer, crouching behind the trunk of an elm tree. The starter motor whined, and this time the engine started and he revved hard to keep it running. There was a dull clunk as he found first gear. A moment later, the car edged forward with a soft crack of breaking ice. She glanced round the tree in time to make out the lettering before the vehicle roared off into the darkness: *Abwehr 24.*

Chapter Twenty-nine

Schenke was woken by the phone ringing in the hall. He made to get up and answer it, and discovered Karin's arm lying across the side of his chest, forearm folded up towards his shoulder. He felt the warm press of her skin against his back and could not help smiling at the evening he had enjoyed before his concerns robbed him of an easy sleep. The phone continued to ring, and he eased her arm up and moved away from her as she mumbled in protest. He shuffled towards the phone and lifted the receiver. The clock on the wall marked the time at just after three in the morning. He felt a sense of foreboding as he cleared his throat.

"Schenke."

"Inspector Horst Schenke?"

"Who's this?"

"Hauptmann Rauch, Tegel precinct. I understand that you are an acquaintance of Count Harstein, who lives at thirty-four Tirpitzstrasse."

"He's a family friend, sir . . ." An icy tingle gripped the back of Schenke's neck. "What's happened?"

"There's been an incident at the count's home. Your name was mentioned."

"What kind of incident?"

"A break-in. I regret to inform you that the count, his wife, and their two servants have been killed."

Schenke frowned. He had heard the words, but they could not possibly be true. And yet who would call him with such news if it wasn't true? He could not reconcile Rauch's statement with the import of his message, nor find any words of his own in response. There was silence from the receiver before the tinny voice spoke again.

"Inspector? Are you there?"

"Y-yes. Yes, of course. Killed?"

"I'm afraid so."

"Murdered?"

"Yes."

Then an obvious omission occurred to him. "The Harsteins and their servants, you say?"

"That's right. I'm sorry for your loss."

"No one else? You've found no other bodies?"

"No . . . Why do you ask?"

Schenke thought quickly, deciding what might be wisest to say to the other policeman at this stage. "There was a house-guest staying with them. A young woman."

"We found no one else. The house was searched from attic to cellar."

"I see. How were you alerted to the break-in?"

"The countess called the precinct to say there was an intruder in the house. She asked for you before she was interrupted by a man purporting to be her husband, but the police officer taking the call was suspicious. A while later there was another call. A woman. Could be the one you mentioned. She didn't leave her name, but confirmed the address and said the police should come at once. My man raised the alarm. We were on the premises no more than fifteen minutes later. The duty doctor was called in as soon as we found the bodies. Nothing could be done for any of them."

"And there was no sign of the woman?"

"No. Do you think we should be regarding this woman as a suspect?"

Schenke considered this for a moment and decided against it. There was no possible reason that he could think of for Ruth to turn on the Harsteins and the servants. "Not if there is proof the house was broken into. In fact, I am concerned for her safety. She was likely to have been the second caller, and since the Harsteins are dead, she is in danger."

"We'll look into that. Do you have her name? And a description?"

Schenke did not answer. An image of his slain friends filled his head and he felt a wave of nausea clench his guts painfully. He forced himself to breathe deeply and think professionally. It was vital that he did so in order to deal with the crime, but also to distract him from the swelling storm of grief and rage that was brewing in his heart.

"I'll tell you what I can when I get there."

"Inspector, the matter is in our hands. You can be sure we will deal with it. It might be best for you not to come while the crime scene is fresh, as it were."

Schenke could tell that Rauch was trying to spare him the details.

"I am a Kripo inspector. There is nothing I have not seen in my time in the service. Besides, this touches on a case I am investigating. It is vital that we work together on it."

"As you wish, Schenke. But I warn you, it is not a pretty sight."

"I understand." Before Rauch could dissuade him any further, he added, "I'll be there as soon as I can."

He hung up and strode back to the bedroom, pulling his clothes on as quickly as he could. On the dresser was the belt and holster containing his Walther P38. He fastened the belt around his waist and then drew the weapon and inserted a clip. "Darling, what's happening?" asked Karin.

He saw that she was sitting up, the quilt drawn to her neck.

He wanted to tell her, but did not trust himself to keep control of his feelings if he did so, and at that moment he needed to be as calm and collected as he could be under the circumstances.

"There's been a development in the case."

"What kind of development?" she asked, then saw the look of anguish that crossed his face. "Horst, what's happened? Tell me."

"Later. I have to go." He made for the door, then turned back and kissed her forehead. "Stay here. Don't answer the door to anyone but me. Clear?"

"Yes, but why—"

"Please do as I say, my love. Please."

She tried to speak but he was already moving towards the door and there was only time to call out, "Be careful."

Schenke broke into an uneven jog as he made for the Pankow precinct, where his section was normally based. He forced himself on even though his injured knee began to ache almost at once and the pain surged through the joint. By the time he reached the precinct, beads of sweat were running down his temples and he had to recover his breath before signing out one of the pool cars. As he drove from the courtyard and onto the street at speed, the rear of the car slid out across the black ice, and it was only a frantic countersteer, an instinctive maneuver from his racing days, that saved him from losing control.

He drove as fast as he dared along the dark, deserted streets of the capital, straining his eyes to pick out the way ahead in the dim light cast by the masked headlights. Alone in the vehicle, he was tempted to give vent to his feelings, and forced himself to concentrate on his driving, just as he had back on the racetrack, when there had been no room for distraction in the pursuit of victory and survival. The roar of the straining engine, the lightning-quick shift of gears and the application of the right amount of brake as he steered through bends took him back to a long-suppressed memory of sitting in the cockpit of his sleek Mercedes Silver Arrow.

He reached the house on Tirpitzstrasse shortly before four o'clock. There were several cars, a police truck and dark figures outside in the street as he drew up. He quickly climbed out of the car and strode to the open gate. He could see that all the rooms in the house were illuminated, despite the blackout. And even though the shutters were still in place, light spilled out of the half-open front door and other points around the house as policemen searched the grounds with torches.

"Halt!" one of the uniformed men at the gate commanded as he saw Schenke approaching. "Who are you? What is your business here?"

Schenke reached inside his coat for his badge. "Inspector Schenke. Kripo."

The policeman flicked his torch on and shone it on the badge, then into Schenke's face.

"Turn that away from me, you fool!" the inspector snapped, squinting at the bright light. "Who's in charge here? Hauptmann Rauch?"

"Yes, sir. He's inside."

Schenke advanced up the driveway and climbed the familiar steps into the house. There were several men in uniform standing in the hall. He saw the epaulets on an officer in a long overcoat and approached him.

"Hauptmann Rauch?"

The officer, tall and thin, broke off from the conversation he was having with one of his men and turned with a frosty look at being interrupted.

"Who are you?"

"Inspector Schenke, sir."

The other man's expression changed abruptly to one of strained sympathy. "Look here, Schenke, there's no need for you to have come. We have this in hand and you can be sure we'll do our best to catch the bastard responsible. I'm sorry for your loss of your friends," he added in a brusque manner that made Schenke want to punch him. But he forced himself to keep a professional veneer as he responded.

"Since I'm here, sir, I might as well do what I can to assist the investigation."

"That's not necessary. We have our own Kripo section on the way now. They can manage." Rauch patted him on the shoulder. "You should go home and I'll call you once we have a clearer picture of what happened. I'm sure this has come as a shock to you. Best you get over that first, eh?"

The urge to hit his superior was stronger than ever, but Schenke spoke again in a calm, deliberate tone.

"As I said on the telephone, I believe this case is connected to mine, sir. I am here in an official capacity, as well as a personal one. There'll be time to grieve later. I have to find out what happened here. Unless you have found her, the woman I mentioned has to be located. I believe she might be in grave danger and there isn't time to waste."

Rauch regarded him. "You're a cold one, Inspector. I would think any normal man would be too shocked by such a loss to even contemplate carrying on as if nothing had happened."

"Sir, I am very aware of what has happened. I just don't want there to be any more loss of life because I did not act in a timely fashion. Has there been any sign of the woman?"

"Nothing more than I mentioned earlier."

"I see." Schenke paused before he made his request. "Can I see the bodies, sir?"

Rauch shook his head. "This is a crime scene. On my patch. And you are connected to the victims. There is a clear conflict of interest, so I cannot permit it."

"But sir—"

"No, Schenke. That's my decision. This is my precinct. I have authority here. I think it's time you left."

Schenke felt for Müller's letter of authority and realized he had left it in his jacket in the apartment. "I'll take this up with my superiors, sir."

"You do that. In the meantime, my decision stands." Rauch took a step forward and placed his hands on his hips, challenging Schenke to defy him. The inspector could see there was nothing he could say to change the other man's mind, so he tried a different tack.

"Very well, but will you at least give me some information that may help with my case? A few questions, sir."

"All right. What do you want to know?"

"How were they killed?"

"Why do you ask?"

"It concerns the methods used by the man I'm after, sir."

"They were bludgeoned. Blows to the head."

"All of them?"

"Three of them. One was stabbed."

In his mind's eye Schenke saw Gerda's body laid out in front of the medical examiner. He recalled the misshapen line of her skull and the shattered mass of congealed blood, brains and bone that indicated the brutality of the murderer. It was clear that the way he had chosen to kill his victims was not merely opportune, but deliberate. He took pleasure in breaking open their heads. Schenke was certain the same man had killed them all. And Ruth was still in danger.

That led to another matter. The killer must have known that Ruth, the only witness to have a clear view of his face, had been taken to the Harsteins' house. But how? Had he followed them from the precinct? It was possible, but how could he have known who was in the car when it left Schöneberg? Searching his memory of the evening before, Schenke recalled that the streets had been empty. He could not remember any vehicle tailing them. If they had not been followed, then the only other explanation was far more frightening. The man he was looking for was either in his section, or being fed information from someone close to the team.

The obvious candidate had to be Brandt. He, after all, had driven them to the house. Unless it was someone known to Ruth. Had she made contact with anyone since she arrived there? he wondered. It seemed unlikely, and he realized he was trying to avoid the possibility that it could be one of his team that was responsible for the night's murders. He had worked alongside most of them for years, carefully vetting anyone who applied to join the section. Even Brandt, new as he was, did not seem capable of the kind of treachery that Schenke now envisaged. But then again, in this world you never really knew anyone else. There was always a mask, something hidden from others. And if not Brandt, then who else could have betrayed him?

"Is there anything more?" asked Rauch.

Schenke put aside his deliberations. "Sir?"

"Any further questions?"

"Not for the moment."

"Good. If there is anything, then call me at my precinct." Rauch shook his head. "It's a terrible business, Inspector. You have my sympathy. You can be sure we will do all we can to catch whoever is responsible."

"Thank you, sir." Schenke bowed his head in farewell and took a last look round the hall of the house that had once felt like a home to him, trying hard not to dwell on the memories of his time here. His heart ached and he could not bear it anymore. He turned and walked out of the house and down the driveway to the gate without looking back.

Passing the policeman on duty outside, he hurried towards his car, fearful that the emotions building up inside him would break before he was safely out of sight. He slipped into the driver's seat and closed the door quickly behind him, then folded forward, forearms braced across the steering wheel as he cradled his head and fought to control his grief.

A minute or two later, he sat up abruptly, adjusted his hat and turned the ignition. The engine coughed and purred into life and he pulled out into the middle of the street. His first thought was to return to his apartment and seek comfort in Karin's arms. But then he dismissed the idea. Such solace must wait. He had to get to Schöneberg, where he could think while he waited for the rest of his team to arrive for the day.

At the end of the street he turned right, towards the center of Berlin and Schöneberg beyond, and accelerated into the night, his face set in a determined expression. He had driven over a kilometer before he heard something stir in the rear of the car, and a moment later a hand grasped his shoulder.

Chapter Thirty

"Shit!" Schenke shouted, and instinctively pulled himself away from the hand. The car swerved, and he just managed to correct the steering and hit the brake pedal so that it skidded into a bank of snow at the side of the road, throwing him against the wheel while the person behind him was propelled forward into the passenger seat.

As the engine stalled and died, he thrust himself back and turned in his seat to grab their collar. With his other hand he wrenched out his Walther and jammed the barrel into the writhing body.

"Don't move, you bastard. Or I'll blow a hole right through your heart!"

He could feel the other person gasping for breath, but not resisting, and he released his grip and reached up to turn on the interior light. He saw that the dark coat was shabby and the person was slightly built and trembling.

"Don't shoot me," a woman's voice said.

He withdrew his gun and sat back in his seat in astonishment. "Ruth?"

She eased herself round, sweeping her hair out of her eyes, and stared anxiously at him.

"I could have killed you. What the hell were you doing in my car?" Schenke demanded.

"I didn't want to show myself until we were away from the police at the house."

Schenke returned the automatic to its holster. "What happened back there? Where were you when my friends were killed?"

"I'm sorry. There was nothing I could do to save them. I barely got away with my own life."

"Tell me what happened."

She recounted the events as fully as she could, to the point where she had noted the markings on the intruder's car.

"Abwehr 24?" Schenke repeated. "You're sure of it?"

"Yes."

"Then it's a car assigned to military intelligence. There should be a log entry for whoever used it last night." He smiled grimly. "If so, then we've got him. Did you get a good look at him? Enough to identify him as the same man who attacked you?"

"Yes. I think so."

"Think? That's not good enough. You have to be sure."

She nodded deliberately. "I'm certain it was him. Although there was something different about him . . ."

"He's probably tried to change his appearance. The question is, how did he know where to find you?"

Ruth shot him a suspicious look. "I was wondering the same thing."

"You think I had something to do with it?"

"I'd be a fool not to consider it. You took me to the house and told me I'd be safe there."

He swallowed his anger at the accusation. "I swear it was nothing to do with me. They were my friends. They were like family to me."

"I'm sorry." She looked away.

Schenke breathed deeply before he continued. "The killer must have discovered your identity from the morning newspapers."

"Even if he saw a paper, how did he know I was at your friends' house?"

"How indeed?" Schenke responded through clenched teeth. "It's possible that he's one of us, a policeman. We'll know the truth later, when the team come on duty. I'll drive there now. If you see him anywhere in the precinct, tell me at once."

"Trust me, I will."

Schenke stared at her. "I'm not sure how much I do trust you. Nor anyone else. Not at the moment." He thought of everything that had happened from the moment he had been assigned to investigate the murder of Gerda Korzeny. There was so much that he did not yet understand about the forces at work. He turned his attention back to Ruth.

"What happened after the killer drove off? What did you do then?"

"I waited a minute, maybe two, to make sure he wasn't coming back, then I returned to the house and called the police."

"And yet you didn't remain there until they arrived."

"How could I? See it from my point of view, Inspector. I'm the only person alive from a house with four bodies inside. How suspicious do you think that makes me look? And then there's the fact that I'm a Jew. The police tend not to look on us with a great deal of affection. How was I to know they wouldn't jump to conclusions and think I was the killer?"

She had a point, Schenke conceded. But then again, how could he be sure that she hadn't killed them herself for some reason? However unlikely, it was remotely possible. And to the first police to arrive at the house, such a scenario would look very possible indeed, given that they had no reason to tie the killings to those Schenke was investigating.

"So where did you go?"

"I left the house and hid behind some bushes farther up the street. I didn't know what else to do. There's a curfew for Jews. If I'd tried to find shelter and was picked up, I'd be in serious trouble. All I could think of was that you would be sure to come at some point. Then I'd turn myself in to you. When you arrived, I couldn't see if it was you at first. Until that policeman shone his torch in your face. I tried the car and found you'd left the door unlocked. I slipped inside while no one was looking and waited until you came back."

"Why didn't you let me know right away?"

"I told you. I wanted to be sure we were clear of the other police first."

Not for the first time, he felt a stab of sympathy for her plight, and some shame for being part of the apparatus that persecuted her kind. He noticed she was shaking so much her teeth had started to chatter. "You must be freezing. You've been out in the cold too long."

He restarted the engine and turned the heater to full, then took off his coat and handed it to her. "Cover yourself with that."

"What about you?"

"You need it more than I do for now. Let's get going."

They reached the Schöneberg precinct at quarter to five and parked the car in the yard before entering by the rear entrance and making their way through to the section's temporary office. To Schenke's surprise, Brandt was not the only officer at his desk. A short distance away, Liebwitz was reading through some documents. He lowered them, stood up and bowed his head as soon as he saw his superior.

"Sir, if I may speak with you?"

"In a moment, Liebwitz."

"But it's important."

"I'm sure it is, but there is something I have to deal with first. Turn the heater up so Frau Frankel can get warm. And make her something hot to drink."

Liebwitz glanced at the woman. "Inspector, Frau Frankel is a Jew. I am a member of the Gestapo. There are certain protocols that govern the relationship between Jews and Aryans."

Schenke was in no mood to waste time on confrontation. He was beginning to understand how Liebwitz's mind worked and how to deal with him. "Tell me, do the protocols cover the relationship between police officials and witnesses?"

"No, sir."

"Then I don't see what your difficulty is, given that Miss Frankel is a witness in an important murder case. It is in the interests of the police investigation that she is not permitted to die of hypothermia. Right?"

"Put like that, you make a good point, sir. I shall see to her needs. Then may I speak to you?"

"Once I have finished one other item of business."

"Very good, sir. Miss Frankel, if you would follow me, please?"

Ruth raised an eyebrow. The abrupt transition in the Gestapo man's manner had confused her. Understandably, thought Schenke. Liebwitz had that effect on everyone, until they got accustomed to him.

Brandt was reading a document, perhaps trying not to draw attention to himself. Schenke pulled up a chair and sat opposite him.

"How did the night duty go?"

The young man sat up as his inspector addressed him. "Fine, I guess, sir. I was about to go off duty."

Schenke pointed at the clock on the wall. "Not for an hour or so yet. Six o'clock is the time your duty shift ends."

"Yes, sir."

"Brandt, did anything of note happen last night? When you returned here after dropping me at my apartment. Anything you think you should bring to my attention?"

The probationer swallowed nervously. "There was a call from an official at the Reich Main Security Office, sir. Hauptsturmführer Bremer of the Gestapo."

"And what did he have to say?"

"He said that the Gestapo wanted to question our witness." Brandt nodded towards Ruth on the other side of the room. "He said he had orders to take her into their custody. I explained to him that she was no longer at the precinct."

Schenke felt a sickening sense of anticipation. "Did you tell him where she had been taken?"

Brandt flinched under his superior's stare. "I told him that he should speak to you if he wanted to know, sir."

"Quite right. And what then?"

"He ordered me to tell him. He threatened me . . . He said he'd have me taken in by the Gestapo if I wasted any more of his time."

Schenke exhaled bitterly. "Go on."

"I said that I had driven you and the Frankel woman to a house in Tegel, sir."

"Did you tell him the address?"

"I think so. Yes, sir."

Schenke leaned forward and rested his forehead in his hands. "Oh shit . . . Do you have any idea what you have done, you fool?"

"Bremer said it was too late for him to do anything during the night and he would call you first thing in the morning to take the matter up with you. That's how he left it, sir. I swear."

Schenke raised his head slightly. "Brandt, I'm convinced the man claiming to be Bremer is the man we are hunting. The same man who needed to eliminate our witness, and you led him right to her."

"But she's still safe, sir." Brandt glanced across the office. "There's no harm done."

"No harm?" Schenke's lips pressed together in a thin line and he barely restrained his rage. He kept his silence, not trusting himself to speak for a moment. "I placed my friends in danger when I asked them to take the witness in. It was a risk, I know. But now four people are dead, and our witness was lucky to escape with her life, all because your nerve failed you when you thought you were being threatened by the Gestapo."

The blood drained from the young man's face and he shook his head. "I . . . I didn't mean to—"

"It's too late for that. And there's no time to deal with you now. But just so you know, there is no place on my team for fools and cowards." He stood up and glared at the hapless probationer. "I suggest you do your best to stay out of my way in the meantime, if you know what's good for you. Clear?"

"Yes, sir."

He left Brandt to stew in his guilt and shame and joined the others sitting beside the stove, where Ruth was clutching a steaming mug.

"How are you feeling?"

"Warmer. And safer. But should I feel safer?"

"I hope so."

"That's not very reassuring, Inspector."

There was nothing he could say to assuage her concerns, and he turned to Liebwitz. "I haven't been entirely open with you, Scharführer. Müller ordered me to release Miss Frankel from custody last night. Instead, I took her to a friend's house. Yes, I know that there are rules against taking in Jews, but we've already established that she is a witness rather than a Jew as far as we are concerned."

"Yes, sir."

"I had hoped she would be safe there, but thanks to Brandt, the killer tracked her down. She managed to escape. Others were not so fortunate. However, Miss Frankel managed to identify the car the killer drove away from the scene. It belongs to the Abwehr. As soon as the others get here, we'll go to their headquarters, check the log and wait for our man to arrive. Failing that, we'll take him at his home."

"The Abwehr?" Liebwitz mused.

"What is it? Is this something to do with the matter you wanted to speak to me about?"

"Yes, sir. It concerns the party badge. I checked the partial number against the records held at party headquarters yesterday evening. I kept one of the secretaries back to provide a preliminary list of badge holders based on the assumption that we were only missing one digit. I told her to find the details and report to me at the precinct. Once that was done, I told her to begin work on another list based on missing two digits."

"I'll bet she loved you for that."

"I don't think so, sir. If anything, she didn't seem happy at the prospect of assisting me."

"I can't imagine why, with your irresistible charm. Anyway, what did you discover?"

"The numbers on the badge signify that it comes from a batch awarded in January 1935. I have the list of names associated with 8940 to 8949, sir."

"Good work."

"Sir, there's one name in particular that I think you should know about, given what I have read of the investigation documentation so far. I felt it was important that you should know as soon as you arrived. I've left a copy of my report on your desk."

"Why not just call me?"

"You have not given me your home telephone number, sir."

"Have you not slept, then?"

"No, sir. It seemed to me this line of inquiry was more important than sleep."

"And the name?"

"Dorner. His gold badge has the number 8941."

Schenke felt his residual tiredness vanish. "Oberst Dorner?"

"He was a hauptmann at the time the badge was awarded to him, in recognition of his services in helping to suppress the SA leadership."

Schenke recalled the action that had resulted in Dorner's award clearly. Hitler's faction, backed by the SS, had eliminated Ernst Röhm and his closest followers and taken over the organization he had led, leaving the Führer without any remaining challengers to his authority. It was likely that Dorner had earned the coveted gold party badge by commanding one of the death squads sent out to assassinate the SA's senior officers. Perhaps that was where he had first discovered an appetite for murder. The Kripo would discover the truth soon enough.

"We need to arrest him at once. I want you and Brandt to get over to Abwehr headquarters. Take your sidearms. You're to wait outside and keep the main entrance under observation while I gather Hauser and the others. If Dorner turns up, make no attempt to arrest him until I get there. If he is already inside the building and leaves before we arrive, follow him, but don't let him spot you."

"Yes, sir."

"I'll see that Miss Frankel is put under guard before I join you with Hauser and the others," said Schenke. "Oberst Dorner, we're coming for you."

Chapter Thirty-one

The car containing Liebwitz and Brandt was waiting a short distance from the main entrance of the Abwehr as Schenke pulled over on the opposite side of the entrance and parked. The two sentries at the double doors stiffened to attention as an officer stepped up from the sidewalk and passed inside the building. There were a handful of other figures on the street. The dashboard clock read 6:50. The first glimmer of the pre-dawn twilight was shading the sky. Schenke half turned to face Hauser, while Persinger and Baumer leaned forward from the rear seat.

"Listen, if Dorner is the killer, he's going to be dangerous. He may be armed. I don't want to give him any chance to resist when we arrest him. We go into his office and the first thing we do is get the cuffs on him. That'll be your job." He indicated Persinger and Baumer. "Hauser, you're good with your fists. You watch him while the others restrain him. If he makes a move, knock him down. I'll cover the door. Last line of defense if he gets through you three."

"He won't," said Hauser.

"What if he goes for his gun?" asked Baumer.

"Then we go for ours. He can't get us all. I want him alive if possible. Shoot to disable if you can. Otherwise shoot to kill. But bring him down him in any case. We can't let him escape. Clear?"

The three men nodded and Schenke took a moment to clear his mind of everything except the task at hand. "Let's go."

They climbed out of the car and Schenke told the others to go over to the entrance while he spoke to Liebwitz and Brandt. Liebwitz tried to roll the car window down as his superior approached, but the mechanism was frozen so he opened the door and stepped out into the street, giving a quick salute. Schenke touched a finger to the brim of his hat in response.

"Any sign of Dorner?"

"Three men who match the description have entered the premises since we got here, sir."

"Have any of them come out?"

"No, sir. People have only entered the building."

"They're early risers in the Abwehr. That's how Canaris likes it, so Dorner is probably inside by now, and at his desk. We're going in to make the arrest. I want you to cover the doorway from the yard at the side. Brandt will cover the front. If Dorner comes out alone, that means he's managed to get away from me. Give him a chance to surrender, but if he resists or tries to run, shoot him. Disable him if possible. Understand?"

Liebwitz nodded. Leaning down to look at Brandt in the passenger seat, Schenke pointed a finger. "Did you get all that?"

"Yes, sir." The probationer nodded.

Schenke gave him a hard stare. "Don't screw it up, Brandt. There's enough blood on your hands already."

He strode across the street to join the others waiting at the entrance. They fell in behind him as he advanced up the steps and showed his badge to the sentries, who nodded them through. At the reception desk, the duty clerk looked up with a frown.

"What is the meaning of this? Who are you?"

"Inspector Schenke of the Kripo. We're here to arrest a suspect."

"You'll have to sign in and state who you are visiting, sir. That's the rules."

"We haven't time for that. I know where I'm going. We'll see ourselves up." Schenke leaned over the clerk. "And you'd do well not to call anyone to alert them to our presence. If our man gets advance warning, I'll hold you personally responsible."

"Yes, sir."

Schenke hurried towards the elevators. One cage stood open, so he waved the others inside, slid the door closed and eased the lever that sent the elevator up through the building. When they reached the top floor, he led the way down the corridor to the office he had visited a few days before. He paused outside, unclipping the strap over his holster and indicating to the others to do the same. Then, turning the door handle, he surged into the office.

Sturmbannführer Schumacher looked up from his desk. "Schenke! What is the meaning of this?"

Schenke ignored the SS officer and crossed to the door leading to Dorner's office. There was no one in the room, but a coat and hat hung from a stand in the corner, and smoke from a cigarette stub curled into the air from the ashtray. He turned back to Schumacher.

"Where is he?"

Schumacher stood up and leaned forward on his desk. "What's going on, Schenke? I demand you explain the reason for this intrusion."

"I asked you where Dorner is."

"Oberst Dorner," Schumacher laid stress on the rank, "has left the office for the moment."

"Where has he gone?" Schenke demanded.

"He went to collect a copy of the morning intelligence briefing. Shall I call up to the typing pool and get him on the line for you?"

"No. We'll wait here."

Schumacher sat back down. "Make yourselves at home. Coffee, anyone?"

Baumer made to raise his hand, but his sergeant gave him a warning glare and he let his hand drop.

"We're fine, thank you, sir," Hauser responded.

Schenke stood by the door while the others arrayed themselves opposite, ready to spring forward the moment Dorner entered. Schumacher regarded them with suspicion. "You all look very grim. I daresay the four of you might manage to deal with the Oberst. Anyway, what's all this about? What's he supposed to have done?"

"It doesn't concern you, Sturmbannführer. We need him for questioning."

"About what?"

"I can't disclose that."

"Dorner is a good National Socialist. We've known each other since we joined the party nearly ten years ago. I can't think of any reason why he should need to be arrested. I take it that is your intention."

Schenke gave him an uncompromising look, then sat down on the edge of the desk with his back to the SS man and waited.

A few minutes later, he heard voices approaching down the corridor. There was a tap on the door before it opened and the clerk from the reception desk stepped inside. Behind him came Admiral Canaris, who halted as he looked round at the Kripo men.

"Horst. What's going on here?" he demanded.

Schenke rose, as did Schumacher. "We're here to make an arrest, sir."

"Arrest? Arrest who?"

There was little to be gained by discretion, Schenke decided. "Oberst Dorner."

"On what charge?"

"May I speak to you in private, sir?"

"What?" Canaris raised his eyebrows and then sighed irritably. "Very well, out in the corridor." He turned to the clerk. "You can go."

The clerk saluted and hurried back down the corridor towards the elevators. Canaris waited until he was out of earshot before rounding on Schenke. "Explain yourself."

"I'm sure you can guess the reason, sir."

"Indulge me."

Schenke drew a breath. "I have reason to believe that Oberst Dorner is responsible for the murder of Gerda Korzeny, along with those of at least six other people, as well as an attempted murder."

Canaris shook his head. "Preposterous."

"We have an eyewitness who places him at the scene of some of the attacks, sir. We have other evidence. More than enough to arrest and charge him."

The admiral's eyes glinted with anger, but he managed to keep his expression neutral as he spoke in an undertone. "I would advise you to take your men and get out of here before Dorner returns. He must not find out you are in the building. I'll deal with Schumacher."

Schenke shook his head. "Absolutely not. Dorner is wanted for murder. I don't understand—"

"You don't have to understand. Just obey my order and get out of here."

"No." Schenke was bewildered. "Why would you give such an order?"

"I can explain later. But you're in danger of putting one of our military operations in jeopardy. You have to trust me. I'll explain everything later. You must leave. Now."

They were interrupted by the bell that announced an elevator stopping on the floor. A moment later the gate rattled open and Dorner stepped out. He stopped dead as he saw Canaris and Schenke outside the door of his office.

"Too late," Canaris muttered.

"Oberst Dorner!" Schenke called out, keeping his voice calm. "I need a word with you."

The three men stood still for a beat, and then Schenke began to reach inside his coat for his pistol. Dorner dived back into the lift and wrenched the metal grille into place. Schenke drew his Walther and ran down the corridor, calling for Hauser. He heard the door open behind him, and the thudding of feet.

Dorner drew a pistol from his belt. He cocked the weapon, thumbed the safety off and took aim as he worked the control lever with his other hand. "Stay back!"

Schenke raised his own pistol, but before he could pull the trigger, there was an earsplitting explosion and a short tongue of flame spat from the muzzle of Dorner's weapon. The bullet passed through the grille and struck the wall close to Schenke's head, plaster bursting over his cheek as he swerved aside.

Hauser sprinted past him, pistol pointed as he shouted, "Drop it! Open the door!"

Dorner fired again, and this time found his target. Hauser spun round and sprawled onto the floor, his pistol flying from his hand. The elevator had begun to descend, and Schenke caught one last glimpse of Dorner's face before the cage was gone and only swaying cables moved in the shaft. He dropped to his knee beside his comrade and eased him onto his back. A dark patch surrounded a tear in the shoulder of Hauser's coat, and blood welled up, glistening on the wool. Hauser moaned. "Shit, that stings."

Canaris came striding towards them. "Get after him! I'll see to your man. Go, Schenke! Go!"

Schenke stood up. "Persinger, Baumer, down the stairs!"

They rushed towards the opening to the side of the elevator shafts while Schenke tried to recall the layout of the building. He hit the button to summon another elevator and then ran on, past the stairs, towards the window at the far end of the corridor, pain shooting through his knee. Doors opened and people looked out to see what was happening. He reached the window, fumbling with the stiff catch before the ice surrounding the frame gave and it swung open.

A blast of bitterly cold air rushed over his face as he leaned out. He was looking down into the yard at the side of the building. By the faint light of the approaching sunrise he saw several cars parked by the far wall, and the foreshortened forms of a handful of figures, including the unmistakable black hat and leather coat of his Gestapo colleague.

"Liebwitz! Up here! Liebwitz!"

The Gestapo officer looked up, his face pale against his clothing.

"Dorner's on the run! He's armed. Cover the side entrance!"

Liebwitz drew his weapon and took position directly in front of the doors. Schenke ran into the nearest office at the front of the building, thrusting aside a naval officer. More uniformed men looked up in shock from their desks as he ran the length of the office and wrestled with the latch of the window at the end until it came loose. Thrusting it open and leaning out, he saw Brandt standing at the main entrance.

"Brandt! Here!" Schenke waved an arm as the young policeman looked up. A coal delivery truck was passing along the street in low gear, the engine revving loudly. "Dorner's on his way down! Watch out for him."

Brandt shook his head and held his hands up to his ears; he couldn't make out what Schenke was saying. At that moment, the doors burst open and Dorner came out of the building, pistol raised, shouting. He brandished the weapon at the soldiers on sentry duty and fired two shots in the air before they dropped their rifles and backed away, hands raised. Brandt froze. Covering the soldiers with his pistol, Dorner hurried down the steps onto the sidewalk and began to run along the street.

Brandt recovered from his surprise and drew his own pistol before giving chase. The roar of the coal truck's engine died away for a moment as the driver changed gear, and Schenke cried out, "Stop him! Don't let him escape!"

At the sound of his shout, Dorner glanced round and saw the policeman in pursuit. He stopped abruptly beside a car, turned, took aim and fired. The bullet went wide, and Brandt, twenty paces away, lowered into a crouch and fired two shots back. From his position high above, Schenke saw one of the shots strike Dorner in the leg, while the other shattered the rear window of the car. Dorner went down, a hand clutched to his leg, and crawled around the front of the car, pistol at the ready.

"Got him!" Brandt glanced up with a triumphant grin. "Got him, sir!" He sprinted towards the car. Schenke saw Dorner raise his head, catching sight of his pursuer, and then level his pistol.

"Brandt! Be careful!"

Brandt hurried round the front fender of the car, and drew up as he caught sight of Dorner with his weapon raised. There was no warning. Dorner fired three times in quick succession, and Brandt's body jerked under the impact. The last bullet struck him in the face, and his hat leaped from his head along with a burst of skull fragments and brain matter. The young man fell onto his back, limbs splayed, blood pulsing across the icy sidewalk.

"No . . ." Schenke gasped. "You fool. You stupid damn fool."

He was angry at the young man's recklessness, but he understood it too. Brandt had been desperate to redeem himself, to earn his superior's approval after what he had done in contributing to the murders at the Harstein house.

The two soldiers on sentry duty had retrieved their rifles and were approaching the car cautiously. Behind them, Liebwitz rounded the corner of the building and began to run towards Brandt's body, passing the soldiers. Schenke shouted a warning as Dorner peered over the hood of the car. Then, abruptly, the Abwehr officer lifted his pistol, jammed it to the side of his head and pulled the trigger. No shot came, and he tried again, and again, but the clip was empty. Finally he threw the weapon out into the street and slumped back against the radiator grille, staring at the sky in dejection. Liebwitz edged towards the car, kicked the pistol away and shouted at Dorner to raise his hands.

Chapter Thirty-two

"It's a flesh wound," the doctor reported as he packed up his medical kit and snapped the clasps into place. "The bullet passed through the oberst's thigh. It missed the arteries, but he's lost quite a bit of blood and there may be some nerve damage in the longer term that might leave him with a limp."

"That won't trouble him," Schenke responded. "He's not going anywhere. As long as he can make the walk to the guillotine, that's good enough."

The doctor raised an eyebrow at the policeman's tone. "What's he done to deserve such a fate? Buggered the Führer's dog?"

"You'll find out soon enough." Schenke folded his arms. "Make sure you complete the paperwork before you leave the precinct. I'll try and get the payment made as soon as possible."

"That would be nice. It being Christmas and all. I'll be off. Make sure the patient . . . the prisoner gets some rest when you're done with him, and have the wounds checked morning and night. If there's any problem, call me."

The doctor left the interrogation room. Dorner was sitting in a chair on the other side of a plain wooden table, his wounded leg propped up on a stool. His bloodied uniform trousers had been cut away and the middle of his thigh was covered in a dressing, through which a small red stain had already seeped. He had been given a prisoner's blanket and clutched the coarse woollen folds about his body. His face looked white and he seemed a little dazed. Schenke felt no compassion for the man responsible for so many murders. The death of Brandt and the wounding of Hauser fueled his anger. He struggled to contain his feelings as he prepared for the interrogation.

"Is Dorner in fit shape to be questioned?" asked Liebwitz, as if Schenke was the only other man in the room.

"I say that he is. And if he's fit enough for the Kripo to question him, then I daresay that's good enough for the Gestapo. You and your colleagues have even fewer scruples over such matters, I am given to understand."

Liebwitz pursed his lips. "It's not about scruples, sir. It's about ensuring the most effective means of extracting the information required. The correct way of applying pain usually works for us. What is less effective is interrogating someone who is in a delirious or semiconscious state. As such, they might give up false information, or irrelevant details."

Schenke regarded Dorner coldly. "Well, that's a risk we may have to take."

Dorner glowered from across the table. "Do your worst, Inspector. I'll say nothing that will incriminate me."

"We'll see about that. What do you think, Liebwitz? Shall we use some Gestapo methods? What would you recommend?"

Liebwitz considered the suggestion for a moment before he replied. "A beating with rubber truncheons is the most effective way to break the subject down. Then progression to electric shocks almost always yields results. That's what I learned in training."

"And have you ever had the chance to put your training into practice?"

"Yes, sir."

Schenke stifled a feeling of revulsion. "Did it work?"

"Yes, sir. I was a good student. I found the prescribed techniques most efficient."

"I see." Schenke saw Dorner shift uncomfortably as he listened to the exchange. "If I need to employ the fruits of your training, then I will, assuming the Oberst fails to cooperate."

"Shall I fetch the equipment from the Gestapo department, sir?"

"Not yet. I'll let you know if I think that's necessary."

"Very well, sir."

Schenke pulled up a spare chair and sat opposite Dorner. Liebwitz remained standing to one side. Behind them, set into the wall, was a narrow strip of darkened glass. Beyond, in another smaller room, sat Ruth and Frieda, the latter ready to take notes.

"Let's begin . . . It's nine thirty-five a.m., for the police log. Oberst Dorner, do you know why you are under arrest?"

It was a standard question, designed to prompt the suspect into giving up further incriminating information. Most, in Schenke's experience, did just that, but he doubted Dorner was the kind of man to play into their hands so readily.

"Why don't you tell me, Inspector?"

"Very well. At present you are being held in protective custody, pending the drafting of the charges."

"What charges?"

"Six counts of murder. One of assault, with seven other possible murders, which are currently being investigated."

"Murder?" Dorner frowned, and then to Schenke's surprise he almost looked relieved. "Are you mad? We went over this when you came to question me about Gerda. I told you I had nothing to do with her death. And I've certainly had nothing to do with any other murders. You've got the wrong man, Inspector."

"That's what the guilty usually say, but we have the evidence to place you at one of the crime scenes."

"What evidence?" Dorner demanded.

"You lost a party badge when you attacked the woman on the train. We traced it back to you."

"But I haven't lost my badge."

"Really? Where is it, then?"

Dorner thought for a moment. "Back in my office."

"We'll be sure to check that," Schenke replied drily. "In any case, we have your description from the woman you assaulted, who was an eyewitness to the four murders you committed last night."

"Last night?" Dorner suddenly laughed.

"I fail to see why you consider a capital charge so amusing, Oberst Dorner."

"It's amusing, you dolt, because last night I was at a reception for military intelligence officers at the Soviet embassy. I have witnesses who will state I was there."

Schenke felt a sinking feeling. "Really?"

Dorner nodded. "Admiral Canaris for one, though there were plenty of others present, not to mention all our Russian friends."

"We'll look into that after the interrogation," said Schenke. "What time did the reception go on to?"

"Until the early hours. There was a lot of vodka being put away."

"What time precisely did you leave the embassy?"

"No earlier than three in the morning. I remember because I saw the time on a clock and knew I'd have to get some sleep as I needed to get a report written for the admiral for this afternoon." He gestured at his leg. "That's not in the cards now."

"I saw you shoot one of my men dead, and wound another, and there were several witnesses to that."

Dorner's expression hardened. "That was self-defense."

"You were on the run when you shot them. If you're innocent, why did you bolt? Is that the reaction of an innocent man? I doubt that is how the court will interpret it."

"Look, I saw you go for your gun. I have enemies here in Berlin. People who would happily see me framed for a crime I hadn't committed. You know what it's like right now. The capital is rife with political factions jostling for influence. It's easy to make enemies, sometimes without even knowing it, and if someone has enough power they can have you plucked off the street and make you disappear into the night just like that." He clicked his fingers. "I reacted to a threat. I panicked and ran."

"And shot at me and wounded Sergeant Hauser, and then killed Brandt."

Dorner nodded. "Like I said, I panicked."

"I find it hard to believe that an army officer can panic so easily."

"We're only human." Dorner smiled.

Schenke stared at him for a moment and then slapped his hand down hard on the table, making Dorner flinch. "That is bullshit! You ran because you are guilty. Because you knew the game was up and we'd caught you. You shot at my men because you were desperate to escape us and evade justice. We know you are a murderer. Stop playing your damned games and admit it. If not, I'll let my Gestapo friend fetch his toys and go to work on you, while I sit back and enjoy the show, you sick bastard."

The outburst seemed to shock Dorner for a few beats, and then the arrogant smile returned. "As I said, Inspector. I have not murdered anyone. And I'll take my chances in court with respect to your sergeant and the fool who stepped out in front of me brandishing a pistol. A good lawyer might well persuade the judges to spare me from the guillotine. If you don't believe me about last night's murders, then call Canaris. Ask him where I was. He'll vouch for me. Him and every other man in the room. Go on, call him and let's get this charade over with."

The earlier doubt flowed back into Schenke's mind. What if Dorner was speaking the truth? What if he wasn't the one who had killed Gerda and the others? But he had to be. Why else would he have run from Schenke and his men? He took a deep breath and eased himself back in his chair, sitting in silence for over a minute before he announced his decision.

"We'll take a break. I've a few calls to make. Let's see if Canaris can confirm your story."

"You do that. And while I'm waiting, send your man there to fetch me something to eat and drink. And some aspirin. I'm still hungover from last night and the lead poisoning isn't helping." He indicated his leg.

The man's arrogance was insufferable, and as Schenke rose to leave the room, he turned to Liebwitz. "No food. Nor water. Nothing until I say so."

"Yes, sir."

"Stay here and watch him."

Dorner chuckled. "I won't be going anywhere. As you pointed out to the doctor."

Schenke paused by the door. "Let's just say I don't want you attempting to harm yourself and escape due judicial process and punishment."

Outside the room, he waited for his anger and frustration

to recede before making for the observation room next door. Frieda and Ruth looked up as he entered.

"Did you get all that, Frieda?"

She tapped her shorthand notepad. "Every word, sir, but the bastard's lying."

"I hope so." He turned to Ruth and saw that she was looking at him anxiously. "What's the matter?"

"That man in the room. He's not the one who attacked me."

"What?"

Frieda turned towards her. "Oh come on, my dear. He has to be."

Ruth shook her head. "He isn't. I'm sure of it. His face is different. So is his voice."

"It was nighttime," said Frieda. "The light in the carriages was poor. And he could have been disguising his voice."

Ruth considered this. "No, I'm sure of it. That's not the same man."

Schenke had listened to the exchange with a growing sense of dread. There had been something in Dorner's manner when he denied involvement in the murders that rang true. And now this. But he had to be guilty of something, otherwise why had he been prepared to run and shoot his way out of the Abwehr when he spotted Schenke? Not to mention turning his pistol on himself when he knew he could not escape.

"All right, I'm sure you could both do with a break. Frieda, take Miss Frankel to the office and get her a drink and something to eat. I'll need you both back in here when we resume the interrogation."

There was a knock on the door frame and he turned to see Persinger.

"You've got visitors, sir. Admiral Canaris and one of his

officers are waiting in the office. The admiral wants to speak with you at once. I told him you were interrogating the prisoner and couldn't be interrupted."

"Quite right."

"Thing is, he insisted. I don't think he'll take no for an answer, sir."

"All right, I'll come." Schenke turned to Ruth. "We'll deal with the identification issue when I get back. Have another good look at him and see what you can recall."

"I-I'll do my best."

"That's not going to be good enough. You have to be certain either way. Nothing else will do. Clear?"

"I understand."

He followed Persinger to the stairs leading to the ground floor. As they passed the canteen, he heard a group of policemen inside singing a carol and he glanced through the double doors. A small fir tree had been set up in the middle of the room and decorated with chains of colored paper. Around it the men had arranged chairs and benches, and they sang lustily as they held bottles of beer in their hands. He felt a moment's envy that they were free to start celebrating Christmas while he and his section were still working hard to resolve the murder investigation. Moreover, while these men went home to their families and enjoyed the next few days, Brandt's family would be in mourning, while Hauser would spend Christmas in the hospital and there would be an empty space at his table.

As he entered the Kripo section's office, he saw the admiral standing by the stove. At his side was Schumacher. Both still had their coats on. Their hats had been placed on Schenke's desk, along with their gloves. As soon as Canaris saw the inspector, he cleared his throat and spoke loudly.

"We need the room; the rest of you, out."

Some rose from their desks immediately and left, while others looked to Schenke and waited for him to give a discreet nod before they obeyed the instruction. As the door closed behind the last man, Canaris glared at Schenke from beneath his bushy white eyebrows. His face reminded Schenke of a hawk sizing up its prey.

"I warned you to leave Dorner alone. Now one of your men is dead and another is wounded."

"Sir, I have reason to believe Oberst Dorner is a murderer. We had to arrest him before he could claim any further victims."

"You still think he's your killer?"

The specter of doubt was looming ever more menacingly.

"He is our prime suspect, sir. We have evidence to link him to the crimes."

"You may have evidence, but I can assure you it does not prove that he is the man you are looking for."

"With respect, sir, how can you be so sure?"

"Because the man's a bloody spy. He's working for the British. They're paying him to betray Germany. We've known about it for a while, and have been feeding him false intelligence to report to his paymasters. Not only that, but he's been under constant surveillance. If he'd murdered anyone, I'd know about it."

"A spy?" Schenke felt the ground beneath him was dangerously thin and might crumble at any time and pitch him into an abyss. He ran a hand through his hair as he tried to consider the implications of this new information. If he was wrong, then the killer was still at large, and one man was dead and another wounded for nothing. And now it seemed that he had fatally undermined an espionage operation.

"A spy," Canaris repeated firmly. "Or at least he was. Now, thanks to you, his treachery is exposed. Oh, he was already worried that we were on to him. That must be why he reacted as he did when he saw you with me earlier. We'd hoped to get him to transmit one final set of false reports before we confronted him and tried to turn him and make him a double agent. There's a chance we can still do that, if you hand him over to the Abwehr. Immediately."

"Impossible," Schenke responded. "He's a murder suspect."

"Horst . . ." Canaris lowered his voice. "Do you think a spy would moonlight as a murderer? Think about it. Why take the risk?"

"Why does any murderer take the risk, sir? Being a spy does not preclude the possibility that one is a murderer also. In fact, having taken the first step in betraying his country, I would think such a person might find other crimes easier to commit."

"Is that what you think?" Canaris frowned. "Spies are criminals? Let me tell you something, Horst. Spies often have to take the greatest personal risks in the service of their country, and they rarely get the gratitude they deserve. You are a policeman, a good one by all accounts. But you are not a spy and you do not understand my world. I am telling you, Dorner is not your man."

"We can settle this simply, sir. Four people were murdered last night. Dorner claims he was at a reception at the Soviet embassy. He says you were there also. Is that true?"

"Yes."

The bluntness of the answer was shattering, but Schenke made one last effort.

"He says that he was there until three in the morning. Can you vouch for him?"

"No. I left shortly after one. But you were also there, Schumacher. I saw you arrive with Dorner."

"That's so." Schumacher nodded. "But I left before you,

sir. I'd had too much to drink and I had work to do first thing in the morning." He smiled self-deprecatingly. "I'm afraid there's only so much vodka I can take at one sitting."

Canaris turned to Schenke. "There, you see? We can confirm Dorner's alibi. And not just us, but all of those attending last night. And now that we have established that he is not a murderer, but merely a traitor, we'll need to take him into our custody. I'd be grateful if you'd arrange that at once, Inspector."

They were back on formal terms, Schenke noted. "I'm sorry, Admiral, but I will do no such thing. Even if Dorner has nothing to do with the murders, there will now be a separate investigation into his killing of one of my officers, and the wounding of another."

"But we know why he did that. He was compelled to flee. Most men in his position would have done the same."

"That doesn't alter the fact that he acted unlawfully, sir."

"Unlawfully?" Canaris laughed. "My God, but you are a man out of time . . ." He composed his features and continued. "Look, Schenke, we have an opportunity here to use this man for the benefit of the Reich. In our hands he might save German lives, and do great damage to our enemies. Surely that outweighs the death of your officer? Bitterly regrettable though that is."

"As you pointed out, sir, I am a policeman. My job is to uphold the law. Dorner has broken the law. My duty is clear. Until I receive orders from my superiors at the Reich Main Security Office, I will hold him here and charge him with whatever crimes he has committed. That is the end of the matter."

Canaris shook his head. "You will regret this . . . Very well, I'll take the matter up with your superiors at once. Good day." He and Schumacher picked up their hats and gloves and strode back through the office towards the door leading into the precinct's reception area.

Schenke stood in silence, too shocked to react. In front of him, on top of some other folders and paperwork, was Liebwitz's report. It was a summary of his search for the details relating to the badge. At the bottom of the page was a list of names against the serial numbers of gold badges, with Dorner's second from the top. Schenke glanced over those below, and when his gaze fixed on the last name, next to the number 8949, he felt an icy chill close round his heart.

Chapter Thirty-three

"Sir!" he called out to Canaris. The admiral and Schumacher stopped and turned.

"What is it?"

Schenke's mind was racing as he spoke. "If you want to make your offer to Dorner before you leave the precinct, I would have no objection."

He saw Canaris hesitate, so he gestured towards the door. "I can take you to him now if you wish."

Canaris considered the offer before he nodded. "Very well. You seem to have come to your senses. Let's go, Inspector."

Schenke led them across the reception hall, where his team were waiting, and down the corridor, past the canteen where the off-duty policemen were singing "Silent Night." At the end, they descended the stairs to the interrogation rooms and the cells. Despite the heating pipes, the air was colder and clammier here, and the admiral fastened the top button of his coat as they passed the first cells. Schenke closed the observation door as he passed by and then ushered the two men into the interrogation room, where Dorner was seated. Liebwitz stood to attention and threw his arm out to salute Canaris, who ignored him.

"Admiral," Dorner bowed his head, "Schumacher. I'd like to say it's good to see you, but I daresay the feeling would not be reciprocated."

"Dorner," Canaris responded flatly. "I think you know that I regard you with contempt for the traitor that you are, so let's not waste time with pleasantries. The inspector here says that you are being held on murder charges. We've furnished him with an alibi for last night. I daresay you can provide your own for the other killings. The only death you have caused, as far as I can see, is that of the Kripo officer. There may be some accommodation we can come to over that, provided you cooperate fully with the Abwehr. I'm here to offer you a deal."

"A deal?" Dorner looked surprised.

"In future, you work for us. You will feed the British with false intelligence that we supply. You will continue to carry out any further such duties I give you. You will not attempt to flee Berlin. You will not attempt to tip the British off in any way. If you do, I will give the order myself to have you put up against a wall and shot. Those are the terms. Any questions?"

"Yes." Dorner smiled. "Do I get to keep their money and draw my army salary?"

Canaris's expression became frigid. "This is not a moment for levity."

"If you gentlemen don't mind," said Schenke, "I'll leave you to discuss your arrangement. Liebwitz, with me."

They left the room and Schenke closed the door behind him before he rounded on the Gestapo man. "That report you left on my desk about the badges; why didn't you tell me about Schumacher?"

"Who, sir?"

"The man in there with Canaris and Dorner."

"Schumacher?"

For a moment Schenke's weary mind assumed that Liebwitz was playing ignorant, then he recalled that there was no reason for him to know anything about Schumacher. The name had never been mentioned to him during the investigation.

"All right, I want you to get back up to the office as fast as you can. I need you to call party headquarters and confirm that the man at the bottom of the list and the officer in that room are the same person. Then I'll need the badge. Go."

Liebwitz nodded and turned to stride back down the corridor with his peculiar long-legged gait. Calming himself, Schenke entered the observation room. The two women were sitting a short distance from the viewing slot, drinking from mugs. The light on the wall indicated that the speaker link to the interrogation room was off. Schenke closed the door to the corridor.

"Miss Frankel . . . Ruth. I need you to look into the next room and tell me what you see."

She seemed confused. "But I told you already, that's not the man I saw. I'm certain of it."

"Have another look. Please."

She pulled her chair to the slot and sat down. Schenke crouched beside her, his gaze switching between following what was going on on the other side of the glass and watching her face for a reaction. As Canaris and Dorner haggled over the terms of the deal, Schumacher looked on, his back to the viewing glass.

Ruth turned away and shook her head. "I'm still convinced it's not him. I'm sorry, but you've got the wrong man."

"Just a moment." Schenke reached up and turned on the speaker, and there was a crackle before the admiral's voice filled the observation room.

". . . no chance of that, I can tell you. Count yourself lucky that you are being given the chance to avoid a firing squad."

Dorner folded his arms. "I know my potential worth to you. If this is played the right way, we'll have the British dancing to our tune and—"

Schenke flicked the intercom switch and cleared his throat. "Admiral, you have a few more minutes. Then I must ask you to leave so that we can complete our interrogation." Canaris and Dorner looked towards the speaker on the wall, and then Schumacher turned. Schenke flicked the switch to cut the microphone in the observation room, while keeping the line from the other side of the glass open.

There was a beat, and then Ruth let out a gasp and recoiled from the window, her eyes widening in terror.

Schenke put his hand on her shoulder. "What is it, Ruth? Tell me."

She pointed through the glass. "It's him. *Him*. The one who attacked me. The one who killed your friends."

"We need more time with the Oberst," Canaris was saying. "Please leave us to complete matters here . . . Inspector?"

Schenke ignored the feed from the other room as he focused on Ruth. "Which one? Tell me."

"The one closest. I'm sure it's him. But he's different . . . His hair was darker. Longer."

"Could it have been cut?"

She shook her head. "It was a different color."

"A wig, then?"

She nodded. "Yes, I think that's possible."

He looked from Ruth to Frieda. "Then he's our man."

"What are we going to do, sir?" the policewoman asked quietly, as if the men in the next room might overhear her.

"Schenke?" Canaris demanded.

Schumacher was staring at the glass, a calculating expression on his face. "Sir, the offer has been made and I think it's best we let Oberst Dorner think it over. The Kripo need to complete their interrogation, and we have to inform Reich Main Security Office about Dorner. I think we should leave now."

Canaris gave him a sharp look. "It is for me to decide what we do, Schumacher."

"I'm sorry, sir, but I think we need to let Müller know as soon as possible."

"I don't give a damn about . . ." Canaris restrained himself before continuing in a calmer tone. "You're right. I've said what I needed to say here. We've better things to do with our time. Dorner, I don't imagine you'll have much difficulty in coming to a decision to work for us, given the likely alternative. Come, Schumacher, let's go."

Dorner gave a cynical smile. "I'll be seeing you both later."

Schumacher darted a final glance at the viewing glass before he followed his superior towards the door.

"Shit," Schenke whispered through clenched teeth. "He's on to us, I'm sure of it." There was one way to be sure. He turned to Ruth. "Will you help me? Please."

She could not disguise her fear as she tore her gaze from the glass partition, but she nodded and gave Schenke a determined look.

"Frieda, get her up to the reception hall at once. I'll buy us a few seconds. Find Liebwitz. Tell him to bring his report and the badge to me at once."

He flicked the intercom switch open and spoke. "Admiral, I have a question."

Canaris paused. "Well?"

Schenke ushered the two women out of the observation room into the corridor before he responded. "What do you want me to do with him once we've finished the interrogation, sir? Shall I have a car take him to the Abwehr office?"

"Yes, I should think that will do," Canaris replied, then

sighed irritably. "I'm not going to have a conversation with a bloody piece of glass." He reached for the door handle.

Schenke hurried out into the corridor at the same time as Canaris and Schumacher emerged from the interrogation room. At the far end of the corridor the two women climbed the last few steps and passed out of sight.

"That's better," Canaris said tersely. "Now listen to me, Schenke. I want this interrogation concluded as swiftly as possible. I'll have a car sent over to wait outside. I'm not giving you any excuse to delay handing Dorner over to me a moment longer. I'll speak to Müller and have him authorize the transfer of the prisoner to my custody. And if you try to delay the matter, you'll be answering to him. Müller is not known for his tolerance of insubordination. You don't want him referring the matter to his superior. Heydrich is not called the man with the iron heart for nothing."

"I'll do my duty, sir. You can depend on it."

"Good. Let's be off."

Schenke led the way. As they ascended the stairs to the main corridor of the precinct, he heard a loud series of cheers, and a moment later policemen spilled out of the canteen, some still clutching bottles, talking and laughing as they prepared to go home for Christmas.

"Make way there!" Schumacher shouted. "Out of our bloody way!"

"That'll do, Schumacher," the admiral admonished. "Let these fellows go first."

Schenke saw the hunted gleam in Schumacher's eyes as he glanced up and down the corridor, as if looking for another exit. But the only way out was to follow the crowd into the reception hall and through the precinct's main entrance. Schumacher stared ahead as he waited for the last of the policemen to emerge from the canteen, and then the three of them followed a distance behind.

Once the admiral and Schumacher were outside, it would

be easy for the latter to flee, Schenke realized. He had to find a way of preventing him from leaving the precinct. The high-spirited crowd moved closer to the archway leading into the reception hall. Frieda and Ruth were waiting by the counter outside the door to the Kripo office. Schumacher edged Schenke aside and began to clear a path through the throng as he and Canaris made for the entrance. The door of the office opened and Liebwitz stepped out. He saw Schenke and raised the report for his superior to see. Schenke pushed through to him, jostled by the drunken policemen as he passed by.

"The badge. Where is it?"

Liebwitz reached into his waistcoat pocket and took out a paper evidence envelope. Schenke snatched it and turned towards Schumacher, who was already halfway across the hall. He drew a quick breath and called out, "Sturmbannführer!"

Schumacher looked over his shoulder, then thrust aside the man ahead of him, who lost his balance and went down on his knees. He was up again in an instant, face twisted in anger as he raised his fists and swayed drunkenly, heedless of the danger of striking a superior officer. A gap opened in the crowd around the two men.

"Sturmbannführer!" Schenke called again, forcing his way through the throng. He approached Schumacher and held out the envelope. The din in the hall began to fade as the crowd's attention fixed on them. "You lost this."

"What is it?" Schumacher demanded.

"Something you mislaid recently."

"I don't know what you're talking about."

Schenke unfolded the top of the envelope and inverted it. A small gleaming object tumbled into the palm of his hand, and he held it up for Schumacher to see. The SS man's eyes widened in shock and he took a half-step backwards, shaking his head. "I've never seen that before. It's not mine."

"I believe it is," said Schenke. "It was traced back to when it was awarded to you in 1935." He glanced at the badge. "Number 8949. It's yours. Or it was, until you lost it when you carried out the attack on that train a few nights ago. Isn't that right, Miss Frankel?" He turned, and Ruth shrank away.

"Is this the man who attacked you?" Schenke asked.

Her bottom lip trembled. Then she nodded sharply. "That's him."

"Jewish bitch!" Schumacher bellowed. His hand went to his holster and he snatched out his pistol, then he grabbed the collar of Canaris's coat and wrenched the admiral towards him, thrusting the muzzle of the gun against the side of his head.

"Get your hands off me!" Canaris shouted.

"Shut up! Shut your mouth and do exactly as I say, if you want to live."

He glanced around at the policemen. "Get back! All of you, get back! Or so help me, I'll blow the admiral's head off."

Some of the men recoiled, pushing back from the man with the gun. Others were unclipping their holsters and drawing their weapons. Liebwitz did likewise, advancing through the crowd and lowering himself into a slight crouch as he took aim with his Luger.

"Put your guns down!" Schumacher ordered. "And get away from the door."

Schenke positioned himself between the SS officer and the entrance and raised his hands, still holding the badge. "It's over, Schumacher. We know who you are. You can't hope to escape."

"We'll see." Schumacher thrust Canaris forward. "Move aside, Inspector."

"Let the admiral go, and put the gun down."

Schumacher aimed at the ceiling and fired. Plaster cascaded over the nearest policemen. He pushed the muzzle harder against the admiral's temple.

"I mean it! You'll do exactly what I say. Have a car sent round to the front. Now!"

"There's no point. Where will you go? Give up. Let me have the gun." Schenke extended his hand.

"Back!"

He froze. There was silence in the hall, the only sound the labored breathing of the SS man.

"Shall I shoot him dead, sir?" Liebwitz asked. "I can make the shot."

"Try it and the admiral dies with me," warned Schumacher.

Schenke turned to Liebwitz. "No! No shooting."

More of Schenke's men, weapons drawn, came out of the office to investigate the gunshot. They took aim as they fanned out, while Baumer hurried round the crowd to take up position in front of the door, pistol raised. Schumacher eyed them warily as he backed up into the corner of the hall.

"Call them off, Schenke."

"I could, but it'll make no difference. We'll catch you, just as surely as night follows day. You're finished. Put the gun down."

"Do as he says," Canaris added.

Schumacher looked from side to side fearfully. A soft, frustrated keening came from his throat, then his eyes fixed on Ruth. "You . . . I should have killed you when I had the chance."

"You should have," she replied coolly, though Schenke saw that she was trembling. "But you didn't, because I fought back. Face it, I got the better of you. Me, a Jew."

"That's one thing I can put right."

His arm snapped out towards her. Two shots detonated deafeningly at almost the same instant. The first struck the woodwork at the top of the counter, which exploded into a shower of splinters. The second entered Schumacher's head and whipped it backwards, his body crashing against the wall as Canaris dived aside. Schenke saw the dark hole in Schumacher's forehead. The white plaster behind him was splattered with bright blood and clots of brain tissue. His mouth worked slowly for a few seconds, and then his eyes rolled up and he slumped down and rolled to one side, his pistol clattering onto the floor.

Liebwitz approached, still aiming at the SS officer as smoke curled from the muzzle of his weapon. He used the toe of his shoe to kick the other man's gun out of reach before he lowered his own, straightened up and announced, "He's dead."

Schenke cleared his throat. "Well done."

Liebwitz shrugged as he removed the magazine and cleared the chambered round, catching the bullet deftly. "Like I told you, sir. I'm a crack shot."

Chapter Thirty-four

Two of the uniformed officers were still cleaning the blood off the wall when the Gestapo arrived. Schumacher's body had already been removed and now lay on a stretcher in one of the cells while it was decided what to do with him. The Gestapo squad pulled up outside the entrance to the precinct: a Mercedes staff car followed by a covered Opel truck. As soon as the vehicles came to a stop, black-uniformed men armed with rifles hopped down from the rear of the truck and trotted up the steps and into the reception hall. Out of the staff car stepped Oberführer Müller. He followed his men inside and strode up to the sergeant on duty at the desk, who rose from his stool, stood to attention and gave the party salute.

"Where is Inspector Schenke?" Müller demanded. "I want to speak to him at once."

"Yes, sir." The policeman indicated the door to the Kripo section's temporary office. "In there, sir."

Müller swept past him, opened the door and entered the room. Some of those working at their desks looked up, then, realizing who their visitor was, abruptly stood. Schenke did the same.

Müller pulled his gloves off as he paced over, ignoring the others in the room, except for Liebwitz, to whom he nodded as he passed.

"Schenke, why did you not inform me immediately about what has happened here? Why did I have to find out from Ritter?"

Schenke noticed the Gestapo squad in the hall beyond. He turned to his superior. "The incident took place barely an hour ago, sir. There were arrangements I had to oversee first. I only returned to my desk a few minutes ago. I was going to call you in a moment. But now that you are here, what can I do for you, sir?"

"I want Dorner, and I want Schumacher's body. And I want all documents relating to the investigation."

Schenke could not hide his surprise. "Why?"

"It is not your place to question my orders, Inspector."

"Begging your pardon, Oberführer, but the Kripo is obliged to store all records within the department's archive, as well as keep copies at the precinct. That is the standard procedure. Particularly in serious criminal cases like this one."

"Don't quote procedure at me. The Reich Main Security Office has taken over all policing and security matters and we do things differently. You obey the orders of a superior officer, and you do not question them." He turned to Liebwitz. "Is that not the case, Scharführer?"

Liebwitz assumed his customary blank expression. "Sir, the inspector is right. Despite the hierarchy of rank, the procedures of the criminal investigation department have not been legally subsumed by the authority of the Reich Main Security Office. As far as I understand it, that is a matter of law."

Müller stared at him for several seconds. "You and I will discuss this later, Scharführer."

He turned to Schenke. "Whatever that fool says, I will be taking Dorner and Schumacher's body with me." He patted his holster and indicated the armed men in the hall. "This is my authority. If you have any complaints, put them in writing and submit them to headquarters. And see how far that gets you."

Schenke had no wish to cause a confrontation between his officers and the Gestapo squad waiting in the hall. He knew that those working closely for the regime tended to act first and have others endorse the legality of what they had done later.

"Sir, I already have instructions from a superior officer. Admiral Canaris has ordered me to hand Dorner over to the Abwehr once I have finished interrogating him."

"Canaris?" Müller frowned. "The admiral be damned. I am your superior and I am ordering you to hand Dorner to me."

"With respect, sir, his rank is superior to yours."

Müller managed to contain his anger. "Inspector, I swear to you that you will regret your audacity . . . Very well, then. You want this from a higher authority than Canaris? I can do that."

He picked up the receiver on Schenke's desk and dialed a direct line. There was a short delay before Schenke heard a faint click and Müller stood a little more erect.

"Sir, it's Müller. I'm at the Schöneberg precinct with Inspector Schenke of the Kripo. He says that Canaris has given him orders to hand Dorner over to the Abwehr . . . Yes, sir, I told him that. He insists that the admiral outranks me . . . Yes, sir, that's why I called you . . ." Müller thrust the receiver at Schenke. "He wants to speak to you."

Schenke took the phone. He spoke as calmly as his nerves permitted. "Inspector Schenke."

"Inspector, it is a pleasure to speak with you," a high-pitched voice responded. "My name is Reinhard Heydrich, chief of the Reich Main Security Office and deputy to Reichsführer Himmler. Is my name familiar to you?"

"Of course, sir," Schenke replied, his guts clenching. Anyone with knowledge of the party's higher echelons was familiar with the man at the end of the line.

"And you recognize my voice?"

"Yes, sir."

"That is good. Müller tells me that you have challenged his authority based on the fact that Admiral Canaris's rank takes precedence."

"That's right, sir."

"I see. I am sure that you will agree that my authority supersedes that of Canaris."

"Sir, I—"

"If it would help to convince you, Inspector, I could refer the matter to my superior, the Reichsführer. I think we can agree that he outranks the admiral. No?"

"Yes, sir. He does."

"And since I am his deputy, in nearly all matters, I think we can assume that he will endorse whatever order I give you. In which case, I order you to obey Müller in every detail. Is that clear?"

"Yes, sir."

"Then the situation is resolved and the business of our conversation is concluded. Good day."

The line went dead. Schenke replaced the receiver and looked across the desk to Müller.

"Well?"

"I will do as you say, sir."

"Good. Before you take me to Dorner, I want to see the body."

* * *

The cell was unheated and damp. It was rarely used to hold prisoners. Live ones at least. Schenke led the way into the cramped space. Müller followed. Their breath curled from their lips in wispy plumes as they took up position either side of the stretcher lying in the middle of the cell. The body had been covered with an old sheet and the cloth over the head was dark with dried blood.

"Let's see him," Müller ordered.

Schenke took hold of the corner of the sheet and peeled it back. It was stuck where the blood had soaked through and congealed beneath, and he had to tug it before it came free and revealed Schumacher's face.

Müller's expression betrayed no emotion as he stared down, but he spoke quietly. "It's a pity we lost him. Schumacher was a good SS man, and a loyal party member."

"He was a murderer, sir."

"Well, yes, quite. But no one's perfect. We're all human, Inspector Schenke. With human failings. You, me, him . . ."

Schenke felt a cold rage fill his body. "My failings do not include raping women and bludgeoning them to death. Of course, I only speak for myself."

"Be careful, Inspector. Having lost the services of one officer, it would be unfortunate to have to dispense with another."

Schenke was exhausted, and a peculiar melancholy had settled on him since the shooting. In an alert state he might have been more cautious, and now he realized it would be dangerous not to keep his thoughts to himself. He wondered if those who suffered from the human failings Müller mentioned included the Führer and all those who followed him.

Müller's sneer faded and his piercing gaze glinted dangerously in the glare of the bare bulb that lit the cell. "I see that we may have to deal with you some day, Schenke. Just as we have dealt with all those who refuse to be part of the

Führer's dream of making Germany great again. A spell in the camps usually does the trick, one way or another. I'd reconsider your attitude if I were you."

He went to the door and snapped an order to the Gestapo men waiting outside. "Get the body in the back of the truck."

They filed in to pick up the stretcher. As they did so, a piece of skull fell onto the floor. No one moved.

"I believe that belongs to you," said Schenke.

Müller eyed him, then bent and scooped up the bone fragment and tossed it onto the stretcher. He drew the sheet back over Schumacher's face. "Get him out of here."

His men left the cell and made their way along the corridor towards the stairs.

"Dorner," Müller announced. "Where is he?"

Schenke led the way. They passed several doors before they came to the interrogation room. Slipping back the bolt, he swung the door open. Dorner had been left in the charge of a uniformed officer, who stood and saluted as he saw his superior. Dorner smiled.

"Ah, Schenke. I wondered when you'd come back. I think I heard a shot earlier, but this dull fellow has refused to explain. Not a word from him this last hour or so."

Schenke stepped aside to reveal Müller and his men. Dorner's smile faded.

"What the hell is this? What's going on?"

Müller clicked his fingers and pointed. "Take him."

Two of the Gestapo men approached Dorner, who reached across the table and locked his fingers over the far edge. "No!" One of them grasped his shoulders and tried to pull him free; the other raised his rifle and slammed the butt down on the knuckles of Dorner's right hand. He grimaced, but did not cry out or release his grip. He looked up at Schenke desperately. "Where's Canaris? Get Canaris!"

Müller shook his head. "The admiral won't be able to save you, I'm afraid. You're going to pay the price for betraying the fatherland, Oberst Dorner. Once we've had a chance to put a few questions to you back at Gestapo headquarters. I think our methods will be more direct than those of the police. You'd sell out your own mother by the time we're done . . . Get him out of here."

The rifle butt came down again, and again, before Dorner's bloodied, numbed fingers released their grip. A single blow was enough to deal with the other hand. The two Gestapo men pulled him from the chair. The heel of his wounded leg landed jarringly, and he let out a pained gasp.

"Call Canaris!" he shouted. "Tell him where they've taken me!"

He was half dragged, half carried from the room, pinned between the two men. Müller touched the brim of his uniform cap.

"Our business here is concluded, Inspector. For now."

He turned and followed the rest of his squad out into the corridor.

Schenke watched the dark uniforms as they climbed the stairs. He caught one last glimpse of Dorner, hanging limply between two men, and a moment later they were gone.

"Sir?" The policeman was still standing by in the interrogation room. "Sir, what do we do?"

"Do?" Schenke shook his head. "What can we do? Nothing. Nothing at all."

Schenke returned to the section's office. The desks had been shoved around and empty filing boxes littered the floor. Persinger was sitting on a chair clutching a bloodied handkerchief to his head.

"What happened?"

"They took all the paperwork, the evidence bags, everything," said Frieda. "Threw it into mail sacks they'd brought with them. Persinger tried to protest—"

"Bastard hit me with his rifle," Persinger interrupted angrily. "Fucking coward. I'd like to see him try that again if our paths cross."

"Pray that they don't," said Schenke.

He glanced round the room; there was nothing left related to the investigation. He patted the outside of his trouser pocket, feeling for the small paper bag containing the badge. But that served no purpose anymore. It was simply a small trophy to mark the end of Schumacher's killing spree.

The remaining members of his staff were looking at him, waiting for some instruction to bring order back to the chaos around them.

"It's over," he said. "Our work here is finished. We found the killer. No more women will die at his hands. And those he murdered have been avenged. We should take some satisfaction in that." He glanced from face to face. "You did a good job. I doubt there is a better team in the criminal investigation department. We pride ourselves on our duty and our ability. That has been hard won, and in this case paid for with the blood of one of our own. Given time, Brandt would have made a fine comrade. Instead, we shall be burying him after Christmas. Now get your coats and go home. Return to your families and hold them close. I'll see you back in our office at Pankow." He shook his head. "There's nothing more. That's all I have to say."

They were still. Frieda cleared her throat. "Sir, if we are as good a team as you say we are, that is because of your leadership. We know what this has cost. Hauser was wounded. Brandt is dead. But some of the victims were close to you. Like family. If there's anything—"

"Thank you," Schenke intervened. "I appreciate the thought. But the best way to honor the dead is to do our job as best we can." He made himself smile faintly. "I wish you all a peaceful Christmas, and new year, I hope."

Liebwitz was the first to move. He put on his black leather coat and hat, then came across to Schenke and held out his hand.

"It has been interesting working with you, sir."

"Interesting?" Schenke could not help a small smile. Scharführer Liebwitz was a man with more talents than he had appreciated on their first meeting. In another life, he might have made an excellent criminal detective.

"Yes, sir. Very interesting indeed. Farewell." He shook the inspector's hand once, then bowed his head and left the office without looking back.

One by one, the others wished Schenke a good Christmas. Frieda was the last. As she turned to leave, he called to her.

"Frau Frankel. Is she still in the building?"

"I took her to the canteen before the Gestapo turned up. I wanted to make sure she had a warm meal before she left."

"Thank you."

Schenke took a last look around the office, without fondness or regret. The room would revert to a common room soon enough, but he doubted the precinct's policemen would forget the day's events. He slipped his coat on, picked up his hat and made his way to the canteen.

Only a handful of men were left: those in no hurry to return home, and the few who were unfortunate enough to be assigned to the afternoon and evening shift. Ruth was sitting beside the stove, her hands cupped round a large mug. He sat down next to her, putting his hat on the table and running a hand through his hair.

"You look tired, Inspector."

"Yes . . . exhausted. Now that the investigation is over, you can call me Horst."

"In my mind I called you and the other policemen a number of names when we first met." She ventured a smile. "But I think I like Horst best."

"Good, and thank you, Ruth. It was because of you that we caught the killer. If you hadn't had the courage to fight back, Schumacher would still be free to continue murdering women."

She spoke quietly. "But it was also because of me that your friends were killed."

"That was nothing to do with you. One of my men allowed himself to be tricked into revealing where you were. If anyone is to blame, it was him. And he paid the price for it."

"I was sorry to hear he had been shot dead."

Schenke considered Brandt for a moment. He had been earnest, but lacking in wits at times. In the longer term, if he had got through his probation period, he would have made a mediocre detective. It was possible that Schenke would have eventually transferred him to the uniformed police. But it was fruitless to speculate. Brandt was dead, and his family would grieve his loss, like so many families had grieved since the war began. Their sons had died in battle. Brandt had died in a different kind of battle, part of an endless conflict that went on regardless of whether Germany was at peace or at war. The difference being, to Schenke at least, that fighting crime was a just cause. War, on the other hand . . .

His thoughts reminded him that no one had informed Brandt's family yet. It was his responsibility to do it. He was the only one in the section still on duty. It was a task that weighed heavily on his heart. He resolved to see to it once he left the canteen.

"Me too," he responded to Ruth. "Me too."

He rubbed his eyes and clenched them shut for a moment to ease the ache. When he opened them again, he regarded her thoughtfully. "What happens to you now? Are you going back to your home?"

"My home?" She gave a dry laugh. "My home these days

is a room I share with a woman old enough to be my grandmother. She snores like a pig. But she is a family friend and I am grateful to her for taking me in. We have barely enough food to survive, and no coal for the stove. . . . That's my home."

"I'm sorry."

"It's no worse than many of my people have to suffer."

Schenke felt another pang of guilt over her situation. It was easy enough to turn aside from the abuse of a faceless people; far less so when it was an individual sitting in front of him.

"I say 'my people,' but we are Germans too," she continued. "Despite what the Nazis say. Despite what they do to us. And when they have finished with us, who do you think they will turn on next? Intellectuals? Those policemen who think the law is above the party, maybe? Be careful, Horst."

He smiled faintly as she addressed him by his first name for the first time. "I am careful. It's you who needs help." He reached inside his coat and took out his wallet. There was over two hundred marks inside, as well as some food coupons he had been saving. He slid the notes and coupons across the table. "Here. Take this. It's all I have with me. And the least I can do for you."

She hesitated, glancing at the handful of other policemen in the canteen. "You could get into trouble for helping me."

He shrugged. "I'm too tired to care about that now. Besides, you need it, and it's the right thing for me to do. Please take it."

She swept the notes and coupons into her hand and tucked them deep into her coat pocket. "I'd better go. My friend will be worried. She needs to know I am safe."

She drained her mug and dabbed her lips as she set it down on the table. "You're a good man, Horst. It's of some comfort to know that there are still good people in Berlin. Aryan people."

Her words pricked his conscience. "I hope we meet again someday. Under happier circumstances."

"So do I."

"If you ever need my help, in any way, you can find me at the Kripo office in the Pankow precinct. Remember that."

"I will."

She rose from the table and pulled her coat about her before doing up the buttons. Schenke stood up too.

"I'll walk you out."

They left the canteen and made their way down the corridor and across the reception hall in silence, glancing briefly at the faint smears on the wall where Schumacher had died. Outside, on the steps, Ruth turned to him, rose up on her toes and kissed him on the cheek.

"Goodbye," she whispered into his ear.

He was surprised by the sudden move, but then smiled and reached for something to say. "Merry Christmas . . ."

"We don't celebrate that, Horst. We don't celebrate much at all anymore."

She held him tight for a moment, then released him and turned away, darting down the steps onto the sidewalk and walking swiftly along the street.

It was snowing again, and tiny flakes swirled in the light gusts blowing over Berlin. Schenke glanced round quickly to make sure no one had seen the brief embrace, then watched her until she turned the corner and disappeared. He still felt the warmth of her lips on his cheek and a sense of loss at her departure. If the fates willed it and they ever met again, he would be glad of it. She had a fierce resilience he admired. That, and something more. He thrust the dangerous thought aside and went back inside.

The sergeant was replacing the receiver on the front desk. He raised a slip of paper.

"For you, sir. I thought you'd left. I was about to go after you."

"What is it now?" Schenke asked wearily.

"That was Gruppenführer Heydrich's secretary."

"Oh?"

"Heydrich wants to speak with you."

Schenke reached for the receiver, but the sergeant shook his head.

"No, sir. He wants you to present yourself at his office. Immediately."

"Immediately?" Schenke sighed to himself. "I suppose I should have expected this . . ."

But first he would make that call to Brandt's family. They deserved to know about his death at once. Heydrich could wait.

Chapter Thirty-five

"The Gruppenführer is expecting you, sir." The secretary, a tall, slender man in an immaculate uniform, indicated the double doors on the far side of the anteroom and led the way across the carpeted floor. He raised a hand to halt Schenke, and then tapped twice on the right-hand door and opened it.

"Inspector Schenke is here, sir."

"Show him in."

The secretary stepped neatly to one side and ushered Schenke through.

Heydrich's office was a large paneled room. A window overlooked Prinz Albrecht-Strasse, and one wall was taken up by a rack of pigeonholes, almost all of them filled with papers. His desk was a huge walnut affair, but there was nothing on it but an inkwell and penholder and the form that he was working on. Behind him, a large framed portrait of Himmler looked down on the room, rather than the usual picture of the Führer that most officials hung in their offices. A revealing detail, thought Schenke.

As the inspector approached his desk, Heydrich lowered his pen and sat back. His gaunt face, long nose and slender frame made him appear taller than he was. A high forehead and smooth skin gave the appearance of his flesh being stretched over his skull. What struck Schenke most was his startlingly blue eyes and piercing gaze. In another man that might be an attractive feature, but Heydrich radiated no warmth or humor, just a steely ruthlessness.

He looked Schenke up and down without giving any indication of his mood.

"Inspector Schenke, thank you for taking the time to come and see me." His lips twitched in what might have been a smile. "It's always a pleasure to welcome a sporting hero of the Reich."

"That was several years ago, sir."

"Nonetheless, you were something of an inspiration to those of us who followed motor racing." He folded his hands together. "Of course, that's not the only thing I have come to know about you in recent days."

He paused, long enough for Schenke to feel anxious about just how much he knew, and then continued.

"You have performed a significant duty for the Reich. You have caught the man responsible for several murders that we know of, and possibly more that have yet to be uncovered. At the same time you exposed a spy in the Abwehr, and while that may have been an inadvertent action, it was a useful service all the same. I know Admiral Canaris claims that he might have been able to turn Dorner to our cause, but I tend to think that a man who betrays his country cannot be trusted ever again. Dorner is a traitor and richly deserves to die a traitor's death. And yet even in death he might be of some service to the Reich."

"How might that be, sir?"

"You have found the killer you were searching for. A name is required to present to the public. As far as my department is concerned, it would be best if the murders were attributed to Dorner, since we are already going to have him tried and executed for espionage. Schumacher is dead, and I see no reason why his actions should be made public knowledge and thereby damage the reputation of the SS."

"Because he's guilty of the crimes he committed, sir. That's the reason."

"And his death is adequate restitution for those crimes."

"What of the families of his victims? Don't they have a right to know who was responsible for the murders of their loved ones?"

"What does it matter what they think they know? They need a name to pin the guilt on. So we'll give them one. It could be any name. Schumacher, Dorner . . . Schenke. Pardon my little joke, but it makes no difference. A name is a name. All that matters is that we provide one and everyone is satisfied. Whether it reflects the actual truth or not is irrelevant. What matters is the effect it has. By using Dorner in this way, the victims' families have a name they can hate, and the reputation of the SS is protected."

"Sir, aren't you forgetting something?"

"What would that be?"

"The truth is relevant to me. Some of the victims were my friends."

"Then your knowledge of the deception is a burden for you to bear. You and those in your section who know the truth. But what is the truth without evidence? And all the evidence is here in the Gestapo's archives, where it will remain. You don't own the truth anymore. We do. That said, if any word of this leaks out to a wider audience, I will know precisely which individuals to hold responsible. And punish. Do I make myself clear?"

"Abundantly, sir."

"I am delighted to hear it." Heydrich smiled thinly. "Then I think we are agreed on the resolution to this unfortunate matter. Let me explain to you how our little predicament is going to play out."

He leaned forward. "This evening's press will carry a feature announcing that the killer who has been stalking the capital's railways has been caught. The article will also state that Dorner was a spy who had infiltrated the Abwehr. Canaris is not going to like that, but it will serve to remind him to take more care over who works for him in future. It pleases me that the Abwehr is tarnished while those in our department are portrayed as effective upholders of the law. Elsewhere in the newspaper will be a small item, an obituary, praising the sacrifice of SS man Schumacher, who was killed during the apprehension of Dorner. That is what you will read, and you will not challenge that account, privately or publicly. Moreover, once this meeting has concluded, I want you to return to your office and write up the official investigation report. Make sure that it matches the version I have given you. You will submit it to me as soon as it is done. Do you understand all of this, Schenke?"

He understood well enough. The truth would be another casualty sacrificed at the shrine of the party's need to be infallible. "Yes, sir."

"There is an additional service you have performed. You will recall that you were assigned to the investigation of the Korzeny woman because you would be seen as unattached to any of the party factions. As things have turned out, Goebbels no longer has to fear that he might be blackmailed over his affair with Gerda Korzeny. For now, at least." He nodded. "It's a satisfactory outcome. You have done well, Inspector."

"Sir, with respect, there are others who contributed more to catching Schumacher than I did. The eyewitness in particular. Were it not for her, he would still be at large."

Heydrich stared at him without expression. "You are talking about the Jewess."

"Yes, sir. She deserves some kind of recognition for her help."

"She deserves nothing. She is a Jew. We are not in the business of helping Jews; quite the opposite. No doubt she has already crept back into whatever sewer she emerged from. Think no more about her. Besides, success is about leadership. You led your section in the investigation and it is through your influence that Schumacher was caught. Dorner too, for that matter."

"Not Dorner. Admiral Canaris was already aware that he was a spy."

"That's what he claims." Heydrich gave a shrug. "It could be that he was attempting to cover his back. What do you think?"

It was an awkward question, and Schenke thought quickly. It was not his place to comment on those in positions of superiority. Besides, Canaris was Karin's uncle, and he owed it to both of them not to compromise the admiral's reputation.

"I do not have enough information to hazard any opinion, sir."

"Yet you have met the admiral on a few occasions, and I believe you know his niece quite well. Surely an astute criminal inspector would be able to make some kind of judgment of his character?"

"I find it hard to believe that a man would be elevated to head of the Abwehr if he did not have a first-rate mind, sir."

Heydrich regarded him silently. "A cautious answer. That's good. Cautious men are to be prized. Which brings us to two other matters. Firstly, I have been following your progress, via Müller. It seems he regards your professional skills highly. Your political judgment less so. He says that you have made some unwise comments that indicate a certain ambivalence towards the party. I hope that is not the case. The Reich needs men of proven ability in all fields. I note that you have not applied to join the SS yet. Most policemen of your rank have seen fit to do so. Why not you?"

"A criminal investigator's duties are time-consuming enough without having to worry about politics, sir."

"You think you can discriminate between your profession and the party? Whatever you might believe, that is not possible. The party is the supreme organization in Germany. It comes first in every sphere of life. The future of the Reich depends on people understanding that, and placing their belief in the party. There is no room for equivocation in the matter. It would be wise for you to embrace that thought. Especially in view of the opportunity I have asked you to consider. Despite Müller's reservations, I am pleased to offer you a post in my office. I need men who can hunt down enemies of the Reich. You have proved your worth in pursuing criminals, and I am confident you will do well if you accept the post. It will mean a promotion, and it will mean applying to join the SS . . . What do you say?"

It was a generous offer, thought Schenke. Perhaps too generous. It was possible that Heydrich subscribed to the philosophy of keeping his enemies close, and that this was a ploy to lure Schenke into a position where he could be watched closely. And then there was the nature of the work that Heydrich was involved in. Schenke had little desire to be drawn into hunting down the political opponents of the regime. To his mind there was a clear line to be drawn between those who committed crimes and those whose crime was failing to subscribe to the values of the party.

"I need time to think it over, sir."

Heydrich's eyes widened fractionally. "There is no time. I need an answer now. Accept, or turn it down. Which will it be?"

"In that case, I must turn the offer down, sir."

A flicker of irritation crossed the other man's face. "Tell me why."

"My abilities, such as they are, are of greater service to the Reich if I remain in the Kripo. It is what I was trained for, and while I am honored by your offer, I cannot in good conscience accept if it means abandoning my section at a time when we are already at full stretch dealing with Berlin's criminals."

"I see . . . You have a pretty high opinion of yourself, Schenke. Too high, if I may say so. You slipped up, according to Müller."

"Did I?"

Heydrich looked amused. "Müller said that the Jew had knifed her attacker. If that was the case, it occurs to me that all you had to do was examine Dorner's side when you arrested him. Then you would have known you had the wrong man."

Schenke looked down. It was true. But by the time Dorner had been taken to the precinct, the evidence against him had seemed overwhelming. It had not occurred to him to check. As for Dorner, he could not have known about the stabbing, otherwise he would have used it to exonerate himself. In any case, Schumacher would have been identified thanks to the badge. But it was still a humiliating oversight.

"You see, there is nothing that escapes my attention, Inspector. And if you think you are irreplaceable, you are mistaken. Few of us are. The Kripo would fill the vacancy very easily. But you have made your decision. I will concede that not many men would have had the guts to reject such an offer from me in person. The Reich needs men of courage. It is for that reason that I accept your rejection without consequence. I would suggest, however, that you consider your priorities and your beliefs carefully in future. If you err from the acceptable path, I will find out about it. I always do. And I will not be so forgiving next time."

He paused to let the weight of his words sink into Schenke's mind, and then he gestured to the form in front of him. "The second matter is more simple. It seems that Scharführer Liebwitz was much taken by his brief attachment to your section. As soon as he returned to the Gestapo, he put in for a transfer. It's unusual, to say the least, to request what many would regard as a demotion. Normally I would dismiss it out of hand. However, I understand that Liebwitz is something of an oddity. His colleagues do not get on with him, and Müller was happy to approve his application. I believe you lost one of your men. Would you be content to accept Liebwitz transferring to your section?"

This was a surprising development, since Schenke had considered Liebwitz a Gestapo man through and through. While it was true he had a blunt manner about him, there was no doubting his eye for detail and willingness to work long hours. In some ways he seemed more of a machine than a man. But he also appeared to be without guile, and it would be good to have a dependable man on the section. It was possible that he was a plant, but the crassness of such an attempt to keep an eye on Schenke made that unlikely. It was more plausible that he annoyed his superior, as Heydrich had said.

"I'd be pleased to have him, sir."

"Good." Heydrich signed the form. "There. It's done. And our business here is concluded." He raised his right hand. "Hail Hitler."

It was a challenge, Schenke realized, and it was best to play it safe. He lifted his arm in a straight line to the fingertips. "Hail Hitler."

It was early afternoon when Schenke returned to Schöneberg. He called Karin to let her know he would be home for Christmas Eve. As he was the only person in the office, he had no one to disturb him as he sat at Frieda's typewriter and wrote out the concluding report of the investigation, according to the directions that Heydrich had supplied. It did not sit easily with his conscience to corrupt the truth of what had happened, but he had no choice. If he refused to do it, then someone else in the section would have to, and Schenke would have a black mark against his record. He had already pushed his luck in his exchanges with Heydrich and had no wish to repeat such an encounter with the ruthless head of the Reich Main Security Office.

Once the report was complete and checked carefully, he sealed it in an envelope addressed to Heydrich's office and placed it in the message tray at the reception desk. Feeling exhausted and cold, he stepped into the street and made his way to the S-Bahn station to catch the train home.

Dusk was closing over the capital as he reached the station, where he bought a copy of the evening edition of *The Attack* before boarding his train. As it rumbled away from the platform, he unfolded the newspaper. Sure enough, the lead story had the headline "Murderous Traitor of the Abwehr" above a picture of a disheveled Dorner being held up by two Gestapo men. Schenke scanned the details and flicked through the pages until he found the smaller article about Schumacher, which proclaimed that the officer had died fighting the enemies of the Reich. A wave of revulsion swept over him and he tossed the newspaper aside and looked out of the window. He could see his own face in the reflection, gaunt and weary, and he let his gaze focus beyond to the passing buildings. Already the blackout curtains were being drawn to plunge Berlin into darkness for the night.

"Sir, the window blind, please." A conductor was looking down at him.

"Yes, of course." Schenke pulled the cord and tied it around the catch at the bottom of the window frame.

"And your ticket."

He held it up to be clipped. The conductor did not move on, however.

"Do you mind?" The man indicated the newspaper.

"Help yourself."

He nodded his thanks and began to read the front page. Schenke soon found his presence uncomfortable. "You can take it away with you, if you like."

"Thank you, sir. Much appreciated." The conductor tucked the newspaper into his coat.

"Ogorzow!" a voice called out from the end of the carriage. "No loitering. Get on with your job!"

"Bloody supervisors," the conductor muttered as he caught Schenke's eye.

"Don't I know it," Schenke replied.

The conductor moved down the carriage and Schenke closed his eyes. He found himself slipping into a comfortable, hazy warmth, and sat up abruptly, blinking. If he fell asleep, he'd miss his stop. He forced himself to keep his eyes open and rubbed his cheeks vigorously until the temptation to sleep had passed.

He left the train at Pankow-Schönhausen. Night had fallen and the loom of freshly fallen snow and the slits of vehicle headlights provided enough illumination for him to see his way to the apartment block. He shivered as he walked, succumbing to the strain of the previous days. Now that there was no need to focus his attention on the investigation, his exhaustion made itself felt without pity. His legs were stiff and leaden as he climbed the stairs to his apartment and walked down the corridor to his front door. He found that it was unlocked. The entrance hall was warm, and a moment later Karin appeared in the lounge doorway.

"Horst!" She smiled in delight, then the smile faded. "You look dreadful."

"Thank you." He closed and locked the door before removing his gloves and hanging up his coat, hat and scarf. "Something smells good."

"I thought I'd cook a special meal for Christmas Eve."

"The accepted term these days is Julefest."

"Not in this apartment, and not between us, my love."

She kissed him on the lips. He was reminded of another kiss, earlier in the day, and forced the thought aside as he followed her into the kitchen and sat down at the small table opposite the cooker. Three pans were simmering on the burners.

"Pork in cream sauce, potatoes and a selection of winter vegetables," she explained. "It's all I could come up with at short notice."

"Sounds wonderful . . . Thank you."

She stepped over to him and cradled his cheeks in her hands. "I thought you might be pleased about the investigation being over . . ."

He looked up at her and related the full details of the events since he had left the apartment before dawn. He concluded by describing his meeting with Heydrich. She listened attentively, and when he had finished she said, "I'm so sorry for the loss of your friends. As for Müller and Heydrich, they are evil bastards. Like all of those who work for Himmler."

"That's true."

"Finally you admit it." She squeezed his shoulder and turned back to tend to the cooking.

"It's made me think, Karin. What is the value of being a criminal investigator in a state run by criminals? I have dedicated myself to doing what I think is right, and enforcing the law. But what is the point of that? I want to be a good man, but how can I be when I serve at the pleasure of the likes of Müller and Heydrich?"

"Be careful where that line of thought leads you, Horst. There are others who think the same way, but it is dangerous to share such ideas." She looked over her shoulder. "It is a dark and perilous path. Be wary of it unless you are certain it is what you want. In the meantime, all a good man can do is be true to his conscience and survive."

She gave the pork a quick stir. "I think we're ready."

As she served up their meal, an air-raid siren sounded in the distance.

Karin looked up. "Should we pay any attention?"

The thought of abandoning the food and making their way down to the cold shelter beneath the building was not appealing. Besides, the enemy had only dropped propaganda pamphlets so far. If they wanted peace, they would be foolish to jeopardize their chances by killing German civilians celebrating Christmas.

"No. Let's enjoy this evening, my love."

The siren continued as they ate in silence, and he wondered if the danger was real, a false alarm or a drill. Who could tell anymore?

A Note on Police and SS Ranks

When the Nazi party took power in 1933, they brought with them a highly organized paramilitary organization that supplemented the official police and military apparatus of the state before steadily supplanting the authority of the official bodies. In the case of the police, all the regional forces were eventually amalgamated into a single corps. The uniformed police, the Ordnungspolizei (Orpo), retained their usual duties for the most part, but many officers were formed into special battalions for rear-echelon duties in lands occupied by the Reich. The criminal investigation department, the Kriminalpolizei (Kripo) comprised highly trained officers who dealt with the more serious crimes. They were the elite of the German police service.

However, with the Nazi party taking on ever more power, the Kripo was drawn into their net. In September 1939, as the Second World War began, Heinrich Himmler completed the last stage of taking control of the state's security and police services when he established the Reich Main Security Office in Berlin, under his protégé Reinhard Heydrich. The Kripo now formed one of two divisions of the new security police department, under Heydrich. The other division was the Geheime Staatspolizei, or Gestapo, the state secret police.

Himmler's SS organization began life as a small force of bodyguards tasked with protecting Adolf Hitler. However, its functions and the number of staff serving the organization rapidly expanded. The SS spread its tentacles across society, eventually becoming a state within a state and at the same time making every effort to recruit into its ranks the members of the organizations it took over. Officials were encouraged to join and take on SS ranks roughly equivalent to their rank in their original organization. Many policemen were eager to do this, but surprisingly there were plenty of officers, even at a senior level, who refused to join the SS on principle, even if this led to them being regarded with suspicion by the Nazi party.

For the sake of clarity, the hierarchy of SS ranks (and their military equivalence) held by characters mentioned in the book is as follows:

Reichsführer SS Himmler
Gruppenführer (Major-General) Heydrich
Oberführer (Colonel) Müller
Sturmbannführer (Major) Schumacher
Hauptsturmführer (Captain) Ritter
Scharführer (Scrgeant) Liebwitz

The Kripo and the Orpo had their own ranks, which I have rendered into English equivalents for the sake of clarity.

Kriminalinspektor (criminal inspector)
Kriminalassistent (sergeant)
Orpo Wachtmeister (sergeant)

Author's Note

For writers of historical fiction, one of the tricky challenges is the attempt to re-create a different time and place, as well as the very different worldview experienced by the characters in the story. Given a regime as extreme as that of Germany under Hitler and the Nazi party, it takes a considerable amount of research to get the details—and, more importantly, the feel of the time—right. Nazi Germany was a place where the slightest public criticism of the leading political party might result in a person being sent to a camp, or even executed. From 1933, when the party came to power, they moved swiftly to take over every aspect of society. Choral societies, pigeon-breeding clubs, rambling associations—all were brought within the orbit of the party and used to spread its propaganda. "Ideology" is too ambitious a term for what lay behind "Nazism"—it was never a coherent or cogent system of thought. In truth, it was a vehicle for scooping up the resentments and prejudices of a broad range of demographics. A vote for the Nazis (while elections still counted for anything) was essentially a populist protest vote, of the kind we are all too familiar with today.

As a consequence, the regime was riven by competing factions, whose relationship to their leader was based on the principle of obeying orders before they were given, in order to curry favor. Much is made of the glib claim that "at least the trains ran on time under the Nazis," in reference to what is assumed to be a feature of the German character—efficiency. In truth, Nazi Germany was not a well-oiled machine so much as a creaking kleptocracy, riven by corruption and intimidation at every level.

In his seminal account of the period, *The Third Reich Trilogy*, Richard Evans points out the distinction between the "normative" and "prerogative" state. The former is bound by the rule of law, respect for traditions and the authority of knowledge. The latter is characterized by contempt for the law, and disdain for any conventions that stand between those who subscribe to the prerogative state and their exercise of power. Given that the Nazi party was a very broad church, politically, for much of its life, I would argue that the real struggle in Germany at that time was not so much between left and right, but between the supporters of the normative state and those of the prerogative state. There are many echoes of that same struggle in the present, and it is by no means certain that the normative state has the upper hand.

Blackout presents that dark time in all its grim paranoia. I hope that the reader can be sensitive to the perils that a character like Inspector Schenke must negotiate as he carries out his quest for justice. If that is challenging enough to show for Schenke, it is harder still to try to portray the experiences of those who were singled out as enemies of the people. Besides the Jews, the Nazis targeted the disabled, gypsies, homeless people, Communists, socialists, Social Democrats, Catholics, homosexuals and all other categories of humanity deemed to be inferior or opposed to the so-called "master race." But it was their conceptualization of the Jews, and the fanatical determination to destroy the Jewish race, that reveals the very darkest stratum of Nazi Germany.

When re-creating this era, I had to adopt a few conventions in order to give the novel as much of an authentically German feel as I could. I wanted to put some distance between my reconstruction of Nazi Germany and the thick accents, heel-clicking and barked "Heil Hitlers!" of so many films (and not a few novels). Not only is the past a foreign country, but one has to take account of differences in culture as well. There are some attitudes and words that do not easily translate into English. For example, there is no German word for "sir"; one would use a specific rank and name when addressing a superior. There is also no equivalent of "fuck," in the way that it is used in the English-speaking world. Similarly, a phrase like "piss off" carries far more weight in Germany than it does in Britain. And then there is the matter of formality. Germans are far more likely to address other people as "Herr" or "Frau" followed by surname than they are to use first names, until becoming well-acquainted. There is accordingly a more nuanced meaning to these modes of address than can be translated into the English "Mr." or "Mrs." In these and other cases, I have used the German words to signify such cultural differences. I have also rendered some ranks and terms in German to emphasize the setting. The same goes for references to the Führer. "Leader" does not do justice to this title, chosen by Hitler himself. He was *the* Leader, and the title "Führer" was his identity, every bit as specifically as any proper noun.

My thanks go to my good friends Peter Krämer—who walked me through the nuances of German society—and Timoor Daghistani—whose comprehensive understanding of small arms saved me from any embarrassing errors. I must also thank my wife, Louise, whose eagle eyes scanned each chapter as it was written, and who made sure that I attempted to represent female characters as accurately as any male writer can.

Visit our website at
KensingtonBooks.com
to sign up for our newsletters, read more from your favorite authors, see books by series, view reading group guides, and more!

BOOK CLUB
BETWEEN THE CHAPTERS

Become a Part of Our
Between the Chapters Book Club
Community and Join the Conversation

Betweenthechapters.net

Submit your book review for a chance to win exclusive Between the Chapters swag you can't get anywhere else!
https://www.kensingtonbooks.com/pages/review/